Ragis

Book Four of the Gemeta Stone

Ragis

Book Four of the Gemeta Stone

Donna Migliaccio

Ragis: Book Four of The Gemeta Stone
SECOND EDITION

Copyright 2018 by Donna Migliaccio

ISBN: 978-1-7338389-6-2

Cover Design by Melissa Williams Design
Frost ©2019 Linus, Adobe Stock

Interior Formatting by Melissa Williams Design

Edited by Catherine Lenderi

Published by Donna Migliaccio

donnamigliaccio.com

For my fellow theatricals, who gave me both the encouragement and the backstage elbow room to write this series

ACKNOWLEDGEMENTS

The long-term encouragement and support I've received from so many quarters while writing *The Gemeta Stone* series continues to be a boon and a blessing.

Thank you to:

Roger Yoerges and J. Fred Shiffman at Capital Talent Agency;

My editor, Catherine Lenderi, who also provided invaluable assistance with the *Kentávron* language;

My cover designer and formatter, Michelle Argyle of Melissa Williams Design, who continues to delight and amaze me with her beautiful work;

My trusty beta readers Rikki Boyce, Philip L. Harris and Joan L. Haines;

Macallister Stone and the community at AbsoluteWrite. com;

My readers, who inspire me to keep going;

My family, who buoy me up when I'm feeling down;

And finally, my husband John: my rock, my shelter and my touchstone. Here's to another 25 years!

CHAPTER ONE

"There they are again," Torrin said, and stamped an angry forehoof. "Look at them. It's as if they're mocking us."

Kristan Gemeta tightened his hold on the rail as another wave struck the wine ship, making it roll alarmingly. The centaur crew braced themselves as well, but their gazes never left the eastern horizon, where Kristan's warship wallowed in the swell, loose sails flapping in the wind. On either side of it, silhouetted against the rising sun, were the sleek, predatory forms of Olaf's and Sigurd Sigurdson's ships, for all the world like a pair of wolves chivvying a large and lethargic ewe.

Kristan's heart knotted at the sight. Bad enough that the Northmen had stolen his ship. Bad enough that they'd taken his retinue and the eleven centaurs he'd rescued along with it. Bad enough that they'd forced him into this mad pursuit on an unseaworthy vessel in dangerous winter waters. Harder to stomach was the knowledge that his friend Olaf had betrayed him and that his own sister Melissa had been the instrument of that betrayal.

Worst of all was the nagging of his own conscience, reminding him how he had shrugged off Melissa's desperation to find her husband Nigel, turned his back on Olaf's pleas for help, and underestimated the gravity of Sigurd's threats.

"Why are we just sitting here?" Chári demanded from the tiller. "They're only a few miles ahead, and we've got a good wind. We can catch them."

Torrin shook his head, in frustration more than denial. "As soon as we get too close, they'll hoist sail and leave us in their wake, just as they've done for the last two days. We're wearing ourselves and this boat out trying to catch them."

Astéria, the leader of the captive centaurs, turned up her hands in a helpless gesture. "My peoples and Kreestan's knights," she said, her anxiety making her command of the common tongue more tenuous than ever. "If only they get free, they fight."

Torrin muttered something in *Kentávron*, and his fierce gaze landed on Nolle, huddled in her cloak at the rail. In response, she whimpered and pressed close to Kristan, as if seeking his protection. He sidestepped her touch but could not blame the Wiche girl for being frightened. All the centaurs were staring at her, their huge, shaggy bodies more forbidding and their musky odor more oppressive than ever. Even Astéria, who had always been kind to Nolle, looked grim.

"I can't," Nolle whined. "That Sigurd will shoot at me again."

"*Ochi*. He not know," Astéria said. "You make yourself bird. Or feesh. He not shoot at feesh."

"It's too far. It's too windy, and the sea is too rough."

"She could at least try," one of the male centaurs muttered, with a pointed look at Kristan. The other centaurs murmured their agreement, and Kristan had to fight the urge to cringe, just as Nolle had.

He could not blame them either. He had offered the dwindling centaur population of *O Tópos* hope—hope in the form of twelve new centaurs, twelve fresh opportunities for mates— and offered it right in the midst of their rutting season. *And then I bungled it*, he thought bitterly. *Bungled it through my own ignorance and arrogance, the way I've bungled everything on this cursed journey.* Another wave slapped the hull, splattering him afresh with salt water. He thrust his hand beneath his soggy cloak and took hold of the Gemeta Stone. *I wish this Stone could do what Sigurd wants. Send him and that traitor Olaf and their thieving crews back where they came from. And they can take my two-faced sister with them—*

His guts cramped, the first warning of an oncoming seizure. *Not now. Not now.*

He clenched his fingers tight around the Stone and forced himself to breathe, to count the breaths, to control his rising rage. "If we can close the distance between the ships, Nolle, will you try to get aboard? Please," he added, in a low voice only she could hear. "We're all depending on you."

His tone was pleading, and he despised himself for that, but it had the desired effect: Nolle swallowed hard, then nodded.

"Right, then," Torrin said. "Let's get the sail up, secure the lines and then take up oars. We'll catch these Northmen if it's the last thing we do."

Within moments the sail blossomed like an enormous white flower before the wind. The crew grunted and strained at the oars, adding more momentum as the ship surged through the waves. Ahead, sails unfurled aboard the warship and the Northern vessels, but more slowly, and Kristan wondered if his men and the captive centaurs were still imprisoned below decks. "Port oars up," Torrin shouted, hurrying aft to adjust their course.

The ship heeled sharply to the left, and Kristan grabbed hold of the rail. Nolle was not so quick; she lost her balance and reeled across the deck. One of the centaurs let go of his oar long enough to grab her arm and sling her back toward Kristan. "Keep her under control," he snarled.

Kristan pushed Nolle against the rail. "Hold on and behave yourself. If you were to go overboard, I doubt the *Kentávron* would stop to haul you out—not now."

Nolle's chin jutted. "I was behaving. I just fell. Why is everyone being so mean?"

I'm not going to explain centaur carnality to you in the middle of a chase, Kristan thought. "Never mind," he said aloud. "Just do as I say."

Were they gaining? He leaned into the wind, as if by sheer will he could make the ship go even faster, although he did not know what would happen if they did catch up to the Northmen. They shot past a cluster of small islands fringed with trees. By the Stone, they *were* gaining. They were close enough he could see the Northmen laboring at their oars as well as their sails, close enough to make out Sigurd at the helm of the warship.

"We steal their wind!" Astéria shouted from her oar. Indeed, the Northern sails were sagging slightly as the centaur vessel came between it and the brisk westerly wind. The centaurs at the oars cheered, and Torrin let out a roar of triumph that made Kristan jump.

And just as suddenly, they lost speed. Torrin's jubilant cry spiraled into a groan as the sails fluttered and drooped. Kristan looked astern, where a second Norwinn warship had swung from behind the islands, diverting the wind into their own sails. The centaurs bellowed their fury as they lost way. Ahead, the Northmen's flotilla fled toward the horizon.

"What do you think you're doing?" Torrin shouted, as the Norwinn warship heaved to near them.

"What do you think *you're* doing?" someone on board yelled back.

I know that voice, Kristan thought.

A moment later, his suspicions were confirmed as a rangy, red-haired man pushed his way past the staring seamen lining the rail. Sir Nigel Demitt, First Advisor of Norwinn, squinted at the centaur ship and suddenly grinned. "Well, you're a long way from home, Torrin," he called. "And in pursuit of our Northern friends as well. Surely they weren't poaching on *O Tópos* too."

Torrin flicked a glance at Kristan, then cupped his hands around his mouth. "No," he shouted back. "Bring your ship closer, so we can talk."

"But they're getting away!" Chári wailed. The other centaurs raised their voices in outraged agreement.

"They won't go far," Kristan said, so sharply that everyone

turned to look at him.

Nigel's mouth dropped open. "Kristan, what are you—"

"Look," Kristan went on, ignoring him. He pointed toward the Northern ships. "Why do you think they waited for us last night? Why do you think they're waiting for us now? They want us to follow them, right around the southeastern shoreline, then north into Stratheden waters."

"What for?" Nigel asked. "What's going on?"

"I might ask you the same, First Advisor."

Nigel drew himself upright, his easy grin hardening into tight-lipped sullenness. "I'm following your Reach's orders, my lord."

"Is that so? Are you aware that my Reach abandoned her post in Norwinn to find you?"

He was not prepared for the sudden, joyous light that brightened Nigel's face. "She did? Where is she now?"

Silently, Kristan pointed toward the Northern ships. To his annoyance, Nigel gaped again. "She's with Olaf? But how—"

"I'm in no mood for explanations now, First Advisor. This *Kentávron* ship isn't suited for a sea voyage. I want yours."

As both seamen and centaurs began protesting, a white-whiskered man with a weather-seamed face pushed forward past Nigel. "If I may, First Advisor." He swept off his wide-brimmed hat and managed a bow to Kristan, in spite of the rocking of his ship. "My lord, my apologies, but that would be ill advised."

Kristan squinted at him. "You must be Commander Pratchett."

Pratchett looked startled, then pleased, and Kristan was sourly grateful for the sleepless nights he'd spent memorizing his realm's military rosters. "Yes, my lord, thank you. My lord, we ran aground off the Terrafina lighthouse some days ago. Holed our hull in three places and weakened the keel considerably. We patched her as best we could, but she needs extensive repairs. We've been limping back to Moordock in fits and starts. The ship's holding together, but just barely." He shot a black look at Nigel. "I wouldn't have tried to pursue the Northmen just now, but Sir Nigel insisted."

"My orders were to find the Northmen and open up discussions with them," Nigel said with an equally hostile stare.

"Very well," Kristan said, fighting the urge to shriek. "In that case, Pratchett, I'll want all the provisions you can spare. Water, food, blankets, weapons—all of it."

"But you said your ship wasn't seaworthy, my lord."

An irritable muttering rose from the centaurs. "It's not my ship," Kristan said. "And regardless of its seaworthiness, we have to press on. Hand over the provisions, and quickly. I don't want to waste more time."

"I'm coming with you," Nigel said. "Pratchett, I'm going to gather my things. Bring the ship closer, so I can transfer along with the supplies."

"As you wish, First Advisor," Pratchett said. His face was expressionless, but there was no mistaking the pleased gleam in his eyes. He and Torrin bawled orders to their crews, and as the ships were lashed together, Kristan turned back to study the Northern flotilla. The three vessels still waited, rocking in the swell, and Kristan's heart swelled with anger at the sight, setting his pulse hammering so loudly in his ears that the noise of the provisions being transferred aboard was almost obliterated. It was not until he felt the ship heave beneath his feet that he realized they had cast off from the warship. He turned to see it moving away to the west, the centaurs stowing the fresh stores with Nolle getting underfoot, and a few steps away, Nigel watching him warily, a knapsack slung over one shoulder.

"I didn't dare disturb you," he said. "Your face looked like thunder."

Kristan only glared at him.

"Torrin told me a bit of what happened. I'm sorry, Kristan. Melissa ordered me away, and my pride was hurt, and I acted like a child. I wanted to make her sorry. I had no idea she'd leave Norwinn to look for me, not after she'd been so ill."

All the reproaches Kristan had been framing died unsaid. "Ill? What do you mean, ill?"

It was Nigel's turn to stare. "She miscarried, Kristan. For the second time. It happened a little more than a fortnight ago. I thought . . . I thought perhaps she'd written and told you."

Torrin was calling orders; the sail went up and the centaurs scrambled to their oars, but Kristan could only reach blindly for the rail as the ship surged forward once more. *No.* His lips formed the word but made no sound. He shook his head and faced into the wind. Nigel joined him at the rail. "She didn't want to worry you, Kristan. It's why she didn't tell you about Olaf. She wanted to confirm the rumors before she said anything. She said if it were all true, it would break your heart."

Everyone is keeping secrets from you. The bitter idea twisted Kristan's guts. "How kind," he said. "And so I've blundered along like an idiot, making mistakes everywhere I turn, all because everyone wants to spare me the knowledge of what goes on in my own realm. What kind of delicate blossom do you think I am? Are you afraid I'll dissolve into tears, or take to my bed at the first sign of bad news?"

"That's not why—"

Kristan rounded on him. "Then what is it? I'd appreciate your telling me, since the same thing has been happening in both Dyer and Norwinn. By the Stone, for all I know Hogia is falling to bits as well."

His voice had ratcheted up, both in volume and pitch, and he realized that everyone on board could hear him. The centaurs at the oars looked at him sidelong; Torrin and Astéria, busy with the sail, paused to listen; at the tiller, Chári stared at him openly. Even Nolle, her face stuffed with filched provender, had frozen in mid-chew and was gawping at him.

"*Ragis*," Astéria murmured.

There's that word again, Kristan thought, but before he could say anything, Nigel spoke up, his face almost as red as his hair. "Kristan, I'm sorry—"

"Never mind," Kristan said. "Never mind. The damage is done. Leave me alone."

Nigel retreated to the stern, and Kristan faced out to sea again, feeling every eye on the ship like a glowing coal against his back. He fought down the nauseating rage and concentrated on the Northern ships and their captive. As the cold winter sun mounted into the sky, they maintained their tantalizing distance, slowing when the centaur ship slowed, quickening their pace whenever Torrin caught a favorable wind. By mid-afternoon Torrin ordered the oars away. "No point in killing ourselves," he said. "The sail alone will do. No," he went on, over his crew's groans and protests, "we'll batter our ship to bits at this rate, and the Northmen will still be ahead. Half of you stay on deck to help with the sail. The other half, rest and eat. At dusk we'll change places, and if the weather allows, we'll sail into the night. Maybe then we can catch them unawares."

He relieved Chári at the tiller and steered the ship while talking quietly to Nigel. One of the centaurs brought up a small brazier and grilled some of the salted fish from the Norwinn warship's borrowed stores. Sitting on their haunches around the brazier, the centaurs ate it, wrinkling their noses at the unfamiliar taste. They washed their meal down with draughts from what remained of their strong red wine, then shared out the blankets and slept, some in the shallow hold, and some on deck, clustered together for warmth. Astéria joined them but ate little, offering much of her share to Nolle, who devoured it greedily and then fell asleep snuggled between Astéria's and Chári's warm flanks.

Kristan stayed where he was, standing lookout and signaling to Torrin when he spotted waves shoaling, or if their quarry changed course. As dusk gathered and the centaurs woke and relieved their comrades, he was surprised to see lights spring up on the sterns of all three ships. He beckoned to Torrin, who gave the tiller to Chári, and came to the bow with Nigel. "What do you think that means?" Kristan asked, pointing at the Northern ships.

Torrin grunted. "They're going to sail through the night, and they want us to follow."

"Why?" Nigel asked. "Do you think they'll try to run us aground?"

"Unlikely. They want Kristan, remember? It's in their best interest to keep him safe. I think we can follow them with confidence." He jerked his chin at Kristan. "Let Astéria have the lookout. It's time you rested."

"I'm not tired."

"With respect, my friend, it's clear that you are. You may be StoneKing, but on my ship, I'm the master, and I say stand down."

With ill grace, Kristan did as he was told. The centaurs lit the brazier again and cooked more fish. Kristan forced himself to choke down a few bites, along with ship's bread dipped in water to soften it. He was cold and weary, but the idea of being squeezed in amongst the sleeping centaurs below decks set his skin prickling. He found a quiet spot against the starboard hull and sat there, huddled in his cloak. A few moments later, Torrin and Nigel joined him. "Here," Torrin said, throwing him a blanket. "That cloak may have been plush once, but it's pretty scruffy now."

"I have your people to thank for that."

Torrin snorted out a laugh and settled himself on Kristan's left, while Nigel sat, somewhat diffidently, on his right. "They were, perhaps, a little overzealous. But they meant well. Don't hold it against them."

Kristan did not answer. Nolle had joined Astéria in the bow, and the pair of them were silhouetted against the darkening sky: Nolle's face tipped up in earnest scrutiny, Astéria's neck bent at a tender angle as she spoke to the girl. Torrin let out the tiniest sigh, and Nigel chuckled. "You like that Astéria, don't you?" he said.

Torrin ducked his head, smiling. The gesture was so

youthful, so abashed, and yet so hopeful that Kristan could not help but smile a little himself. "I do. If she returns my feelings, I . . . it would be a good thing for *O Tópos*, for my people. I've only ever had one wish: to find a life mate. If I did, it would create the right conditions for more couplings among my people. True couplings that would result in births. More births, more children, more growth. More strength. We could finally come out of hiding and take our place as a people to be recognized and reckoned with. We could become a nation of *Kentávron*, instead of a gathering of curiosities, dying a slow death."

"And a dozen new centaurs could do all that?" Nigel asked.

"Given time, I believe it could happen. What luck the princess of Malchea was so eager to make an impression on you," Torrin said, looking at Kristan. "What if she'd decided to keep Astéria for herself, as a pet?"

"Princess Jelena would have had difficulty keeping her," Kristan said. "I told you, Astéria tried to trample me when we first met. Serle got between us and scolded her off like a wayward sheep."

"Who's Serle?" Nigel asked.

"My squire."

"He must be an impressive lad, if he was able to stand up to her."

"Just the opposite. Dealing with Astéria is one of the few things he can do without botching the job. Maybe it's because he used to be a shepherd. He kept cooing nonsense at her until she calmed down. *To paidí eínai treló*, that's what she kept calling him."

Torrin laughed. "That means 'the boy is crazy.' You've attracted some interesting followers, haven't you? A Wiche girl and a crazy boy."

"And Gabriel's son."

"What?"

"Or at least, I think so. Mali Uzuri told me she had a cousin who had to flee Seagirt because he got another man's wife with child—which fits with what little I know of why Gabriel was hiding in the Exilwald." Kristan shook off the rising shadows and hurried on: "Desta is the image of Gabriel. But he's an ill fit in the Uzuri family and lives under a cloud because of his birth. He stowed away when we left Seagirt, and we only discovered him when it was too late to do anything about it. I'll have to find a place for him somewhere..." His voice drifted off as Nolle turned from Astéria and pulled something from her pocket. She lifted it to the moonlight and studied it. It glowed a faint blue in her fingers.

"What's she got there?" Torrin asked, following his gaze.

"A scrying ball," Kristan said, through the pang he still felt over its loss. "I gave it to her as payment for helping me with Astéria."

All three of them watched as Nolle stared into the ball, as if trying to see what lay within its depths.

"How did you end up with such a thing?" Nigel asked.

"A gift, long ago," Kristan said. Simeon's face, eyes cold and calculating, swam through his memory, and he could not bring himself to say more.

Nolle's eyes glittered in the moonlight, reflecting the light shining from the ball, but her mouth was tight with frustration. Suddenly, she thrust the ball back into her clothing and, with a few muttered words, transformed into a seagull and flapped her way to the top of the mast.

Nigel let out a grunt of surprise. "Neat trick, that."

"It's been useful," Kristan said.

All three fell silent as they watched Nolle's gull-form, its feathers ruffled for warmth against the cold wind. "Maybe you could send her ahead, to check on your ship," Nigel said. "See if Melissa... if everyone is all right."

"She's afraid to fly that far," Kristan said. "And she's frightened of Sigurd."

"Despite everything that's happened, I can't believe Olaf would stand by and let any of your people or mine be harmed,"

Torrin said. "We'll have to trust in that."

Nigel blew out a long sigh. "I just want Melissa back. Just to tell her how sorry I am. To ask her forgiveness."

Kristan remembered how he had opened Melissa's message to Nigel and was overcome with self-loathing. "She feels the same way," he murmured.

"I wish I could take her someplace where we could talk, and be alone. Where we could find ourselves again." Nigel hunched deeper into his blanket, his eyes squinted against the wind. "Where no one would disturb us, and I'd have the time and the quiet to make her understand that I don't care if we never have children." He flicked a rueful look at Kristan. "Perhaps that's wrong of me, Kristan; I know heirs to the Gemeta line are necessary. But even if Melissa can never bear children, I don't care. All I need is her."

In the bow, Astéria stared intently ahead, then looked back to Torrin and pointed toward the horizon. "*Vlépo éna fws,*" she called softly. "Light."

Nigel craned his neck. "That's the Terrafina beacon—it's on the southernmost point of Norwinn. Once we round the point and turn north, we'll be headed toward Stratheden waters."

"Terrafina—that's where Pratchett said you ran aground, isn't it?" Torrin asked.

"The same. If you're right about the Northmen, we can follow their lead and make it through the shoals safely."

Torrin stood up to watch as Chári, her lips pressed tightly together, navigated them past the Terrafina beacon. Kristan stood as well, captivated by the sight of the steady light shining through the darkness ahead of them. "I've seen it on maps, and mentioned in Norwinn's reports," he murmured. "I always wondered what it looked like."

"In daylight it's not much to see," Nigel said, joining him at the rail. "Just a rough stone tower about the height of four men standing on each other's shoulders, but by night it's a welcome sight."

"What keeps the light going?" Torrin asked.

"Two keepers, working in shifts," Nigel said. "On top of the tower is a beacon, partially enclosed by glass windows. The keepers stoke the fire through the night, and during fog and storms. During the day, they sleep. I got to know them when we were grounded here. Pratchett barely gave them the time of day, but I thought they were interesting fellows." His mouth gaped in an enormous yawn. "Well, there you have it. The southernmost point of your realm, Kristan." He settled onto the deck, pulled his blanket over his head, and soon his breathing deepened to a light snore.

Tired as Kristan was, he was too riveted by the sight of the beacon to close his eyes to it. As they swept past it, he clung to the rail, hair whipping around his face. Something about the small tower, upright against the wind, its light sure in the darkness, seemed familiar.

Heather, he thought. *It's like Heather.*

He slipped one hand into his pocket, wondering if the blue ring he had purchased in Seagirt had survived its dunking in the Mor, and the mauling of his clothing at the hands of the *Kentávron*. It was still there, smooth against his fingers. Even as the touch of it heartened him, even as he slid it onto his finger, a scoffing voice in his head berated him, saying, *Why do you keep it? To keep part of her with you? If you want to keep her safe, better throw it into the sea, along with whatever she's meant to you.*

"What about you, Kristan?" Torrin asked softly. "What do you wish for? If you could go anywhere in the world, do anything you wanted—what would you do? Where would you go?"

To Heather, Kristan thought. *I would find Heather. I'd sit with her, talk to her, hear her voice, look into her eyes, feel the touch of her hand, and find comfort at last.*

But he dared not say the words aloud.

Torrin kept his own silence, and when Kristan glanced at him, he discovered the centaur prince had turned slightly to watch Astéria in the bow. His handsome face was taut with desire, and his whole body seemed to yearn toward her. He jumped a bit when he caught Kristan's gaze. "I know, I know," he said, with an abashed smile and shrug. "*To paidí eínai treló*, like she called your squire, eh? Except I'm crazy with love."

An uncomfortable memory shifted in Kristan's brain. "She called me something once. More than once. Under her breath, and she didn't look happy when she said it."

"What was it?"

"*Ragis.*"

Torrin drew back slightly, his brow furrowed. "She said that?"

"Yes. What does it mean?"

"Well . . . it's an old word. Its meaning is a bit . . . obscure."

Torrin averted his gaze to the Terrafina light in the distance. It was clear he did not wish to answer. Kristan's skin prickled with unease, and the sensation made him brusque. "Stop dithering, Torrin. Tell me what it means."

Torrin looked at him then, his expression grim. "*Ragis* means cracking. Shattering. On the brink of madness."

"Ah." Kristan turned away, fumbling beneath his cloak for the Stone.

Torrin stepped closer and ducked his head so he spoke almost in Kristan's ear. "Do you think . . . do you still believe . . . what you told me when we parted last summer?"

Kristan tried to laugh, but all that came out was a thin, hysterical giggle. "Are you asking if Astéria is right? Am I losing my mind?"

"You know what I mean."

Resisting the urge to recoil from Torrin's nearness, he lowered his voice to a murmur. "If you're talking about Daazna, then yes. Yes. I know he isn't dead. He haunts me. He's in my dreams; sometimes I hear him even when I'm awake."

They studied the distant beacon in silence. At last, Torrin breathed a heavy sigh. "When I left you on Hogia's shores last summer, I wondered if I'd ever see you again. I thought you might seal yourself in one of your castles, and one day, I'd hear a rumor that you were dead by your own hand."

"I can't do that," Kristan said absently. "The Stone won't let me."

"So you've tried."

"Even thinking about it was too much." Kristan tugged on the chain of the Stone. "This thing hates me. Its touch used to comfort me, but now it's like a block of ice in my hand."

"My poor friend. No wonder you look so haggard. Is there anything I can do?"

"No," Kristan said, then shook his head. "Yes. I don't know. Torrin, I'm so angry all the time. So angry that I make myself . . . sick."

"The fits, you mean? They haven't gone away?"

"They're worse than ever. The last one . . ." Kristan's throat knotted up so tightly at the memory that he could barely speak. "Never mind. Never mind. I don't want to talk about it."

"If you told me, perhaps it would help."

"No. I can't bear talking about it. Leave off, Torrin."

"Isn't there anyone you can talk to?"

Heather . . .

"By the Stone, will you let me be?" Kristan's voice went ragged. "That's all I want. Not to be interrogated, scrutinized, or judged. Just leave me alone." He stumbled toward the stern. Ignoring Chári's sidelong glances, he leaned against the rail. In the distance, the Terrafina beacon was no more than a bright pinprick in the darkness, but he stood gazing at it until it was swallowed by the night.

CHAPTER TWO

"I need to talk to you."

Ravelin only applied himself more vigorously to his bowl of porridge.

"I said I need to talk to you."

Isobel's insistent whisper was like a wasp buzzing next to his ear, and Ravelin resisted the urge to swat the annoyance away. "I've no interest in what you have to say," he muttered to his spoon.

Isobel leaned over him to snatch up a spare spoon from the table. "Not even if it's about your little friend?" she hissed.

He glanced up at her then. Isobel's eyes were red-rimmed and puffy, her skin an unpleasant yellow in the morning light, but her lips were pressed into a hard, determined line. She let the spoon slip from her fingers and it fell to the floor, its soft clatter lost in the din of the soldiers at their breakfast. "I'm telling her I'm sick today," she told him as she stooped to fetch the spoon. "I'll stay in my room. Come to me there."

"I'll be on maneuvers with the others."

"Find a way." Spoon in hand, she moved toward Heather, who sat at another table with her knights and maidservant, her back to Ravelin.

Heather's hair was braided into its customary, neat circlet around her head, but a few tendrils had escaped the orderly arrangement and lay in soft swirls against the nape of her neck. There was something so sweetly tantalizing about the escaped locks that it was all Ravelin could do not to fling down his stodgy meal, stride across the room, and seize her.

A virgin.

He had never imagined she would be untouched. He had long ago accepted the fact that he would have to make love to a woman he found unattractive; long ago resigned himself to the idea of dining on crumbs from the StoneKing's table, if it meant gaining control of Hogia's army. Discovering she was intact had stunned him, and like a spotty-faced juvenile, he had fled from her into the woods, and spent himself with his own hands rather than despoil her.

Lianna, his virgin bride, had betrayed him. Since then, all the women he'd taken had been no better than whores in his eyes. But now . . . now it was as if he had been given a gift, a second chance. Now another virgin bride was within his grasp, and he was filled with a ravening hunger for her, and the resolve that this time, no one would deprive him of his prize.

Across the room, Isobel stood at Heather's side, eyes downcast and chin trembling as she spoke. Heather turned to her with an inquiring expression that deepened into concern. She gestured toward Bayla, but Isobel shook her head. At last, Heather nodded, and with a show of feebleness, Isobel made her way to the staircase and ascended, shooting a surreptitious glance at Ravelin as she left. Heather and her knights pushed away from the table and rose. Bran and Jerrold nodded to their captains, who called the troops to order. The hall burst into activity: the soldiers cleared and stacked the tables, then threw on their cloaks and gloves, while Bayla went to fetch Heather's things. Alone for the moment, Heather headed for the door, and Ravelin hastened to join her.

"Good morning," he said. "I trust you slept well."

She avoided his eyes. "Well enough. And you?"

"Well enough," he echoed. "What's the matter with Isobel?"

"She says she doesn't feel well, so I excused her from today's exercises. I offered to leave Bayla with her, but she said no.

Cook and his assistant will be in the kitchen, so she won't be completely alone. I expect she's still suffering the effects from what happened yesterday."

"So am I," Ravelin said with a meaningful smile.

The color rose in Heather's cheeks. At that moment, Bayla arrived bearing their cloaks, making further pursuit of the subject impossible. He stayed close as they went outside, where the troops had assembled into their customary two columns. Already on horseback, Bran waited at the head of one and Jerrold at the head of the second. Wearing curiously smug smiles, the two knights glanced from him to a cluster of perhaps a dozen soldiers standing apart from their fellows, armed with bows and arrows.

"Cook says we need more meat for the pot," Heather said, meeting Ravelin's gaze at last. "These men need instruction in woodcraft, as well as additional practice with their bows. Reach Seachlan, I wonder if you'd lead them in a hunting party, rather than participate in today's exercise."

Her manner was brisk and impersonal. *She doesn't want to be around me*, Ravelin thought. *She's ashamed of what happened last night.* He gave her a curt nod, knowing full well his frustration showed in his face. Heather's grim expression softened. "It's just . . . it's just that you know this area well," she said. "And you're the most skilled hunter among us."

"As you wish," he said, unable to suppress a grin. "My skills await only your . . . desire."

This time Heather flushed to the roots of her hair. "We'll be to the southwest," she said. "You should do your hunting well clear of us." She whirled and strode across the courtyard so quickly that she was nearly running. She snatched Skapi's reins from Bayla, swung into the saddle, and kicked the white horse into a brisk trot through the lodge gates. Her maidservant, knights, and men fell in behind her. Within moments they were gone, and Ravelin turned to the hunting party, rubbing his hands together. "Right, you lot. Keep up or be left behind."

Eschewing his own mount, he led the men on foot to the north, badgering them to move faster, stay quieter, keep their eyes and ears open, and their bows at the ready. The men stumbled over themselves in their haste to obey while Ravelin directed them first this way and then that, in a twisting, turning route that would thoroughly baffle anyone not familiar with the terrain. Overhead, the clouds grew low and thick. Navigating their way back to the lodge without the sun would be even more difficult. Hopelessly confused by midday, the group startled a herd of deer and became even more muddled as Ravelin urged them after their quarry. He fell back and waited as the men charged ahead in pursuit. As soon as their voices faded, he hurried back to the lodge.

By the time he reached the courtyard gates, a light snow had begun to fall. He let himself into the lodge and hesitated just within the doorway, listening. The clatter of pots and the sound of idle chatter from the kitchen told him that the cook and his assistant were busy with preparations for the evening meal. He crept upstairs to the women's bedchamber and tapped at the door. Soft footsteps approached, and the door cracked open. Isobel peered out at him. They stared at each other without speaking, and he found himself revolted by her puffy eyes and sniffling nose.

"Speak," he said.

"Is that all you have to say to me?"

"Don't be tiresome," he said, shoving past her into the room.

She closed the door and leaned against it. "What happened here wasn't my fault. You have to understand that."

"I've no interest in discussing the matter. You said you had news."

Isobel held out a piece of tightly folded parchment. "This is what Lady Heather has been hiding in her boot all this time. I found it on the floor last night. She must have dropped it when she was undressing."

Ravelin snatched it from her hand and unfolded it. Still

attached to one edge was a fish-shaped blob of red wax, impressed with the StoneKing's seal. One side bore a letter he recognized: Heather's request to the StoneKing for the use of the lodge, with the scribe Bastian's elegantly lettered *Approved* at the bottom. The writing was scored through by a single bold stroke of ink.

He turned the parchment over. On the opposite side were a few lines, in Heather's untidy handwriting:

> *My lord:*
> *Ravelin Seachlan has proposed marriage to me.*
> *Unless you have some objection, I will accept his offer.*
> *Heather Demitt*
> *Lady Commander of Hogia*

At the bottom of the page, in Bastian's hand, was once again the single word: *Approved.*

A shout of triumph boiled up in Ravelin's throat, but he choked it back and contented himself with reading the brief message and its even briefer response again.

He had let her go. The StoneKing had released her from whatever bond lay between them, and he had done it with an impersonal finality that bordered on cruel. *Perfect*, Ravelin thought. *It couldn't be more perfect. She's been carrying it like a hidden wound. How it must have destroyed her to receive it. How her feelings for him must be teetering on the edge of hatred. And after last night . . . all I need is one final push and she'll be mine, and the army will be mine, and just a single step beyond that and Hogia's throne will be mine too.*

"You lied to me," Isobel said.

He had been so absorbed in the letter that he had forgotten she was in the room. Her eyes were locked on him in a savage glare. "How did I lie?"

"You told me we'd be together. Once you had your kingdom back, we'd be together. But you proposed to her. You offered marriage to that common little slut!"

"Keep your voice down."

"When were you going to tell me? Or was I to find out when you announced it to the world?"

"I thought maybe she'd mentioned it to you already."

It was a lie, and Isobel knew it as well as he did. "Don't make me laugh," she said, her voice scaling up. "Do you think the Lady of the Sword and I lay here at night and exchange girlish secrets? I doubt she's even told her maidservant. She must have written to the StoneKing hoping he'd say 'No, don't do it, I love you,' but all she got was his approval." Her mouth twisted into a bitter sneer. "And my guess is, she's keeping you dangling while she makes up her mind. How things have changed. You used to take what you wanted, but now the mighty Seachlan waits with his cock in his hands while a common girl decides whether she'll deign to have him."

He grabbed her by one arm. "I said keep your voice down. I told you I'd do whatever it takes to get my throne back. If it means I have to marry her to get control of the army, then that's what I'll do."

"But what about me?" Isobel grabbed his hand, tearing the parchment he still held. "I've done everything you wanted, and more. What's going to happen to me now?"

He shoved her away, and Heather's message fluttered to the floor. "I might have kept you as my mistress, but I've no interest in that option now. Why don't you peddle your used wares in Stratheden? Maybe some of your former customers will take you on."

For a breath she stood motionless, her hands clenched, her mouth twisted with rage and grief. Suddenly, she lunged at him, swinging wildly. One fist clipped his ear; he caught it and twisted it behind her back. She cried out, and he grabbed her by the throat with his free hand. "How dare you, you whore?" he snarled in her ear. "How dare you raise your hand to your lord?"

"I'll tell her," Isobel said in a strangled whisper. "I'll tell the little fool about you and me; I'll tell her what you've been doing, what you've been planning—"

He tightened his fingers about her neck, choking off her words. Eyes bulging, she clawed at his hand, kicked and struggled against his grip until he knocked her legs out from under her and bore her silently to the floor. Pressing the full weight of his body along hers, he pinned her down and locked both hands around her neck. She bucked and thrust against him, an action so similar to their lovemaking that he felt himself growing hard. "Whore," he muttered, squeezing his fingers tighter still. "You whore."

Even after Isobel had stopped struggling, even after her eyes had filled with blood and gone still, Ravelin kept his hands clenched tight around her neck, hissing imprecations. In time, his hardness lessened. He released his grip and spat in Isobel's face. "Whore," he whispered. "See what you made me do."

He rolled onto his back. Once he had caught his breath, he got to his feet and crept to the bedchamber door. He cracked it open and listened for a few moments. Far off in the kitchen, someone laughed.

He felt like laughing himself, but remembered that time was short and Isobel's body still lay behind him. He briefly considered leaving it where it was, to be discovered when the army returned from the day's drill. *Perhaps they'll blame one of the cooks*, he thought, then immediately rejected the plan. *No good; the cooks will vouch for one another. And if I try to carry her out and throw her down the ravine, one of them might spot me.*

His gaze fell on the garderobe door, and a cruel idea struck him.

Inside the chilly little room, he removed the thick slab of wood with its round hole, a seat for those relieving themselves. Holding his breath against the stench of piss and shit, he peered down the dark, rectangular stone chute. Far below, a square of light glimmered: the end of the chute, the ravine beyond it, and far below, the River Strath running fast and cold, creating the border between Hogia and Stratheden. The chute was narrow; *but then*, he thought with a grim smile, *Isobel is narrow too.*

Back in the bedchamber, Isobel lay as he had left her, one arm bent behind her back, her legs askew, her dead eyes glaring at the ceiling. Her gray cloak hung from a peg; he snatched it up, spread it on the floor next to her and, with his feet, rolled her onto it. He found her pack at the foot of her bed, rummaged through it, and extracted several long, woolen stockings. He picked up her slippers, which had come off during the struggle, and put them inside the pack. He knelt beside Isobel's body, tucked her knotted fists against her sides, and with one of the stockings, tied her arms to her body. He rolled her up in the cloak, covering her face with its hood. Using the remaining stockings, he bound the cloak tightly about her, so she made a neat bundle.

He sucked in a deep breath, heaved her wrapped body over his shoulder, and staggered to his feet. As quietly as he could, he carried her into the garderobe. Panting a bit, he eased her, headfirst, into the hole. It was a snug fit, but her shoulders and hips passed through easily enough. Grunting with the effort, Ravelin clung to her ankles and raised her legs high, so she would slide down as straight as possible.

Then he let go.

A muffled thumping marked Isobel's passage down the garderobe chute. The sound receded, then suddenly stopped. With a muttered curse, Ravelin peered down the hole, but he could no longer see daylight at its bottom. Isobel's body was jammed in the chute.

He swore, softly and vehemently. There was no way to reach her, to shove her further down. He fought back his rising panic. *No matter. No matter. There'll be a search for her, but no one will think to look there.*

He lifted his head and listened once more. From the kitchen came the distant sound of chopping and conversation. He went back into the bedchamber to clear away any signs of his death struggle with Isobel. The piece of parchment, torn along one edge where Isobel had snatched at it, lay on the floor. Ravelin picked it up, folded it into a tight packet, and stuffed it down the leg of his boot. He gathered up what he could find of Isobel's things and crammed them into her pack.

He ducked into the garderobe, threw Isobel's pack into the hole and squinted after it. Not even a glimmer of light showed from below. *Well and truly stuck*, he thought. *She'll be hung up in the chute until she rots and falls to pieces, and by then, this lodge will be sitting empty again*. He replaced the wooden seat, then paused as a malicious thought filled his head.

"One last salute to my dear Isobel," he whispered, and pulled down his leggings.

Outside the lodge, snow was falling steadily. A thin layer already covered the ground as Ravelin crossed the courtyard, hurried out the gate, and onto the trail. Although he was shaking from his exertions, he forced himself into a loping run, and as he ran, the snow came down harder and harder. In spite of his exhaustion, a strange exuberance filled him. By the time he reached the place where he had left his hunting party, he was grinning. No sooner had he settled on a rock to catch his breath than one of the hunters trudged over a rise in the near distance. "There you are, Reach Seachlan," he called, waving one arm.

"I missed mine," Ravelin called back. "Did anyone else bring one down?"

"Three altogether, sir. Two bucks and a doe. The others are butchering them now."

"Excellent. I'll be there as soon as I catch my breath. She led me on a merry chase."

The man nodded and walked off. Tilting his head back, Ravelin reveled in the pressure of Heather's note against his calf, and the sensation of snow patting his hot cheeks and forehead like small, approving hands.

CHAPTER THREE

The storm came up suddenly, surprising everyone. Heather and her knights had to scramble to assemble the troops from their various positions in the day's exercise, and by the time they were in ranks and quick-marching back to the lodge, the snow was coming down in thick squalls that snatched the hoods from their heads and whipped their cloaks about their legs. Skapi kept dancing sideways and snorting, as if trying to dodge the snowflakes, and it was all Heather could do to keep her from bolting. Beside her, Bayla's horse plodded along with its head down, while Bayla herself huddled miserably in the saddle.

"We'll be there soon," Heather said.

Bayla tried to smile. "I hope Reach Seachlan had good hunting before this storm blew up. A nice piece of roasted venison would go down well."

"A tankard of ale would go down even better," Sir Bran said, drawing up on Heather's right.

"Where's Jerrold?" Heather asked.

"At the rear, my lady, keeping an eye on the stragglers."

Very good, Heather started to say, but an icy blast snatched the words from her mouth, and she contented herself with an encouraging nod as she clutched her hood about her face.

At last, they were through the gates. Heather waited until all the men were in ranks and accounted for, then dismissed them into the lodge. "Give me your horse and go inside," she called to

Bayla over the wind, and waved off her maidservant's protests. "Do as I say; your lips are blue with the cold."

"My lady, I'll see to the horses," Jerrold said, but she shook her head. She, Jerrold, and Bran led the mounts into the stable. Ravelin and Isobel's horses stood quietly in their stalls, along with the placid pack horses, and their warmth and tranquility seemed to soothe Skapi's ill temper. She stood still as Heather removed her tack and rubbed her down, and even laid her head on Heather's shoulder.

"Glad to be out of that weather," Bran remarked as he unbuckled his mount's girth.

"It's going to be a bad night out, for man or beast," Jerrold said. "I'm glad we've all got a warm place to sleep." He jerked his chin at the new roof over their heads. "The men did a good job repairing this place."

Heather only nodded as she cleaned Skapi's hooves. She wished she could stay in the stable with the warm, drowsy animals, rather than go into the noise and activity of the lodge. Ravelin would be waiting for her. Throughout the day, she had fought back the memory of his hands and lips on her flesh, and instead, thrown all her energy into the day's exercises. Now, however, with the prospect of a long evening cooped up indoors, she did not see how she could avoid seeing him, not unless she sequestered herself in her room like a timid child. Perhaps she could go over the rosters with Jerrold and Bran, or start drafting her report on the maneuvers to Kristan—

With a gasp, she jerked upright, startling Skapi. *Kristan. The message. Where is the message?* She had been so distracted when she had stripped off her clothes the night before that she had forgotten about putting the folded parchment under her pillow; had not thought about stuffing it into its accustomed place in her boot when she had dressed that morning; had not missed its pressure against her leg until this very moment.

"Something wrong, my lady?" Bran asked.

"No . . . no. Skapi nipped me a bit, that's all."

Jerrold shook his head. "She's never been broken in properly, that one. A shame Sir Walter had to leave with the job half done."

"There's nothing wrong with Skapi," Bran protested. "She's just high-spirited."

As the two debated her horse's merits and shortcomings, Heather portioned out water and hay for Skapi, then stood absently stroking her smooth, white hide. *Maybe Bayla found it. No, she would have given it back to me right away. Surely it didn't work its way out of my boot during maneuvers. When did I feel it last? Right before Callum and his men arrived, wasn't that it? Or did I lose it when . . .*

Her face went hot at the memory of Ravelin yanking down her leggings.

"—up on the tower again, my lady," Bran said.

She spun to face him. "What? What was that?"

Startled, Bran stepped back. "I was just saying it was too bad we can't light another signal fire tonight, my lady. Not in all this wind and snow."

She sagged against Skapi. "Sorry, Bran . . . sorry. I was a thousand miles away."

"If you don't mind my saying so, you've looked tired all day, my lady," Jerrold said. "It's probably just as well that our maneuvers were cut short. A good night's sleep will set you right again."

The stable door flew open and Bayla whirled in, her clothing and hair shot with snow. "Bayla, where's your cloak?" Heather said. "You'll catch your death out here."

Bayla's face was pale. "My lady, I can't find Isobel. She's not in our room."

"Oh, she's probably shirking as usual," Bran said. "Did you check the garderobe?"

Bayla ignored him. "Not only that, her things are gone. Her cloak and pack."

"Are you sure?" Heather demanded. "Her horse is still here."

"Yes, ma'am. I asked Cook if he'd seen her, but he said he and his man had been in the kitchen all day and only came out when Reach Seachlan and his hunters came back."

"All right. Go back inside and get dried off. I'll be right in."

"Do you think she went out, my lady?" Bran asked. "Went for a walk, maybe, and lost her way?"

Jerrold snorted. "Walk? That one?"

"Well, she took her things, remember? She's run off." Bran lowered his voice. "Out of shame, I'll wager."

Heather was already out the door, wincing against the stinging snow. With her knights on her heels, she crossed the courtyard and entered the lodge's kitchen. Bayla stood warming her hands before the fire, while Cook and his assistant muttered excitedly as they carved a haunch of venison. "You two never saw Mistress Isobel today, correct?" Heather demanded.

"That's right, my lady," Cook said. "I thought I heard someone on the stairs around mid-morning, and figured she was coming down for a bite to eat, but she never showed, and we got so busy after Reach Seachlan brought us all the venison that I never gave it another thought."

"Wait here," Heather told the knights. She hurried through the main chamber, where her men were setting up the tables, faces bright at the prospect of a fine dinner. She took the stairs two at a time and nearly ran into Ravelin on the landing.

"Well, good evening," he said, smiling.

Without answering, she brushed past him and strode into her bedchamber. Her own bed and Bayla's were neatly made, but Isobel's was a rumpled mess. Heather walked around it, not certain what she was searching for. Isobel's blankets were puddled at the foot of the bed, and she pulled them off, revealing Isobel's boots on the floor beneath. Heather turned to the hearth. The fire had died, but when she held one hand over it, a faint warmth still rose from the ashes.

"Looks like it's gone out," Ravelin said from the doorway. "I just poked up the fire in the next room; why don't you go in there to warm up while I start a fresh one here?"

"This fire hasn't been out long," Heather said, more to herself than to him.

"Looks as if it wasn't banked before you left. Naughty Bayla."

"It wasn't banked because Isobel stayed behind today. And now she's missing." Heather stood up, gnawing on her lower lip.

"Missing? You're sure she's not somewhere around the place?"

"No one's seen her since this morning. Her horse is in the stables, but her things are gone."

Ravelin's eyebrows went up. "Oh." He moved toward her, then stopped. "Heather, I'm afraid this may be my fault."

An uneasy tingle ran up her arms. "Explain, please."

"You may already know this, but Isobel and I ... before Daazna, that is—"

She waved one hand impatiently. "Yes, I'm aware of the swath you cut through the ladies of your court." Ravelin lowered his head, looking so chastened that she relented and moderated her tone. "Go on, please."

"Last night she came to my bed. She asked me not to hate her for what she'd done; she told me she'd do anything to make it up to me. I was still angry at her, and I—" His voice faltered, and he looked at her with pleading eyes. "I'm not proud of what I did, Heather."

"What did you do?"

"She wouldn't go. She tried to get in bed with me. I was afraid she'd wake the other men and they'd see me with her. I didn't want her, Heather; I haven't wanted any woman for months, not until last night—"

"Leave last night out of it," Heather said. "What did you do?"

"I told her to get out. I told her to leave me alone. And then I told her that for all I cared, she could go peddle her wares across the border in Stratheden."

Heather fixed him with a steely glare. "And then what happened?"

"She went back to her room. I saw her at breakfast, but we didn't speak." He spread his hands helplessly. "You don't think she took me at my word, do you? Took her things and crossed into Stratheden?"

"How close is the nearest Stratheden outpost?"

"Three miles or so. You take the trail south and then bear east. There's a bridge over the Strath and the outpost is on the other side. She could have walked it, I suppose, although I'm surprised she didn't take her horse."

"If she walked, why didn't she wear those?" She pointed at Isobel's boots.

Ravelin's face went pale to the lips, and for some moments he did not speak. "You're right," he said at last, his voice strained. "Why wouldn't she have worn her boots? Unless . . . unless she left before the snow started. Unless she wanted to present herself at the outpost looking her best."

With a frustrated shake of her head, Heather started from the room, but Ravelin caught her arm. "Heather, I swear to you I never meant to wound her—I only wanted her to leave. I was afraid someone would see us and tell you she'd been in my bed. A month ago, I wouldn't have cared. But after last night—after we'd been on the tower together—I realized how much was at stake. I couldn't stand to lose you, Heather."

She pulled loose and hurried downstairs, with Ravelin behind her. The soldiers had settled at the tables, eager for their dinners; Bayla, Bran and Jerrold lingered in the kitchen doorway, looking anxious. They stepped aside as she and Ravelin came into the kitchen. "Bring as many lanterns as you can find," Heather said to Bayla, then turned to the knights. "Bran, I'm leaving you in charge here. Jerrold, pick ten men who can sit a horse and aren't afraid to venture out in this mess, then join me in the stables. I want mounts for every man. We'll use the pack horses if we must."

"Surely, you're not mounting a search party?" Ravelin said. "In this weather, it would be madness."

"Not a search party, no," Heather said. "I want to pay a call on the Stratheden outpost."

She pulled up her hood and left them all in mid-protest. Buffeted by the wind, she made her way back to the stables, where she pulled the horses from their meals and began outfitting them in tack still damp from the day's work. They swelled their bellies against the saddle girths, but she elbowed them mercilessly and pulled the cinches tight. By the time the men joined her, she had a half-dozen confused and irritable horses ready to go. "Get the rest tacked up," she ordered, moving on to Skapi, who had laid back her ears and was showing every other sign of resistance. "Does Bayla have those lanterns ready?"

"Bran is lighting them," Bayla said, entering the stables red-cheeked and gasping from the wind. "He'll have them ready for us at the kitchen door."

"Bayla, you don't need to come."

"Your pardon, my lady, but if you don't have Isobel as an escort, you should at least have me."

"All right, all right. Skapi, stop it," Heather said, grabbing at the halter as the white horse tried to rear.

"Here, let me hold her while you get her saddled," Ravelin said.

"Reach Seachlan, you don't have to come either."

Ravelin lowered his voice below the noise of the men readying the horses. "I know the way to the outpost; you don't. Besides, this is partly my fault."

Heather heaved the saddle onto Skapi's back. "It's mostly your fault," she said through her teeth, but her words lacked heat. "If she's there, we'll bring her back—and you'll apologize for what you said."

Ravelin's eyebrows knotted and he opened his mouth to retort, but then he paused, as if considering what she had said. "Very well," he said. "If she's there, I'll apologize."

His sudden change of attitude was gratifying, if a little surprising. In short order, the other horses were ready, and everyone pulled on their gloves and cloaks, drew their hoods up, and led their mounts into the storm. At the kitchen door, they paused long enough to take the lanterns that Bran passed to them. "My lady, please be careful," he called over the wind.

"It's not far, and we'll be staying on the trail," Heather said. "Meantime, see if you can get the signal light going. If Isobel got lost, maybe it'll help her find her way back."

Bran peered doubtfully toward the tower. "It's not going to be easy in this wind, my lady."

"Do the best you can. Reach Seachlan, lead the way. Jerrold, take the rear and make sure everyone stays together. Bayla, stay with me. Let's go."

They crossed the lodge's courtyard in a slow-moving clump, heads bent, lanterns aloft. Once on the trail, they nudged the horses into a reluctant trot. Heather urged Skapi alongside Ravelin's mount, and he squinted at her from the depths of his hood. "At least the wind is at our backs," she said, raising her voice to be heard.

"It'll be in our faces on the return trip. And the snow is pil-ing up fast."

They spoke no more, concentrating on moving the horses forward. Heather turned frequently to make sure the group stayed together; periodically, they paused to leave a lantern at a turn in the road as they descended toward the Strath. At last, the bridge was before them. An iron-barred gate stood at the far end, with King Aldo's sun-and-crown insignia worked into the design. Just beyond the gate was a sturdy little hut, and beyond that a barren yard, with a low stone barracks on one side, a stable and two or three outbuildings on the other, and at the far end, a single and slightly more elegant structure, with Aldo's banner snapping from a pole in front of it.

As the Hogians crossed the bridge, their horses' hooves set-ting up a muffled clatter on the snow-covered boards, Heather peered down at the Strath. It was still moving fast, although a thin glaze of ice had formed near the shore and around the foot of the bridge. Ahead, two soldiers emerged from the hut, carrying pikes and a lantern. "Halt!" one cried through the wind. "Identify yourself!"

Heather threw back her hood. "Heather Demitt, commander of Hogia's army," she shouted back. "I need to speak to Commander Callum. It's urgent."

The soldiers conferred together, then one hustled off. "Wait there," said the other, his grin evident even through the blowing snow.

"Bastard," Ravelin said as they huddled against the dual miseries of their exposed position and the damp chill rising off the river below.

In time, the second man returned, and, with his comrade, swung the gates open and waved them ahead. "Last building on the right," he shouted as Heather came abreast of him. "He says he'll see you, Lady, but your men'll have to wait in the lee of the barracks." With a malicious grin, he jerked his thumb at the low stone building. "We have no comfortable doxy-houses here."

A low growl rose from the men behind her, but Heather merely nodded and led them through the gates and toward the barracks. More soldiers assembled in the doorway to watch them file past, heads bent against the wind, and gather on the opposite side of the building. The barracks were of a dugout design, with walls so low that someone on horseback was still exposed to the weather, so Heather gave the order to dismount. "I'll be as quick as I can," she said as she handed Skapi's reins to Jerrold.

"I'll come with you," Jerrold and Ravelin said in unison.

"You'll stay here," Heather said. "All I want is to find out if Isobel is somewhere in this encampment. If she is, I'll want to talk to her without any men around." She started toward the outbuilding the gate guard had indicated, but to her surprise, Bayla fell in with her. "Bayla, stay with Jerrold."

"My lady, for appearance's sake I should go with you. You shouldn't meet with Callum alone. And if Isobel is here, I might be able to help persuade her that running away isn't the solution."

As they approached the little building, its door opened, framing a figure just within. It was Callum's pockmarked captain, and he grinned as they blew past him into the snug room.

"Come in, come in," Callum said. He was sitting with his heels propped on the table before him, while his stocky captain lounged in a chair opposite. The captain rose, goblet in hand, and gave them a mocking bow, but Callum stayed as he was. "What a pleasant surprise, Commander. And you brought your lovely maidservant as well. My captains and I were just enjoying a little wine before bed. Please, sit down." He gestured toward the seats vacated by his captains, then reached for a heavy earthenware jug that stood in the middle of the table. "May I pour you both a dram?"

"Thank you, no," Heather said, taking one seat as Bayla slid into the other. "I won't keep you long. Commander, one of my people has gone missing—"

The pockmarked captain clucked his tongue. "One of Hogia's finest? Gone astray?"

"No. It's my traveling companion. Isobel."

Callum pulled a comic face. "Really? Izzy's gone and gotten herself lost?"

"We came back from the day's exercise to find her gone, along with her pack. I don't think she's gone far; she left her horse and her boots behind." She fixed Callum with a somber stare. "Is she here? I'd like very much to talk to her."

"Well, well," the stocky captain said. "The stringy old ewe has run off and left her little lamb behind."

"Is she here?" Heather repeated.

Callum shrugged. "I haven't seen Izzy. Either of you seen Izzy?"

"Let me think." The pocky captain tapped his finger against his chin. "The men said there was a wild sow rooting around in the woods this morning . . . you think maybe they mistook it for her?" He guffawed at his own wit.

"Maybe she's hiding," said the stocky captain. He drained his goblet, slammed it on the table, and dropped to his knees beside Bayla. "Izzy?" he called, thrusting head and shoulders beneath the table. "You here?"

"Commander, it's no joking matter," Heather said. "If Isobel isn't here, I'll need to mount a search immediately."

Callum only smirked in response. At the same moment, Bayla went rigid.

"Well, she's not under here," said the stocky captain from beneath the table. He put his head out and grinned at Bayla. "Nice legs, though."

For a long moment Bayla stared at him, then her mouth curled into a faint smile. "Your goblet is empty, Captain," she said, and reached for the wine jug.

The pockmarked captain laid one hand on her shoulder. "I'd like a drink from a different jug," he said, and slid his hand down to her breast.

Before Heather could react, Bayla seized the jug and brought it down hard on the stocky captain's skull. He collapsed without a sound as she swung round and slammed the jug into the second captain's face. His eyes rolled up into his head, his legs buckled, and he crumpled to the floor. Bayla replaced the jug and looked demurely at Heather. "Sorry to interrupt, my lady."

Heather gazed at her maidservant, at the two unconscious captains, and then at Callum, who gaped at her from across the table. She rose and drew her sword slowly and without menace. "Commander, you've mocked and insulted me. You've allowed your subordinates to put their hands on my maidservant. You've refused me even the common courtesy of a straight answer to a simple question. I'm going to ask you one more time: Is Isobel here?"

Callum took a long look at the sword in her hand, then raised his eyes to hers, his face set in an expression of grudging admiration. "No."

"Are you sure?"

"She isn't here."

"Is there any chance that she's elsewhere in your camp? In an outbuilding? In the barracks?"

"No," Callum said again. "If you want to search the buildings, I give you permission. I'll even escort you. But I swear to you, one commander to another—Isobel isn't here."

Heather breathed a silent sigh. "Then I feel bound to tell you that we'll begin searching for her as soon as day breaks tomorrow. And that search will include this entire area, including your border."

"As you wish. I'll give orders that you aren't to be hindered in any way." Callum stood and extended his hand to her. "I've handled this situation poorly, Commander Demitt. Put your sword away, and let's start over."

Bayla rose, her eyes narrowed suspiciously, but Heather sheathed her sword and put her hand into Callum's big paw. "Thank you for your time, Commander. And I hope Bayla didn't do your captains any lasting damage."

"I doubt it," Callum said. He craned his neck to look at both men, who were stirring and moaning softly on the floor. "They're a couple of hardheads. That was neat work, Mistress Bayla."

"I had a good teacher," Bayla said with a sidelong glance at Heather.

Callum's mouth twisted into a wry grin. "Clearly. Commander, I'll pass the word among my men to keep an eye out for your comrade, but I must be blunt with you: If Isobel wandered off and didn't find shelter before this storm hit, I doubt you'll find her alive."

"I appreciate your honesty, Commander. Thank you for your help, and good evening."

They left Callum pouring himself another goblet of wine and watching sourly as his two captains struggled to their feet. Outside the wind had died somewhat, but the snow was still falling thick and fast, and the men and horses waiting alongside the barracks wore a coating of white on their heads and shoulders.

"What's the news?" Jerrold asked. "Have they seen her?"

"No," Heather said. "She's not here."

Her satisfaction over gaining Callum's respect was already fading, overwhelmed by worry and a nagging sense of failure. Isobel was still missing. She found it hard to believe that Isobel—haughty, lazy Isobel—would strike off on her own into the wilderness. *Without a horse*, she thought; *without even a decent pair of boots. What was she thinking? Where was she heading? Was she distraught enough to have done something so foolish?*

As they made their way back across the bridge and onto the trail, she remembered the night before: her terse words to Isobel, the sound of muffled sobs in the darkness. Her spirits sank even lower. *If she had been one of your soldiers, you would have treated her more kindly. But you didn't like her, and you resented being saddled with her on this trip. She was your responsibility, and you turned your back on her.*

She was distantly grateful they'd had the foresight to leave lanterns along their path. The snow was falling so thickly that it was difficult to make out the trail, and in places it had piled into hock-high drifts. Callum's words echoed through her brain, summoning visions of Isobel staggering through the snow, or shivering against a tree, or collapsed and covered with a veil of white. The last image was unbearable. The lodge loomed ahead, every window bright with candlelight, and, suddenly hopeful, she kicked weary Skapi into a faster gait. As they filed into the courtyard, the lodge doors opened, silhouetting Bran's sturdy form. "Did she come back?" Heather called. "Is she here?"

"No, my lady," Bran said, and even though she could not see his face, she heard the strain in his voice. "No luck at the Stratheden outpost?"

A knot rose in Heather's throat. "None."

Bran's shoulders slumped. Skapi was already heading eagerly toward the stables; as they rounded the corner of the lodge, Heather saw that the tower beacon was not lit. "What in the—why isn't there a signal fire?"

"My lady, the snow is so thick—" Jerrold said.

She threw herself from Skapi's back and flung the reins at him. "Take care of her while I deal with this," she snarled, then plunged across the snow-covered courtyard and mounted the tower steps in rising fury.

Two soldiers were huddled at the top, struggling to light a handful of kindling from a lantern. "This beacon is supposed to be lit," Heather shouted, startling them so badly that they jumped. "Why isn't it lit?"

Both men snapped to attention, faces wrung with anxiety. "Sorry, ma'am, sorry," said one. "We've been trying and trying, but the wind kept blowing it out, and now the snow is so thick and wet that the wood won't light."

Heather swore and snatched the lantern from them. "Grown men and you can't even light a simple fire? Go inside, the both of you. You're no use to me."

As the men retreated, shamefaced, Heather knocked the accumulation of wet wood, scorched kindling and snow from the basin. The men had carried up plenty of firewood and piled it in a corner, and Heather stripped off her gloves and rooted through the mass for the driest wood she could find. She laid a quick fire in the basin, then snatched up a branch of pine. She clawed off a chunk of bark the size of a man's hand, then filled it with smaller chips and dried pine needles. She lit the bundle from the lantern and thrust it into the basin. For a few moments, the little flame glowed and spread, and Heather blew on it, fed it more tinder, cajoled and swore at it, but the snow and wind were relentless, and in spite of all she could do, the flame went out. Again, she scraped together a handful of tinder; again, she lit it from the lantern, this time dripping some of the lantern's oil onto the mound. She shoved the brave little blaze into the basin, but the heavy, wet snowfall snuffed it. Back to the woodpile she went, but her hands were numb and fumbling, her fingernails blue with the cold, and the snow was thicker than ever. Crouching over the lantern, she tried to light the scanty wad of tinder, but she was shivering so hard that the lantern rattled and swayed, and she could not do it. It was no good, no good, no good—

Someone moved the lantern aside, grasped her shoulders and lifted her to her feet. She swung around with a snarled oath and raised her fists to strike, but Ravelin only enveloped her in his arms. For a moment she struggled to free herself, but then she sagged against him and began to weep; silent, gulping sobs that shook her whole frame. The snow swirled around them, masking them from sight, but for once Heather did not even care who saw them. She let Ravelin hold her while she cried tears of guilt and shame and helplessness, and he cradled her against his chest and patted her back, murmuring words of solace.

At last, her tears over, she raised her head to look into Ravelin's face. For some reason she expected him to be looking down at her, with a comforting expression in keeping with his kindly words, but he was not. He gazed into the distance, his eyes squinted slightly against the snow, a little smile on his lips.

CHAPTER FOUR

"No offense to you, but I'm sick of the sight of your warship's backside," Torrin muttered as he, Nigel, and Kristan stood in the bow of their ship, following the track of the Northern flotilla.

"We must be nearly there," Kristan said. "Olaf said this *sprunga* is in some cliffs north of Hull's Contrivance." He pointed to the shoreline off their port side, where the waves smashed and churned at the foot of steep headlands.

"I hope so. I'm not certain how much longer our vessel will last." Torrin glanced toward the shallow hold, where two centaurs stood hock-deep, bailing seawater, while two more struggled to patch the growing cracks in the wineship's hull.

"At least the fleet from Hull's Contrivance has left off following us," Nigel said. "They didn't look any too pleased to see us in Stratheden waters."

"If they have any sense, they've headed back to their own port, such as it is," Torrin said. "The sea's gone an ugly color, and I don't like the look of those clouds."

"Ring 'round the moon last night too. Captain Pratchett told me it's a sign of rain or snow."

"As long as it's not a storm. I'm not sure how this ship will fare in a storm."

The two went on discussing the weather, but Kristan was barely listening. Ahead, Olaf's ship and the captured Norwinn warship had changed course; now, instead of bearing north, they had turned slightly westward, angling toward shore. And were they slowing? They certainly seemed to be looming much larger on the horizon.

Astéria was at the rail, craning her neck, with Nolle beside her. "They're stopping!" the Wiche girl cried suddenly. "Look, everyone, they're stopping!"

Torrin shaded his eyes against the meager afternoon sun. "They certainly seem to be. What do you want to do, Kristan?"

"We ought to rush them," one of the male centaurs said. "Get between them and the ocean, and push them in toward shore."

"And then what?" Chári said from the tiller. "Run them aground and risk of drowning our brothers and sisters?"

Not to mention my men and horses, Kristan thought bitterly. The longer they had been at sea, the more the mingled scent of musk and frustration rose from the *O Tópos* centaurs. They had chafed at Torrin's refusal to overtake the Northmen, and for his part, Torrin was sometimes brusque as well, clearly torn between watching their quarry and watching Astéria.

Torrin was watching him now, waiting for an answer. "Get within hailing distance," Kristan said. "I doubt they'll allow us any closer."

He nodded to Chári, who brought the ship's nose to the northwest. As they closed on the Northmen's vessels, Nigel leaned over the rail. "Odd," he murmured. "Look at that cliff face just beyond them . . . see the big discoloration that runs down it? If Dell were here, he'd probably give us a lecture on rocks and sediment and . . ." His voice drifted off and his eyes went wide.

"That's no discoloration," Kristan said, his own voice hushed. "It's the *sprunga*."

Reaving, Crack, *sprunga*—none of the words fully encompassed the sheer enormity of the rift that cleaved the rock face. At its base, where the waves churned and swirled, it was large enough to swallow even the Norwinn warship whole. The great gap soared upward through the stone, three times the height of the warship's tallest mast, and tapering to a point at its summit, with a series of smaller cracks running out from it. It was as if an enormous spear had risen from the ocean, stabbed through the rock, and then withdrawn, leaving its imprint like a giant scar. A shudder of pure dread ran up Kristan's spine.

"*O Astéria mou,*" Torrin whispered, but it was an expression of awe rather than terror.

"Olaf said they saw it open up before them during a storm," Kristan said. His voice was trembling, and he had to steady it before continuing: "He said it was large and deep enough that both his ship and Sigurd's could shelter inside."

"Imagine watching that thing being born," Nigel said. He was grinning, as if the prospect pleased him. The other centaurs had paused in their labors to study the huge fissure, but they seemed intrigued rather than frightened, and Nolle was so excited that she was almost dancing. "There it is, there it is!" she cried, scampering from bow to stern in her glee.

No one is afraid of it but you, Kristan berated himself. *Why are you so afraid?*

"Kreestan!" Astéria called. She pointed to the captive warship. Sigurd stood in its stern, with a white-faced Melissa at his side. Sigurd had one hand on her shoulder; the other beckoned to them in a manner that was almost friendly. Nigel made a sound halfway between a groan and a growl, and pressed against the rail, as if by doing so he could make the ship move faster.

"StoneKing!" Sigurd bellowed over the boom of the surf. "Come closer so we can talk, but let's have no tricks. I haven't harmed a hair on your sister's head, but I won't hesitate to push her overboard if you try anything."

"Bastard," Nigel said through his teeth.

"Come to my starboard, between my brother's ship and this one," Sigurd said.

Kristan nodded to Torrin. The centaurs furled the sail and used the oars to maneuver their craft closer to the Northern fleet. Sigurd's ship stood off the Norwinn warship's port bow, while Olaf's vessel bobbed to starboard, his men waiting at their oars, and Olaf himself, somber and still, at the tiller. Torrin nodded to him as they passed, while Nigel glared, but Kristan averted his head.

Sigurd brought Melissa to the rail and stood looking down as they came alongside. "You're lucky your vessel made it this far, StoneKing, but it's taking on water fast. I doubt it'll last much longer."

"Melissa, are you all right?" Nigel called.

She nodded, her eyes brimming with sudden tears. Her lips formed the words *I'm sorry*, but she made no sound. She looked to Kristan, but he was only dimly conscious of her gaze. The *sprunga* loomed in the distance, like a great mouth waiting to be fed, and he could not tear his eyes from it.

"Yes, look at it," Sigurd said. "You'd think the thing was hungry, the way it gapes, but it's spit us out time and again. This time, with you aboard, maybe it'll swallow us down."

Kristan had to shut his eyes against the *sprunga* so he could think. "I've told you it won't work. Don't make this worse than it already is, Sigurd."

"It can't get any worse for us, StoneKing. Now, I'm going to sling a gangway between our ships. You'll secure it on your side, and then we'll trade your crew for mine, one at a time, turn about. You'll stay right there, in plain sight, until the trade is over, and then you'll come with us. Into the *sprunga*."

Kristan's mouth went dry; his tongue was like a piece of leather. He gripped the Stone in one fist and forced his numb lips to form words. "I'll do nothing until I have proof my people are unharmed."

"Fair enough." Sigurd turned to one of his crew and held a brief conversation. The man trotted off. "I wouldn't delay too long, StoneKing; the weather's beginning to turn, and I think your *hestur-verur* friends are going to have a hard enough time crossing the gangway as it is."

Kristan turned to face Olaf. "Listen to me. This won't work. Do you understand, Olaf? It won't work."

"We have to try," Olaf said. "I wish I could make you understand that."

His face was expressionless, as if a stiff mask had fallen over it. Kristan's scalp crinkled with sudden anger. "Very well. When I'm proved right, and all this is over, are you prepared to deal with the consequences?"

Olaf nodded.

"Don't be an idiot, Olaf," Nigel said. "Don't you understand that every ship in Kristan's realm will be after you?"

"When you took the *Kentávron* prisoner, you turned against me and *O Tópos* as well," Torrin said. "It's not too late to make things right, Olaf."

"What would you have me do?" Olaf said. "Take up arms against my own people? My own brother?"

"Do what your heart tells you to do."

"I have. Just as he has," Olaf said, jerking his chin at Kristan. "He put your friendship before mine. The *Kentávron* before the Northmen, when the Northmen were in greater need."

"I gave you all the aid I could," Kristan said.

"Everything but what we needed most."

"Enough," Sigurd called. "Here's one of your men, StoneKing. Question him as you want."

Some of the crew wrestled Sir Geoffrey up to the rail. His arms were bound behind his back and his mouth was tight with rage. "Get your hands off me, fools; where would I run?" He looked over the rail at Kristan and his face flushed. "My lord—and Prince Torrin too. A thousand, thousand apologies."

"Never mind, Geoff. Tell me if the others are all right. Has anyone been mistreated or harmed?"

"There was some scuffling at first, my lord—"

"Sir Geoffrey—my people," Astéria cried. "How they do?"

"They're fine," Geoffrey said. "A little seasick from being kept in the hold, but fine otherwise. Some of the knights got knocked about when the ship was taken, my lord, but all in all, we're in good shape. And the Northmen treated your sister kindly." The look he shot Melissa was anything but kind. "Let her come up on deck for air and all."

"Very good," Kristan said absently. He turned back to Sigurd. "Set up your gangway."

"My lord, surely you're not going with them?"

"Geoff, I've no choice."

"Put him back with the others," Sigurd said to his men, and turned to Torrin. "Once we're away, you can let everyone out of the hold, but not until we're out of range."

Torrin scowled. "We're not going to shoot at you."

"No, you're not, and you're not going to follow us either. Your word, please."

"Or what?"

"Or I'll take one of yours with me as insurance." Sigurd grinned at Chári. "Maybe that pretty one at the tiller."

"I'd like to see you try, *kópane*," Chári muttered.

"Very well," Torrin said. "You have my word. I won't release our people in the hold until you're away."

As the centaurs secured their oars, the Northmen produced their gangway: planks lashed together to form a rough bridge and fitted with rope handrails. They fastened it to the rail of the warship and then swung its end down to the centaurs, who secured it. "It's awfully narrow," Nigel said to Torrin. "Are you sure your people can pass over it safely?"

Sigurd tossed them a loop of a sturdy rope. "Have each one put that around their middle, and we'll help haul them up."

"Very well," Torrin said. "Who's first?"

"I go," Astéria said. "I speak to my people. I tell them what happens, and they are free soon."

"You won't be able to get them out," Nolle piped up. "They can't climb the ladder."

"You change them like before."

"But I want to go with Kristan," Nolle said. "I want to see

the *sprunga*."

"You'll board the warship with everyone else," Kristan said, "and you'll do as Prince Torrin and the knights tell you."

"But—"

"You come with me now, Nolle," Astéria snapped. She stood at the foot of the gangway, slid the loop of rope over her head and around her waist, and beckoned to Nolle. Eyes downcast, Nolle ducked beneath the rope and stood in front of her. With one hand on Nolle's shoulder, and the other gripping the rope, Astéria nodded to Torrin. "I ready."

"Be careful," Torrin answered, his face suddenly drawn with anxiety.

"Haul away," Sigurd called to his men. Slowly and carefully, Astéria and Nolle ascended the gangway. As they reached the top, the Northmen reached out to help them onto the deck, but Nolle hopped down by herself, looking surly. "Easy," Astéria called back to the other centaurs. "No worry."

One of the Northern crewmen took her place on the gangway and descended, swiftly and easily, bringing the rope with him. As he stepped onto the deck, he gestured Sigurd's warship closer. "Sick of that Norwinn tub," he muttered. "It'll be good to be back on our own ship. Well, who's next?"

"You go, Nigel," Torrin said.

Nigel started eagerly forward, but then hesitated, and turned back to Kristan. "Will you be all right? I mean . . . you're sure the Stone won't . . . won't do something?"

Fear turned Kristan's tongue bitter. "You mean send the Northmen back home and me along with them? How kind of you to care."

Nigel's mouth went tight. "Of course I care. All of us care. You're the StoneKing. What would we do if something happened to you?"

"What, indeed?" Kristan said with a tiny shrug. "Don't trouble yourself, Nigel. One way or another, this is going to end badly. It's just a question of how badly. Go on . . . and put things right between you and Missy. Neither of you is any use to me if you're quarreling."

He waved Nigel off and went into the bow to wait as the exchange continued: centaurs ascending from their leaking craft into the Norwinn warship; Northmen descending, crossing the centaur vessel's deck and leaping gratefully into Sigurd's ship, which had drawn up by the wineship's stern. Turning his back on the activity, Kristan huddled in his cloak. The wind had died to a light breeze, and the slack sails of the warship flapped listlessly. On Olaf's ship, the crew waited in silence. His fists on his hips, Olaf stood looking at the *sprunga*, but the sight of it made Kristan's skin crawl. He gripped the Stone in one fist and fixed his gaze instead on the seawater rising about his ankles.

"*Fiskur.*"

He looked across the water into Olaf's blue eyes.

"I'm sorry for all this," Olaf said.

"Are you?"

"We had to try. I don't expect you to understand, but we had to try. And if you're right—if it doesn't work—I swear you'll never be troubled by the Northmen again."

Without answering, Kristan turned back to the gangway. Only Torrin was left, and, at the top of the gangway, Sigurd waited. Torrin settled the loop of rope around his waist, then nodded to Kristan, and raised one hand in solemn farewell. Kristan nodded back, and Torrin ascended to the warship. As soon as he was aboard, Sigurd swung down to the deck and cast the foot of the gangway loose. As Torrin and the centaurs lifted it into the warship, Sigurd clapped his hands. "To your oars, *hundar.* It's time to go home."

With a clatter of oars and a roar of glee, Sigurd's crew took up their posts. Sigurd bowed mockingly to Kristan and gestured him aboard the Northern vessel. He even held out his hand to assist, but Kristan ignored it and leaped clumsily across the gap by himself. Sigurd hesitated only long enough to yank away the sodden patching in the wineship's hold, then jumped into his own ship. "Sorry about your vessel," he called to Torrin, who watched grimly as the ship sagged deeper in the water, executed a sluggish half-turn, and sank beneath the next wave.

Sigurd strode across the deck, slapping shoulders, making jokes, his eyes gleaming and his teeth white in his ruddy face. On Olaf's ship, the men had also made ready to leave, but more quietly, and Olaf took the tiller without a word.

"Pull away!" Sigurd shouted. In unison, the men dug their oars into the water and the two ships surged toward the *sprunga*, leaving the Norwinn warship in their wake. Kristan had one last glimpse of the anxious faces lining its rail—Torrin, Astéria, Nigel, and Melissa—then Sigurd stepped before him, blocking his view. "Look at her," he said, pointing toward the *sprunga*. "I called her a mouth, but maybe I'm wrong. Maybe she's not a mouth at all. Maybe she's a great *kunta*, all gaping and ready for us. Maybe all we have to do is ram ourselves into her and she'll do whatever we want."

The Northmen rowed hard, caught the crest of a swell, and rode it, whooping. Kristan could only cling to the rail, mouth desiccated by fear. The *sprunga* seemed to bound toward them like a great beast, and it took all his self-control not to shriek and bolt to the stern to elude its maw. Within moments they reached the churning froth around the *sprunga's* mouth, and Sigurd shoved him aside to direct the ships into the dark recess within. "Oars at the ready! When the next wave hits, we'll let the greedy slut suck us in," he cried, then turned to wave to Olaf. "Follow me, *litli bróðir!*"

With a rumble and a roar, the wave caught them, slewing them sideways. On the starboard side, the rowers dug in to correct their trajectory; on the port, the oars came out to fend off the rocks that lay like jagged teeth around the mouth of the *sprunga*. With a splintering crash that knocked Kristan off his feet, Sigurd's ship struck the side of the opening, rebounded, and then rushed into the gap. As Kristan rolled to his hands and knees, Olaf's ship came careening after them, its sinuous prow striking their stern with such force that everyone aboard went tumbling. The impact sent Kristan hurtling against Sigurd; they slammed to the deck in a snarl of arms, legs and cloaks.

And then all was silent. Kristan lay on deck staring at the ceiling of the *sprunga* high overhead: a dark, shining surface dotted with small, ragged shadows that shifted uneasily as the two ships drifted deeper into the gap. At last, the nose of Sigurd's ship bumped up against a barrier and stopped, and when Kristan sat up, he saw that their prow had reached the end of the passage and was snubbed against the rock. Olaf's ship eased up behind them, giving them a gentle nudge. The two ships lay in a quiet line, stern to prow, with the walls of the *sprunga* rising close around them. It was as if the sprunga had molded itself around the shapes of the two ships; its sides were no more than an arm's length away, its roof tapered high enough for the masts to clear.

For some moments no one spoke or moved. "Well," Sigurd said at last. "Here we are."

His voice was overloud and rang with a sneering bravado that made Kristan want to clap his hands over his ears. He felt certain the *sprunga* was listening, breathing lightly and evenly as a cat watching an unwary mouse. On the other ship, all was quiet but for Olaf's reassuring murmurs. In time, Sigurd's crew got to their feet, secured their oars, and talked nervously amongst themselves as they peered about the *sprunga's* interior. They spoke in their own language rather than the common tongue, with the word *kunta* repeated frequently, mockingly. *Don't*, Kristan wanted to tell them. *Don't insult it. Don't provoke it.*

The crew's snickers rebounded off the *sprunga's* walls, as if the sprunga shared in their laughter, but the echo sounded different: a low chuckle that sent a chill through Kristan's body. Gripping the Stone in both hands, he cringed against the ship's hull, trying to make himself as small as possible.

Sigurd's hand fell on his shoulder. "Stand up, StoneKing.

Stand up and let the *sprunga* see you." Kristan did not move, and with a shouted oath Sigurd yanked him to his feet.

As one, the shadows overhead shifted and then boiled to life, squeaking and fluttering. Kristan tried to recoil, but Sigurd held him in place. "What, are you afraid of bats?" With a bellow, he waved one arm at the ceiling. Panicked, thousands of bats swirled down from the ceiling, squeaking and fluttering wildly. Everyone aboard the ships ducked and shouted and swatted at the tiny creatures. Like living smoke, they swarmed toward the fading daylight beyond the *sprunga's* entrance. A breath later, they were gone, leaving the cavernous interior of the *sprunga* more silent and ominous than before.

"Well, go on!" Sigurd said. He shoved Kristan toward the bow and the *sprunga's* nether wall beyond it. Kristan landed against the rail, the slick, dark rock so close that he could smell it, feel its dankness like clammy hands against his face. He wanted to run, but the thought of turning his back on it was more terrifying than facing it head-on.

"What would you have me do?" he said. His tremulous words echoed off the stone.

"What do you mean?" Beneath its veneer of bluster, Sigurd's own voice was suddenly uncertain.

Kristan looked at him over one shoulder. "You made me come here because you thought the Stone could send you and your men back. I'm not Wiche—I have no powers. So tell me what you want me to do."

Sigurd stared at him for several long moments. Beyond him, Olaf stood in the bow of his own ship, silhouetted against the fading light beyond the *sprunga's* entrance. A few bats fluttered back inside and settled uneasily onto their overhead roosts.

Sigurd took a menacing step forward. "Use your Stone. Send us back."

"The Stone is a talisman. I wear it around my neck, and it protects me from magic. I don't know how to make it do what you want it to do. If you know some way, then tell me."

The wind outside chuckled and moaned across the mouth of the *sprunga*. More bats returned, chittering softly, leathery wings whispering as they regained their perches, huddling together. A flicker of wavering light caught Kristan's eye; a trio of the creatures, each surrounded by a faint unsteady glow, circled overhead. They did not land, but flitted back and forth, as if watching. A few men hunched their shoulders and peered up at the bats, faces pinched with disgust.

"Do as I say," Sigurd said. "Use your Stone."

"How?"

"I don't know how!" Sigurd shouted. "It's your Stone! Do something!"

"Touch the *sprunga's* wall, Kristan." Olaf's voice was soft, reasonable. "Your touch can undo spells. I've seen you do it."

Outside the wind gusted, sending a low howl ricocheting off the rock walls. More bats hurried inside, but the trio overhead still did not land. Nolle's amber eyes gleamed within one wavering shape, but Kristan could not tell who the other two were. He gripped the Stone in one hand and stretched the other toward the *sprunga's* back wall. Cold rose off it in waves. Teeth chattering, Kristan hesitated, only a finger's width from touching the wall.

"Do it!" one of the men cried. "Touch the wall!"

Sigurd strode forward, grabbed Kristan's wrist and thrust his hand against the slick, clammy rock. It was as if an icicle had pierced Kristan's palm; the cold shot through his hand, his wrist, up his arm to his shoulder. It crawled down his neck and sides, penetrating his guts, his brain. Another muttering chuckle sounded, but this one was inside his head.

His jaw clamped shut against the knot of terror and rage rising in his throat, against the heave and churn of his guts, and the incipient cramping of his calves. Sigurd did not seem to feel the cold; he was swearing horribly and straining to keep Kristan's palm pressed tightly to the wall. As Kristan tried to twist free, something swooped past his face and suddenly materialized into the furious form of the boy Desta. "Get off him!" Desta cried, drawing a knife. "Get off him!"

With his free hand, Sigurd knocked Desta to the deck. Another form dropped from the ceiling: Serle, eyes wide as he tried to peel Sigurd's fingers from Kristan's wrist. "Let him go, please, sir. He don't like it; he don't like to be touched."

Sigurd elbowed Serle aside. Desta scrambled for his knife, but Sigurd kicked him in the ribs. At that moment Nolle materialized, eyes flashing, forefinger pointed at Sigurd as she snarled the words of her shift spell. Kristan had a single glimpse of Sigurd's startled face before the Northman's figure blurred and shrank down to that of a large, angry-eyed bat. The crew cried out and cringed away from the flapping, helpless creature.

Nolle bared her teeth in a fierce grimace, struggling to hold the shift. "I wish I could make it stick," she hissed. "Make you stay a bat forever. Then you could live here in your precious *sprunga*."

Olaf leaped from his ship and shoved forward, white-faced. He and his men joined the semi-circle of Sigurd's crew, whose shouts had faded to mutters as they watched their transformed captain flail and squeak.

Kristan sank to his knees and pressed his icy hand to the Stone. "Stop it, Nolle."

Nolle did not answer. Her face was growing ashen. Desta stood over the Sigurd-bat with his knife at the ready. Serle crouched at Kristan's side, hands poised as if desperate to lay them comfortingly on Kristan's shoulders. The Sigurd-bat let out a furious chittering and heaved itself onto the joints of its wings, for all the world like a man propping himself on his elbows. One of Sigurd's crew let out a high, hysterical giggle.

Bucking furiously, the Sigurd-bat opened its mouth, showing an uneven row of sharp teeth. With a sudden hiss, the spell collapsed, and Sigurd finally materialized, flat on his back, arms and legs waving, purple-faced with rage. Nolle's eyes rolled up into her head; she tottered backward and fell. Like an angry bear, Sigurd lunged on hands and knees toward her. Serle cried out and tried to pull Nolle out of reach as Desta slashed at Sigurd with the knife, catching the sleeve of the Northman's tunic. Sigurd slammed one elbow into the boy's midriff, sending him flying, then grabbed Nolle by the ankle. Shouldering through the watching men, Olaf grasped his brother's arm, but Sigurd twisted free, and dragged Nolle from Serle's grasp. With a shrill cry that spiraled into a yowling screech, she abruptly shifted into her cat-form and raked one forepaw across Sigurd's nose. In a blur of claws and fur, she fled behind Kristan. Serle joined her there as Sigurd roared and advanced, but Desta charged at the Northman yet again. Kristan grabbed the boy by the collar, slung him in the bow with Serle and Nolle, and threw out both arms protectively. "Don't hurt them!" he cried. "I'll do whatever you want, only don't hurt my children!"

Sigurd loomed over him, breathing hard, blood dripping from the claw marks scoring his nose. "*Your* children?" he snarled. "Your little band of freaks? I ought to knock you down and drown all three."

Kristan did not move. He was suddenly, strangely calm. "I'll do what you want. I'll try to summon the power of the Stone. But touch any one of these children and I won't be responsible for what happens afterward. I swear it."

Sigurd feinted toward Nolle's cat-form. She hissed, ran up the serpent-like prow, and stood at its end, back arched, fur standing out all along her spine. Desta let out a hiss of his own and brandished his knife, but Kristan quelled him with a glance. Serle stayed where he was, chin trembling.

"*Bróðir*, leave them alone," Olaf said gently. "If the StoneKing says he'll try to help, he will."

"He'd better." Sigurd backed up a few steps and waved one hand dismissively, but his fingers shook, and his face was pallid and sweating.

Kristan turned toward the prow. Nolle's shift form still perched there, shivering. Serle cowered by the hull, white to the lips. Desta still clutched his knife and watched the Northmen with a distrustful eye. "Desta, put your knife away and stand aside," Kristan said. "Nolle, come down from there. Go wait with Serle. Serle, calm her down, please. Desta, stay with them."

"Yes, my lord," Desta said.

"Yes, my lord," Serle whispered.

Nolle slipped past Kristan, and he had just a glimpse of her wild eyes within the shift form. She slunk to Serle, who crouched and put his arms around her. Desta stood over the two, one hand on the hilt of his knife, the other nursing his side where Sigurd had struck him.

"Now be still," Kristan told the three of them. "This will be over soon."

"Please, sir," Serle said. "Please be careful."

"Nothing will happen," Kristan said, but he was not so sure.

Once again, he clutched the Stone in his right hand and stretched out his left. Once again, the terrible chill seemed to leap from the *sprunga* wall, but he clenched his teeth and placed his fingertips on its surface. He was afraid, but without Sigurd pinning him in place, the sense of panic was gone. The rage was still present, but it had subsided to cold calculation. *Breathe*, he told himself. *Control it. Use it.* He let his palm slide flat against the rock and shut his eyes.

This time he did not hear the laughter. He heard nothing, nothing but the faraway crash of surf, the squeaking of the bats, and the anxious breathing of the Northmen as they stood watching him. *Not mine*, he thought. *This Reaving, this Crack, this sprunga is not mine. It cares nothing for me.*

The idea calmed him even further. *These Northern fools. What do they think is going to happen? That I'll mutter Wiche words, snap my fingers, and everything will be as it was?* Bitter resentment welled in his chest. *If it wasn't for Sigurd, these men would have given up long ago. They'd have found themselves some land to work and women to make a home with; maybe they'd even have families by now. But he wouldn't let them give up. He's kept them believing there's still a chance. And now he's tangled me in his net of promises and lies. He's mocked me, man-handled me, made me follow him out here in the dead of winter on a fool's errand. Send him back? I'll see him dead first.*

In the darkness of his mind's eye, a faint memory stirred: Olaf telling him of the day their ships had been lost in storm, how they had prayed to their gods for deliverance, how Sigurd had cursed both his men and the gods for abandoning them.

An idea came to him, an idea that made him smile even as his guts twisted in protest and the Stone went cold in his fingers, colder than the *sprunga's* wall beneath his other hand.

Control it. Use it.

Kristan opened his eyes. He stepped away from the wall and turned to face the Northmen.

"What happened?" Olaf asked. "*Fiskur*, what happened?"

"Nothing happened," Kristan said. "Just as I told you."

"Try again," Sigurd said.

"No."

"I said try again."

"And I said no." He walked unsteadily to the stern and peered past Olaf's ship toward the mouth of the *sprunga*. Serle and Desta tagged after him; Nolle, still in her cat-form, leaped ahead and poised herself on the rail. The light outside had faded to an ominous, leaden gray. For a few heartbeats Kristan studied it, then deliberately reached out and ran his hand over Nolle's fur. With a hiss, the spell collapsed, and she rose up next to him, grabbing his hand. Tolerating her touch for the moment, he turned back to Sigurd. "Did you see that?" he said. "That's the limit of my power—and the Stone's. I can undo a simple spell. But what happened here, with this Reaving, this *sprunga*—that was a greater magic. *Tabi'a*. I told you that before." His guts were churning, from both the pressure of Nolle's hand and from the knowledge of what he was about to say. He pulled his fingers free of hers and pointed at Sigurd. "This *sprunga* is your doing."

"What?" Olaf breathed.

"You told me about the storm, Olaf. The storm that brought you here five years ago. You told me your men cried out to the heavens for help. I think this Reaving heard. I think it opened for them. But you also said when your men cried for help, your brother cursed them, and your gods, and your fate." He settled himself against the rail. "Maybe the Reaving heard that too. Maybe that's why you can't leave."

"What are you saying?" Sigurd demanded.

Kristan shrugged. "I think your punishment for those curses is to be trapped here forever. And that means your companions are trapped as well."

The color drained from Sigurd's face. The men were silent, but some pursed their lips and nodded, as if Kristan had spoken aloud thoughts they had nursed in their hearts over the years. The children pressed as close to Kristan as they dared.

"No." Olaf's voice was little more than a strangled whisper. "That's not true. That's not true."

Kristan said nothing. He waited.

With a sudden shriek of despair, Sigurd turned and flung himself at the *sprunga* wall. "*Hóra!*" he shouted, pounding both fists into the unyielding stone. "*Kunta! Slepptu okkur! Slepptu okkur!*"

Olaf tried to pull him away. "*Bróðir, nei. Vertu róleg.*"

Sigurd's voice scaled up to an inarticulate scream. He struck the *sprunga* wall again and again. Overhead, the bats stirred but still clung to their roosts. The crewmen pressed closer to Sigurd, like a pack of wolves surrounding their wounded leader. "Get back!" Olaf shouted, shoving at them. "Get away! Go back to your stations!"

The men shuffled to their oars, but their eyes were still on Sigurd as he sank to his knees, his back to them. Knotting his bleeding hands in his hair, he rocked back and forth. His breathing was high-pitched and labored, as if he had run a long way. Olaf leaned over his brother and spoke in his ear, the soothing rumble of his voice a counterpoint to the keening sound his brother made. Some moments passed. Finally, Sigurd nodded, and, with Olaf's assistance, got to his feet. He stood in the bow facing the *sprunga's* wall as Olaf made his way to the stern. He paused beside Kristan but did not look at him. "We'll take you back now," he said. "Back to your ship."

"Very well," Kristan said.

Olaf's sea-blue eyes welled with sudden tears. "I see what you did," he whispered. "Kristan, you're my friend. He's my brother."

Kristan's stomach churned, but he kept his voice steady. "Your brother is no friend to me. And no friend to you, or to these men."

Olaf said nothing. After a moment he gestured to his crewmen, and they filed after him onto their own vessel. Sigurd's men still watched their captain, as if waiting for orders, but he only lifted his gaze from the rock wall to the bats settling quietly on their roosts.

"Let's go, then," Olaf said. As his crew shoved their oars against the *sprunga* walls, backing the ship toward the narrow opening, he stood in the stern, guiding them with small, spare gestures.

Sigurd said nothing, did nothing. He stood in the bow as if he had been nailed there. One of his men finally came to the stern to navigate. "Get out of the way," he said, not unkindly, and with a jerk of his thumb, directed Kristan and the children amidships. Nolle and Desta hurried to obey, but as Kristan followed at a more measured pace, he found Serle close at his side. "Sir, what happened?" the boy whispered. "What happened?"

"Find something to hold onto," Kristan said. "Keep low and out of the way. This is going to be rough."

Like a midwife birthing twins, the waves yanked the Northern ships from the *sprunga*, one after the other. The crews strained at the oars to escape the breakers at the *sprunga's* mouth, finally pulling free of the dangerous shallows. They plunged toward the Norwinn warship, which pitched and pulled against its anchor in the distance. "Ooo," Serle said, and clamped his hand to his mouth as the sea heaved about them. Even Desta and Nolle looked discomfited, but Kristan merely braced his legs and lifted his face to the wind. *Done*, he thought in grim satisfaction. *Done*. He flicked a glance toward Sigurd. The Northman still stood in the bow, but he had turned inboard, and his storm-gray eyes bored into Kristan's. *And now you know*, Kristan told him silently. *Now you know not to trifle with me.*

The warship was on their starboard now. Olaf turned his own vessel aside and waited a short distance away as Sigurd's men brought their ship as close as they dared. Centaurs and knights alike lined the rail and peered down at them. "Send down the gangway," Kristan called.

"At once, my lord," Sir Mitchell called. Torrin and some of the other centaurs heaved the gangway over the side, and two of the Northern crew hustled to secure it. "Let's go," Kristan said, giving Serle a push as the loop of rope descended as well. "Take Nolle with you. I'll follow with Desta."

They made their way across the slippery deck as both crews made ready for the transfer. Serle stepped up on the gangway, Nolle tucked herself behind him, and Kristan secured the rope around them. "Slowly and carefully," he said, and stepped clear. As the two were guided aboard the warship, Desta suddenly cried out.

Kristan turned just as Sigurd bore down on him. He grabbed Kristan by the throat, forced him against the rail, and bent him backward over it. "Let go of him!" Desta cried, and then the boy was on Sigurd's shoulders, scrabbling at his hands. The extra weight toppled all three over the rail. Kristan had only enough time to think *not again* before they plunged into the icy, surging sea.

The shock drove the breath from Kristan's lungs. He squirmed free of Sigurd's grasp, kicked out with both legs, and shot to the surface. "Bear off, bear off, you'll crush them!"

someone shouted. Just over his head, the gangway swung loose and crashed against the warship's side. Desta's dark head bobbed up nearby; the boy's eyes were round with terror. With a few strokes, Kristan was at his side. Desta scrabbled at him, trying to get a handhold, but Kristan wrapped one arm about the boy, rolled him onto his back and cupped his hand around Desta's chin. "Lie quiet and don't fight," he said. The boy's eyes rolled upward and fixed on Kristan's face, and incredibly, he did as he was told.

Sigurd's ship had pulled wide, giving them space. Olaf's ship was swinging toward them. Fighting his way through the waves, Kristan gained the side of the warship where the gangway dangled. Sir Walter was halfway down it, with Kennet and Matthew holding it steady above. "Grab for the gangway," Kristan told Desta, treading water as he waited for the next wave. "Here we go. One, two . . . three." He heaved the boy up, and Desta seized the lowest plank of the gangway and clung to it, his skin ashen with cold. Another wave caught Kristan in the face and drove him under; he came up coughing. Overhead, Walter had passed Desta to the other knights and was leaning down again, stretching his hand toward Kristan.

A short distance away Sigurd surfaced, but just barely. His head was thrown back and his hair swirled around it like seaweed around a rock. His broad hands rose from the water and slapped its surface ineffectually. His mouth opened and closed, like a landed fish, but his eyes were glassy, as if his life was already fading. He was only a few strokes away; Kristan could have reached him easily, but he stayed where he was, treading water with mindless efficiency even though his arms and legs were growing numb.

"Help him!" Olaf shouted.

On board Sigurd's ship, the men sat motionless, watching.

"Help him!" Olaf cried again. "*Fiskur*, help him!"

Fiskur.

The old nickname was like a sudden, hard slap, reminding

Kristan of Olaf's loyal presence throughout last summer's struggles. *You could do it*, he thought, but the reasonable voice inside his head was far away, barely more than a whisper. *Swim, Fiskur. Swim over and save him, just like you saved Desta. Just like you once saved Olaf.*

But stronger than the slap of memory, stronger than the urge that had sent him to Desta's aid, stronger even than the knotting of Kristan's guts was his cold detachment as he watched Sigurd sink and then bob up again. This time only the Northman's nose and gaping mouth pushed above the surface; his swatting hands and glazed eyes were just below the waterline. "*Fiskur*, please!" Olaf cried. "Please!"

He deserves it.

In spite of the cramping pain, Kristan's thoughts were oddly serene. *He kidnapped your people. He forced you to follow him here. He put his hands on you. Now he can pay the price.*

"Sigurd!" Olaf cried. "*Bróðir!*"

His ship was closing on them, just as Sigurd's own vessel swung further off. Sigurd's crew crouched over their oars, backs to their drowning captain, eyes on the eastern horizon.

"*Fiskur!*" Olaf's voice was shrill.

Kristan continued to tread water, even though the muscles of his legs and arms were seizing up. Once more, the water closed over Sigurd's open mouth. With a final soft gurgle, the Northman sank from sight.

Olaf screamed, but his crew stayed quiet. There was no sound from Sigurd's ship but the clopping of its oars as his men pulled away. Those aboard the warship were equally silent.

A patch of small, delicate bubbles formed on the surface where Sigurd had disappeared. They floated in a cluster for a few breaths, like a watery flower garden, then one by one dissolved into the surrounding spindrift.

Just like that, Kristan thought. *Simple.*

Then the cramps came on him hard, as he knew they would. His thighs knotted so violently that they slammed into his belly, rolling him onto his side like a foundering ship. Seawater rushed up his nostrils, gushed into his mouth through his clenched teeth, filled his ears so he could no longer hear Olaf's cries.

Simple, he thought as he sank. *Simple.*

At that moment fingers snarled in his hair, dragging him back to the surface. "Got him!" Sir Walter shouted. "I've got him!"

Other hands were on him then, snatching at his clothes, his spasming arms, his jerking legs. His knights clung to the dangling gangway as they passed him from hand to hand: Walter to Kennet, Kennet to Geoffrey, Geoffrey to Matthew to Mitchell, all of them grunting, cursing, nearly weeping as his thrashing body fought their touch. He was almost to the deck rail when something slammed into the hull right by his head and stuck there, quivering from the impact: Olaf's ax.

"Curse you, StoneKing! A thousand, thousand curses on you all!" Olaf cried, somewhere out of Kristan's line of vision. His voice caught on a sob. "Sigurd! *Bróðir!*"

Olaf's voice faded as Torrin and Astéria grappled Kristan aboard and fell with him to the deck. "He's gone blue with the cold," Melissa gasped as she hurried to help. "And Desta's just as bad."

Another cramp rippled up Kristan's belly. He rolled onto his right side and found himself an arm's length from Desta. The boy was huddled into a tight, shivering ball, his eyes squeezed shut, his coppery skin faded to ash.

"We need to get them out of these wet clothes," Nigel was saying, but his voice seemed very far away. "Nolle, Serle: fetch some blankets."

Footsteps hammered across the deck and faded.

"What about the Northmen?" Marcus said. "What if they attack us?"

Kristan's skull beat a rapid tattoo on the deck as another spasm shook him. Through the pain, the full impact of what had happened pierced him like a sword of ice. *By the Stone, what have I done?*

"They're headed east," Dell called. "Olaf's crew is putting up their sail, and Sigurd's boat is already nearly out of sight."

A fresh wave of cramps jerked Kristan onto his back again. His pain-bleared vision showed him his knights standing in a ring around him, staring, just as Sigurd's men had stared at their leader as he writhed in bat-form before them.

What have I done?

"Oh, my lord," Sir Mitchell said in a surprisingly small voice. "Are you hurt? What's happening?"

"It'll pass," Torrin said, laying one hand on Kristan's shoulder. Kristan's belly knotted at the touch, and through his clenched teeth came a sound somewhere between a snarl and a whimper. He bucked Torrin's hand off and rolled onto his side again, his biceps bunching so hard that his forearms struck his chest. He tried to grab for the Stone, but his fingers cramped into claws and the Stone slid away and landed on the deck by his ear. The sound rang through his head like the clang of a hammer on an anvil, and he shut his eyes against the pain.

Walter let out a decisive grunt. "Standing here staring is doing no one any good. I'll get a fire going in the aftcastle galley. Strip those wet clothes off them and use the blankets to rub them down, then bring them to me as fast as you can." Something thumped against the deck near Kristan's head. "Great heavens, what's gotten into the boy?"

Kristan forced his eyes open. Desta was kicking and struggling as Nigel tried to pull off his boots. "Oh, you would, would you?" Nigel said through gritted teeth. "Hold still, you little rascal." He tossed the boots aside, pinned Desta down with one knee, and yanked off his sodden tunic.

Astéria tried to lay her hand on Kristan's forehead, but he struck out at her. Another spasm took him, arching his spine, snapping his head from side to side. "*Ragis*," Astéria almost whimpered. "*O ragis, ragis . . .*"

"*Astéria mou*," Torrin groaned. "Kristan, we have to get you out of these wet clothes. Forgive me. We'll be as quick as we can. Melissa, Astéria, the boots first. The rest of you knights, help me hold him down."

He knelt and cupped Kristan's head tight between his hands as the knights pinned his arms and legs to the deck. A memory swelled like a great blister in Kristan's brain, a vision of manacles and chains, of being stripped and stretched before a crowd of chanting, counting, laughing soldiers, of Daazna's fingers digging into his skull as the Wichelord chanted the words of the *éigniú anam*—

No. No no nonono . . .

His boots were off, and someone was fumbling at the fastenings of his tunic.

You were a pretty boy once, but now you're hideous, with your scars and your twisted body. So repulsive . . .

He tried to knock the hands away, but he could not raise his arms—

. . . ragis . . . ragis . . .

Someone knelt by his head and then Serle's soft voice was in his ear, murmuring *hush hush* and singing bits of his foolish little song: *Rest your woolly head in your woolly bed*—

And his tunic was open, and the air was icy on his exposed chest, and someone sucked their breath in through their teeth, and someone else swore softly—

Hideous . . .

And then Nigel said, "Oh . . . oh," in a strange, strained voice, and Desta began to sob. The sound pierced Kristan's own suffering and he rolled his eyes toward Desta, who lay naked and spread-eagled and weeping on the deck, fists clenched, eyes squeezed shut.

"Well, I'll be switched," Geoffrey said.

Marcus snickered. "I knew. I would have said something, but my instructions were to hold my tongue."

A great smeary wave of gray surged up in Kristan's brain,

and the taste of betrayal, bitter as ashes, filled his mouth. He cramped and gagged and choked but nothing came up; *nothing ever comes up.* The last of his clothing was stripped away and a final paroxysm of rage and shame and despair shook him from scalp to toes. Everything dwindled, swallowed up by the wave: the staring eyes and the pitying murmurs and Desta's sobs and Marcus' derisive laughter and Serle's silly little song. A thin, high buzzing filled his ears, and his tongue felt thick and swollen and too big for his mouth, and it was as if he was sinking, sinking in the sea once more.

After a while the wave rolled back a bit. He was lying on his side in a bunk in the aftcastle, his naked body swaddled in blankets. Desta huddled on the bunk opposite, watching him. Walter crouched by the stove, muttering under his breath as he tried to coax more heat from it.

"I'm sorry, my lord," Desta whispered. "I'm so sorry."

"Because you deceived me?" Kristan said, his voice no more than a croak. "Or because you were born a girl?"

Desta's chin trembled. "Both," she said.

Kristan coughed; a barking, bubbling sound that brought Walter to his side bearing a steaming cup. "Can you sit up, my lord? I have some broth here that might ease your chest."

"Leave me alone," Kristan said, and turned his face to the wall.

CHAPTER FIVE

His body ached, as if someone had driven cold iron spikes into each joint. Voices kept asking him questions and he wasn't certain what he said in response, or if he had responded at all. Again and again, Sigurd's drowning face flicked through his brain; again and again, he heard Olaf's cries of anguish, and he closed his eyes against the sight and covered his ears, as if by doing so, he could somehow make the images and sounds disappear. He tried to count, but could not fix on a single subject; he tried to recite lists, but fragments of military rosters mingled with calculations of taxes and tables of exports, until his brain roared with their cacophony. His mind vomited up a mélange of images and sounds: Nolle's glittering eyes as she cast her spells, Astéria's fumbling attempts at the common tongue, Quinn Logan clucking irritably over a report as Bastian's quill scratched on parchment nearby. At last, even those images tumbled into darkness, and he was frightened, but then his mind's eye showed him the little Terrafina light shining ahead, and as he yearned toward it, a lump in his throat, it transformed into Heather, holding a lantern high and peering at him through the night.

He had a vague sense that Geoffrey and Nolle were arguing: Geoffrey demanding that Nolle loan Desta a dress and Nolle snapping out that she was bigger than Desta and Desta had her own clothes, and what difference did it make anyway. He thought he had snarled out to leave the child alone and let her wear what she wanted, but when he finally raised his head to look, Desta was gone, and Melissa was sitting on the bunk, weeping softly as she asked his forgiveness for deceiving him. *Leave me alone*, he told her, or thought he told her. He shouted for Serle to bring him dry clothing and then was wracked by a coughing spell that seemed to go on forever. When at last he opened his eyes, he was alone, and his clothes were stacked neatly on the opposite bunk, but he could not remember who had brought them. He dressed, found his damp boots and cloak near the fire, pulled them on, and staggered out on deck.

The bitter wind hit him like a slap and his fuzzy wits sharpened somewhat. Torrin stood nearby, in close conversation with Astéria. When he caught sight of Kristan, his brow knotted. "You should be in bed, my friend," he said.

Without answering, Kristan leaned over the rail, searching the horizon. The sky was gray, the sea was gray, and he wanted very badly to see the little Terrafina light. He wondered if they had already passed it, and he was struck by a strange melancholy. He scanned the deck, trying hard to bring his thoughts into some kind of rational order. "Astéria," he said, "your people are unharmed?"

"Yes, Kreestan. No one hurted them." She nodded toward the centaurs working at the lines, laughing as Marcus joked and capered to amuse them. "They are happy to see these new *Kentávron*. This will be a good thing. Torrin's people and my people."

"And we'll go for the others soon," Torrin said. "As soon as we have some ships better suited to the sea."

Kristan squinted at him. "Others? What others?"

"The rest of Astéria's people."

"Don't we have all eleven?"

Torrin flicked a glance at Astéria. "You didn't tell him?"

Astéria ducked her head. "Not yet," she said very softly. "I wait . . . I see if he do as he says first."

"There are more?" Kristan said, hardly believing his ears.

"There are," Torrin said. "A small colony of *Kentávron*, less than a hundred, far west of Malchea. They'd heard rumors of *O Tópos*. Astéria was leading a search party to find out more. They'd stopped for water on an island, and that's where they were captured."

"I see." A knot of anger swelled in Kristan's throat, so that he could barely speak. "I see. I'm sorry I wasn't worthy of your trust, Astéria."

Astéria hung her head. "I should have told you, Kreestan. You do so much for us—"

"She was trying to protect her people—" Torrin interjected.

Kristan slammed his hand on the rail. "By the Stone, I'm sick to death of deceit and treachery!" His voice, high and querulous, echoed around the deck. Everyone went still. "Is there anything else? Any other bits of news I should know? Any more surprises in store?" He raked the entire group with a savage glare. "No? Because I swear to you, the next time I'm lied to . . . the next time someone deceives me—"

"*Ragis*," one of the centaurs whispered.

Sigurd's drowning face rolled before his eyes; Olaf's anguished cry of *bróðir* rang in his ears. His insides twisted, and he bit down hard on his lip. *No. No. Controlcontrolcontrol . . .*

"Kristan," Torrin said gently.

"Never mind. Never mind." He took a deep breath and stumbled over to Mitchell, who was at the tiller with Chári. "Get us back to the Mor. To Moordock. Unless someone has sold it out from under me, there should be a centaur ship still docked in the harbor. Torrin and Astéria can take their people home, my Reach and her First Advisor can take up their duties again, Marcus can go on to Needwood and drink himself into a stupor, Dell can go off wandering the world—" Phlegm rattled in his chest, and a fit of coughing doubled him over. Moments passed before he could draw a proper breath, and in the interim, he felt every eye on deck boring into him. By the time he straightened up, his head was spinning, and he could no longer remember what he had been saying. "Where are we? Where's the light?"

"What light, my lord?" Mitchell's face was wrung with pity.

"The Terrafina light. Where's the Terrafina light? We should be there by now."

"My lord," Kennet said, appearing so suddenly on Kristan's right that he jumped. "My lord, we're barely under way. We're making for the harbor at Hull's Contrivance."

"I don't want to go there," Kristan said. He knew he sounded like a petulant child and tried to moderate his tone. "Why are we going there?"

Kennet swallowed hard. "Your pardon, my lord, but you should see a healer; you've had a bad spell, and that cough—"

"I don't want to see a healer!"

Geoffrey rose up alongside Kennet. "The weather's getting a bit restless, my lord," he said, and, as if in answer, the sea gave a sudden heave. Kristan reeled and would have fallen, but Geoffrey caught him by the arm and set him on his feet again. "We have to revictual as well. We didn't plan on a voyage of this length, and our supplies are almost gone. The horses ate the last of the hay yesterday."

"The horses . . ." He had forgotten them, forgotten about his own Malvo. "How are they? How is Malvo?"

"All doing well, my lord, considering how long they've been cooped up below. It was close quarters, with all of us sharing the same space. Nigel, Matthew, and Walter are down there now, mucking out," he added, raising his voice over the rising wind as Kristan wobbled toward the entrance to the hold.

Its hatch had been removed, and a foul smell welled from its depths. One of Astéria's centaurs stood over it, his nose wrinkled. Someone below handed up a wide wooden bucket filled to the brim with mingled straw and filth, and the centaur took it to the stern and heaved its contents overboard. Serle was at the stern as well, being sick over the side.

"The boy's got no sea legs at all," Matthew said, his head and shoulders filling the hatchway. "He tried to help but we were afraid he'd just make more of a mess, so Walter sent him on deck."

"Where are the other children?"

"Nolle's in the rigging with Dell. A school of dolphin went by and they both climbed up for a better look. Desta's down here with us. He's—sorry, *she's*—working like a dog, my lord. She's good with the horses. Malvo minds her when he won't listen to any of us." He grinned and raised his hands for the empty bucket as the centaur returned. "*Efcháristó*, Zosimos. My lord, please don't," he added quickly as Kristan moved to follow him into the hold. "It's not healthy down here."

"I want to see Malvo."

Matthew looked as if he was going to argue, then thought better of it. Kristan descended after him, trying to breathe lightly. It was no good; the smell was so thick he could taste it, and his mouth filled with saliva, as if he would be sick himself. Choking it back, he peered into the gloom, and finally made out Nigel and Sir Walter, stripped to the waist and smeared with filth. "Greetings, my lord," Walter said, pausing to lean on his shovel. "Welcome to our erstwhile bedchamber."

Nigel was scooping dirty straw into a large basket. "Eleven centaurs, ten horses, and our own people all sharing this little space. I don't know how you did it."

"We were extremely polite to each other," Walter said, grinning. "No, my lord, it was Matthew's doing. He ran this place like a barracks: everything in order, everyone with a job to do. And the Northmen weren't unkind; they usually kept the hatch propped open, so we could get some light and air, and they helped us keep the place mucked out and gave us enough to eat and drink. But the horses didn't much like it."

The horses were in their narrow stalls, heads drooping, bodies braced against the roll of the ship, but in spite of their glum attitudes, their coats gleamed from currying and their manes and tails were braided into intricate patterns. "That's the centaurs' doing," Matthew said. "When they got bored braiding their own hair, they worked on the horses."

Malvo was in one of the nearest stalls. Desta stood with him, letting the big horse lip oats out of her hand. At Kristan's approach, she stepped aside, avoiding his eyes. Malvo's ears flicked up, but when Kristan put out one hand to stroke the broad, black nose, Malvo swung his head out of reach. "So that's the way of it with you as well?" Kristan muttered. By reflex he put his hand to the Stone for comfort. It was unpleasantly clammy.

"He's just cross, my lord," Desta said in a small voice. "He's been down here a long time."

The ship gave a sudden heave to port, and they all staggered. "Storm's worsening," Nigel said. "It's just as well we're making for Hull's Contrivance, although I wonder what kind of a reception we'll get. Those Stratheden warships we saw earlier didn't look very welcoming."

"We'd better leave this for later and get up on deck," Walter said, pulling on his tunic. "Mitchell's going to need every hand."

"I'll stay with the horses," Desta said.

"Let me go first, Kristan," Nigel said. "And Walter can follow you up. You're still very pale."

Kristan made his way up the ladder and heaved himself onto the deck. The effort brought on another fit of coughing, and he had to bend over and clutch his knees until it passed. When he straightened up, Walter and Nigel were already in the rigging with the other men, the centaurs were at the lines, and a dark mass was looming off the starboard bow. "Stratheden, my lord," Mitchell called from the helm, where he and Chári were both laboring to keep the ship on course. "The harbor entrance is just ahead."

Kristan looked forward and gasped. The entrance to Hull's Contrivance was an appalling sight: two great rocky promontories that towered on either side of the channel, like a pair of enormous hands cupped and waiting to clap any unwary vessels between them. "By the Stone," he said under his breath, then reeled as the ship lurched again.

Instantly, Geoffrey was at his elbow to steady him. "Mitchell will get us through this safe and sound, my lord; you can rely on it. He's shortened the sails so much there's barely enough cloth to cover a baby's backside, but he'll get us through." He pointed to the aftcastle. "You should get out of this weather, my lord. Your sister is already in there with Nolle and Serle."

Again, the ship plunged and rolled, and a wave crested deck-high, but Kristan was so stunned by the sight of the harbor entrance that he could not move. The upthrusts of rock were nearly overhead now, looming far above the warship's highest mast. "By the Stone," he said again, tilting his head back to study them. Everyone else on deck, knight and centaur alike, peered up as well, sheltering their eyes from the pelting rain as the ship passed into Hull's Contrivance.

At that moment, there was a splintering crash on the starboard side. The entire ship pitched to port, sending everyone skidding and sliding across the deck. Kristan fetched up against the rail so hard that it knocked the wind from his lungs. He heard the children squealing in the aftcastle. "What's going on?" one of the *O Tópos* centaurs yelled. "Are we aground?"

"*Ti symvaínei?*" Astéria cried, holding tight to her sister Gaia.

Melissa appeared in the doorway of the aftcastle. "What's happening?"

"They're attacking us!" Dell shouted from the bow.

The ship's hull seemed to drag in the waves. Torrin had taken Mitchell's place at the helm and was shouting instructions; Mitchell was up in the rigging with Nigel, Kennet, Walter, and Matthew. All five were plucking desperately at the reefed sails, trying to loosen them, while the centaurs stood ready at the lines. Kristan had one glimpse of a low-walled escarpment on the starboard shore, and on it, a thing like a gigantic bow lying flat on a great wheeled cart. Soldiers in red and gold were laying an enormous, arrowlike bolt across it. The faint ratcheting of a winch being wound came to his ears.

Marcus was atop the aftcastle, almost capering with fear. "Hurry up! They're going to shoot again!"

The reefed sails suddenly swelled open and the ship lunged forward. Just as it did, there was a deep, thrumming vibration and something slammed into the stern. The impact hurled Marcus to the deck at Melissa's feet. From the hold, the horses set up a terrible commotion, neighing and stamping and kicking at their stalls. The warship tilted slowly to starboard, and its sudden, vigorous progress faltered. Geoffrey swore and raised his voice to a roar. "Serle! Come tend to your master!" He scrabbled toward the hold as Serle and Nolle came tumbling to Kristan's side. "I'm here, my lord, I'm here!" the squire gasped.

"Both of you hold onto the rail," Kristan said.

"Is the ship sinking?" Nolle demanded.

"I don't know," Kristan said, but the warship was tilting even more, and Geoffrey's face was white as he stared into the hold.

"Malvo," Serle moaned. "All our horses."

Ten horses, Kristan thought. *By the Stone, why am I counting now?*

Geoffrey shouted for help and thrust his head and shoulders into the hold. Astéria, Gaia, and some of the other centaurs came hurrying to his aid, their hooves slewing on the slanting deck. In spite of the turmoil, Kristan stood still, more figures ticking through his head.

Twenty-five centaurs.

Melissa was trying to help Marcus to his feet; Nigel was in the bow with Dell; the other knights were leaning over the rail, screaming and waving their arms at the Stratheden soldiers.

Eight men. One woman.

Geoffrey straightened up, pulling Desta from the hold by the collar of her tunic.

Three children.

Kristan blinked. Out of the methodical counting, an idea

was taking shape.

Desta kicked free of Geoffrey and slid across the deck to Kristan. Tears streamed down her face, mingling with the rain and the salt spray. "My lord, the water's coming into the hold. I untied the horses, but they can't get out. Malvo . . . he's going to drown. They're all going to drown."

The warship lurched, knocking everyone off their feet. Boards snapped and groaned as fingers of foam-flecked water forced their way through the splintering deck. Ashore, people came running to watch.

"She's breaking up!" Geoffrey shouted.

"We're sinking," Serle whispered.

Kristan turned to Nolle. "Ten horses," he said. His tone was surprisingly calm. "Twenty-five centaurs. Eight men. One woman. Serle and Desta. And you. Can you do it?"

Uncomprehending, she gaped at him. He pushed his face close to hers. "Listen to me. Ten horses. Twenty-five centaurs. Eight men. One woman. Serle and Desta, and you. Can you do it? And can you hold it long enough for everyone to get to shore?"

He felt the shock of realization go through her skinny frame. "I . . . I think I can."

"Come with me."

Together they clawed their way up the deck until they gained the aftcastle. Bracing himself in the doorway, Kristan boosted Nolle onto the poop deck above and then sagged, his breath rattling in his chest. She clung there, hardly able to stand because of the extreme angle. The ship was almost on its beam ends; the sea was surging and crashing against the boards.

"Remember," Kristan said. "Ten horses. Twenty-five centaurs. Eight men. One woman. Serle and Desta, and you."

"But what about you?"

The ship gave a terrible groan and began to roll. Kristan struggled to maintain his handhold. "Just do it," he gasped. "Do it now."

Nolle raised one hand. Her amber eyes lit with a strange, determined fire as her lips formed the words of the shifting spell. A wave slammed into Kristan, breaking his grip on the door, and he tumbled headfirst into the sea.

Third time this trip, he thought as he fought his way back to the surface. *Ridiculous.*

Through water-bleared eyes, he glimpsed Nolle straddling a corner of the aftcastle, her arms upraised. All around her, men and centaurs and horses thrashed as the sea tried to swallow them. A series of waves slammed into him, knocking him down and up and down and up again.

At last, he broke the surface. The ship was gone. All the drowning figures were gone. The face of the sea was covered with floating planks and casks and crates. Among them were dozens of struggling fish. Most lay on their sides, lashing their tails, beating the water with their fins. Each one was surrounded by an eerie, wavering blur. Kristan spat out a mouthful of water and took a deep breath. "Swim!" he shouted with all his might. "Swim toward shore!"

One of the fish, a large one, managed to right itself and surged toward him. Within its shimmering blur, he saw Sir Kennet's shocked face. "No!" he cried, kicking away from it. "Keep off; you'll break the spell! Gather the others! Make for shore!"

The big fish curved away from him, flopping awkwardly. Another wave was cresting just over Kristan's head. He caught a deep breath and let it take him under, roll him, push him. He swam with it as long as his air held out, then kicked to the surface. Ahead in the surf tumbled the wavering glow and glittering fins of the fish. Beyond lay the shore of Hull's Contrivance.

A wave caught him and pushed him under. He tumbled and rolled, struck bottom, surfaced. Again and again, the waves drove him down, but each time he surfaced, the shore was closer, the waves weaker. The water grew shallow and foamy as churned milk. Within it, the shifted fish-forms were harder to see.

A final wave thrust him onto the shore. He crawled out of the surf, coughing up seawater. All around him shimmering fish flailed in the swallows, beating the surf into spindrift. He flung himself toward the nearest one, and in one motion, scooped it up and hurled it as far up the beach as he could. In midair it shifted into Serle's scrawny form, all sprawling arms and legs, and the boy landed with a thud. Kristan plunged on to the next fish and lobbed it, and Torrin slammed into the wet sand, upright but hock-deep. Next was Sir Kennet, who landed hard on his back and lay gasping. Trying to keep count, Kristan lurched through the shallows, slinging the fish-forms ashore: *Walter, Astéria, Mitchell, one of the O Tópos centaurs, three horses.* All lay stunned where he had hurled them, twitching and gaping, as if unable to remember how to breathe air or use their arms and legs.

Kristan floundered into the icy surf once more. *Geoffrey, Chári, Dell.* He was wheezing; his fingernails had gone blue. *Malvo. Marcus. Four more centaurs.* He stood upright and looked wildly around for Nolle. She could undo the spell in an instant, but he could not find her. Bracing against the breakers, he continued tossing the flopping fish toward the shore. *Four, five, six horses. Three centaurs.*

People were running onto the beach, crying out in disbelief as the transformed took their own shapes again. A wave knocked Kristan's legs from beneath him; with the salt water stinging in his eyes, he picked out a fresh cluster of the fish-forms and flung himself toward them. *Melissa, Matthew, Desta, more centaurs, more horses.* He had lost count; panic squeezed his chest tight. Panting, he staggered to his feet and wiped his streaming hair from his face. On the beach some of his party had risen and were helping others; an officious-looking soldier in red and gold was making his way toward Sir Kennet, bellowing questions.

Kristan looked all around, but there were no more fish. "Nolle!" he tried to call, but his voice was no better than a croak. "Nolle!" His knees buckled, and at that moment, the sodden form of a tabby cat swirled past him in the foam, its legs and spine rigid, its eyes open, its teeth clamped together and bared in a snarl. He grabbed its tail and with a hiss, the shift collapsed, and he was holding a handful of Nolle's skirts. She rolled in the water like a stick of driftwood, facedown and then faceup, her skin deathly white. He pulled her into his arms and dragged her toward the beach. Walter and Geoffrey met him into the shallows; Walter grabbed Nolle around the waist, bent her stiffened body over his folded arm, and pounded on her back, while Geoffrey helped Kristan out of the water. "Is that everyone?" Kristan gasped. "Is that everyone?"

"Every single one, including all the horses," Geoffrey said. "Dell, Serle, and Desta are rounding them up. We lost everything but the clothes on our backs, but that's nothing compared to all these lives. Well done, my lord; oh, well done."

"It was Nolle's doing," Kristan said. "Not so hard, Walter; you'll hurt her."

"Not in this lifetime," Walter said. "This girl is as tough as leather."

Nolle's eyelids fluttered and the terrible rigidity of her body abruptly eased. She coughed weakly, then vomited up an astonishing amount of salt water. "That's the way," Walter told her, supporting her forehead with one large hand. "Bring it all up."

A sudden roar of angry voices dragged Kristan's attention up the beach. More soldiers had joined the first one, and they stood with pikes at the ready. The first soldier, who looked as if he was some kind of commander, was nose to nose with Kennet. As the two bellowed at each other, the pikemen, Nigel, Mitchell and Matthew added their voices to the din.

"You fired on us without warning!" Kennet was jabbing his forefinger at the commander. "You destroyed a Norwinn warship!"

The commander's jaw jutted at a truculent angle. "You entered our waters without permission."

"Are you blind and deaf, as well as stupid? We weren't trying to attack you—we were trying to make our way out of the storm!"

"Well, what about him?" The commander pointed at Kristan. "You Hogians may welcome Wiche in your country, but they're outlawed in Stratheden."

Nigel guffawed. "Wiche? Him? Why, you great fool—"

"We saw what he did." The commander gestured toward the centaurs, who had gathered in a clump further down the beach. "We saw how he conjured those . . . those freaks out of the sea."

Torrin's head snapped up. With a face like thunder, he gestured to his comrades, and all twenty-five centaurs started toward the Stratheden soldiers in a slow, menacing trot. The commander and his men, and all the other gawkers on the shore, backed hurriedly away. The soldiers formed a rough unit, pikes at the ready, but Torrin grabbed the nearest one and tore it from the man's hand.

"We are not freaks," he said. His voice echoed off the cliffs. "I am Torrin, prince of the *Kentávron* of *O Tópos*." With the pike, he pointed toward Melissa. "This woman is the Princess Melissa, Reach of Norwinn, and sister to the StoneKing. And that—" He swung the pike toward Kristan. "That is the StoneKing himself."

Kristan pushed back his sopping cloak to expose the Gemeta Stone, but it took all his strength. Unable to straighten into the kingly bearing the situation demanded, he turned away, trying not to cough. There was a long silence, broken only by his wheezing.

"Now you've done it," Marcus said, his voice comically fearful. "You've made him angry. No telling what he'll do, when he's angry."

Melissa picked up the thread. "He'll want to see your lord. You should send a messenger ahead, to warn King Aldo you've sunk the StoneKing's ship and he's not happy about it."

The commander threw back his shoulders. "I told you, you entered—"

"If I were you, I wouldn't dawdle," Nigel said. "When the StoneKing gets quiet like that, it's not a good sign."

"He turned me into a slug once," Marcus added in a hoarse whisper.

"Very well," the commander said. Kristan turned back in time to see one of the soldiers running at full speed down the beach. As he followed the soldier's progress, he finally noticed the enormous wooden gantries perched like giant birds between the docks and the foot of the cliff. Beside them stood a pair of burly men who were watching the proceedings with folded arms and skeptical expressions. The messenger had a quick word with one of the men, then stepped onto a small railed platform just within one of the gantries. One of the burly men took hold of the crank of a nearby windlass. As he turned it, the platform rose, with its single occupant clinging to the rail.

Walter had wrung the worst of the water from his cloak and was bundling Nolle in it, but he paused to watch the activity. "Awfully small platform for such tall scaffolding."

"That one's just for foot traffic," Geoffrey said. "Look up at the cliff's edge. See those big platforms? They're attached to heavy chains, and the other ends of the chains are fixed to those tall columns you can just see beyond that bunch of gawkers looking down. They're a kind of capstan—the people here call them whims. They harness horses to them, the horses walk around the columns, the chain winds and lifts the platform. King Aldo breeds enormous draft animals just for that purpose. That's how they get all their goods from the harbor up to Hull's Contrivance. When the StoneKing sent Kennet and me here last summer, we got to see the whims in action. Impressive."

They all watched as the little platform rose up the cliff side, its sole occupant hanging on grimly as the wind and rain buffeted him. "Windy up there," Walter said. "Down here in the harbor you'd hardly know it was storming."

The little platform had barely reached the cliff's top before the soldier leaped clear, gesturing frantically. A moment later, he dashed off again, and with a clatter and groan of chains, the two large whim platforms began to descend.

"Follow me, please," the commander said a bit stiffly.

He barked an order, and his soldiers formed ranks along either side of Kristan's company, hemming them in. "Don't like that much," Geoffrey muttered.

"Nor do I," Torrin agreed, and said something in *Kentávron* to the other centaurs. Heads high, they fell back, formed two lines of their own, then trotted forward. They moved to the right and left of the Stratheden lines, effectively pinning the soldiers between themselves and the knights. Torrin and Astéria took up positions just in front of Kristan; Melissa and Nigel placed themselves to his right, with Dell and Marcus on his left. Walter came just behind, carrying Nolle. Serle and Desta followed him, and the rest of the knights, with the horses in tow, brought up the rear.

With a scowl, the commander gestured to his soldiers, and the entire cavalcade followed his rigid back toward the whims. Marcus eyed the Stratheden soldiers suspiciously. "I don't know about the rest of you, but I'd feel better if my sword wasn't at the bottom of the harbor right now."

"Quiet," Nigel hissed.

Kristan bent his head and concentrated on maintaining his footing in the sand. To prevent his legs from giving way, he adopted a stiff-legged walk, but there was no stopping his shivering, nor the insistent rasp that came from his lungs. "Brother," Melissa said, her voice far too loud, "give me your arm; the sand is too slippery for me." She grabbed his arm, keeping up a solid wall of silly chatter: *I'm so cold, aren't you cold too, but of course you're never cold*, while at the same time she braced her shoulder against his side, supporting him when he stumbled. His skin crawled at her touch, but he was grateful for her assistance, and regretted the harsh words that had passed between them.

After a few moments, the sand gave way to broad flagstones,

and just ahead the great platforms were settling with a screech of chains and a series of gentle thumps. The Stratheden soldiers stepped aside, and one of the attendants opened two wide gates in the railing of the nearest platform. "If you'll enter, please," the commander said with a slight bow.

The knights led the horses on first and when they were settled, the rest of the company filed aboard. They arranged themselves so Kristan was completely surrounded, sheltered from both the weather and the eyes of the Stratheden soldiers, who were filling the second platform. The closeness of his companions, combined with the mingled odors of wet centaurs, wet horses, and wet clothing, made Kristan's guts ache, and he put his hand to the Stone and closed his eyes. There was a double clang as the gates of the platforms were closed, then someone called out a command in a booming voice. *Probably one of the attendants*, he thought; *no doubt a commanding bellow is requisite for the job.* With a lurch, a shudder, and a groan, the two platforms rose from the shelter of the harbor into the full force of the storm. Everyone pressed close as the wind and rain lashed at them, and someone let out a little squeak as the platform swayed. Kristan slit his eyes open but could not see beyond the broad shoulders of his companions.

"Look at that sea," Matthew said. "Quite a view from here."

"I wouldn't care to go out in that again, not even as a fish." Walter smiled down at Nolle, who was half asleep in his arms. "That was a good trick, my girl."

"Quiet," Kristan murmured. Everyone around him started, then smiled with relief. *They thought I was only half-conscious,* he mused. *I have to pull myself together to deal with Aldo.* "If they've outlawed Wiche here, let's not draw their attention to Nolle."

"But they think you're Wiche," Melissa said.

"Let them think what they want," Geoffrey growled. "If they're frightened of him, so much the better."

Mitchell grinned in spite of his chattering teeth. "It did

look as if you were working magic, my lord—turning fish into humans and centaurs and horses."

"Keep your voices down," Kennet said, indicating the other platform with a jerk of his head. He hunched his shoulders against a particularly brutal blast of wind and leaned close to Kristan. "My lord, do you think Aldo will help us? Everything we had is at the bottom of the harbor. We've no supplies, no dry clothing, not even a sword amongst us."

"I've got my knife," Serle piped.

Marcus cuffed the boy across the top of the head. "Quiet, you."

Kristan closed his eyes again. *No money either. What a splendid way to show up on Aldo's doorstep: stranded, penniless, and sick into the bargain.* He was wracked with another bout of coughing, just as the platforms bumped to a stop at the cliff's edge. At a barked order from the commander, the whim attendants opened the gates of the Stratheden soldiers' platform, allowing them to form into ranks on either side of the other platform. They waited there, glowering, pikes at the ready, as Kristan and his company disembarked. Around them were gawkers of every stripe: men, women, and children, merchants and soldiers, seamen and tradesmen. Even the horses at the whims seemed to be staring at them. The sight of so many eyes made Kristan's numb skin prickle. He forced himself to look past the staring people and study his surroundings.

On either side of the platforms were the great whims, wound about with chains, with the massive horses that drove them waiting patiently in harness. A low, snug stable was only a few steps beyond, as well as a sturdy little building that looked as if it might be the whim-keepers' shelter. A plume of smoke rose from its chimney, making Kristan think longingly of a warm fire and dry clothes.

Just ahead was the castle town of Hull's Contrivance, its houses and shops gray and low to the ground, as if hunching their shoulders against the wind. Beyond the town rose the castle itself, but in contrast, its towers and battlements were all jags and points, an echo of the toothed cliffs that lined the coast. On first glance, it was impressive, but a second look showed crumbling parapets, missing shingles on the pointed roofs, and banners that, while they snapped bravely in the strong wind, were tattered and faded.

"My lord," Kennet said in a low voice.

With an effort, Kristan brought his attention back to the people surrounding them. More soldiers were approaching, parting the onlookers like a wave. Behind them was a group of men on horseback. At their head was a tall, spare old man wearing an opulent, fur-trimmed cloak and a spiky golden crown that echoed both the castle's spires and the nearby cliffs. Beneath the crown the man's long, iron-gray hair was scraped back and bound into a tight braid, making the hollows at his cheekbones and temples even more pronounced. He reined up before the group and raked them with a stony glare that finally settled on Kristan. "I would have known you," he said, his voice as deep and hollow as an old bell. "I would have known you anywhere, Kristan Gemeta. You're the living image of your mother."

Waxy dead face cradled in the pillows . . . stop it. Stop it.

"Greetings, Aldo Hudnall," Kristan answered. His own voice was hoarse; his wits still felt thick and slow. "My apologies for intruding on you without notice."

"And mine, for the unpleasant welcome you received." Aldo's gaze flicked toward Torrin and the ranks of centaurs with him. "You're far from home, Lord Gemeta. And in strange company. My men said your ship was escorted by Northern vessels."

"Not escorted," Kristan said. "We had some . . . business to transact."

"Did you? Their ships have preyed on our shores for some years now. And I understand you're allied with them."

"No," Kristan said again. "That alliance is over." Sigurd's drowning face swelled up like a bubble before his eyes, and a faint warning cramp knotted his guts.

Aldo's thick, bristling brows drew together. "Is this a recent development?"

"Yes." He did not trust himself to say more.

"Do you break alliances so easily, Lord Gemeta?"

"Not without provocation."

"And were you provoked?"

"I was."

"I see." A grim smile curled Aldo's lips. "Circumstances being what they are, you might say we were provoked as well."

"How so?"

"By the continued presence of Hogian troops on our north-western border."

"But we've always had outposts on the border," Matthew protested.

Aldo turned a hard stare on him. "I said troops, young man: a sizeable contingent of them, concentrated in one area of the mountains, not half a day's march from here. They've been in residence for some time now."

Kristan struggled to focus his thoughts. By reflex, he reached toward the Stone, but a flash of blue on his hand startled him. He realized he was still wearing the ring he had purchased in Seagirt.

And there's a request from Lady Heather asking permission to use your northeastern hunting lodge. Bastian's voice creaked through his brain, along with a vague memory of the old scribe hastening through a checklist. "It's a training exercise," he said aloud. "I gave permission for it."

"Yes, that's what your girl commander said when I sent a unit to investigate—"

Kennet let out a small noise, somewhere between a yip of joy and a whimper, like a starved dog surprised by the sudden scent of food. Kristan's heart began hammering so hard he felt sure everyone must hear it. *Heather. Heather is at the border. Heather is half a day's march away.*

"—but they've been there far longer than she claimed they'd

be," Aldo went on. "Every night they light a signal beacon, a beacon Ravelin Seachlan built just to goad me. With them on my very doorstep, and you and your Northern comrades skulking around my harbor, not to mention the avidity with which you snap up crowns and thrones, what was I to think?"

Again, Kristan thought. *There it is again.*

Nigel made a rude sound with his lips, Geoffrey said something in a growling mutter too low to hear, and several centaurs stamped, their musky scent growing stronger. Kristan half turned to glare at them, knotting his hand around the Stone more tightly. At the action, a murmur ran through Aldo's retinue, and Kristan's fatigued brain finally found clarity in a single thought: *They're frightened. Aldo and his people are frightened. Of the centaurs, yes, but mostly they're frightened of me. Of the Stone.* "Lockward in Malchea thought the same," he said aloud. He was so weary that his voice had dropped to a low rasp that sounded somehow menacing. "I'll tell you exactly what I told his daughter: my plate is full." He took a step forward; Aldo and his retinue recoiled. "I have no interest in your kingdom. All I want is to return to Fandrall. But you sank my ship out from under us."

One of Aldo's courtiers leaned from the saddle to whisper in the old man's ear. Aldo smirked and muttered something back. Other courtiers pressed close around him, shaking their heads and adding their murmurs to the first man's. Kennet bent his head close to Kristan's ear. "My lord, we don't need a ship. You heard what he said. Our own border is close at hand."

"We could cross into Hogia," Matthew agreed in a whisper. "Regroup and rest in Needwood, then continue home overland."

"You said one of our vessels was still in Moordock," Torrin added. "We could go there with Nigel and Missy, then make our own way back to *O Tópos.*"

"Wouldn't it be faster to travel by land?" Melissa asked. "Faster and safer?"

With a dismissive wave to his courtiers, Aldo turned toward him once more, and Kristan held up a hand to silence his own people. As he did, the ring caught his eye again. *Can I bear it?* he wondered. *Bear seeing Heather again?* He sensed the rest of his party pressing in on him, as if by their sheer mass they could force his decision.

"Alas," Aldo said. "Unlike you, I have only one kingdom and its resources are stretched too thin to simply give you one of my ships."

A knot of annoyance formed in Kristan's throat. With difficulty, he swallowed it. "Are you suggesting I buy a ship from you?"

"As I've already pointed out, you entered our waters and our harbor without permission."

"Everything aboard my ship, including what funds I carried, is at the bottom of your harbor."

"Perhaps we can arrange a trade instead. For example, that hunting lodge on my border, where your army is holding its exercises—suppose you let me take possession of that, and I'll give you a ship and supply it as well."

Kristan could not suppress a wheeze of bitter laughter. "That lodge, and the land it sits on, is worth far more than any ship."

Aldo shrugged. "Then I can't help you, Lord Gemeta."

"Then we'll cross into Hogia and onward from there."

His words were greeted by a murmur of approval from the members of his own company, but Aldo merely smirked. "You'll have to pass through my kingdom to do so, Lord Gemeta."

Kristan nodded. "With your permission."

"I don't think I care to give it."

Another, different murmur sounded from his companions, and Kristan fought back his own rising anger. "Why not?"

"Do you think I'm a fool?" The outburst brought warning hisses from his retinue, but Aldo only bared his teeth in a sudden, snarling grin. "Do you think I'd let your prying eyes roam through my kingdom, looking for its weaknesses? You may have fooled others into thinking you're a warrior, Gemeta, but to me you're just a cunning sprat who was born to one crown, had the second presented to you, took the third with the help of your Wiche Stone, and snatched up the fourth at the first opportunity. Only time will tell if you can keep all four, StoneKing, but in the meantime, I'll be damned if you'll get your hands on mine."

The outburst so stunned Kristan that he could not speak, but the rest of his party more than made up for his silence. Torrin snarled something in *Kentávron*, just as Melissa hissed "How dare you?" and the centaurs and knights let out a collective rumble of ill-contained anger. The children had wedged between the knights to watch; Serle was gaping and Desta was flushed with outrage, but Nolle wore a scheming expression Kristan knew well. Even though she was still shivering and pale from her earlier exertions, one hand had crept from beneath her cloak, and her gaze was fixed on Aldo. An idea glimmered in Kristan's fogged brain. *It might work*, he thought, *but she's already fatigued. We'll have to be careful.* He cleared his throat, lightly but deliberately. Nolle glanced at him. He shook his head, ever so slightly, then jerked his chin toward Desta. Nolle's eyes narrowed. As if sensing the silent exchange, Desta looked at Kristan, curiosity replacing the anger on her face. Kristan nodded at her, then at the eastern road, then at Nolle, and lightly fluttered the fingers of both hands. Comprehension flooded both girls' faces. Kristan gestured Desta to his side and leaned down so his mouth was at her ear. "See that road headed west?" he murmured. "You're going to fly that way until you're out of sight, then find a place to hide and wait for us. We won't be long."

Desta nodded. Kristan turned back to Aldo. "I'm distressed that our first meeting has gone so poorly. Our realms have been at peace, and I hate to jeopardize that. However . . ." He darted a warning glance at Nolle, then raised both hands over Desta, in a fair imitation of Nolle casting her shift spell. The entire

Stratheden retinue flinched back.

"Wiche is outlawed in my realm!" Aldo cried.

"That's unfortunate," Kristan said. "*Marra marra marra-patta.*"

He said the words slowly and deliberately. Behind him, Nolle echoed the words in a whisper. Desta's slim figure wavered, and a breath later, a sleek young hawk stood on the ground where she had been. "Desta," Kristan said, "kindly take a message to Commander Demitt. Tell her we're traveling to the lodge from Hull's Contrivance, and if we haven't arrived by sunup tomorrow, she's to initiate an attack on Stratheden. Go now."

He clapped his hands. Many of the onlookers cried out, and one of the soldiers lunged at Desta, as if to grab her, but the hawk-form was already in the air, and the soldier went sprawling. Desta caught an updraft and wheeled high overhead as other soldiers fumbled for their bows, but before a single arrow could be nocked, she straightened her course and shot away toward the west.

Kristan watched the small, flickering form until it disappeared among the trees, then turned to Aldo, whose eyes were nearly popping out of his head. "Now, Lord Hudnall, I'll need dry clothing for my company, arms for my men, tack and saddles for my ten horses, plus four additional mounts from your stables. Riding mounts, not those big whim horses. I also want two pack ponies loaded with food and water. Lanterns too."

"You . . . you . . ." Aldo breathed.

"It would be better not to argue. My knights tell me it's a half-day's travel to my lodge. The longer you delay our departure, the less likely we'll make it there by sunrise."

Aldo stormed off, barking orders to his courtiers, who streamed behind him, protesting and remonstrating. A fresh bout of coughing doubled Kristan over, and his company watched him worriedly until it passed. "My lord, why don't we wait over there?" Kennet asked, with a jerk of his thumb toward the whim-keepers' quarters and the stable. "We can get the horses wiped down and at least be out of the weather ourselves."

Kristan nodded. The Stratheden soldiers stood back and let them pass. As they went by the great whims, Kristan touched Nolle lightly on the shoulder. "That should be long enough. Let her go."

Nolle twirled one forefinger, then breathed a heavy sigh and stumbled a bit. Walter caught her by one elbow. "Nicely played, my lord," he said.

"If it works," Kristan said. His own knees were shaking, and he wanted nothing so much as to sit down.

"You were bluffing?" Melissa asked in a whisper.

"Like a practiced gambler," Marcus said. "Nolle is too weak to hold a shift for long, and Desta doesn't know the way to the lodge, but Aldo doesn't know that."

"Keep your voice down," Kristan said.

"Although I'd love to see Heather come charging to our rescue," Marcus went on, more quietly. "I'll wager she'd do it in a heartbeat, no questions asked."

Heather.

As the other knights and some of the centaurs took the horses toward the stable, Kennet turned to the men loitering near the door of the whim-keepers' quarters. With a hard stare and a jerk of his chin, he dismissed them, then opened the door into the snug little building. Inside, a cheerful fire crackled in the hearth. "Why don't you sit there, my lord?" Kennet said, indicating a chair close to the fire, and Kristan sank into it.

As the rest of the company warmed themselves, talking quietly, he sat with his eyes closed, turning the blue ring around and around on his finger. *Heather.* He allowed himself to imagine her, alert and upright on the horizon, holding a lantern high. The sight comforted him, but then the vision swirled and smeared and became instead the little Terrafina lighthouse, and he was in the water again, with waves churning all around him. Beneath the surface something clamped on his ankle. *Sigurd,* he thought, and tried to kick loose, but a second hand gripped his other ankle, then his knee. The hands clawed up his back, climbing him like a ladder, forcing him under. Water filled his mouth and nostrils and he could not breathe. As he fought to free himself, the hands landed on his shoulders, and a low, bubbling laugh sounded in his ears.

He jerked awake, gagging on the thick phlegm in his throat, and Sir Kennet recoiled. "I'm sorry, my lord, so sorry to wake you, but everything's ready for our departure. Once you change clothes, we can be on our way."

He proferred a stack of folded garments, and Kristan realized that they were alone in the whim-keepers' house. "Where is everyone?" he croaked.

"Dressed and waiting outside. Would you like me to help you? Or I can send for Serle."

Kristan shook his head. Alone, he fumbled into the clothes: too big for him, but dry and warm. There was also a cloak, gloves, and a broad-brimmed hat, all made of heavy, oily wool of a drab gray. When he joined the rest of his company, he found they were all wearing similar garments. Even the centaurs were outfitted in the cloaks and hats. "We're not pretty, but at least we're dry," Nigel said, from the back of one of the borrowed horses.

Malvo was waiting, for once not fighting Serle as the boy held onto his bridle. Kristan heaved himself into the saddle and took up the reins, then realized Aldo was standing nearby with his courtiers, glaring at him with utter hatred. Even though he wanted nothing so much as to turn his back and ride away, Kristan forced himself to gather his wits and face the man. "Events have taken an unfortunate turn, Lord Hudnall. Perhaps in time we can mend this rift."

Aldo snorted. "It's all one to me, Gemeta. Be on your way. Get out of my kingdom."

There was nothing more to be said. Kristan turned Malvo toward the western road. The Stratheden soldiers jeered a bit as his company passed by, and some of the bystanders half-heartedly pitched rocks at them, but within moments they had passed beyond the outskirts of Hull's Contrivance. "Miserable place," Torrin said.

"Stubborn old fool," Kennet said. The sour remark was so out of character that they all stared at him. "He's never gotten over his defeat in the Stratheden war," Kennet went on. "The land the lodge sits upon used to be his, but he had to cede everything west of the Strath as part of his treaty with Hogia. That's why he wanted it, my lord. It's no good to him; it would have been wiser to ask for arable land, or a trade agreement, or something equally useful, but his pride wouldn't let him. Pride was his downfall then, and it will be again, mark my words."

As Hull's Contrivance disappeared into the distance, the road grew steeper, and the trees grew thick on either side. Just ahead, in the waning light, a small figure crept from the underbrush and raised one hand. Mitchell blew out a sigh of relief. "There's Desta."

"Poor thing, she's shivering," Melissa said. "And no wonder—she's still in those wet clothes. Did we think to bring a change for her?"

"I took some extra clothes when the man in charge wasn't looking," Serle said. "They're in my pack."

"Give to me," Astéria said. "I help her. Kristan, we build fire?"

"I don't think we should stop, my lord," Kennet said, while Kristan was still trying to sort out an answer. "We're still in Aldo's territory, and no telling what he might do if we slow down enough to give him a chance."

Kristan nodded, grateful to have the decision made for him. Melissa and Astéria hurried Desta back into the underbrush while the rest waited. Walter took the opportunity to light some of the lanterns and pass them to other members of the party. Kennet took one, and Kristan was staring stupidly at its yellow flame when Astéria and Melissa reappeared, with Desta trailing behind. She wore a disgruntled expression and what looked like a page's uniform, faded and threadbare. "I'm sorry," Serle said, handing her a hat and cloak. "Everything else was too big, and I didn't think you'd want a dress."

Desta only tossed her head. She mounted up and as the company started off once more, she brought her horse abreast of Malvo. "I did as you told me, my lord," she said.

He knew he should praise her—she had done well—but no words came. He managed another nod. "Leave him be," Geoffrey said, rather sharply, and Desta fell back, eyes downcast.

They plodded on through the night, stopping once to rest the horses and have a bite to eat from the supplies Aldo had grudgingly provided. The simple act of dismounting threw Kristan into another coughing fit. He brushed off the offers of assistance and sagged beneath a tree. Even at rest, he could not seem to draw a full breath. Serle brought him some food, but the stale bread and hard, dry cheese from their Stratheden supplies made him choke. He contented himself with cautious sips of water from a battered tin mug, and watched as his company mingled and murmured. Nigel and Melissa sat thigh to thigh on a fallen log, their ridiculous floppy hats masking their faces only slightly as they kissed. Some centaurs had already paired off, and fed each other bites of food and drank from the same mug. Nolle, Serle, Desta, and Gaia giggled as they played some sort of counting game. The knights joked quietly together, and Torrin and Astéria stood a little apart from the rest, facing each other, their hands joined and their faces nearly touching as they whispered in *Kentávron*. No one bothered Kristan; no one spoke to him. Other than a few quick, sidelong glances, no one even looked at him. *And that's the way you wanted it*, Kristan scolded himself, even as melancholy descended on his heart like an iron weight. *You made them afraid to speak to you, to touch you, even to look at you. You wanted them to leave you alone, and you got what you wanted.*

He closed his eyes and leaned his head against the tree trunk. *Heather was never afraid of me. She never hid things from me. And she always said what she thought. I could always depend on her to say what she thought. What would it hurt, what would be the danger, just to sit with her, talk to her—*

A nightmare vision of Heather in Daazna's arms billowed up in his mind's eye. He gasped and jerked upright. The action made him cough: whooping, rattling paroxysms that made his chest ache and his head spin. When he was finally able to catch his breath and look up, he found the entire company clustered around him. "Maybe I was wrong, my lord," Kennet said, his face wrung with worry. "Maybe it wouldn't hurt to build a fire and rest until daylight."

"We could mount a watch," Torrin said.

"Mitchell and I could head back down the trail a bit," Geoffrey offered. "Keep an eye out for any sign of pursuit."

Their pitying gazes were like skewers through his flesh. "Mount up," he said, his voice no more than a wheeze. "Talking doesn't get us any closer to Hogia."

In near silence, the company hurried to secure packs and remount. Malvo snorted and tossed his head as Serle fumbled to untie him, until at last Desta stepped in. Grasping Malvo's bridle, she brought the big horse under control, loosened the reins, and handed them to Serle. With barely a nod to acknowledge his murmured thanks, she returned to her own mount.

It took Kristan three attempts to haul himself into the saddle, and once there, he was breathless and dizzy. He clung to the front of the saddle and closed his eyes, waiting for the world to stop spinning. Through the ringing in his ears, he caught snatches of whispered conversation:

". . . barely eaten in days . . ."

". . . hallucinating . . ."

". . . *ragis* . . ."

". . . brought a healer on maneuvers with them, maybe . . ."

". . . if he'll consent to be treated . . ."

"... perhaps she can talk sense into him ..."

"... *ragis* ... *ragis* ..."

The hissing, buzzing voices swirled around him. As if beset by bees, he flung up one hand. "Quiet!" he cried, but when he opened his eyes, only Kennet was near him. The rest of the company, packed and mounted, waited on the road.

"I'm sorry, my lord," Kennet said. "I was only asking if you were ready to go. Everyone is assembled."

"Of course," Kristan said. "Of course."

He nudged Malvo onto the road with the others, and they set off again, silent but for the creak of leather, the jingle of tack, and the faint crackle of their cloaks. Kristan stared into the darkness, trying to focus on the way ahead, but again and again, his attention wavered; again and again, Malvo's steady, rocking walk turned into the pitch and heave of a ship's deck, and the gleam of a lantern became the glow of the little Terrafina light. In time, he heard voices and sensed Malvo slow to a stop, and raised his own voice in querulous inquiry. "It's the last outpost before the border, my lord," Walter answered, from somewhere just in front of him, but the knight's figure was no more than a smear of shadow. Kristan rubbed his eyes and finally made out a few low buildings, the glow of torches, and, beyond Walter, Kennet in conversation with a large man bundled in a blanket.

"Yes, she's still quartered in the lodge just up the mountain," the man said, sounding both gruff and sleepy. "She may be out and about already, even though it's not yet dawn."

"War games, I heard?" Kennet said. The eager tremor in his voice belied his casual manner.

"Not now. One of her attendants went missing two days past, and they've been up before the sun and out after dark trying to find her."

Walter sat straight up in the saddle, eyes wide. "Her? Who?"

"A woman named Isobel. Wandered off right before a snowstorm and hasn't been seen since." The man pointed into the distance. "See that light? That's the lodge watchtower. You cross the bridge, there, and follow the road up the mountain. You'll be there before dawn breaks."

Kennet gathered up his reins. "Thank you for your help, Commander Callum."

Callum shrugged. "Gathering up strange creatures seems an odd task for a knight of your repute, Kennet. To be honest, I'm surprised Aldo let you pass through. Those things—" He jerked his head at the centaurs. "They look Wichie to me, and Aldo despises all things Wichie."

"*Wiche*," Nolle muttered under her breath. Nigel shushed her.

"I do as my lord commands," Kennet said stiffly.

"You always have," Callum said, pulling a face halfway between a grin and a grimace. "Be off with you, then. And watch out for that lady commander. She doesn't brook much nonsense."

As the company moved onto the bridge, Kennet brought his horse alongside Malvo. "Almost there, my lord," he said. "That's the Strath just below us. Once we've crossed it, we'll be in Hogia, and the lodge is only a few miles further, an easy ride up the mountain."

"Who this woman everyone talk about?" Astéria asked.

"The Lady of the Sword," Kennet said. His eyes were wistful.

"Her name is Heather Demitt," Marcus said drily.

"She's the commander of the StoneKing's army in Hogia," Geoffrey added.

"She is soldier?" Astéria asked.

Nigel grinned. "She is indeed, and my sister too. It'll be good to see her again."

"You'll like her, Astéria," Chári said, and put her hand to her chest. "She's *aderfí psyché*—the sister of my heart."

With a final clatter of hooves, the last of the company moved from the bridge back onto the snow-covered trail, but rather than the soft, unbroken carpet of white they had been traveling, the way ahead was a slushy mess. "There's been a lot of movement here," Dell said, examining the road by the thin dawn light. "Not just on the trail, but off through the trees."

"Search parties, I suppose," Mitchell said.

"I wonder what happened to Isobel," Melissa said. "From what little I remember of her, I can't envision her wandering off. Not in this weather."

"Not in any weather." Matthew looked at Sir Walter sidelong, a little grin on his face. "You looked as if you had a bad moment there, my friend. I had no idea you harbored feelings for Isobel."

Walter snorted. "I don't care two figs for Isobel. I thought he was talking about Bayla."

"Ah, that's right," Matthew said, the teasing light still in his eyes. "I forgot about the flurry of letters you two have exchanged."

"She must think I've dropped off the face of the earth. I haven't had a chance to answer her last letter."

"And you've probably been carrying it next to your heart all this time." Mitchell snickered, then ducked as Walter aimed a cuff at his head. The rest of the company laughed, all but Kennet, who was leaning forward in the saddle, his eager gaze fixed on the road ahead. A quiver of jealousy stirred low in Kristan's guts, but he fought it back and raised his own eyes to the lodge's beacon. Sometimes the trees blocked his view of it; sometimes the angle of the road obscured it for a few moments, but then it would reappear, still bright, still steady, and growing closer with every step. As they neared the crest, it rose above the trees again. Ahead was a battlemented gate, with two men in Hogian red and black standing guard. "There it is," Kennet said, pointing at the lodge beyond, but Kristan could not tear his gaze from the watchtower. A small figure stood on its summit, facing east, silhouetted against both beacon and the breaking dawn. A shaft of sunlight pierced the treeline and sparkled on a coronet of bright braids, and Kristan's heart seemed to turn over in his chest.

At their approach, the guards had lowered their pikes men-acingly, but when Walter shouted a greeting, their faces lit with delighted grins of recognition. One man sprinted for the lodge; the other saluted as the company surged through the gates and reined up in the courtyard. More soldiers came running, but Kristan ignored them, craning his neck to see the figure on the tower. It was no good; this close the angle was too acute, and he turned Malvo away from the gathering, away from the doors and the lodge and the noise, and urged him toward the rear of the courtyard and the watchtower rising over it.

CHAPTER SIX

"It won't do any good, my dear."

Heather jumped as Ravelin rose up next to her on the tower. "We've done everything we can," he went on. "Two days of searching, sunup to sundown, and not so much as a single footprint. I'm afraid we have to accept that wherever Isobel is, she's beyond our help."

"We can look a little longer. We've supplies for another day or two."

"We'll need them for our trip home. As it is, we'll have to augment our provisions by hunting along the way." He took hold of her shoulders and turned her to face him. "We were supposed to start home yesterday. If we delay much longer, your father is going to think something's happened to us."

"We can send a messenger," Heather said stubbornly.

"Or we could just go home." Ravelin bent and kissed her lightly on the forehead. "Go home, and start planning our wedding."

"I haven't said yes yet."

He cupped her face in his hands. "The very fact that you said 'yet' fills me with hope." This time he kissed her lingeringly on the mouth.

Her skin prickled, and she tried to pull away. "Don't. Someone will see."

"Everyone is busy with their breakfasts."

"Go and get yours."

"I'm having mine." He buried his face in her neck, nibbled at her earlobe. "Just a little bite of something delicious." His hand ran down her back and came to rest just beneath the curve of one buttock. "Just a handful of something sweet and fresh."

She caught her breath as his fingers sank into her flesh. "How I love to hear you gasp," he murmured in her ear. "How I love to make your heart hammer and feel the heat rising from you. I can wait as long as you can, my darling. I can stave off my hunger with these little morsels until you're ready to admit your appetite is the equal of mine. And what a feast we'll have then."

His mouth fastened on her neck, but through the roaring in her ears, Heather heard a sudden burst of other sounds. "Stop . . . stop," she gasped. "Listen. Something's happening."

Still holding her tight, Ravelin raised his head. A slight frown creased his face. "What is all that?" he muttered as the cacophony of excited voices, banging doors, and thudding footfalls rose from the lodge.

A knot of sheer joy caught in Heather's throat. "Isobel . . ."

Ravelin's frown deepened. "What about her?"

"She must have been found. Or she's come back, one or the other. It doesn't matter. Come on!" She broke free of his arms and ran down the tower steps. She was almost at the bottom when the kitchen door burst open and a flood of familiar faces poured out in the courtyard: Nigel and Melissa, Torrin and Chári, Kennet and Walter and Matthew, Dell and Marcus, all grinning, all calling her name, and just beyond them, at the far end of the courtyard, sitting still as a shadow on Malvo's back—

"Kristan," she breathed.

Before she could do or say more, the others were on her. Melissa grabbed her in a fierce hug; Nigel, laughing, put his arms around them both before Chári shouldered the pair aside, clasped Heather's face, and kissed her, first on one cheek and then the other. Torrin picked her up and swung her in the air like a child, Marcus clapped her on the back and Dell smiled shyly, and then Kennet, Walter and Matthew were lined up in front of her, bowing, and Kennet caught her hand and went to one knee, his eyes full of tears.

But she could not respond; she could not do anything but stare at Kristan. He had not moved. His face was haggard, his gaze cold and distant. Two boys ran up to him, with Sir Geoffrey and Sir Mitchell just behind. All four tried to help Kristan out of the saddle, but he did not even look at them. He dismounted, and a spell of loud, ragged coughing overwhelmed him. The sound shocked those around Heather into sudden silence. They drew back as Kristan limped toward her. He stopped a few strides away and put his hand to the Stone.

"Kristan," she said again. Her voice was trembling.

"Commander," he said. His gaze lifted slightly. "Reach Seachlan."

Ravelin was standing just behind her. "My lord," he said, and bent into a deep bow.

Kristan's mouth tightened into a bitter smile. At that moment Heather knew, without the slightest doubt, that he had seen everything.

* * *

Kristan sat close to the fire in the kitchen, but he could not get warm. He had been cold so many times before: teeth-chatter-ingly cold, joint-achingly cold, but now it was as if the chill had pierced his very marrow. He could not move, could not so much as shiver.

And so he sat still as a gravestone while everyone in the lodge bustled about him. In a distant way, he was aware that the arrival of his company had thrown the entire place into a furor; he knew hunting parties were being hastily assembled, that squads of men were out cutting evergreen boughs for makeshift beds, that some kind of temporary shelter was going up to house Malvo and the other horses, and that the cook and his assistant were hissing at each other while they tried to sort out how to stretch already-meager supplies to feed all the additional mouths.

Through it all, people kept asking what he wanted them to do, how he thought they should proceed, how to handle this or that. Through it all, he was coaxed to eat something, drink something, lie down and rest. Serle tried to give him a bowl of porridge, Walter a tankard of beer, Geoffrey a blanket, Melissa a cushion, and then they all stood murmuring just out of his line of sight. Through it all, he had said not one word. He stared at the fire and saw not the dancing flames, but Heather, her head flung back and her spine arched as she quivered in the arms of the man who held her, and sometimes the man was Ravelin and sometimes it was Daazna, and sometimes the man lifted his head and smiled at Kristan and whispered *you can watch would you like that?*

And then Heather herself was standing before him, and at her side was a nervous young man with a cup clutched between his hands. "Kristan," she said, "this is Ammus, the army's healer. He's got a draught that might ease your cough—"

"Clear this room," Kristan said, without raising his eyes from the fire. Footsteps shuffled quickly toward the door. "Not you, Commander," Kristan added. He waited until the room grew quiet and he could sense Heather's silent, anxious presence just to his right. He opened his mouth to speak, to call her *whore* and *betrayer* and *false friend*, but his voice failed, and he was overwhelmed by a fit of coughing. When it was done, the words were gone, and he had to struggle to find others to replace them.

"My reception in Stratheden was less than cordial," he finally said.

"Kennet told me a bit of what happened."

"Aldo interpreted the presence of my troops on the border as hostile. Did you give him any reason to think so?"

"I did not."

Another coughing spell came on him, and when at last he raised his head, he discovered her crouched in front of him, face soft with pity, one hand extended as if to lay it on his knee. He recoiled, and a finger of spite prodded his guts. "Aldo mentioned a signal fire. I assume this is the same fire I saw in the watchtower?"

She stood upright, crimson creeping up her face: the same deep, guilty shade her face had turned when she had first caught sight of him.

"I lit it to guide Isobel, if she was lost in the woods."

"Was it the first time you lit it?"

She cleared her throat. "No. It was lit twice before."

"Why?"

"The first time was just a little fire—when we first arrived, Rav . . . Reach Seachlan burnt some rubbish that was in the basin."

"Were you aware that the signal was built for the express purpose of goading King Aldo?"

"Reach Seachlan told me that, yes."

"Did Reach Seachlan light it the second time?"

"I lit it."

"Why?"

"Commander Callum . . . he's in charge of the outpost at the bridge—"

"I know who he is."

Her fingers curled into fists. "He came to the lodge that night. His manner toward me was . . . insolent."

"And that's why you lit the signal?"

"Callum insulted my men. He insulted me, and Reach Seachlan, and you."

"I see. You were willing to risk our shaky peace with Stratheden over an insult?"

As she struggled to frame a response, he finally noticed how drawn she was. The blue eyes he had longed to see were wary and shadowed with fatigue. Her mouth, once so ready to curve into a smile, was pinched tight. "I was wrong," she said at last. "I should have controlled my temper."

Kristan turned back to the fire. "Explain this Isobel situation."

"Three days ago, she said she wasn't feeling well. She stayed in the lodge while we went on maneuvers. When we came back, she was gone."

"And there's been no sign of her since?"

"None. I spoke to Commander Callum and no one at the outpost has seen her either. I must add that he's given me every assistance in our search."

"I'm glad to know that fence, at least, has been mended. What do you think happened to her?"

Heather did not answer. He turned to look at her and found that she had caught her lower lip between her teeth. The familiar sight was like a stab to the heart. "Well, what?" he said, more sharply than he had intended.

"The night before Isobel disappeared, Commander Callum paid a visit to the lodge. He told my knights, Reach Seachlan and me about some . . . unsavory activity that took place here when Isobel and the other courtiers were in residence."

"Be more precise."

"She was running a doxy house," Heather almost snapped. "I understand why; they'd been here for months and were out of food and supplies. They did what they had to do to survive. I assured her that the information would be kept secret, but I believe she was humiliated all the same."

"To the point of running away?"

"Rav . . . Reach Seachlan says—"

"Oh, by all means call him Ravelin."

The savage mockery in his voice startled him. Heather reared back, as if he had slapped her. "He and my knights . . . they think that's what she did, but it doesn't make sense. All of her things were gone except her horse . . . and her boots. If she was going to run off in the dead of winter, why would she leave her boots behind?" She spread her hands in entreaty, but he stared past her at the fire.

"When did you plan to return to Needwood?"

"My original plan was to start back yesterday, but I wanted to keep searching."

"I understand your supplies are low."

"I've sent out hunting parties to augment—"

He flicked one hand irritably. "I'm aware of all the activity. How many men do you have here?"

"Approximately two hundred."

"Sir Jerrold is your senior knight, correct? Is he a good leader? Levelheaded?" He said the last words with acid emphasis.

"He is."

"Then tomorrow we'll head back to Needwood, but Sir Jerrold will stay behind, with a contingent of fifty men. If there are objections—from Callum or anyone else—the answer is that they're continuing the search for Isobel, but the real reason is to keep watch. Their presence may dampen any retaliation Aldo may be contemplating. In five days' time, if everything stays quiet, Sir Jerrold can lead the bulk of them back to Needwood, but he's to leave a contingent of a dozen, under a steady man's command, in residence at this lodge until further notice. Any questions?"

"None. It's a good idea."

"I'm glad you approve—"

His sardonic response died on his lips as another spasm of coughing besieged him. It was a bad one, doubling him over in his chair, its bubbling bark making his head ring. When he could sit up again, Heather's face was twisted with concern. "Kristan, should you be traveling at all? We can stretch supplies a bit longer, so you can rest here for a few days, and Ammus assures me that his draught—"

"Tomorrow, I said."

She drew herself upright, the distress in her eyes fading to neutrality. "As you wish."

"I trust you're seeing to sleeping arrangements for my company?"

She winced. "It's going to be a bit uncomfortable, I'm afraid.

All the outbuildings were torn down long ago, so my soldiers have been camping in the great hall. Torrin says he and his people can squeeze into a corner there. Upstairs, there's a large communal bedchamber where Reach Seachlan and my knights and captains slept, and a private room Isobel and Bayla and I were using. My captains will move downstairs to make room for the men of your party—"

"What about the women?"

"I'm having a corner of the big room curtained off. Melissa and I will sleep there, along with Bayla and that little servant girl—"

"There are two girls. Nolle is the one in skirts; the dark-skinned one in boy's clothing is Desta."

Heather blinked. "Oh. Nolle and Desta will sleep with us, then, and you'll have the private room—"

"You five women use the private room. I'll sleep elsewhere."

"But—" He fixed her with a cold stare, and she cleared her throat. "Very well. Would the curtained-off section suit you?"

The thought of being in the same room with Ravelin made Kristan's skin crawl. "No," he said and pointed to a little room just off the kitchen. "I'll sleep in there."

"But that's where Cook and his assistant sleep—"

"There, I said." His guts were starting to roil. *Controlcontrol-control* . . .

"But it's no bigger than a closet—"

"It's sufficient for one night."

"But you can't sleep in the k—"

"Be silent!" he shouted. Heather drew back, eyes wide. "I've told you what I want, Commander; now do as I say. Have your cook and his assistant remove their things from the room. Do it now."

Her hands clenched into fists. "As you wish." Her features hardened. "My lord."

It was as if the two words struck the earth, opening an enormous chasm between them, deeper and wider than any

Reaving. Heather seemed to be receding from him, her small, sturdy figure dwindling into the shadows. His hand twitched toward her, but his arm was too heavy to move; his mouth opened and closed, but his brain refused to give him the words to repair the damage. Heather wheeled and marched out of the room, and Kristan turned to the fire, too numb to do more than stare at the crackling flames.

* * *

Heather strode into the main hall. Torrin, Melissa, and Nigel were in a tight clump in the middle of the room; nearby, Dell stared dreamily at the ceiling, Ravelin and Marcus muttered together in a far corner, and the three children of Kristan's company slumped amongst a motley collection of packs and cloaks near the hearth. Heather finally picked out Cook and his assistant lingering in the shadows and gestured them over. "You two go get your bedrolls. You'll be sleeping with the soldiers tonight."

Cook gaped at her. "But my lady—"

"Do it now and don't argue!" Kristan's savage tone echoed in her own voice, and Cook's face went slack with surprise and hurt. She grimaced and raised a placating hand. "Sorry. Quickly and quietly, please. The StoneKing will be staying in your little room tonight."

"In the kitchen?" Melissa almost squawked.

"Ma'am, we have to get up so early to make breakfast," Cook protested. "I'm afraid we'll disturb his sleep."

"He doesn't sleep," the girl Nolle said. "Hardly at all."

"Shut up," hissed the gangly, freckled boy next to her.

The girl Desta gave the boy a light push. "Take him his pack, Serle."

Serle looked at the welter of belongings around them. "Wh . . . where is it?"

"You're sitting on it," Desta said wearily.

Serle got to his feet, heaved the pack onto his back, and stumbled after Cook and his assistant, who were headed into the kitchen so cautiously that it was almost comical. After a few moments, they returned, their bedding heaped in their arms. "He didn't say anything," Cook said in answer to her inquiring look. "He didn't so much as turn his head. That boy was chattering away, but he never said a word, just looked at the fire."

"Very good," Heather said. "Dismissed." She watched grimly as the pair found a place for their bedrolls in the stacks along the walls.

Torrin came to her side and put a comforting hand on her shoulder. "I'm afraid that wasn't a very pleasant meeting for you."

"No." She resisted the urge to shrug him off; the show of sympathy had brought a knot into her throat, and with difficulty, she swallowed it down.

Nigel and Melissa joined them. "We heard him shout at you," Nigel said in an undertone. "I'm sorry, sister. He's bone-tired, and about as sick as a man can be and still be on his feet."

"Then why doesn't he rest and get better?" Heather almost snapped.

"You know how he is."

"He wants to be rid of us all," Melissa said, in a voice so soft, it was nearly inaudible.

Nigel kissed the top of her head. "That's not true, and you know it."

"He just wants to go home to Fandrall," Torrin said. "Try not to be angry with him, Heather; he's not himself."

She blew out an irritable sigh. "Do you know where my knights are?"

"Upstairs with Kristan's bunch," Nigel said. "I think they were trying to sort out how to section off the room for the ladies."

She started for the stairs. "I'd better tell them not to bother."

Desta jumped to her feet. "I'll go for you, my lady," she said, and before Heather could answer, the girl bounded up the staircase and disappeared into the upstairs room.

Heather gazed after her. "Striking child."

Nigel grinned. "She's Gabriel's, or at least Kristan thinks so."

"Gabriel's? Are you joking?"

"Not a bit. Take a closer look when she comes back downstairs. The resemblance is uncanny."

"Great heavens. Where did she come from?"

"She's Dyerian," Melissa said. "She stowed away when we left Seagirt."

"What in the world were you doing in Seagirt?"

Mouth trembling, Melissa looked at the floor, and Nigel pulled gently at one of her wavy brown locks. "We had a little lovers' quarrel. I'll tell you more later. Don't look like that, Missy; it's all in the past."

"What about the other boy?"

"He's Kristan's squire and completely inept at the job," Nigel said. "I think he used to be a shepherd."

"And where'd that one come from?" Heather said, jerking her head at Nolle. The girl had produced a blue glass ball from somewhere in her skirts and was peering at it.

"Nolle? Kristan never said. She's Wiche—a shape-shifter. A bit stroppy, but she's been invaluable on this journey."

"What's that in her hand?"

"It was Kristan's," Melissa said. "One of his teachers gave it to him when he was small, and he's always treasured it, but for some reason he gave it to Nolle before he and Astéria went to *O Tópos*. Maybe his knights can tell you more."

"Astéria? Is she one of those new centaurs?" Heather asked, turning to Torrin.

To her surprise, he blushed. "She is indeed."

"Where did they come from? And where are they now?"

"Where they came from is another long tale. Astéria can tell you during dinner. Right now, they're all out helping with the hunt. Chári's idea."

"Next question?" Nigel said with a grin.

"What are Dell and Marcus doing here? Why aren't they in Dyer?"

"Kristan dissolved the partnership Reach and left Raul in charge," Melissa said. "I don't know what happened, except that Dell seems perfectly happy about it and Marcus just the opposite. Maybe one of Kristan's knights can give you the full story."

"It sounds like you've had quite a journey." Heather's anger had receded enough that she was finally able to smile. "It's so good to see you all. You've no idea how I've missed you. If only Olaf were here, we'd be complete."

The sudden, stricken look on all three faces hit her like a blow. "What?" she demanded, her voice rising. "Has something happened to Olaf?"

"He's not hurt or dead, if that's what you mean," Nigel said. "But I don't think we'll be seeing him again."

"Why not? What happened?"

"Let's find someplace quiet," Nigel said. "I'll try to explain everything."

Marcus and Ravelin had left the lodge, so the four moved into the corner the pair had vacated and huddled there, while the hall rang with the comings and goings of human and centaur alike. In a hushed tone, Nigel explained about the centaurs and the Northmen's theft of the warship, with Melissa adding a comment here and there. She was subdued and sad, but it was Torrin's silence that troubled Heather most. Through the whole recitation, he stood with arms folded and brow knotted.

"I can't believe it," Heather said when Nigel concluded. "I know Sigurd deserved it tenfold, but I can't believe Kristan would do that to Olaf. Not after last summer. Not after everything Olaf did for him."

"Nor I," Nigel said. "But perhaps he was stunned. The water was freezing. He was going under himself when Kennet dragged him out, and then he had one of those fits—"

"It was awful," Melissa whispered. "I thought it would never end."

"And ever since, he hasn't been right. Oh, he pulls himself together when the need arises—his handling of Aldo was nothing short of masterful—but then he fades away, and sometimes when he comes back, he doesn't seem to know where he is. He kept talking about going back to the lighthouse at Terrafina."

"Can't you do something, Heather?" Melissa pleaded. "He's always listened to you. Maybe you can get him to rest and accept a healer's care once we're in Needwood."

Heather bit her lip, remembering Kristan's hateful gaze, his bitter words.

"Please try," Torrin said, breaking his silence.

"All right," she said. "I'll do what I can."

Melissa hugged her, and Nigel squeezed her shoulder. "Let's go upstairs," he said, taking Melissa by the hand. "I'd like a look at these sequestered sleeping quarters of ours."

When they were gone, Heather turned to Torrin, who was frowning at the floor. "There's something more, isn't there?" she asked.

His face colored again. "It's . . . Heather, I'm not sure I should tell you. I haven't told a soul. But it's been weighing on my mind." He glanced around, then drew her deeper into the shadows. "Kristan believes Daazna isn't dead."

Heather stared at him. "Torrin, I saw Daazna's body. We all did."

"I know. But Kristan believes it all the same. He told me just before we parted company last summer." He lowered his voice to the merest whisper. "And I'm afraid it's affected his mind. Astéria noticed first; she says he's *ragis* . . . breaking apart."

Heather's stomach knotted. "Torrin . . . oh, Torrin, what can we do?"

"I don't know. I just don't know. I've tried to talk to him, but he keeps me at arm's distance. He can't seem to tolerate anyone near him but those three odd children, and sometimes not even them." He put his hands on Heather's shoulders. "I know you love him—not as a king and lord, but for himself. And I know in my heart that he loves you."

A vision of her message, with its terse, impersonal APPROVED appended to it, swam before her eyes. "I don't think he does, Torrin. Not anymore."

"Heather, please. If not for him, then for his realm. What will happen if he's unable to rule? It'll all fall on Melissa's shoulders, and she's so young, and unwell herself."

Heather breathed a long sigh. "I'll try," she said. There was nothing more she could say.

Torrin kissed her forehead. "You're the bravest person I know," he said. "You'll find a way."

He went away to join the rest of his people. Heather hurried upstairs, determined to immerse herself in work. In the main bedchamber Mitchell and Geoffrey were arguing genially about how to make enough room for nine more men to lay their heads. Desta and Nolle stood by with armloads of blankets as Walter and Bayla laid out beds of evergreen boughs. Walter caught sight of Heather first. "Looks like we'll all have to turn over in unison, my lady," he said.

"It's only for one night," Bayla said, glancing at him shyly.

Walter beamed back at her. "We've all had worse beds. We'll be fine."

"Where are Bran and Jerrold?" Heather asked.

"Bran went out with Dell and a few soldiers to cut more boughs," Mitchell said.

Geoffrey let out a grunt. "Every evergreen within three miles will be stripped bare."

"Jerrold's in there," Mitchell added, jerking his chin at the smaller bedchamber.

When Heather entered the next room, she found Jerrold stoking the fire, Melissa and Nigel emptying out her pack, and Kennet on his knees, smoothing the blanket atop Heather's bed. There was something so tender in the gesture that it brought her up short.

"Everything all right, my lady?" Jerrold asked, and Kennet's head snapped up. His adoring gaze made her ashamed at how easily she had forgotten his feelings for her.

"A word with you, Jerrold," she said, turning her back on Kennet for the moment.

"Five days?" Jerrold repeated when she told him Kristan's orders. "I doubt old Aldo will try anything, my lady, no matter how warlike he's feeling. Callum told me the whole country is strapped for money, and the military gets by with scraps and tatters."

"All the same, it's what the StoneKing wants."

"It'll be dull as dirt here."

"You'll have to hunt for your meals until I can send supplies back to you. And there's repair work to keep you occupied as well."

"Yes, my lady." Jerrold scratched his chin thoughtfully. "Ma'am, do you want us to keep searching for Isobel? To be honest, I don't know where else to look for her."

Heather sighed. "Send out a patrol each day, just to keep up appearances. Maybe she'll turn up yet."

"Heather, is there anywhere I can hang this to dry?" Melissa said, holding up a wrinkled, damp dress.

"I'm afraid all of us have wet clothing in our packs," Kennet added.

"Let me talk to Cook," Heather said. "Maybe we can string a clothesline in the kitchen after dinner."

She hurried out. As she started down the stairs, she realized that Kennet was on her heels. "My lady, are you sure the StoneKing wants to sleep in the kitchen?" he asked.

"He was quite clear on the subject." She hated the peevish sound of her voice, but Kennet's sorrowing face as he caught up to her made her feel even more sullen.

"I'm sorry he shouted at you," he said.

She shrugged. "He's the StoneKing. He can do as he likes."

"And I'm sorry I haven't written. This trip was so sudden, and so much longer than any of us expected."

She raised her hand to wave off his apology, when a sudden thought struck her. She stopped halfway down the stairs and faced him. "How long?"

"My lady?"

"How long have you been traveling? When did you leave Fandrall?"

Kennet began counting on his fingers. "Let me see . . . half a day from here, then three days' sailing from the Terrafina light, another few days along Norwinn's southern coast, two days' sail to the Mor from Seagirt, three days in Seagirt, and five days before that on horseback . . . that'd be about twenty days, my lady."

He left Fandrall before my message about Ravelin arrived, Heather thought. *He didn't see it. He never saw it.* "You're sure, Kennet?" she said aloud, putting her hand on his arm.

He went red to the tips of his ears. "Yes, my lady."

For the first time in days, Heather's spirits lifted. "Thank you, Kennet; that's good to know. Now if you'll excuse me, I'd better go talk to Cook." She turned to continue her descent and saw Ravelin at the foot of the stairs, watching her. Kennet saw him as well and stiffened to his full height.

"Kennet," Ravelin said with a smile and nod. "Good to see you."

"Reach Seachlan," Kennet said, eyeing Ravelin coldly before turning to Heather. "Excuse me, my lady. I'll be getting back to work." He turned and strode back up the stairs.

"Well, well," Ravelin said as Heather joined him. "I don't suppose he'll ever forgive me for what happened with Iele."

"For a man like Kennet, who values his honor above all, that may be too much to ask."

"There may be one thing he values more," Ravelin said with a wry smile. "Every time he looks at you, he blushes like a girl." Heather scowled, but Ravelin went on blithely: "I had an interesting conversation with Sir Marcus. Did you know the StoneKing dissolved the triple proxy in Dyer?"

"I heard," Heather said, scanning the room for Cook and his assistant.

"And he's much annoyed with his sister for deserting her post in Norwinn."

"I heard that as well." She spotted the pair idling near the main door and started toward them.

"Did you also hear he attacked a woman in Seagirt?"

Heather spun to face him. "Kristan? That can't be true."

"That's what Sir Marcus said."

"Oh. Marcus." Heather waved one hand in dismissal. "He was probably joking."

"I don't think so. He wept a little when he told me. The woman was his mistress." Ravelin drew closer and lowered his voice. "Apparently, she knew the StoneKing when they were children. Her name's Pansy, or Tansy, or something like that."

Tansy. A sudden memory, painful as a stab, punched through Heather's brain: a summer afternoon in the Northmen's camp near the Mor, Kristan holding both her hands, a rueful smile on his face as he said *she was blonde and green-eyed and had a way of looking at me out of the corners of her eyes that made me weak in the knees. For a while, I thought I was in love with her, and that she loved me . . .*

Her ears filled with a strange buzzing sound that was so loud that she could barely hear Ravelin.

". . . claimed the StoneKing asked for a meeting with her, but then he assaulted her when they were alone . . ."

Her vision blurred into a smear of gray speckled with little black pinpricks. The floorboards seemed to sag beneath her feet and she felt herself falling, falling . . .

"Heather?" Ravelin's face swelled up out of the blur. "Are you all right? You're pale as death." He gripped her arm, steadying her, bringing her back into the room. "Come sit down by the fire. Cook, bring some water for the commander. Hurry."

He walked her to the hearth, sat her on one of the few chairs and stood patting her shoulder until the water arrived. The metal cup shook in her hands, and, with a pitying click of his tongue, Ravelin took it from her and held it to her lips so she could drink.

"Should I fetch the healer?" Cook asked. His voice seemed to come from far away.

"She's all right, probably just light-headed from all the excitement."

Nonsense, Heather tried to say, but choked on the mouthful of water. As she coughed, Cook backed away. "Hope whatever the StoneKing has isn't catching."

"Clear off, you fool," Ravelin barked. "Go about your business."

When they were alone, Ravelin crouched at her knee. "I'm sorry to give you such a terrible blow, my love. I know how you idolize him."

"I don't idolize him," she tried to snarl, but her voice trembled.

"You don't?" He took the cup from her and pushed something into her hands. It was her missing message, now sadly crumpled, torn along one edge and missing its distinctive, fish-shaped red seal. "I found this on the tower the other night. Forgive me for reading it; I didn't know what it was, and I wish I hadn't, because it wounded me to the heart. Did you ask his permission because you hoped he'd say no? Because you hoped he'd say, 'Don't marry him, marry me and be my queen?'"

"I . . . I didn't . . ."

"He approved our marriage. He let you go. Why can't you do the same for him?"

"It's Bastian's handwriting." As soon as she said the words, she knew how feeble they were, how foolish she was. "He left Fandrall twenty days ago, long before my message came. He never saw it."

"My little innocent," Ravelin said, but there was an edge to his pitying smile. "I told you the StoneKing entertained the princess of Malchea. Don't you understand what that means?

He's going to do what any shrewd king would do. He'll make a political marriage and add a fifth kingdom to his realm."

"He wouldn't—"

"Wouldn't he? He was quick to snap up Dyer when he had the chance." Ravelin took both her hands in his, crushing the parchment. "No doubt he thinks he's treated you fairly, given you a fine title and a position of both means and respect. You can't expect more from him. When will you understand, Heather? The young man you loved is gone. In his place is a king, perhaps even a great king, and like all great kings, his eye will always be on gain."

Her tongue was gummy in her mouth, her throat parched in spite of the water. "You don't understand—"

He plucked the parchment from her hand and rose. Without speaking, he folded it back into its former, neat package, thrust it into his tunic and then studied her face for a few moments. "Such dogged devotion," he muttered. "No wonder he values you. But you'll never be to him what he is to you. As long as you refuse to see that, you'll only make yourself miserable, and that's both a loss and a shame. Open your eyes, Heather."

He strode from the hall, slamming the door on his way out. Heather rose, picked up the cup and went to the kitchen, but when she opened the door, the stool on which Kristan had sat was empty. The door to the little pantry was shut, and the boy Serle sat with his back against it, his freckled face wan. "He took his pack in there, ma'am," he whispered as she approached. "Please don't disturb him. I'm hoping he'll go to sleep."

Heather raised one hand to knock.

"Please, ma'am," Serle said, looking up at her with imploring eyes. "He's so sick."

She put her hand down and sagged to the floor beside Serle. The two of them sat for a long time in silence, their backs to the door, listening to the faint wheeze of Kristan's breathing on the other side.

CHAPTER SEVEN

After the lodge finally quieted for the night, Kristan raised his head and listened for a long time. Serle's gentle snore sounded somewhere outside the pantry door, and from the hall beyond came the rumble and sigh of many more in slumber, but that was all.

He had been sitting on his pack in the corner for so long that he was numb all over. Bracing himself against the wall, he rose slowly, then waited some moments until the tingling of his newly-awakened legs subsided. Two quiet steps and he gained the door; a light push and it swung open, and then he was blinking in the faint red light from the kitchen's banked fire. A small, blanketed figure was curled in a shadowy lump before it: Serle, sound asleep. As Kristan moved toward the hearth, the boy stirred, mumbled something in a questioning tone, and then slipped back into slumber.

A step away from Serle's sleeping form, Kristan hesitated, studying the fire. Only a few red coals peeped out from the cloak of ash that covered them, but they still radiated a faint heat. He extended his cold hands toward the hearth. The skin of his fingertips prickled a bit, but the warmth did not penetrate to his cold flesh, his aching bones. The light glinted off the blue ring on his finger. *I should throw it into the fire*, he thought. *Throw it in, watch the metal melt, and the gemstone blacken and crack.* But in spite of his anger, the idea repelled him, and he could not do it. He let his hands drop.

The motion sent a faint push of air against the fire, and a single coal brightened. Kristan fixed his gaze upon it, and in the next instant was high in the rigging of the Northern warship, clinging to the lines, and looking west toward the little Terrafina light glowing in the distance. *Make for the light*, he thought, and as if in answer, the beacon surged toward him. They were almost upon it, and he stretched his hand, as if to take hold of it, but the ship sailed on without stopping or even slowing. *We've missed it*, he said, looking down at Sir Mitchell at the helm. *Go back.*

But the helm was unmanned. There was no lookout in the bow. Irritated, he peered toward the aftcastle and found everyone clustered there: Torrin and Astéria, Olaf, Nigel and Melissa, Nolle and Serle and Desta, all the knights and all the centaurs.

Go back, he called again. *Why aren't we turning back?*

Sir Kennet looked up at him gravely and pointed at the Terrafina light. To Kristan's surprise, Ravelin stood at the foot of the beacon. A long, heavy sword was in his hands, and he swung it hard at the tower. There was no sound, but a spray of chipped stone billowed up from the blow, flickering in the beacon's light. A cold tingle ran up Kristan's spine. *Turn back*, he shouted. *Turn this ship around.*

Astéria pointed at him. Her lips formed the word *ragis*, but she was voiceless. The others only gazed at him blankly. Anger knotted his guts. *Turn back*, he said again. *I command you.*

They did nothing. Beyond them, at the very stern, four figures were taking shape, both familiar and yet disturbing. Three stepped into the light: Ariphele, Phelan, and the old Wiche woman. The fourth shape remained in the shadows.

Make this ship turn back, Kristan told them.

The old Wiche woman waved a dismissive hand. *It's your burden, boy, and your choice to make.*

Turn back. Turn back this instant.

Phelan giggled. *Don't look to me, boy. You'll find your way.*

The empty cup is tainted, Ariphele said, with a mocking

shake of her head.

Kristan wheeled back toward the Terrafina light. It was retreating, its gleam fading into the night.

The Stone is in the way, said a new voice, and then a low chuckle sounded right at his ear.

Kristan froze. His fingers knotted so hard in the rigging that the taut lines dug into his hands.

I see you. Daazna's voice hissed through his brain. *I know what you are.*

The lighthouse was only a bright speck in the darkness now, like a single moth-hole in a blue-black blanket. Even though he could no long see the tower, now Kristan could hear the distant ring of Ravelin's blade against it.

You can watch, Daazna whispered. *Would you like that?*

Kristan's insides cramped, and he knew another seizure was building. *Control*, he told himself. *Controlcontrolcontrol . . .*

Little king, Daazna hissed in his ear. *Little coward.*

Control.

Too afraid to go through the door yourself.

Kristan clenched his teeth against the rising fury. *Control . . .*

Come out, little coward. Come out.

Stop, Kristan cried. He let go of the rigging and clawed out with both hands, as if to grasp the blanket of night and draw the beacon to him. *I am the StoneKing and I command it!*

The light paused in its backward flight and seemed to tremble.

Daazna chuckled again.

Choose, the old Wiche woman called.

Choose, Phelan repeated, and the entire company echoed the word.

Do as I say, Kristan shouted. *Do as I say, or you'll regret it.* He knotted his fists into the night sky and pulled, and the light moved slowly toward him, growing bright and then brighter. He let go of the sky long enough to grab a fresh handful, and pulled again. Waves slammed against the ship's stern as he dragged it backward through the water, straining against the night's resistance.

Watch out for the rocks, Sir Mitchell cried.

You'll run us aground, Torrin shouted.

I am the StoneKing, Kristan screamed, *and I will do what I must!* His insides shuddered and knotted, but he only pulled again, hard, and now the light was rising overhead, impossibly tall, and at its summit its beacon burned bright and brighter—

"Sir . . . oh, sir . . ."

Serle's terrified whimper and the clutch of the boy's hands on his boots jerked Kristan back to reality. He opened his eyes. His fists and trembling arms were silhouetted before him in the bright red light of the roaring, towering kitchen fire. Flames licked out of the fireplace like a dozen crimson and gold tongues, glinting off the blue ring on his finger, leaving glowing trails along the mantel and walls. On the stone floor, fingers of fire reached toward Serle's blanket.

Horrified, Kristan recoiled, dropping his arms. With a sharp crack, the flames shrank to coals.

Serle looked up at him, so pale that his freckles looked like a sprinkling of tiny bruises.

A low chuckle sounded in his left ear. In the same breath, a cramp wrung his guts so hard that he fell to his knees. His outstretched hands twisted open, and the last thing he saw before his senses faded were his dirty, broken fingernails rimmed with blood, and the oozing, half moon-shaped wounds they had carved into his palms.

* * *

"What's the matter?"

The whisper, thin and sharp as a needle, pierced through Heather's leaden slumber. She was too sluggish with fatigue to move, but she managed to slit her eyelids open enough to see a small figure sitting bolt upright in the faint red light of the fire.

Nolle, her sleep-fogged brain suggested.

"What's the matter?" the whisperer insisted. A second small figure sat up next to the first.

"Dunno . . ." Nolle mumbled, as if she were half asleep. "Go back to sleep, Desta."

"What is it?"

"Not sure. Something's not right . . ."

"What?"

"Something . . ." Nolle cocked her head, as if listening to a distant sound. Heather listened as well, but all she heard were the rumbling snores of the men in the next room. The rhythm, like the rush of gentle waves on sand, lulled her back toward sleep. Her eyelids were drooping shut when another sound joined in: Nolle, mumbling strange words under her breath.

"Wait," Desta murmured plaintively. "Me too."

"Oh, all right," Nolle said. She breathed the incomprehensible words again. There was a faint rustle, and then all was quiet. Heather squinted into the darkness, but the girls' silhouettes were no longer visible. *Must have gone back to sleep*, she thought, and shut her eyes again.

She was teetering on the edge of slumber when a knock at the door roused her again. "My lady?" Sir Bran's voice whispered on the other side.

She struggled out of bed, stumbled to the door, and cracked it open. Bran bobbed his sleep-tousled head apologetically. "Sorry to wake you, my lady," he said softly, "but I thought you ought to know. There's been a bit of a disturbance in the kitchen."

"What happened?"

"Not quite sure. Cook smelled something burning and found the hearth all scorched."

"Is Kr—is the StoneKing all right?"

Bayla sat up, rubbing her eyes. Melissa groaned and pulled her blanket over her head.

"I suppose so, my lady. He's still in his room. I took the

liberty of knocking, but he didn't answer. That squire of his was in there, though. He was singing, if you can believe that, but he broke off and told me everything was fine and to go away." He lowered his voice still further. "He may look all innocence, but I think the boy is a sly little sprat. I don't like it, my lady. Not at all."

"I'll be right down," Heather said.

She closed the door and snatched up her clothing. Bayla kicked free of her bedding, made her way to the fire and prodded it to life. As the room brightened, Melissa yawned and propped herself on one elbow. "Where'd the girls go?"

Heather paused in the act of pulling on her leggings. "They're right there . . ."

Her voice trailed off. Desta and Nolle's bedrolls were empty.

Melissa blew out an irritable sigh. "They must have sneaked out."

"But how? I swear they were there a few moments ago."

"They were," Bayla said. "I heard them whispering. And the door was shut until you opened it, my lady."

"They don't need doors," Melissa said. "I'll bet Nolle shifted them both, probably into mice or something like that. Bran thinks Serle's sneaky, but he's nothing compared to Nolle. Who knows where they've gone, or what they're up to?"

Heather fastened up her tunic. "Well, I'm going to find out."

* * *

Rest your woolly head . . .

Serle's little lullaby meandered through Kristan's skull, faint as a sigh, soft as down. A final weak spasm curled his toes, and then the seizure was over. He sucked in a deep, shuddering breath but kept his eyes closed.

"That's the way, sir," Serle said. "You just rest now. Breathe slow and rest." He began to hum again, but the tune was timorous, the notes unsteady. Kristan realized the boy was frightened. He was frightened himself.

He had done something the Stone should have prevented. He had summoned fire. He had somehow drawn it to himself in his dream. Even though he had been too surprised or too feeble to maintain it on waking, he had still worked magic: magic without words, magic without a spell or a charm. True magic.

"*Tabi'a*," he whispered.

"Sir?"

Without answering or opening his eyes, he fumbled the Stone into his hand. It was colder than ever, like a chunk of ice. He pulled weakly at the chain. *Take it off*, he commanded. *Let it go. It's standing in your way.*

But he could not do it. It was as if he feared the snapping of the chain would set him bleeding. As if the Stone was his heart. *Coward. Coward.*

Something rustled near the door. A familiar hiss filled his ears, and he sensed the presence of others in the little room. "What happened?" Desta asked. "Is he all right?"

"He had another fit," Serle whispered.

"Something else happened," Nolle said. "Out in the kitchen. What did he do, Serle?"

Serle cleared his throat but said nothing.

"Tell me," Nolle insisted. "I felt it. Something happened. Something strange."

"Maybe you just dreamed it, Nolle," Desta said.

"Did not. Aunt used to tell me she could taste when something wasn't right. I tasted something . . . something bad. And the hearth is all singed."

A long silence passed before Serle spoke, in a small but determined voice.

"I don't want to say. It would be gossiping."

Good boy, Kristan thought. Someone spread a blanket over him; he rolled on his side and curled up beneath it. Voices sounded in the kitchen beyond.

"You'd better get out of here," Serle told the two girls.

Nolle sighed sharply, but she muttered her shift spell and the faint rustling noise sounded once more, then swiftly faded. Beneath the blanket Kristan could not help but smile. "Mice again?" he murmured.

"No, sir," Serle said. "Some kind of bug, this time. Maybe cockroaches. You sleep, now."

The door to the little pantry opened and shut, and the voices in the kitchen rose: demanding, querulous, exasperated, with Heather's voice sounding the sharpest note. Kristan pulled the blanket tight around his head. The arguing voices outside mingled with the ringing in his ears and the pounding of his head, and he drifted into a leaden torpor, the icy Stone still clutched in his fist.

CHAPTER EIGHT

A *t last*, Heather thought, breathing a sigh of relief as she sank back into Skapi's saddle. Never had she imagined she'd be so grateful for the sight of Hogia's Plain and the grim gray castle towering over the homes and businesses of Needwood.

"Home looks good, doesn't it, my lady?" Sir Bran said.

"It does indeed," she answered. "You'd better ride ahead and let my father know the StoneKing is coming, along with his retinue."

"And all those centaurs too," Bran said with a grin. With a tap of his heels, he urged his horse into a gallop through the thin crust of snow. With another sigh, Heather glanced over her shoulder at the company. Trudging footsoldiers, plodding centaurs, and weary riders looked equally morose.

It had been a trying two days: the brutal cold, demanding terrain, and short supplies would have been dispiriting enough on their own, but Isobel's disappearance, the uneasiness of the StoneKing's party, and Kristan's odd, withdrawn demeanor had cast a pall over the entire journey.

Ravelin had tried to give Kristan his own fur-lined cloak to replace the StoneKing's covering of oily wool, but his offer had been ignored. Other than his constant, wracking cough, Kristan had made almost no sound, and his silence had effectively muzzled the entire company. Even Marcus dared not joke. Conversations were brief and held in hushed tones. The three children, rather than fidget or frolic, fixed their attention on Kristan and matched their ponies' gaits to Malvo's.

They're as strange as he is, Heather thought. She was still puzzled by the scorched hearth in the lodge's kitchen and Serle's stubborn denial that anything out of the ordinary had happened, even though he had been sleeping right in front of it; even though Geoffrey, out of sheer frustration, had gone so far as to try shaking an answer out of him. To everyone's astonishment, the two girls had suddenly materialized out of nowhere and flown at the knight in fury, and then Astéria had shouted at him for laying hands on Serle. Throughout the incident, Kristan had stayed in his little pantry room, doing nothing, saying nothing, and thus setting the troubled tone for their journey.

She reined up and let most of the company pass by. Kristan rode toward the rear of the column, his knights surrounding him but keeping their distance. His hood was pulled well over his head and she wondered if he was asleep in the saddle, but when she nudged Skapi alongside, Kristan's eyes were open and he was studying Malvo's neatly braided mane.

"My lord," she said. In the clear, cold air, her voice seemed too loud. "Needwood is on the horizon. We'll be there before sundown."

He nodded but did not raise his head.

Ravelin reined up on Malvo's other side. "It'll be good to have you visit with us, my lord. I'll move out of my room, so you can use it."

"The room I had before will do," Kristan said.

"As you wish," Ravelin said. "And may I take this opportunity to thank you, my lord? You've made me the happiest man on earth."

Horror jolted up Heather's spine. *No*, she thought. She lifted one hand, to hold off the words she knew were coming, but Ravelin only smiled at her. Kristan looked up at last, peering at Ravelin as if seeing him for the first time. "How so?"

"Why, by giving your approval to Lady Heather." With a

flourish, Ravelin pulled the folded parchment from his tunic. "I made her an offer of marriage some time ago, but she was reluctant to accept it unless you approved."

Sir Kennet's head snapped around. His eyes were wide, his mouth open. The other knights were turning to look, and Melissa, Nigel, and Torrin. "I know she's a great favorite of yours," Ravelin went on blithely. "And I know you've no affection for me, my lord, and deservedly so. Approving of the marriage was most gracious, and in return, I swear I'll be a worthy husband to her."

Kristan drew Malvo to a halt. He put back his hood. A gust of wind set his tangled black curls tumbling, but his face beneath them was motionless, unreadable. He extended his hand for the parchment. "Halt," Jerrold called softly, and the entire column, its progress already faltering, stopped completely.

Slowly and deliberately, Kristan unfolded the parchment. No one spoke or moved. It was so quiet that Heather could hear the paper snap and crinkle in the cold breeze. As Kristan studied it, first one side and then the other, his brow knotted, but only slightly. "I never saw this," he said at last.

Ravelin's smile wavered a bit. "Ah?"

"It must have arrived after we left Fandrall."

"Ah," Ravelin said again. His smile was fixed now, his face pale.

With the same slow deliberation, Kristan turned his head and looked at Heather. His gaze was piercing and yet expressionless, like the lidless stare of a snake. Everyone was looking at her. Her stomach knotted.

Kristan turned his attention to the parchment once more. He read it again, then folded it carefully, and handed it back to Ravelin. A fit of coughing overcame him, and as they waited for it to pass, Ravelin leaned forward in the saddle, his eyes glittering. "My lord," he said as soon as the coughing eased, "do you . . . does the approval stand?"

"Of course," Kristan said.

He lifted his hands to his hood. His fingers were trembling.

Ravelin's grin spread slowly across his face, like honey ooz-ing off a spoon. "Thank you, my lord. Thank you. Perhaps, my lord, if you stay in Needwood long enough for the wedding, you'd honor me by giving your permission in the ceremony? I have no kin and few friends left, and it's only fitting that, as my lord, you should say the words."

Kristan paused, hands upraised as if in surrender. He turned his head toward Heather. For a long, agonizing moment their gazes locked.

"Of course," Kristan said again, and pulled up his hood.

* * *

Control.

Kristan sank his teeth into his lower lip. He squinted, block-ing out the sight of Hogia's landscape, scarred with Reavings that stretched east and west, north and south, and every direc-tion in between.

How I hate this place.

A low chuckle sounded in his ears. He flinched but forced himself to concentrate on Malvo's mane. Clever centaur hands had braided it from poll to withers. In spite of wear and weather, the intricate design was still snug and shining; in spite of his attempts to will the braiding loose, it held firm.

Control. Find the loosest part of the braid. There, near the poll. Concentrate on it. Unwind it. Free it.

The plait twitched. The nearest loop arched ever so slightly, as if trying to lift itself from the design.

Control.

The Stone, tucked deep inside his clothing, was cold as a shard of ice over his heart. A mocking, muttering laugh sounded behind his head, then the sound moved past his left ear until it seemed to be directly before his face.

Breathe. Concentrate.

He had made the decision. He had let her go. But he had never expected the direction she would turn.

Control.

His guts roiled, knotted. He tightened his fists around the reins. He tried to focus on the individual hairs in Malvo's mane, willing them to move. He tried to ignore the taunting chuckle filling his head, to tamp down the jealousy, the rage, the anguish. He tried to halt the twitch and twinge of the oncoming seizure.

Control. Don't think about her. You can do it. You did it by accident last night. You can do it again if you concentrate.

Malvo's black mane blurred before his eyes and became Ravelin's hair, trimmed and combed and shining clean. Ravelin's tall, broad-shouldered, long-legged figure rose in Kristan's brain: his smiling face, his courtly manners, his careful dress.

A nobleman. A legendary warrior but without a mark on him in spite of so many campaigns. Straight and strong and sure.

Hatred prickled Kristan's scalp, set his insides shuddering.

Control. Don't think about him. Unbraid the mane.

The chuckling bubbled up again, louder, nearer. He clenched his teeth so hard his jaw ached, so hard that his temples throbbed.

Hideous. I'm hideous by comparison. Scarred and twisted and sick and half mad and no wonder, no wonder she turned to him. I pushed her away and she turned to him, to my enemy; she turned to the man who killed my father and ruined my life—

With a sharp squeal, Malvo skipped sideways, nearly colliding with Sir Walter's mount. "Whoa, there," Walter said, grabbing Malvo's bridle. "What's the matter with you, boy?"

Malvo shook his head hard, and shuddered all over. He arched his neck and rolled his eyes back toward Kristan.

"Everything all right?" Heather called from the front of the line.

Walter glanced at Kristan. "Fine," he called back. "Something just spooked Malvo. He's fine now."

He released the bridle. Malvo gave his head a final shake,

and then slowly, ears twitching, settled back into his usual steady, rocking walk. A gust of wind set his black mane flying.

The plaits were gone.

A fresh wave of nausea washed over Kristan, and the Stone was so cold that it made him shiver. He was on the brink of another seizure; his toes were beginning to cramp. *What have I done?* The voice in his head was a child's voice, frightened and alone. *What have I done?*

You controlled it.

It was his own voice, at its most cool and arrogant. *In spite of the Stone, you used the Tabi'a power. Now breathe. Control the seizure. Rule it. Rule the Stone.*

He sucked in a deep breath, sending it all the way down to his cramping feet. He concentrated on every muscle, every bone.

Slowly, ever so slowly, his toes relaxed.

* * *

"Why did you do that?" Heather said through clenched teeth.

Ravelin only smiled. "You wouldn't have believed it otherwise. You would have gone on hoping. It hurts now, my dear, and I know you resent me for it, but believe me, it's better this way. Now there's no uncertainty. You know how things stand and you can move forward."

He reached out, as if to pat her hand, but she reined Skapi sideways to avoid his touch. With a shrug, Ravelin rode ahead, still smiling, his shoulders thrown back and his black hair whipping in the wind. *Triumphant,* Heather thought, looking at the easy, confident way he handled his horse. She could feel the others staring at her and fought the urge to pull her hood over her head, just as Kristan had done. *No,* she told herself. *Don't hide. Bear your shame. Ravelin is right. You were a fool.*

She knew how each and every one of them would look: Melissa, Torrin, and Nigel dismayed, Kennet wounded to the heart, her own men baffled. She knew it was only a matter of time before someone approached to question her and was not surprised when hoofbeats sounded close beside her. But when she turned her head, it was Chári.

The centaur's face was flushed with anger. "Have you lost your mind?" she hissed. "You're supposed to be with Kristan, not that *géro árren!*"

Kristan doesn't want me. The words rose in Heather's throat and knotted there, so hard that she could not speak.

"You and he are *enoménoi,*" Chári went on, still whispering. "Coupled. Joined. I saw it last summer. All the *Kentávron* did."

"The StoneKing and I are not *Kentávron,* friend," Heather said gruffly.

"But—"

"Leave off, Chári. I'm a soldier and commander now, not some silly girl."

Chári's mouth went tight. "The girl I knew wasn't silly. She was honest and true. And in love."

"Humans fall in and out of love all the time."

"Then I'm sorry for them." Chári tossed her head and trotted over to the rest of the centaurs. She elbowed her way to Torrin's side and engaged him in earnest conversation. Heather stared straight ahead, ignoring their sidelong looks.

Next was Nigel, with Melissa at his side. "Sister, are you really going to do it?" he asked quietly. "You're going to marry Ravelin?"

"I don't know. I haven't given him an answer."

"But you asked for Kristan's permission. That must mean you're considering it."

Heather shrugged.

"But he's . . . Heather, you know he's never fathered a child," Melissa said in a small, choked voice. "You wouldn't have any babies."

"Given my responsibilities, perhaps that's for the best."

"I don't think you believe that. Not for a moment."

"We can't have everything we want, Melissa. You of all people should know."

The words were cruel, and she was ashamed of them as soon as they were voiced. But she could not bring herself to apologize, and after a few moments of uncomfortable silence, Nigel and Melissa left her, only to be replaced by Kennet. He rode by her side for some time without speaking, stiff-backed and white-faced. "Why him?" he said at last. "Why Ravelin?"

"With respect, Sir Kennet, that's none of your business." His cheeks and forehead flushed red, and she moderated her tone. "I'm a young, unmarried woman whose position requires her to be constantly in the company of men. You know the rumors, the whispering, the glances, the gossip. If I marry, I'll have some protection from all that."

"But why him?"

"What would you have me do? Marry one of my subordinates and run the risk of undermining the discipline I've worked so hard to achieve? Or marry a Needwood merchant, who'll expect me to give up my command to be a wife?"

"But you don't love Ravelin—do you?"

"No."

Kennet's shoulders hunched. "You refused me because you didn't love me."

"This is different. You wanted me to love you in return. I can't. But Ravelin doesn't love me. He expects nothing from me."

"So it's a marriage of convenience, then?"

"I told you, I haven't accepted his offer."

"You know how the StoneKing feels about Ravelin. Is this how you strike back at him for abandoning you?"

Her hand jerked toward her sword, but with an effort, she controlled herself. "You must have a very low opinion of me indeed, if you believe that." She kicked Skapi into a gallop to the very front of the column and stayed there through the last miles of their journey.

In spite of the cutting wind and the setting of the sun, the people of Needwood lined the streets at their approach, craning their necks to see the cavalcade. Kristan kept his face hidden deep in his hood, not acknowledging the faint cheer that rose as he passed. Ravelin, however, smiled and nodded graciously, even though no one was looking at him. The crowd was more interested in the centaurs than either him or Kristan.

They passed through the gatehouse and into the castle courtyard. Colin and Alister waited before the keep's main doors, with the rest of the courtiers ranged alongside them and down the steps. Even Phelan was there, leaning on his staff and looking frailer than ever.

Her soldiers stood in tight ranks on the eastern side of the courtyard, with Sir Eaden, glowing with pride, at the fore. He barked out an order and the men came smartly to attention. To Heather's surprise, her women warriors were assembled with them, mantled in Hogian red and black.

Kristan reined up at the foot of the steps, and the courtiers bent into deep bows as he dismounted. Colin was the first to straighten; he descended the stairs, waving a group of stablehands forward to assist the travelers. "Welcome, my lord," he said, his manner stiff and correct. Kristan put back his hood, and Colin's eyes went wide. "You look like shit," he blurted, and immediately clapped a hand over his mouth, as if to push the words back in.

Everyone gasped, but Kristan only let out a bark of bitter laughter. "I can always trust you to say what's on your mind, Steward Demitt."

Colin's face was nearly crimson with shame. "I beg your pardon, my lord, I shouldn't . . . it's just that—"

"No, no, honesty makes a refreshing change. I expect I do look like shit. I feel like shit. The diet of half-truths and outright lies I've been fed throughout this journey is probably to blame." He threw Malvo's reins at the nearest stablehand and started up the stairs, his gait more halting and graceless than ever. The courtiers shrank back as he passed; his knights hustled, grim-faced, in his wake.

Heather had expected him to go straight to the chamber he had occupied the previous summer—a room adjoining the great hall, large enough to serve as both a bedchamber and a meeting place. Instead, he limped across the hall, shedding his cloak and gloves. His knights collided with Desta and Serle in their haste to recover the garments as Kristan mounted the low dais to Hogia's throne and flung himself into it. Travelers and courtiers alike assembled before him. "Reports, please," he said.

Alister blinked. "Um . . . which would you like first, my lord?"

"All of them. Now."

"The usual packet was going out via runner tomorrow," Colin said. "Would you like to start there, my lord?"

"Fine."

Alister rushed out, casting a look of wild dismay at Heather. His hurrying footsteps faded, and in the silence that followed even the slightest shift in posture and the tiniest sniff seemed as deafening as a clap of thunder. On the throne, Kristan flinched suddenly and batted at his ear, as if some troublesome insect buzzed there. Another spell of ragged coughing overwhelmed him. When it had passed, he leaned back, hands clamped on the arms of the great chair, motionless but for the flick of his eyes as he studied the company.

Colin cleared his throat, and Kristan's gaze bored into him. "What?"

"Sir Jerrold tells me your company has had a long journey. I've arranged rooms for them." Kristan said nothing, only brushed his hand at his ear again. Colin's heavy brows knotted. "Perhaps they'd like to rest and clean up a bit before dinner, my lord."

Kristan glanced toward Torrin, then away. "Since the *Kentávron* are our guests, they can be shown to their chambers. The rest stay."

Colin nodded to Annys and Lily. The two timidly showed the centaurs from the hall, but Torrin remained, his arms folded, his expression pensive. Colin turned back to Kristan. "Shall I have chairs brought, my lord?"

"Why?"

Colin's puzzled expression deepened. "So everyone can sit—"

"Everyone can stand."

"Yes, my lord."

Alister hurried in, carrying the packet of reports. With a bow, he presented them to Kristan and stepped back. As Kristan thumbed through the documents, Heather spread her feet slightly and clasped her hands behind her back in the classic soldier's 'at ease' position, although she felt far from easy. Jerrold glanced at her from the corner of his eye, then relaxed his posture as well; Eaden and Bran did the same, although Sir Kennet and the rest of Kristan's knights stayed as they were, leaning forward slightly as if ready to leap at any command. Melissa clung to Nigel; Marcus slouched, staring at the floor, and Dell studied Kristan, his head on one side. The three children stood quietly enough; Desta's full attention was on Kristan, but Serle looked around the room, mouth agape, while Nolle squinted at Phelan, craning forward like a curious cat.

"Phelan," Kristan said, without looking up from his reading. It was as if he had sensed the force of Nolle's interest.

Phelan started. "Yes?"

"This girl is Wiche," Kristan said, gesturing vaguely in Nolle's direction. "She's willful, but not without skill. Her name is Nolle. While I'm here, you're to teach her what you can."

"Teach . . . teach her?"

"Yes." Kristan thrust the papers at Alister. "Alister, you see that boy there? The one with the freckles?"

"Yes, my lord."

"That's my squire, Serle. He doesn't know how to read or write. Teach him." Kristan's gaze flicked past Heather and landed on her three knights. "Which one of you is Sir Eaden?"

Eaden stepped forward boldly enough, although he swallowed hard before answering. "Me, my lord."

"This report says you've been in charge of training these Needwood women—this Home Guard."

"Yes, my lord."

Kristan pointed to Desta. "Add this girl to their ranks."

Desta's shoulders sagged, but she brightened a bit when he added: "If you had squires training here, I'd ask you to place her with them. As it is, she can assist you teaching the women basic swordplay until we leave."

He turned to Colin. "Sir Marcus has expressed a desire to start afresh here in Needwood. In the next day I'd like you to sit down with him, determine his financial needs, and report back to me."

Colin's brow furrowed deeper, but he nodded.

"Prince Torrin and his people have pressing business elsewhere. Torrin, how long before your company is able to travel?"

"All we need is a day's rest and we'll be ready to go," Torrin said.

"Very well." Kristan's stony gaze fastened on Melissa. "The Reach of Norwinn and her First Advisor are to return to their posts at the same time. Sir Colin, the entire company will need to be outfitted for the journey. Commander Demitt, you're to provide them with an appropriate escort from your ranks. Sir Dell, I believe you wished to travel with them as well."

"I'll make my own way to Norwinn in a few days' time," Dell said, then flinched a bit as Kristan's head snapped toward him. "With your permission, my lord. There are some . . . observations I'd like to make here first."

"As you like," Kristan said. "Torrin, I believe the *O Tópos* wine ship currently in Moordock's harbor will be too small for your company. My Reach will provide you with a ship of your choosing from my fleet, and any supplies you require for your journey."

"Thank you, Kristan," Torrin said.

"Alister, you can forward that packet to Quinn Logan in the morning. Include a note explaining that I've reviewed its contents, and that we'll discuss it more fully once I return to Fandrall."

"I'm sure he'd like to know when that will be, my lord."

"When my remaining business here allows."

"How can I assist with that, my lord?" Colin asked.

Kristan stood up. "To begin with, you should speak to Lady Commander Demitt and Reach Seachlan."

"My lord?"

"Speak to your daughter and her intended. I'm going to my chambers and don't wish to be disturbed."

CHAPTER NINE

"You're not marrying Ravelin!" Colin shouted.

"I haven't given him my answer," Heather said. "Not yet."

"Do you love him?"

"No. And he doesn't love me."

"Then why on earth would you marry him?" Alister said. His expression was wretched. "A man more than twice your age, who's been with more women than you have years, and who will, most likely, be unable to give you children. And you say you don't love each other in the bargain. Why? Why would you even consider such a match?"

"I respect him. And it would be a useful alliance."

"An alliance?" Colin repeated.

"You may not like him, Father, but you have to admit Ravelin Seachlan has been a good Reach. He's been useful, even agreeable, no matter how you've insulted him. I think he could be more helpful still, if he was given some measure of respect."

"Some measure of power, you mean," Alister said. "Heather, think. Marrying you would give Ravelin control of the army."

"What kind of soft fool do you think I am?" Heather said, bristling. "You think I'd allow a husband to dictate how I command my troops?"

Colin slammed his fist on the table. "I refuse to give my consent, d'you hear?"

"I don't believe I asked for your consent."

"No, you didn't," Colin said with a bitter smile. "You bypassed me, your own father, and went straight to your precious Kristan Gemeta. What did you think writing him was going to accomplish? Was it some final, pitiful attempt to get his attention?"

"I am the StoneKing's servant," Heather said as evenly as she could, although her face flushed hot with shame. "Of course I'd ask for his permission."

Colin fell back into his chair and clutched his hair. "Ravelin. You're going to marry Ravelin."

"I told you, I haven't made a decision."

Colin lowered his hands and glared at her. "I don't even know you anymore. You're a stranger to me. My daughter was always willful, but never cold and calculating like this."

"Cold and calculating seems to be the way of the world, doesn't it? If you're finished, I have business to attend to."

Heather strode from her father's work chamber and nearly collided with Phelan. "My dear," he quavered. "Can you spare me a moment? I need to talk to you."

She choked back the swear words rising in her throat. "I thought you'd be busy with your new charge."

"I gave her a few simple spells to try and left her to practice them. Please, Heather. We must talk."

He led her into the chamber where she and Ravelin had planned their war games, where he had proposed marriage to her, where she had so rashly written to Kristan, asking his permission for the match. Overwhelmed with regret and weariness, she sank into a chair.

Phelan sat next to her and put his gnarled hand over hers. "My dear girl . . . are you truly going to marry Ravelin?"

"I haven't given him an answer," she said, for what seemed the hundredth time.

"You know what I've told you about him. About the young woman he was going to marry."

"I remember."

"Do you love him?"

"No," she said, barely suppressing the urge to shriek. "But I have other reasons for considering the match." She sighed at his sorrowful look. "We get along well, Phelan. I think he's changed since you knew him."

The old Wichearte let out a sigh of his own. "He may very well have. He was young and angry then. But dear heart . . . what about Kristan?"

Heather swallowed the knot in her throat. "He's changed too. Whatever Kristan and I once shared is over and done with. You see how he is now. You see how he acts toward me—toward all of us."

"It overwhelms him," Phelan said, more to himself than to her. "I thought I might be able to help, but it's grown beyond me now."

"What?"

"Perhaps there's still time. Perhaps, with a few days more, I can find an answer. But you should step away. Step back where it's safer. Let go, stand clear. I think he knows that. Wants that."

"I don't understand."

Phelan shook his head, not in denial, but as if to clear it. "I must ask you something, Heather. Something very important. Do you want children?"

She sighed. "I know Ravelin can't father a child, Phelan. Perhaps, in my position, I shouldn't have children anyway. I'm resigned to that."

"You may not need to be resigned." Phelan edged closer, dropping his voice to a whisper. "You may not need to be resigned at all. Oh, my dear, I have a confession to make."

"What's wrong?"

"I told you what happened to the girl Ravelin loved . . . I told you what passed between him and his father and me. But I didn't tell you everything." Phelan twisted his fingers in his lap. "I didn't tell you how angry I was when the Seachlans blamed me for the girl's death and banished me. I didn't tell you what I did in revenge."

"What did you do?"

"I decided the Seachlans should be punished. I decided their line should not continue. And I cursed Ravelin. I cursed him so that he could never sire a child. And for all these years, I've held that curse in place."

"Phelan . . . how in the world . . ."

"It's drained my power and driven me half mad, but my heart was hardened against the Seachlans, and I didn't care what it did to me, as long as they suffered." Tears shimmered in the old man's eyes. "I didn't realize how their suffering would affect others—how my hatred for them would spread and spread, like ripples on a pond, like poison through a body—"

His voice caught on a sob, and his spidery old hand clenched tightly around hers. As the Wichearte wept, Heather made wordless, soothing noises, but both her heart and brain were numb.

At last, Phelan raised his tear-streaked face. "If you want a child by him, Heather—if you really want it—I can release the spell. I'd do that for you. Truth be told, it would be a relief to let it go. The bitterness and hating weighs on me like iron . . ."

He folded his arms on the table and buried his face in them. She sat patting his shoulder, squeezing his knobby, veined hand, saying the words again and again: *I haven't given him an answer.* At the same time her mind whirled with images of Ravelin in her bed, Ravelin in her body, Ravelin's seed swelling her belly. *Is this what you need?* she asked herself. *Is this what you want?*

She got Phelan to his feet, put her arm around his bony shoulders, helped him from the anteroom and across the great hall. *Is this what you want?* rang through her head, all the way to his snug chamber with its tottering piles of books, its crooked heaps of papers and scrolls. Nolle sat by the single window, a book open on her lap, a sullen expression on her face. She watched as Heather patted Phelan's hand and released him into the room, as one might release a trapped, frightened animal. Phelan pottered over to the big table near his bed, gesturing vaguely and muttering to himself.

Is this what you want?

And at last, her brain and heart united, and gave her the answer. A strange, numb calm overtook her. She closed Phelan's door, and walked briskly down the corridor.

* * *

The old Wichearte stood shivering and mumbling over his messy worktable, and Nolle allowed herself a tiny, derisive snort. *So this is the great Phelan. This is the Wichearte who's supposed to teach me. The old fool's as addled as a baby.*

At that moment, Phelan's head jerked up, as if in response to her thought, and Nolle quickly pursed her lips into a thoughtful frown and bent over the book in her lap. Her reading skills were rudimentary at best, but even the few simple spells she had been able to make out had not worked. *Like that stupid ball,* she thought, seething inwardly. *I can't See a thing in it.*

Through the veil of her hair, she peered at Phelan, wondering if he'd miss the small items she'd filched from his room. They were nothing much: a small amulet in the shape of a beetle, a little vial of good-smelling oil, a few tiny cockle shells strung together like beads. Her aunt had cautioned her about petty thievery; still, every pocket, nook, and crevice in her clothing was stuffed with little things she'd stolen. It was hard to resist when people were careless with their belongings—especially if those people had insulted or annoyed her.

The old man had his back to her now. When he had first brought her to this room, Phelan had pushed her away from the table with one hand while quickly sliding papers over something on the cluttered surface. He had not been quick enough, though; Nolle had gotten a glimpse of a small, slim book with a rat-gnawed cover of green leather before he'd hidden it. The uneasy expression on Phelan's face had aroused both Nolle's curiosity and her avarice. There was nothing so satisfying than taking something deeply valued.

She watched Phelan carefully. Another book, large and heavy and bound in thick brown hide, lay open at one corner of the table; he drew it in front of him, out of her sight, and a breath later, she heard a thud as he closed it. He turned, and she focused her gaze on the book in her lap, but listened with all her might. Phelan's shambling steps moved about the room, first toward his rat's nest of a bed, then back to the table, then behind her to the shelves near the window, then to the table once more. His footsteps paused now and then, and much noise was made with papers, *but I know what you're about, old man,* Nolle thought; *you're trying to confuse me, but when the time's right, I'll find what you're hiding. You may be a Wichearte, and I may not be able to cast these stupid book spells, but I'm good at finding what people value. I'll find it. Just wait.*

* * *

The muttering, chuckling voice swirled through Kristan's chamber, reverberating from the floor, rebounding from the ceiling, tucking itself into corners, and then leaping past his head with a hiss. Kristan turned with it, tracking it as it moved from wall to window to door.

It slithered across his worktable, slid beneath the bed, and out again. It brushed against the silver pitcher and washbasin, making them chime faintly. It rattled the fire tongs and set the flames of the newly-lit fire fluttering. It tapped the toe of his boot, tugged the hem of his tunic, stirred his tangled hair as it breathed in his ear.

"Not yet," Kristan said, and the awful croak of his own voice startled him and set him coughing. The paroxysm doubled him over, and the Stone swung in and out of his vision like a red pendulum.

The low chuckle was in Kristan's ears and it would not stop. It ran on and on, like a steady trickle of water.

He's here. This place is full of him. Thick with him. He's in every crack and crevice. And he knows I'm here too.

He shivered and rubbed his arms, trying to press the goose-flesh down. *Stop. Don't let him frighten you. He feeds on your fear. For six months, he's been devouring you, bit by bit.*

He caught his breath at last and straightened up slowly. *You have to outlast him. You have a weapon now. You have the Tabi'a. Just a little more time, a little more time to learn to use it, a little more time to get everyone farther away; the Kentávron on their journey, Nigel and Melissa back to Moordock. Keep the children busy with their lessons. And Heather . . . let her go. Let it all go. You can't do it unless you're willing to let it all go, so you can be ready. Ready for the right time. Ready to choose at last . . .*

CHAPTER TEN

"Well," said Nigel. "I suppose he isn't going to come out and see us off."

Torrin blew out a long sigh. Melissa only shivered. Colin, Alister, Dell, and Ravelin said nothing. In the cold dawn light, the massed *Kentávron* stamped and shifted in the courtyard below, impatient to be off. The small contingent of Hogian horsemen and pack ponies assigned to accompany them waited more impassively, eyes on their commander. A small honor guard stood at attention by the gatehouse.

"I knocked," Colin said. "He told me to go away."

"Very well, then," Heather said, and turned to Sir Bran. "See the company safely to Moordock and return with as much haste as the weather and your good judgment allows. Safe journey to you."

"Yes, my lady," Bran said. He trotted down the keep steps, where Sir Eaden waited with his horse. The two knights clasped hands with a genuine camaraderie that Heather envied, then Eaden held the stirrup while Bran mounted.

"Well," Ravelin said, "on the StoneKing's behalf, I wish you all a pleasant journey." Unlike the others, he was smiling, and his whole being exuded an easy confidence. Colin gave him a stony look, but the travelers nodded politely.

With a visible effort, Melissa stood up straight and squared her shoulders. "Goodbye, Colin. Thank you for your hospitality. Goodbye, Alister. Sir Dell, we'll be awaiting your arrival at

Moordock." She turned to Heather, and only then did her composure falter as she opened her arms. "Goodbye, sister."

Heather returned the embrace, but the parting was strained and largely silent. The honor guard saluted smartly as the company passed through the gatehouse, with Torrin and Astéria at the head of the Kentávron, and Bran leading the Reach of Norwinn's contingent. A faint cheer rose from the streets of Needwood at the cavalcade's passage, but that faded quickly. Colin grunted, and he and Alister went back into the keep. Sir Eaden turned an inquiring look on Heather.

"Is the Home Guard scheduled for practice today?" she asked.

"Yes, my lady. Later this morning."

"Very well. I want every soldier not already scheduled for duty to join us for a combined drill. Meantime, these men are dismissed. Go get your breakfasts."

Eaden wheeled smartly toward the waiting honor guard. "Dismissed," he barked, and with a salute to Heather, trailed them from the courtyard. Dell had already moved away, bent almost double as he followed one of the Cracks out of sight behind a cluster of outbuildings. The few courtiers and servants who had come out to witness the departure made their way indoors. Heather watched them go, her hands clasped behind her back. At last, the courtyard was empty.

"An uncomfortable farewell," Ravelin said.

"Indeed."

"A shame the StoneKing sent your brother and the princess away. I'm sure it would have meant a great deal to you to have them present at our wedding."

Heather drew a deep breath. "There will be no wedding."

From the corner of her eye she saw him start. For a few moments he said nothing, and she sensed his rising anger.

"You're toying with me," he said at last. "Teasing me, as women like to do."

"No."

"Is it because your father objects?"

"My father's opposition to the match has nothing to do with it."

"It's your brother, then. Or perhaps the princess Melissa—"

"My decision is mine alone." She faced him then. His forehead was flushed, his mouth set hard. "I'm sorry."

"You led me on." Ravelin's voice was low and guttural.

"I did not. I never said I would marry you."

"That night on the tower—"

"I was weak and foolish. I regret it. I regret making you think I wanted you."

He stepped close, his face twisted into a snarl. "You writhed like a whore when I touched you. How dare you play the virtuous maiden with me now?"

With an effort, she kept her voice level. "What I did was wrong. To marry you would only compound that error."

"Error?" He loomed over her, jaw clenched. A vein in his temple pulsed. Finally, with a bitter laugh, he stepped back. "It's him, isn't it? Your precious Kristan Gemeta. He spits in your face and still you love him. You stupid, stupid girl. You and I could have been something extraordinary. Together we could have wielded such power . . ."

He choked on the words. His hands rose, as if to take her by the shoulders—*or by the throat*, Heather thought. She stood her ground.

"I'm sorry," she said again. "Truly, I am. But this is over."

He spun from her, flung open the keep doors, and stormed inside. With a sigh, Heather faced the empty courtyard. *He's right*, she thought. *I am a fool. But at least I'm a fool by my own choice. And I can live with that.*

* * *

Ravelin scarcely knew what he was doing, where he was going. He stalked through the corridors of the castle, swearing under his breath, scattering servants before him like so much chaff.

The bitch.

He went to his room, stared from the window, and finally slammed his fist against the wall.

She duped me. She played me for a fool.

Nursing his bruised knuckles, he paced the room. He could not stand still. The spacious chamber seemed to close about him like a prison. He strode into the hallway and down the steps to the great hall. A door rose before him; he shoved it open, descended still more stairs, slammed through a second door. He sensed men around him, men who fell silent and stepped from his path. Another door, another descent, this time into darkness. His pulse thrummed in his throat so hard that he thought he might choke. He had to stop and lean against a wall until his head stopped spinning.

It's over. He's won. He's won again, without even lifting a finger.

With a strangled cry that was half rage, half anguish, he clamped his hands to his temples. The sound echoed back, mocking him. On its heels came another sound: a faint, bubbling whimper of fear.

Ravelin opened his eyes—he had not been aware he had closed them—and realized where he was. Around him stretched the gloom of what had once been the castle's interrogation chamber. Across the room, a wan pathway of light led from the little corridor of cells and the castle's half-hidden postern. Once again, the thin whimper sounded from the distance.

Staub.

And all at once, like a jab of lightning through a bank of storm clouds, an idea burst into Ravelin's brain. All at once, he knew what he had to do. Perhaps he had always known.

He crossed the chamber and down the dank little corridor, his boots ringing against the stone floor. On a three-legged stool opposite Staub's cell door, a single lantern stood in a circle of flickering yellow light. Within the cell, all had gone quiet.

Ravelin imagined Staub holding his breath.

"It's me," he said gently.

At first, there was no answer. Ravelin waited, counting his own heartbeats. A dozen passed before something in the cell moved, with a groaning sigh and a shuffling of feet. An instant later, Staub's scarred face rose in the cell door's little barred window. His single eye was wide and still. "My lord," he whispered.

"How have they been treating you, Staub?"

"Well enough, my lord. They feed me. They give me clean straw. They put a light out there because I scream sometimes when I'm afraid of the dark." Staub's voice caught on a sob, and his eye gleamed as it filled with tears. "But they won't let me out. They won't let me out."

"I could." Ravelin stepped close to the cell door.

"Oh, my lord." Staub's fingers curled around the window's bars. His breath was rank in Ravelin's face. "Please, my lord. Please."

Ravelin reached above the door. On the lintel, his fingers touched the cold, sharp edges of the shard of metal Staub had used to stab Uklet so many days past.

"I will, Staub," he said. "But first, you must do exactly as I say."

CHAPTER ELEVEN

Kristan sat at his worktable, his hands spread flat on the polished, wooden surface, his teeth clenched against the wave of nausea that threatened to overwhelm him, his body alert to the incipient cramping of his calves and thighs. He kept his attention fixed on the quill that hovered just at the level of his eyes.

He was vaguely aware of activity in the forecourt of the keep, voices rising and falling in cadence, the measured thump of marching feet, but he ignored it, just as he ignored the cold weight of the Stone on his chest and the biting drag of its chain against the flesh of his neck.

He lifted his gaze to the ceiling, and the quill rose with it. He tilted his head toward the window, and the quill drifted in that direction, as if carried by an unseen hand.

Come out, little king.

The voice hissed in his ear and a faint gust of cold air set the floating feather spinning briskly, like a child's pinwheel in a spring breeze. *Not yet*, he thought, and squinted, willing the quill to immobility. Its spinning slowed, then ceased entirely.

The muttering laugh sounded in his ear. *Not yet*, he told it again, and it slithered to the floor, crawled across the room, and settled into a corner.

Someone rapped at his door; his lips formed the words *not yet*, but he made no sound. Once again, he nodded toward the window; once again, the feather wafted toward the wan winter light that spilled into the room, gray and cold as the ashes of the long-dead fire in the hearth, gray and cold as the fingers Kristan raised to urge the quill on its way. A sudden, stronger draft caught the feather: it flipped against the window, fluttered down and lodged, nib first, between the mullioned panes and the stone ledge. Kristan stared at it, willing it into movement once more, but his stomach heaved and his fingers cramped and the gorge rose in his throat.

"My lord?"

He looked up and flinched. Ravelin loomed over him, his teeth bared in an obsequious grin, his shoulders hunched in a properly servile fashion. "I knocked, my lord, but perhaps you didn't hear. May I have a moment of your time, my lord?"

. . . not yet . . .

"I was wondering, my lord, while you have these few quiet moments, if you wouldn't mind looking over the castle with me."

. . . not yet . . .

"I've been after Sir Colin to allot funds for some repairs, especially to the lowest level—there's been considerable crack-ing of the flooring since last summer—but your steward is very close with the kingdom's money. I know it's asking a great deal, given the expense of restoring your castle in Fandrall, but I'd hate for this one to crumble to bits without your realizing what's going on."

. . . not yet . . .

"No one will bother us. Everyone is outside watching the Home Guard women drilling with the male soldiers. It'll just be you and me . . ."

Ravelin's smiling mouth was still moving, but his voice had dwindled away to a buzz, like flies busy at a bit of rotting food. Kristan stared up at his Reach, at the flash of his teeth showing occasionally between his thin lips, at his eyes, barely blinking and glittering with plans, at the crease of his cheek as he smiled, and it was as if he could read the other man's thoughts, hear them pinging through his brain like flung pebbles, saying *Come with me, come with me down below, come with me and I'll kill you quietly and my kingdom will be mine again—*

And the low chuckle rose over the buzzing of Ravelin's voice, and at last Kristan knew it was time.

Leaning heavily on the table, he got to his feet, stiff and bent as an old man. "Very well," he tried to say, but the words were no louder than a frog's croak.

Ravelin bent closer, his hungry eyes bright, his grin as wide and mirthless as a dog's bared teeth. "I beg your pardon, my lord?"

With a bubbling cough, Kristan cleared his throat. "Very well," he said again. "Show me."

"Excellent, excellent!" Ravelin's cry was too loud, too triumphant, but he recovered by bowing low and gesturing toward the door with a flourish. "Please, follow me, my lord."

Ravelin led the way down the corridor, into the great hall and down one flight of stairs and then another, taking huge strides in his eagerness. He rapidly outdistanced Kristan, who labored behind him, hunched against the weight of the Stone dragging at his neck and the nightmare memories battering at his brain like a swirl of light-baffled bats: *here I stumbled, here I tried to break away, here the guards threw me into the wall and broke my nose, here the Daaznans mocked and spat at me and here here here were the wooden towers and the chains and the manacles and the whip and beyond them the cells and the rats . . . the rats . . .*

The low chuckle rang and rang through his head as Ravelin stood in the middle of what had been the interrogation room. "See here, my lord," he said, pointing at the floor. "See where the great stones have shifted out of true? Maybe it's the cold, my lord, or perhaps the Cracks outside the castle have compromised its foundation." His eyes shone as he stooped to look into Kristan's face, and his fingers twitched as if longing to wrap themselves around Kristan's neck.

"I see," Kristan said, but though his lips moved, he made no sound.

Ravelin let out a short, harsh laugh, then collected himself. "Oh, but this isn't the worst, my lord. Come this way, down by the cells. You'll see. You'll see what I mean."

He struck off toward the dank little corridor, and Kristan shuffled behind him, and as he did, the low buzzing chuckle in his ears rose to a great roar, so that he could not even hear his own footsteps.

* * *

Heather clasped her hands behind her back as women and men alike stepped through the drill. Even though encumbered by bulky skirts and awkward wooden practice swords, the Home Guard kept pace with the regular soldiers, throwing themselves into the exercise with fierce precision. At their forefront, Desta whirled and thrust with the liquid grace of a young cat, but her face was glum. At the other end of the courtyard, Sir Geoffrey stood over Serle, correcting and scolding as the boy stumbled through the exercise with the Hogian soldiers. The other knights of Fandrall stood near the gatehouse, arms folded, watching with interest. Sir Eaden called out the sequence of the drill, his voice bouncing from keep to curtain wall and back again.

It seemed as if the entire castle had turned out to watch the drill; courtiers and servants alike lined the courtyard, clustered in front of the keep steps, and peered out of windows above. Even Phelan was there, standing with Colin and Alister. Nolle slumped sullenly by his side. *Everyone but Ravelin*, Heather thought. *And Kristan.*

A sudden shout drew her attention to the gatehouse. Sir Jerrold was riding in, alone and grim-faced. He caught sight of her, flung himself from the saddle, and hurried to her side.

"What are you doing here?" she asked. "Is all well at the border?"

"Well enough, my lady," Jerrold said, his voice low. "May I

speak to you in private? It's urgent."

She nodded to Sir Eaden. "Carry on. I won't be long."

They retired to the far side of the courtyard. "What is it?" she asked. "Why have you left your post?"

"I brought a small party back with me, but they're a few miles away yet. I came ahead to alert you." The knight was almost wringing his hands. "My lady, we found her. Isobel, I mean. She's dead."

Heather's heart sank. "I've been dreading this news, Jerrie. Where did you find her?"

"In the lodge garderobe, my lady."

"What?"

"Yes, my lady. One of the men noticed that things weren't . . . well, that the chute seemed to be blocked. We tried to push the blockage through, and when that didn't work, I sent men with pikes below to hook it out . . ." Jerrold's mouth twisted into a grimace. "At first, we didn't know it was . . . her. Everything was frozen into a lump . . . her pack and cloak and all . . ."

The gorge rose in Heather's throat. "How . . ."

"There are marks all around her throat, my lady. She was strangled."

"Who would have done such a thing?"

"I don't know, my lady. The day she disappeared, we were all out on maneuvers. Only Cook and his assistant were in the lodge."

"They'll have to be questioned."

"I don't think either of them would do such a thing, my lady; why would they? Do you think there's any chance one of the Stratheden soldiers could have come up from the outpost? Come up expecting Isobel to be . . . to be compliant, and killed her when she wasn't?"

Heather took a deep breath and shook her head. "It seems far-fetched."

"I know, ma'am, but who else would have done it?"

"I don't know. Where is her body now?"

"Coming with the others. We wrapped her up tightly and put her on one of the pack ponies."

"I want her brought in quietly, understand? I don't want everyone in Needwood to know what's happened until I have a chance to question Cook and his man. Off with you, now."

"Yes, my lady." Jerrold started away, then hesitated, took something from his pocket and pushed it into her hand. "Oh. She had this clutched in one fist, my lady. I don't know if it means anything." He hurried off, leaving Heather staring at the small object he had given her.

It was a blob of red wax, dried hard, in the shape of a fish.

Heather's heart seized up in her chest. A dizzying parade of images swirled before her staring eyes: the message from Fandrall, sealed with red wax in the shape of a fish, and on the inside her request, marked APPROVED . . .

. . . the seal wrapped into the message and thrust deep in her boot, its pressure a reminder of what she had lost . . .

. . . writhing in Ravelin's embrace, her leggings about her knees but her boots in place, *in place* . . .

. . . stripping off those same clothes and boots before the fire, so anxious to remove the marks of Ravelin's hands that she had not thought to look for Kristan's message . . .

. . . Isobel later that same night, before that same fire, head bent over something clutched in her hands, muffling sobs . . .

. . . Isobel gone without a trace the next day, leaving her boots behind . . .

. . . Ravelin's face, too close, as he pushed the torn and creased piece of parchment into her hands, murmuring *I found this on the tower the other night*—

He had lied.

He had not found her message there. After he had left her, she had circled the beacon, picking up stray bits of kindling. If the message had been dropped there, she would have found it. No, she had dropped it later, in the bedchamber, when she had hurried out of her clothing, and Isobel had found it, and read it, and wept—

And sometime the next day she had showed it to Ravelin, and he had killed her, and stuffed her body down the garderobe, and wedged her pack after her, missing the boots hidden beneath the bedcovers, missing the fish-shaped seal gripped in her fist—

"My lady? We've finished the exercise."

Eaden was looking at her, his head tilted. The Home Guard and the assembled soldiers were waiting patiently.

"Begin again, please." Her voice was no more than a croak. "I have to go. Carry on."

As Eaden barked an order and the drill started afresh, Heather hurried toward the keep. In the anteroom, the doorward snapped to attention. "Have you seen Reach Seachlan?" Heather demanded.

"He hasn't come out this way, my lady."

Heather pushed past the man into the great hall, empty but for a maid sweeping near the staircase, and a manservant stoking the fire. The door leading to Kristan's chamber stood open, and with her heart in her mouth, Heather strode down the hallway, telling herself *stay calm, stay calm, you could be wrong, it could have been someone else*—

Kristan's bedchamber was empty. His chair was angled away from his worktable, as if he had only just pushed back from the quills and ledgers and papers that littered its top. Of their own accord, Heather's hands rose to her head and knotted in her hair.

"Ma'am?"

Heather jumped, whirled. The maidservant stood timidly in the doorway. "Sorry to startle you, my lady, but if you're looking for the StoneKing, he and Reach Seachlan just left."

"Where did they go?"

"Below stairs, ma'am."

"To the kitchens?"

"No, ma'am, the other way. Reach Seachlan was saying something about the storerooms."

I could be wrong, Heather thought, hurrying down the stairs and through the empty soldiers' hall. *It could have been some-one else. Ravelin could be perfectly innocent.* But the reasonable voice in her head was overwhelmed by the pounding of her pulse.

She opened the door to the storeroom. The chamber below was dark but for a dim yellow glow from a far corridor. "Wait there, my lord, until I light these wall sconces," Ravelin's voice said, echoing faintly against the stone walls. The light flared up. "There, now."

Heather hurried down the stairs, taking her weight on the balls of her feet, and headed toward the dank little hallway. For once, Staub was quiet, and Heather wondered distantly how Ravelin had contrived to quell the one-eyed man's outbursts. "See here, my lord," Ravelin went on, his tone both solicitous and puzzled, "the displacement of the flagstones runs right out this way. At the door of this cell, it's particularly bad."

As Heather stepped into the hallway, Ravelin's head snapped toward her. His expression was fierce, and his eyes reflected the thin light so that they seemed to glow from within. "Who's that?" he demanded.

"It's me." Heather moved into the light, and Ravelin bared his teeth in a mirthless grin.

"Oh, hello, Commander," he said, his tone cool. "I was just showing the StoneKing some of the damage down here. Won't you join us?"

He gestured her closer, with a bow that was almost courtly. Kristan stood with his back to Staub's cell door, one hand to the Stone. As she approached, he turned his head toward her. His face was so pale, it seemed almost luminous.

Ravelin pointed to the floor. "Here, my lord. See how the flagstones are out of line?"

Kristan only stared at Heather. A cold chill flitted across her scalp and was gone.

"Do you see, my lord?" Ravelin insisted.

A faint, sardonic smile curled Kristan's lips. "I see," he said.

Ravelin smiled back. "Now, Staub," he said pleasantly.

A filthy hand shot through the bars of the cell window, snarled in Kristan's hair, and jerked him against the door. Aghast, Heather lunged forward, but Ravelin flung his arms around her. "Stay back, my dear," he said.

Staub's face loomed up in the window just behind Kristan's head. "Don't you move, my lord," he whispered, his single eye glittering. "You just stand quiet and don't move."

His other hand pushed through the bars, and Heather recognized the dagger-sharp piece of metal clutched in its fingers. "Staub, no!" she cried. "Let him go!"

Staub yanked Kristan's head back, exposing his throat. He pressed the crude knife beneath the crook of Kristan's jaw. Kristan did not struggle. One hand was still knotted around the Stone, but the other hung, limp, at his side. His eyes rolled toward her, the faint smile still curving his mouth. She fought to free herself from Ravelin's grasp, but he only held her tighter, pressing her against the wall, trapping her thrashing arms and legs. "He's beyond your help, my dear," he said in her ear, and then, incredibly, kissed her temple. "Let things take their course. It's for the best. He's mad—everyone says so." Heather cried out, in rage and despair, and Ravelin clamped his hand over her mouth. "Hush, now. It'll be quick, I promise you. I'll have my throne and my crown and my kingdom back—and you'll be my sweet little queen." He looked at Kristan and grinned. "You should have thought twice before you trifled with me, Gemeta. After Staub cuts your throat, I'll celebrate by taking your commander's maidenhead. Or maybe I'll do it first, so you can watch. Would you like that?"

Kristan's eyes rolled up and the lids shivered halfway closed. Frothy spittle formed at the corners of his mouth. Ravelin let out a derisive snort. "Are you fainting, Gemeta, like you did when your father died? Or are you having one of those fits people whisper about behind their hands? Stop it," he added as Heather tried to wrest free. With his large hand still fixed over her mouth, he pinched her nostrils together with finger and thumb. "I'd like you to enjoy losing your virginity," he said, giving her a slight shake as she struggled for breath, "but I'd be just as happy to knock you cold and take it that way. You choose."

Defeated, despairing, she stopped writhing, and Ravelin let go of her nose. Still holding her close, he turned back to Staub and nodded. "Go ahead."

Staub adjusted his grip on the crude knife. A strangled moan rose in Heather's throat.

At that instant there was a faint, metallic snap.

Kristan's clenched fist opened. The Stone, gray as lead and trailing its broken silver chain, slipped from his fingers. It landed on the floor, clattered for a moment, and was still.

Staub's hand froze. The knife at Kristan's throat trembled.

"Get on with it," Ravelin said.

Kristan opened his eyes, wide and then wider. The dark irises were like empty black holes in his white face. His gaze drifted to the knife poised at his throat and fixed on it with terrible intensity. A shock of chill air struck Heather like a blow, and behind Ravelin's hand, she gasped.

With a sharp crackle, a film of silvery frost appeared on the knife's point and spread up the rough blade. Staub whimpered and dropped the knife as if it had burned him. It hit the floor and burst into a thousand shards. As Staub snatched his hand back inside the cell, more frost formed on the window's bars, the lock and hinges and nails of the door. A shining coat of ice crawled up the corridor walls, slicked the floor beneath their feet and trapped the Stone in its embrace.

"What is this?" Ravelin said. His breath billowed white before his face. "What Wiche trickery is this?"

Cell doors up and down the corridor creaked and groaned as their wooden surfaces contracted in the bitter cold. The nails in Staub's door squealed against the pressure, and suddenly one popped free, shot across the corridor, and struck the opposite wall beside Ravelin's shoulder.

Kristan turned his dead eyes toward them. As his gaze passed over her, a bone-wracking cold shook Heather from toes to scalp. An answering shudder ran through Ravelin's body.

More nails burst loose as the door behind Kristan began to tremble and buckle. Inside the cell, Staub whimpered. The faint smile on Kristan's lips pulled tighter.

"Run," he whispered.

With a crash, the cell door collapsed. The impact knocked the lantern from its stool; it shattered on the icy floor and immediately went out. Ravelin shoved Heather aside and bolted from the hallway into the chamber beyond. The slick of ice pursued him, slithering across the stone flags, casting a faint bluish light that made it look like a shimmering veil. A few steps shy of the staircase it overtook him, passed him. Ravelin skidded, flapped his arms desperately, and then fell flat on his back. Kristan turned toward him, extended one languid hand and gave his first finger the smallest flick.

Ravelin shot across the icy floor, struck the bottom of the staircase, and bounced back. He tried to rise, but Kristan's hand twitched and Ravelin's legs went out from under him again. This time he landed on his chest. He kicked and clawed for purchase on the slippery floor, but it was as if he had been pinned through the ribs and could not rise. Kristan lowered his hand and tilted his head, and at that same moment Ravelin's body began to turn, slowly at first, like the blades of a windmill before a rising breeze. Heather had a glimpse of Ravelin's face, slack with shock, before it pivoted away, and its place was taken by the soles of his boots. A breath later, she saw Ravelin's face again, then his boots, then face, then boots, then face, then bootsfacebootsface until everything blurred together in a dizzying whirl.

Ravelin let out a bubbling wail of terror. Staub echoed the

cry as he burst from his cell, shoved past Heather, and scrambled down the corridor to the postern, slipping and sliding on the ice. Kristan ignored him, his attention fixed on Ravelin's spinning body. Staub threw himself at the far door until it burst open and he catapulted into daylight. His gibbering, weeping voice faded into the distance. Some dutiful, reasonable part of Heather's brain made a note to assign men to track him down, but the rest of her being was transfixed where she stood, open-mouthed, as the ice crawled up the walls and Ravelin whirled around and around and Kristan watched, his posture for once upright and attentive, like a cat watching the flutters of a wounded bird.

At last, he raised his hand again, this time in a dismissive wave, and Ravelin's spinning body skidded to an abrupt stop. Ever so slowly, Ravelin turned his face toward them. His eyes were shut, and his chin oozed tiny droplets of blood where the ice had scraped it raw. As he lay moaning softly, a thin trickle of drool ran from his lips, down his cheek, and to the floor. "Carrion crow . . ." he said in a bubbling whisper, ". . . what have you done to me now . . ."

Kristan jerked his head. Crackling faintly, the ice crept up the slender rope of Ravelin's saliva. It touched his cheek, then spread swiftly up his face and across his chin, freezing the dew of blood into a crimson sheet. Ravelin flinched and flopped onto his back; he opened his eyes just as the ice reached them. Before he could blink, the orbs were covered with a shimmering glaze. Before he could cry out, the ice thrust relentless fingers into his mouth, up his nostrils. His throat bulged and his back arched. His arms jerked up and his reaching fingers bent into claws.

"Kristan . . . oh, Kristan, no . . ." Heather whispered, pressing her own icy hands to her face.

Ravelin's arms stiffened. A fine hoarfrost coated the hairs on the backs of his hands; his fingernails had turned a sickening gray-blue. His legs shuddered and jerked; his heels beat a sudden, rapid tattoo against the floor.

Then Ravelin's body went rigid.

Slowly, ever so slowly, Kristan turned his head toward Heather. The light from the postern was too thin to lift the shadows that lay in the hollows of his face. It was as if a skull had turned its empty eye sockets upon her, and a scream of utter terror welled in her throat.

At that moment, some faint sound hissed past Heather: a whisper, a murmur, a chuckle. It swept down the corridor like a draft and Kristan turned with it, his head tilted as if trying to hear it better. The sound swirled into the chamber beyond, bouncing and echoing lightly from the walls and ceiling. Kristan moved after it and, without thinking, Heather followed. Her feet slid out from under her and she landed on hands and knees just within the chamber, but Kristan drifted featherlight across the ice, his face raised toward the sound. As he gained the center of the floor, the chuckling murmur skittered around and around the room, and with each pass, it seemed to Heather that the sound was creeping down the walls, until at last it whistled right past her nose. It rustled across the floor toward the staircase and for some moments, eddied and mumbled around Ravelin's frozen body.

"Enough," Kristan said.

The room went quiet, as if whatever was making the sound had stopped to listen.

"Are you finished?" Kristan went on. "Finished with your foolery?"

In the silence, Heather heard the crinkle of gooseflesh rising on her scalp.

"Because I'm ready," Kristan said. "I'm ready for you now."

There was a sudden whoosh of air, as if the walls themselves had been holding their breath, and the sound began again, a rising mutter that twisted and spun like a whirlwind. Suddenly, it lurched across the room toward Kristan. He staggered slightly as it struck him, tumbling his hair and dragging at his clothes, but then he threw up one arm and the sound careened away. It bounced from the far wall and ricocheted back, striking the floor near Kristan's feet. The ice cracked, and the heavy flagstones below heaved and shifted. With a dull clatter, a great ridge of crumbling earth thrust upward, nudging the flagstones out of the way. The mound spread from the middle of the room to the walls at right and left, as if some huge animal were burrowing its way to the surface. Then it began to rise, until it was as high as Kristan's knees, and as it rose, it split along its center like a loaf of baking bread.

"Crack," Heather said, in a voice no better than a squeak. "It's a Crack."

Kristan's eyes flicked toward her. It was just a glance, no more, but enough that she saw his sudden unease. Just as abruptly, he turned to face the great furrow. "Now," he said again. "Now."

The chuckling, muttering sound began. A fine gray mist welled between the lips of the Crack, like a ghostly tongue tasting the air. It spread right and left, until it frosted the Crack's surface, and then it drifted upward, veiling Kristan from Heather's view so that he was no more than a shadow on the other side of it. A few tentative tendrils brushed the ceiling, and then paused, as if waiting.

Slowly, Kristan raised his hands.

The mist quivered, thinning around Kristan's fingers so that his face was suddenly visible beyond it. The sight of his hollow eyes and fierce grin wrenched an involuntary whimper from Heather's throat.

Kristan fanned his hands, opening great rents in the mist. "This is what I feared? This is the stuff of my nightmares?" He laughed softly, echoing the chuckling murmur. "Come on, then."

For several long moments, nothing happened. Featherlike, the mist floated around Kristan's face, touching his cheeks, forehead, and hair as if caressing him. He flinched and drew back, his mouth twisted with disgust. "Stop," he muttered. "Come out and face me."

With a suddenness that made Heather gasp, a thick black fog burst from the Crack, scattering the mist like spindrift. It surged up to the ceiling and struck it, and as it curved like a cresting wave, it solidified into a glutinous sludge. The muck cascaded toward the floor, striking Kristan so hard that he staggered, and as it boiled around his knees, he thrust out both hands as if to ward it off. In answer, the mumbling laughter rose to a roar, and two great gouts burst from the mass and spiraled up his thighs. Kristan's teeth pulled back from his lips; whether in fury or revulsion, Heather could not tell. His upraised hands stiffened into claws. For a breath, the muck around him seemed to draw back, then poured up his body with renewed vigor. It slathered his waist and chest and shoulders, and sent viscous fingers twining into his hair. With a terrible sucking sound, it began to retreat into the Crack, pulling Kristan with it.

"No!" Heather cried, struggling to her feet. "No!"

She skidded across the ice toward him. The sludge bubbled and bloated and spewed out a low, undulating swell that collided with her halfway across the room, knocking her feet from beneath her. She flapped her arms wildly and regained her balance, but then the sludge bulged to the height of her head and slammed into her with such force that she spun across the chamber, ricocheted off the far wall, and landed just at the mouth of the cell's corridor. The wave that struck her was already slithering back to join the main mass. In desperation, Heather flung herself toward the remains of Staub's cell door, looking for something to use as a weapon. As she snatched up a long stave of wood, a faint glitter caught her eye: the Stone and its broken chain, frozen beneath the ice. With a cry of relief, she stabbed the stave into the ice as hard as she could. On the third blow the ice shattered, and she clawed the pendant free. Stone in one hand, stave in the other, she slid and stumbled back to the main chamber. Across the room, the sludge was sinking into the Crack, dragging Kristan with it. Submerged to his chin, his eyes rolled back into his lolling head, he had ceased to struggle.

With a guttural snarl, Heather threw herself toward the mass. A long arm of the stuff shot out at her; she slapped it aside with the stave, leaped clear of the dark wave that followed it, and landed an arm's length from Kristan. The sludge slurped at her knees, its clammy touch raising the gorge in her throat. Flinging stave, caution, and pity aside, she grabbed a handful of Kristan's hair and dragged herself to his side, holding the Stone high. With a gobbling sound, the sludge surged up her thighs and belly; it pulsed between her legs and she was suddenly, forcibly reminded of Ravelin's mouth on her. In fury, she balled her fingers around the Stone and, with all her might, punched her fist through the muck over Kristan's heart.

Her knuckles slammed into him. Spreading her fingers, she pressed the Stone against his chest. He cried out and shuddered all over. At the same moment, the slimy mass recoiled. Squirming like a slug sprinkled with salt, it released them and shrank toward the Crack. Kristan collapsed, and Heather caught him and bore his writhing body to the floor. She pinned one flailing arm and ducked the other, keeping an eye on the bulging, quivering sludge forcing its way back down the Crack's gullet. Three heartbeats passed, and it was gone, and the only sound in the room was Kristan's wheezing pants and the rattle of his heels and elbows against the icy floor. Even that sound softened to an irregular drumming as the ice thinned and faded. Kristan's body spasmed one last time and then went limp. His labored breathing grew more measured, and his grimacing expression eased. Heather placed one hand on his heart. Reassured by its steady pulse, she sat back on her heels. The Stone lay shining on the floor just beside Kristan's left ear, and she lifted it gently. To her surprise, its silver chain was whole again, and looped about Kristan's neck as if it had never been broken. She placed the Stone in the middle of Kristan's chest and stroked the chain smooth. A single link was slightly bent, showing where Kristan had broken it, but otherwise it was as if nothing had happened at all.

Nothing but the Crack, Heather thought with dry clarity. *And Staub's broken cell door. And Ravelin.*

She heaved herself to her feet. Taking care on the tumbled flagstones, she stepped across the Crack and made her way to Ravelin's body. His tortured limbs had gone limp; the rictus of his face had given way to a gentle scowl, although the skin still had a bluish cast. Heather crouched, extended a finger and placed it on his upper lip. The flesh was supple, but it was cold, and not even the slightest breath passed from mouth or nostrils.

"Still dead," Heather said aloud.

Kristan moaned, and she picked her way back to his side. As she bent over him, his eyelids shivered open and he looked up at her.

"Why?" he whispered. "Why didn't you let me go?"

Before she could answer, the door at the top of the staircase burst open and a jumble of voices sounded from the room above. "My lord?" Kennet called. "My lord, are you there?"

"Wait a bit, we need a light," Geoffrey said. "It's black as pitch down there."

"There's daylight coming from the corridor," Sir Eaden answered. "Has someone opened the postern?"

"My lord?" Mitchell's young voice was tight with apprehension.

"My lady?" Bayla echoed.

"Down here," Heather called. "Bring a light."

"A lantern, someone!" Geoffrey barked. Kristan breathed a sigh and rolled to his knees. She held out one hand, but he ignored it and staggered to his feet. Matthew shouldered his way through the doorway, a lantern held high. As he descended, other lights flared at the top of the stairs and a veritable procession followed: knights, soldiers, courtiers. Halfway down, Matthew stopped, staring. The yellow glow of his lantern had reached Ravelin's body. "What . . . what . . ." he breathed.

Others crowded behind him to look. In the circle of light, Heather could see each face and read every expression: the knights incredulous, Bayla and Alister troubled, Colin wary, Dell thoughtful, Serle and Desta anxious, Nolle merely curious. *Not one look of dismay or pity*, Heather thought. *Not one tear.* She glanced at Kristan, waiting for him to speak, to explain, but he, too, was studying the others' faces.

"Mind your feet," she called. "There's a fresh Crack down here and the floor is all jumbled."

"You children stay back," Geoffrey ordered, and waved his arms at others who clustered near the doorway. "The rest of you, go about your business. Go on."

As Matthew descended, yellow lantern light poured across the jagged floor and up the walls, *like beer from a keg after the bung's been pulled*, Heather thought. Dell, Colin and Alister paused to examine Ravelin's body, but everyone else continued past with barely a look.

"Are you all right, my lord?" Walter asked. Kristan nodded but said nothing.

"We were all outside watching the exercises," Mitchell said. "We heard an awful roar, and old Phelan cried out and fainted dead away—"

"No, that happened first," Colin said, joining them. "He was standing right next to me—"

"Dell always said there were Cracks under this castle—" Alister said.

"Were you down here when it happened, my lord?" Kennet asked. The urgency in his voice cut the others off short. In the sudden quiet, Heather heard the rattle of her own pulse.

Once again, Kristan nodded.

Only Dell still stood apart, his attention now on the Crack. Heather watched him absently as he followed its path into the cell corridor.

"Well, there's not a mark on him," Alister said. "On Ravelin," he went on, when no one answered. "His face is a little scraped, that's all, but he's still stone dead."

"But what happened to him?" Colin said.

Kristan's gaze flicked to Heather.

She took a deep breath. "I'm . . . I'm not sure. The Crack opened, and he ran toward the stairs, and then he tripped . . ."

Kristan's eyes narrowed.

"He tripped and fell," Heather went on more strongly. "He landed on his face. He rolled onto his back and twitched once or twice. Then he didn't move again."

"Frightened to death by a Crack," Walter said, and there was no mistaking the amused contempt in his tone. "Well, then."

"All three of you were down here when the Crack opened?" Colin asked. "Why?"

Heather opened her mouth to answer, to tell of Ravelin's betrayal, of the attempt on Kristan's life, but Kristan spoke first.

"He wanted me to see the floor." His eyes were still locked on her and his voice was flat, toneless. "He was showing me where it was uneven and might need to be repaired."

"And then?" Colin asked.

Kristan gave his shoulders the smallest shrug. "And then the Crack opened." Dell rejoined the group, a pensive twist to his mouth, and Kristan's gaze moved to him. "What is it, Dell?"

"The Crack goes all the way down that corridor," Dell said, pointing. "All the cell doors are burst."

"What do you mean, burst?" Eaden said.

"I mean they're in pieces on the floor."

Eaden gasped. "Staub! Staub's loose!" He bolted across the room and disappeared into the corridor.

"There's no one back there," Dell called after him. "The postern's wide open, though."

Eaden returned at a run. "Staub's gone, my lady," he said, panting. "He must have seen his chance and fled."

"Assemble a unit and search the town for him," Heather said. Eaden sprinted up the staircase, taking the steps two at a time. Kristan stepped across the Crack and followed, with Serle, Nolle, and Desta on his heels. His knights hurried to catch up, but Matthew paused alongside Ravelin's body. "My lord," he called. "What do you want to do with him? With Ravelin?"

Kristan stopped halfway up the stairs. He turned slowly and for several long moments, considered Ravelin's body. "Lay him before the throne in the great hall," he said at last. "Arrange whatever rituals and royal trappings are customary upon the death of a Seachlan."

"Royal trappings?" Colin sputtered. "Surely you're not going to give him a king's burial?"

"He was a king," Kristan said. "And the last of his line." He raised his hand to silence the mutters of protest. "Let him lay in state for two days, Colin. No doubt my Hogian knights can advise you as to the customs. On the third day, his body will be taken in procession through Needwood, so the people can pay their respects before we lay him with the rest of the Seachlans."

"But my lord—" Kennet said.

"See to it."

Kristan continued up the stairs, the children dogging his footsteps, and was gone.

"Well," Alister said.

Colin threw up his hands. "I'll never understand how his mind works, not if I live to be a hundred."

Matthew and Walter looked at each other and shrugged; Kennet stood staring at Ravelin's body, his mouth set in a hard line. With one fist, Geoffrey tapped Mitchell on the shoulder. "Come on, lad," he said. "Let's get him shifted upstairs to one of the anterooms and find someone to prepare him for the laying-out."

"The healer can do that," Alister said. "He was helping Phelan up to his room, last I saw him."

"Annys can assist with the appropriate clothing and banners and such," Colin said.

"Let's get started, then. Unless . . ." Geoffrey shot Heather a diffident glance. "My lady? Would you like to . . . did you want to—"

Heather shook her head.

Walter, Matthew, Geoffrey, and Mitchell bent over Ravelin's body, but Kennet stepped back, his features rigid with disgust. "No," he said. "I'm sorry. I can't put my hands on him."

"As you like, friend," Geoffrey said.

Grunting a bit, the four knights heaved the body shoulder-high and bore it up the staircase and out of the room. Kennet followed, his head bowed.

"Well, Uncle, we'd better get to work as well," Alister said to Colin. "The whole castle will be in an uproar and Needwood too, once the news travels."

"So it will." Colin looked down at the Crack and shook his head. "I'll have to get some masons in here to see if this damage can be repaired. Although if this Crack is like the others, there'll be no repairing it. I only hope the whole place doesn't come crashing around our ears as a result." He turned to Heather, clearing his throat. "Well, daughter. You know how I felt about Ravelin, so I won't pretend to grieve. But I'm sorry if . . . if losing your intended gives you pain."

"He wasn't my intended. I declined his offer this morning. Stop," Heather said, holding up a hand as everyone began talking at once. "I don't want to discuss it now. We have more on our plate than you know. Jerrold and a unit from the hunting lodge will be arriving soon. They're bringing Isobel's body; they found her dead a few days ago. Bayla, kindly tell the healer he'll have a second body to deal with."

"Yes, my lady." Bayla's lower lip trembled. "Do you . . . should I tell Annys and Lily? They were her friends."

"Yes, please. But do it quietly. And find Eaden first. Tell him to wait at the gates and assist Jerrold when they arrive."

Colin opened his mouth and she knew he was about to hammer her with questions, and if he did, she was afraid she might scream. "Father, not now," she said, and to her annoyance her voice cracked, and her knees were trembling. Alister put a comforting hand on her arm, but she pulled free and turned her back. "Please, everyone. Just ... just go about your business. Let me be."

"Hush ... no, no questions ... leave a lantern and come on ..." The pitying murmurs faded along with the others' footsteps. Heather shut her eyes and pressed both hands to her face, trying to sort out everything that had happened, everything that had been said, but her mind skipped and whirled and refused to cooperate. Finally, she heaved a deep sigh. "Enough," she whispered. "You have work to do."

She turned, and jumped at the sight of Dell, still standing near her, studying something in his hand. "These are all over the corridor," he said, without looking up. "Little slivers and chips of metal."

With an effort, Heather kept her composure. "Oh?"

"Every door is in pieces, yet I couldn't find a single lock or hinge or bar. Not even a nail. Only these little bits of metal." He looked at her then. His usual faraway expression was gone, replaced with an impatient eagerness. "I never heard of a Crack that could shatter metal."

"Nor I."

He cocked his head like a curious dog. "You're not going to tell me what happened, are you? Phelan knows, I think; when he came to, he was laughing and babbling."

"What did he say?"

"He said his freedom came at a terrible cost. And then he wept, and that was all anyone could get out of him." Dell shrugged. "Heather, I mean you and Kristan no harm. You're my friend, and Kristan has always treated me with respect, even when others didn't. I don't want the knowledge for gossip's sake, nor to use it against either of you. Whatever happened here, I don't care *why*; I only want to know *how*."

"It's not for me to say. Not now. Perhaps not ever. I'm sorry, Dell."

"Ah, well." Dell shrugged again. "At least you didn't lie, or laugh at me. So many people do, you know. I don't mind. I'd rather look like a fool than be one."

CHAPTER TWELVE

In accordance with the StoneKing's instructions, Ravelin lay in state for two days. A great bier, draped in red and black, was placed at the foot of the stairs leading to the throne, and on this, the body had been laid, dressed as if for battle. Ravelin's naked sword lay on his chest, its tip pointing toward his toes, his gauntleted hands wrapped around its hilt. Thick beeswax candles in tall iron holders provided the only light. The large, generous hearth sat cold and empty, and those who processed past the bier shivered in the cold. All the day and night, two soldiers in full Hogian regalia stood guard, one at the head of the bier and the other at its foot.

Heather viewed all this from a distance. She could not bring herself to approach the body; too many eyes were on her, too many mouths ready to ask questions she could not answer. Isobel had been laid out in a nearby antechamber, and Heather lingered beside that lonely bier instead, as if by her presence she could somehow lessen the humiliation of Isobel's end.

Isobel's body was covered from head to foot by a linen cloth that hid her torn and battered flesh and the livid marks around her throat. Heather had given orders that the details of Isobel's death and the discovery of her body were to be kept secret, and the official story that Isobel had wandered off and been lost in the storm seemed to satisfy most. Heather had expected questions from Annys and Lily, but after one brief visit to the room, the pair had stayed away, as if the sight had frightened them into silence. *I wonder how much they've guessed,* Heather thought wearily. *I wonder how much more they could tell. But it's not worth asking.*

She sat with Isobel until she was numb with cold and fatigue and the castle grew quiet as night deepened. In the early morning, Isobel would be laid in Needwood's burying ground, where the frozen earth had already been hacked open to make a grave for her. Her burial would, of necessity, be without ceremony, as Ravelin's elaborate interment in his family's crypt later in the day would take precedence. *Perhaps it's for the best,* Heather thought. *Less notice, fewer questions.*

Someone walked across the courtyard just outside the anteroom, and a moment later, the light from a lantern flickered over the mullioned windows. Other footsteps crunched up to join the first.

"Any luck?"

She recognized Sir Geoffrey's gruff, muffled voice.

"None," Sir Mitchell's lighter tones answered. "The others are checking to see if he's up on the battlements."

Heather sighed. Staub was long gone; she was sure of it. He had run screaming through Needwood immediately after fleeing the castle, frightening the townsfolk badly, but a thorough search of the town, outlying villages and the nearby Plain had turned up nothing. She was rising to open the window and tell the knights so, when Geoffrey spoke again.

"Are we sure he's not in his chamber?"

"The children say no. And Malvo's still in the stable. My guess is that he's somewhere in the castle, but he doesn't want to be bothered."

Geoffrey grunted. "Well. He'll turn up when he's ready, I suppose. This wind is bitter; let's go inside."

Their footsteps scrunched away. Heather sighed again, pressed one hand into the small of her back, and tried to ease her stiff muscles. She took her time arranging the linen cover over Isobel's body so it hung neatly all the way around, then snuffed the candles one by one. When she was finished, she paused at the foot of the bier. "I'm sorry," she murmured, and slipped from the darkened room.

The great hall was silent. Ravelin's bier stood unattended but for the guards. Beyond and above them, the towering throne of Hogia loomed in the shadows. The sight sent a shiver down Heather's spine, and she leaned back against the anteroom door, girding herself to approach the bier. Just then, the three children of Kristan's party came up from the kitchen stairwell and crossed the room. Desta led the way, carrying a candle, with Serle behind her and Nolle a few steps further back.

Desta stopped at the bier. "Excuse me," she said, her voice high and clear in the silence. "Have you seen the StoneKing?"

The guards stared straight ahead.

"I don't think they're supposed to talk," Serle whispered.

Nolle shrugged irritably. "Come on; maybe he's gone back to his room."

The children departed. As their footsteps faded, the guards exchanged a smirk and relaxed, leaning on their pikes. "Getting hungry," one murmured. "When's our relief?"

"Not for a while yet," said the other.

"No other visitors tonight, I'll wager. Off to their beds by now." The guard rested his pike against his shoulder and breathed on his hands. "I'm cold."

The other guard jerked his chin at Ravelin. "Not as cold as he is."

They snickered, and Heather had just opened her mouth to reprimand them when the outer doors of the keep opened, letting in a blast of cold air that fluttered the draping around Ravelin's bier. Three cloaked men entered the hall, putting back their hoods, pulling off their gloves. As they approached the bier, the guards strained to attention, but one of the men chuckled and waved a dismissive hand. "No need for that," he said, and Heather recognized Sir Walter's voice. "At ease."

The guards relaxed, candlelight glinting on their teeth as

they grinned.

The men ranged themselves around the bier, and now Heather could see them: Walter, Kennet, and Matthew, red-faced from the cold. "Well," Walter said. "Still dead."

Still dead. The echo of Heather's own words rang mockingly through her head, and she cringed.

"He's been dead for six months," Matthew said. His tone was light, careless. "A king without a crown is as good as a corpse. The StoneKing should have executed him when he seized the throne."

Kennet said nothing. His posture was rigid as the guards' had been a moment before, while Matthew's weight rested on one hip and Walter was positively slouching.

"Well," Walter said at last. "Goodbye, you piece of shit."

And he spat full in the face of Ravelin's corpse.

One of the guards guffawed. Matthew clapped Walter on the back, and the two went out the way they came. Kennet stood where he was. "Get out," he growled, without looking at the guards.

"But, sir, our orders—"

"Get out, I said. Go down to the kitchens and get warm. You can come back in a bit."

"Yes, sir."

For some time Kennet stood with his hands knotted at his sides. "You were magnificent, once," he whispered at last. "A king to admire, to revere, to serve with both heart and soul. You made me want to be the best man I could be. And you threw it all away." His voice hitched, and sudden tears sparkled in his eyes. "All for a woman. And for vanity. And for pride. And you threw me away as well."

He wheeled and strode from the room. Once his footsteps faded, Heather approached the bier.

The golden candlelight did little to soften Ravelin's sharp features. His mouth was downturned, as if in displeasure at the spittle that dribbled down the side of his face like an errant tear.

Heather lifted a hand to wipe the spit away, then hesitated.

"Touch him if you like."

The hoarse whisper was like a fingernail up her spine. She dropped her hand and slowly turned to face the throne. In its depths, the shadows shifted, and the faint candlelight caught first the glitter of the Stone's silver chain, then the flicker of Kristan's eyes. "Were you going to kiss him farewell?"

"No, my lord."

"Then perhaps you were going to spit on him too."

"No, my lord."

He said nothing, and she took a step toward him.

"Stay back." His voice was icy. "Look away. I don't want to be stared at."

She dropped her gaze to her boots. "People have been looking for you, my lord."

"I know. I've been watching my keepers go back and forth all evening. Strange that no one bothered to look here, on the throne, where one might expect to find a king who's mourning his loyal subject."

The flatness in his tone sent a tremor up Heather's spine.

"Why are you doing this?" she whispered. "Why are you honoring him? He tried to kill you. Why didn't you tell the others he tried to kill you?"

"Why didn't you tell them what I did? That I killed Ravelin. That I opened the Crack and summoned him and tried to face him and failed, failed again, just like I've always failed—" Kristan's voice broke, and a coughing spell doubled him over.

Without thinking, Heather stepped forward. "Summoned him? Who are you talking about?"

He caught his breath and leaned forward, and the candlelight sent shadows leaping beneath his eyes and into the hollows of his cheeks and temples and jaw. "I chose. After all these miserable months of cowering and shrinking, of seeing him in my dreams and hearing him when I'm awake, I finally chose. I thought the power was strong enough to face him—"

"Him?" She suddenly remembered her conversation with Torrin. "Kristan . . . do you think that was Daazna?"

He flinched, as if she had struck him.

"How can that be? You killed him. I saw his body."

"Something of him survived. I knew it the moment I put my sword through his back. I felt him changing, laughing, swirling all around me. And then he was gone. But he didn't go far. I've felt him around me since last summer, but he's strongest here, in this castle."

"But how? How?"

"*Tabi'a.*" The word was so soft she could hardly hear. "True magic. More powerful than any learned spell. He wanted it for himself. And I . . . I showed him how."

He hunched his shoulders and knotted both hands in the tangles of his hair, as if to pull it out. In three swift steps Heather mounted the dais and went to one knee in front of him. "Tell me," she whispered. "Tell me what happened."

"I don't know. Ariphele said it was a *Tabi'a* of destruction— that I manifested it after Daazna cursed me with the *éigniú anam*, and that the Stone was blocking me from using it again. She didn't tell me what I did, only that Daazna was terrified, and desperate to possess the power for himself. And I think somehow he did. When we finally faced each other again, I could feel it coming off him in waves. He dared me to put the Stone aside and match my *Tabi'a* against his. But I was too afraid. Like the coward I've always been, I hid behind the Stone where I was safe, and like a coward, I stabbed him in the back, but he didn't . . . he didn't . . ."

"Die? Kristan, you must know that can't be true. Torrin said—"

"Torrin thinks I'm mad. *Ragis*, that's what the centaurs call me. And now you think I'm mad too. But I swear to you Daazna is still alive. I feel him waiting, and growing stronger while he waits. The only defenses I have against him are the Stone, and this *Tabi'a*—this power of destruction. The Stone doesn't want me to use the *Tabi'a*; it hurts me when I try." He touched it with flinching fingers. "Even now, it's like a knot of ice against my heart. But while it protects me, it leaves everyone around me vulnerable. Too many died for my sake: Martin and Gabriel, Finn Curry, Norwinn's soldiers by the thousands. Night after night, I relive their deaths in my dreams. I won't hide behind the Stone again while others die in my place. The Stone is only a shield, but the *Tabi'a* is a weapon, and my only hope of defeating Daazna, once and for all. But I'm too weak; I tried to take him on and I failed again; I always fail—"

"I'm glad you did."

He reared back. "How can you say that?"

"Because I saw what you did to Ravelin. I don't blame you for killing him; he deserved to die. He killed Isobel and he was going to kill you. I would have killed him myself if I'd had the chance. But you made him suffer first. You tortured him, like Daazna tortured you. The Kristan Gemeta I knew would never have done something so cruel."

"The Kristan Gemeta you knew was a weak fool." She said nothing, only peered into the shadows, trying to make out his face. His knotted hand thumped the arm of the throne. "Don't stare at me. I hate being stared at."

"What are you going to do now?"

"What do you mean?"

"You said you failed. You said you were too weak and you failed. So what are you going to do now?"

He was silent for so long that she wondered if he would answer. "I don't know," he said at last. "Wait. Wait until I'm strong enough to destroy him."

"And when will that happen? Tomorrow? Next month? Next year? Ten years from now? And while you wait for your *Tabi'a* of destruction to grow stronger, what happens to your realm? To your people? What happens when you lose the love and respect of those you depend on? You've already started down that road; what happens when you're so maddened by fear and hate that they're ready to turn on you, the way Daazna's soldiers were ready to turn on him?"

He shrugged. "Then perhaps someone will put me out of my misery. That's what Ariphele asked me to do for Daazna. Will you do it for me, Commander? Will you take your sword and end my suffering?"

"No. Not now. Not ever. You are not Daazna, nor Ravelin. You are my lord, and I swore an oath to protect you." She stood up. "If I must, I'll die protecting you."

He sucked in a hissing breath. "You will not. Next time I face Daazna alone."

"Why? Why, when you wield a power stronger than any *Tabi'a?*"

"What are you talking about?"

"You think you were weak last summer. You're wrong. Others were drawn to you, not because you were a mighty warrior or a powerful king, but because you were kind and just and decent. The Stone wanted you because of that. I carried it; I felt it yearn toward you. I know Daazna destroyed much of your memory, and maybe you can't remember what happened when I placed the Stone around your neck, but I can. The earth *sang*. Your goodness aligned with the Stone's *Tabi'a* of protection, and it made you strong. This other, destructive *Tabi'a* is the opposite of your true nature. It's a weapon, yes, but one that's heavy and warped and poisoned. It doesn't make you strong—it weakens and sickens you."

For perhaps a dozen breaths, he was silent. "Then what am I to do?"

"Turn away from this terrible *Tabi'a*. Fight against the cruelty it breeds in you. Be true to the Stone. To yourself. Gather your friends around you once more and draw your strength from their love. Thousands and thousands of people look to you for leadership. For a new path. For hope. You have to learn to hope again. Because if you're right—if Daazna is somehow still alive—who else can stand against him when he returns?"

In the silence, Heather heard her own heart hammering in her chest. At last, Kristan stood up. In the faint candlelight, his gaunt features looked like those of a dead man, and it took all Heather's self control not to recoil. "You throw my responsibility in my face," he said. "You condemn me to live so I can face Daazna alone, and in the same breath, tell me I'm too weak to meet him on his own terms. And you call *me* cruel."

Her knees were trembling, but she forced herself to stand up straight and tall. "You are not alone. Your family and friends stand by you. Your knights and soldiers are ready to serve. Four kingdoms full of people hunger for a ruler to love and respect, rather than hate and fear. Thousands upon thousands of people will stand with you. Their love will strengthen you, if you'll only let it."

Kristan opened his mouth to respond, but at that moment, something moved at the far side of the room, and they both turned to look. Desta stood just beyond the shadows; she bowed, then hurried to the door leading to Kristan's chamber.

A bitter smile curled Kristan's mouth. "I am discovered. No doubt the rest of my keepers will be on me in a moment. This has been an interesting conversation, Commander, but I will do what I must. Good night."

Heather stood watching as he made his way toward the door leading to his chambers. A small figure stepped out to greet him, and Serle's voice rose in timid inquiry, but Kristan brushed past him without answering. He disappeared down the corridor and Serle followed, closing the door.

Heather turned back to the bier. She picked up one of the pikes left behind by the guards. She stared down at Ravelin's body but did not see it. The two guards came up from the kitchen, muttering and chuckling and wiping their mouths on their sleeves. They froze at the sight of her.

"You left your posts," she said.

"Ma'am, Sir Kennet told us—"

"I don't care what Sir Kennet said; your orders were to stand guard on Reach Seachlan's bier. You're dismissed. Report to Sir Jerrold at once and tell him you've been relieved of duty."

"Oh, but my lady—"

"Tell him you're to be docked a month's pay. Throughout that month, you'll be assigned cesspit duty during the day and the late watch at night. Understood?"

"Yes, ma'am. Sorry, ma'am."

They started to leave, but one guard hesitated. "Ma'am, should we send our relief—"

"No. Tell Sir Jerrold I'm taking this watch until dawn and I don't want to be disturbed. By anyone. Now get out of here."

"Yes, Commander."

Their trudging footsteps faded. Heather crouched beside the bier and stayed there for some time, her forehead cradled in both hands. At last, she rose, took up one of the guards' pikes and placed herself at the head of the bier. Gripping the pike so it stood exactly upright at her shoulder, she blinked the tears from her eyes, focused her gaze somewhere in the near distance, took a deep breath, and began the long wait for dawn.

* * *

Staub fled all night, through the frost-crusted grass of Hogia's Plain, under the bitter black sky without even the moon to light his way. The grass sliced his hands open as he pushed it aside; it cut his palms so that they bled and then froze.

He made the River Mor by dawn. The realm's ferries were snugged up against the banks and he knew he could not cross that way. The river was sheeted with ice, and he ventured onto its treacherous surface, his heart in his mouth and whimpered curses on his lips.

Slowly, so slowly, he made his way across the ice. He was almost to Fandrall's shore when a rotten patch gave way beneath him. He let out a squeal of fear and pain, for the water was so cold it was like being skinned alive, but then his feet touched

the bottom and he threw himself toward the riverbank, breaking the remaining ice with flailing arms. By the time he clam-
bered ashore, he was shaking so hard that his teeth rattled. He
turned his head to the side, bringing his one eye to bear, and at
last saw the forbidding mass of the Exilwald in the distance. His
single eye fixed in a mad stare, he staggered toward it.

CHAPTER THIRTEEN

Under a leaden sky, Ravelin's final procession wound through the main street of Needwood. The people clustered along the route, jigging in place to keep warm, eyes watering in their cold-reddened faces. Some of the men spat contemplatively as the bier rolled by, and some of the women nodded, dour smiles tightening their mouths, but most only glanced at Ravelin and studied the living instead: the stone-faced soldiers marching in formation, the knights riding in grave escort, and especially the courtiers who followed the bier, bareheaded, on foot and on horseback. They muttered to each other as Heather passed, keeping restless Skapi on a tight rein, her expression equally restrained; they nodded in recognition at the sight of Kennet, Walter, and Matthew; they yearned toward the children who rode just to Kristan's right.

But mostly they stared at Kristan. Without the protection of his hood, he felt the full force of so many searching, questioning eyes. He clenched his teeth and stared straight ahead. *Don't look at me. You bruise me with your need, with your hope. Look at Ravelin, look at your dead lord. I'm no more use to you than he is now.*

Serle sniffled.

"Stop it," Desta hissed. "You're the StoneKing's squire. You're not supposed to cry."

"They're just so sad."

"Who, these people?" Nolle's voice was bright with derision.

"You three quiet down," Sir Geoffrey rumbled from Kristan's left.

Something soft and wet touched Kristan's face. He glanced up. Snowflakes were falling from the brooding clouds overhead. As he watched the flakes, a sudden gust of wind sent his hair tumbling into his face.

"They didn't like him," Nolle whispered. "No one liked him. No one's sorry he's dead."

"But they're still sad," Serle said. "It feels like they've been sad for a long, long time."

"Quiet." This time it was Sir Walter, somewhere just behind Kristan. He felt the press of warm horseflesh as Walter drew closer and spoke more quietly. "My lord, I don't like the look of this sky. Do you want to cut the procession short? I doubt anyone here will care."

Kristan nodded, and Walter urged his horse ahead. He drew up beside Heather, and they held a brief, muttered conference while the snow swirled around them. She glanced back at Kristan, and the sorrow in her blue eyes pierced him to the heart.

You made him suffer.

Her rebuke thrummed in his memory, shaming him anew.

You tortured him, like Daazna tortured you.

A knot tightened in his throat.

The Kristan Gemeta I knew would never have done something so cruel.

He longed for tears, to cry out his remorse, his confusion and fear, but his eyes were dry.

Heather called out a series of orders. The procession swung down a side street, then turned again, doubling back to the castle on the town's outer road. The gazes of the townspeople were like pebbles flung against Kristan's back. He hunched his shoulders against the sting.

Geoffrey leaned toward him. "Back at the castle soon, my lord," he said. "We'll bung him in his crypt and that'll be the end of it."

The casual cruelty in Geoff's voice made Kristan want to moan, but at that moment, another voice sounded in his head.

You soft fool. Have you forgotten what he did?

It was his own voice, at its most spiteful. The image of Robert Gemeta's head, splattering blood across Fandrall's castle courtyard, rose in his mind's eye. His guts cramped, suddenly and sharply.

He killed your father, and then stood by while your people were murdered, your castle ransacked, and your family's tomb defiled. Have you forgotten that?

The horses pulling the bier leaned into their halters as the procession mounted the road toward the castle lying just ahead, with the Reavings spread out around it like the spokes of a great shattered wheel.

Your father lies in pieces somewhere outside his castle, thrown into a Crack and buried like so much rubbish, along with your mother and your grandparents and generations of Gemetas.

Another cramp. Kristan grimaced and dug one gloved hand into his belly. The procession clattered onto the drawbridge. Under the lowering sky, it seemed like a long tongue, run out of the gaping mouth of the gatehouse to lap up soldiers and riders and bier alike.

Ravelin killed your father. He would have killed you. Why should he be buried with honor? Why should he lie in a king's grave?

The bier's rattling wheels echoed through the gatehouse and out into the courtyard, where an honor guard stood waiting at the keep's enormous doors. The guards snapped to attention as Ravelin's body came to a halt before them, but their eyes gleamed with cynical amusement.

End this mockery now. Order them to drag Ravelin's body off the royal bier and strip it of its fine clothing and string it up by the neck from the highest tower, and let it hang there, to be pecked by birds and nibbled by rats—

The memory of Gabriel's rat-gnawed face hit him like a blow. His stomach heaved, and bile burned in his throat. *Stop. Stop. Controlcontrolcontrol* . . .

Around him the riders were dismounting, but Kristan's calves cramped hard, and he could not move. Awful visions crowded around him: Finn sitting dead on the banks of the Strath, the army of Norwinn screaming beneath tearing claws and beaks, the old commander whispering *curse you curse you, Gemeta* . . .

"My lord?" Sir Geoffrey was leaning toward him. "Something wrong?"

. . . his sword cleaving Owen's face, crushing his skull . . .

"No," he managed to choke out. "Carry on."

Geoffrey nodded and swung himself from the saddle. Kristan's thigh muscles seized, jerking his feet in their stirrups. Malvo's ears flicked back and he let out a low, rumbling whinny. The snow was coming down harder now, coating the frozen ground and the stone steps of the keep, and as the honor guard descended to the bier, they slipped and slid. Heather snapped out a low reprimand. Quickly, they ordered themselves along the bier; in unison they lifted Ravelin's body and raised it shoulder-high—

And it was not Ravelin but Kristan's mother who lay silent and pale on the bier, and then Simeon's cold gray eyes rose up before him and he saw rather than heard the thin lips whispering *avama* . . .

"What are you waiting for?" Desta muttered to Serle. "Get down and hold Malvo's bridle."

"Sir?" Serle was peering at him, his freckled face drawn with anxiety. "Sir, are you all right?"

His back muscles clenched, pulling him upright. He let out a small gasp. *I can't. I can't do this.*

Now his knights were turning toward him, and at the head of the bier, Heather hesitated, one hand half raised, and the gaze she turned on him was clouded with apprehension.

I can't bear this any longer.

He forced his knotted leg muscles straight and wedged his feet tight in the stirrups. "Carry on," he said again, with all the self-control he could muster, and turned Malvo around. At that moment his calves knotted, rattling his heels against Malvo's ribs. Malvo snorted and broke into an uneven trot.

A commotion broke out behind him, and he was still well short of the gate when Walter drew up on one side of him, Kennet on the other. "My lord, where are you going?" Kennet asked. "Shall we accompany you?"

Kristan's very jaws were spasming now. "No," he said through his teeth. "See to Ravelin."

"But my lord—"

"See to Ravelin, I said."

"My lord—"

"*Leave me alone!*"

His cry startled Malvo into a gallop. It was only the death-like grip of Kristan's cramping legs that saved him from being unseated. As the knights fell back, he hunched over Malvo's neck, his fingers gripping reins and mane alike. The guards dived clear as horse and rider hurtled through the gatehouse and across the drawbridge, and Kristan groaned as his insides clenched and churned.

Suddenly, Desta was racing alongside him, crouched low in her saddle. She reached for Malvo's bridle. "No!" Kristan screamed, flailing one arm at her. "Get away! Go back!"

She reined up, and Malvo thundered on. Kristan clung to the big horse with all his might. Convulsions squeezed and shook him, as if he were in the grip of a great fist, and he whimpered into the warm flesh of Malvo's neck. He did not know where they were going; he did not care. Every jarring hoof-beat seemed to hammer the words *choose choose choose* into his flesh; every jerk and twist of his muscles sent fresh memories into his brain, memories that seared to his soul: Ravelin's frozen features, Sigurd's drowning eyes, Melissa's tears, the children cringing away from him, Malvo flinching under the blows of Kristan's glove, the knights' eyes averted in fear, Heather staring at him in revulsion.

"No," he cried out loud. "I don't want it. I don't want it anymore."

With those words Kristan's stomach gave a single, powerful heave. His mouth filled with bile, so hot and bitter that his whole body went rigid with revulsion. Like a stone, he fell from Malvo's back; like a stone, he tumbled and rolled until he finally fetched up on his hands and knees, opened his mouth, and spewed gouts of stinking gray-green slime onto the snow.

He was sick again and again, until at last his retchings brought up nothing but feeble moans, like the mewing of a newborn kitten. His arms buckled; he toppled onto his side and lay with his eyes squeezed shut, gasping and shivering. His insides felt as if they had been scoured, leaving his body as empty and fragile as a dried eggshell.

Something popped faintly, like the smacking of fleshy lips. He opened his eyes. The mounds of vomit were twitching, squirming. Through his stupor he realized he was lying right on the edge of a Reaving, and that the repulsive substance he had disgorged was straining toward him even as it was sucked into the rift.

Fear rattled down his spine, but his exhausted body would not move. Like a frightened child, he whispered a single, instinctive word.

"Papa."

As soon as the word was spoken, he braced himself for the horror that would follow, but in place of the vivid images of Robert Gemeta's death, only the vaguest impressions flitted through his memory; empty, fleeting outlines that swelled transparent and then just as quickly dissipated, like a soap bubble.

The last of the gray-green substance was shriveling into the Reaving, but Kristan barely noticed. He scrambled through the remains of his memory, trying with all his might to call up the garish colors and sounds and sensations of his father's death.

It was no use. It was gone.

Mumma, he thought, and tensed for the melancholy image of his mother's face, pale and remote in death. Again, there was nothing.

He shut his eyes and sucked in a shuddering breath. He forced himself to think of Martin and Gabriel, deliberately trying to conjure up their horrifying last moments, to hear the thud of the blades biting into their necks, and feel the hot splatter of their blood on his face. He waited for the onset of horror and sorrow and crushing guilt.

His mind's eye presented him with only shades and echoes. The powerful images were gone, faded to shadows like the rest of his memories.

Instead of relief, he was overwhelmed with a shattering sense of loss. *Come back*, he tried to say. *Come back. You're all I have.*

A gulping sob burst from deep in his chest. Something hot streaked down his cheek, following the angle of his scar to the corner of his mouth; he tasted salt on his lips. A mutter from the past echoed through his brain: *He's weeping blood.*

He rolled onto his back, fumbled off one glove, dragged his fingers across his face and then looked at them. His fingertips glistened, not with blood, but with tears.

The sight destroyed what was left of his self-control. Another sob escaped him, and another and another. He rolled onto his side again, curling his arms and legs against his body. His fingers caught in the silver chain around his neck, and as he tried to free them, the Stone slid into his palm.

It was warm.

For a long time, he lay clutching the Stone, wracked with sobs that shook him to his very core. He wept out of grief for his losses, out of remorse for his many cruelties, out of sheer and utter exhaustion. Most of all he wept because the sick rage that had fueled him for so long was finally gone, and its absence terrified him. *There's nothing left*, he thought. *What am I to do now?*

He did not know how long he lay there, alone in his grief, but after a time, a huff of warm breath stirred his hair, and Malvo's long nose loomed into his sight. The horse's black hide was frosted with snow, and he shook his head so hard that his tack jingled, then blew gently through his lips. It was as if he was scolding Kristan for keeping him out in the cold.

Kristan laughed. It was a thin and shaky sound, but in response, Malvo whickered low, as if he were laughing too. Kristan struggled to sit up, but he could barely raise his head. "Help me," he said, his voice no more than a croak. Malvo pushed his nose into Kristan's shoulder, and Kristan placed his ungloved hand on the horse's head.

A tremendous jolt shot through his palm and straight up his arm, a surge of heat and energy so intense that for a moment he couldn't breathe. He snatched his hand back, dizzied by the impact.

A wisp of memory floated through his brain: a pair of steely gray eyes, thin lips muttering.

. . . *avama* . . .

Malvo snorted with impatience and pushed his head out again.

Warily, Kristan pulled off his other glove. He reached out with both hands, and Malvo nudged his soft nose into Kristan's upturned palms.

Avama.

Another shock surged from Malvo's body into his own. He was filled with the horse's strength, the power of his four legs, the tension of tendons and muscles, the big lungs drawing cold air into the deep chest and expelling it out into a cloud of steam. At that moment, beyond the haze of hay-scented breath, he saw himself through Malvo's eyes: a little pale-faced two-legged creature with wild black hair and red-rimmed eyes, mouth dropped open with wonder.

Then the vision was gone, and Malvo was lipping, none too gently, at Kristan's sleeve, and all Kristan could feel beneath his hand was the slick, damp hide and the warmth of the horse's body; nothing more. He got hold of Malvo's bridle and struggled to his feet. Malvo snorted and pulled his head away, as if bored by Kristan's weakness, and Kristan, still unsteady, put his hand out to a nearby tree for support.

As his flesh made contact with the rough bark, another shock of energy burst through him. This one yanked him in two directions at once: rushing up the length of the trunk toward the leaden sky and down into the earth below, reaching outward with the branches and downward into the cold dirt, his toes seeking water and nourishment, his fingers seeking light and sustenance. His muscles stretched with the latent power of buds still unborn, waiting for the right moment to burst forth; his skin seemed to crackle and peel with the dying energy of the few remaining leaves trembling on their stems, ready to drop—

It was too much. Kristan reeled away, afraid his head and heart would explode. He sank to his hands and knees, and this time the snow delivered its blast, a blow that rocketed through all ten fingers and straight into his brain, and he was whirling inside the storm that had brought the snow, deafened by screaming winds, his eyes full of the delicate filigree of ice crystals as they spun and tumbled and fell, joining to create an endless white curtain of cold.

Slowly, the world stopped spinning, and Kristan was brought back to his senses by the wheeze of his own breathing. Another sound joined it, a faint, chiming whir that he traced to the Stone. It was glowing, humming, and when he took it into his cold bare hand, its warmth flowed into him. "Well," he said, with a weak laugh, "I'm glad you're happy."

Somehow he got to his feet again; somehow his eyes focused and found Malvo waiting impatiently; somehow he lurched through the snow and got hold of stirrup and reins; somehow he dragged himself into the saddle. Malvo tossed his head and would have raced off once again, but Kristan managed to rein him in. For some moments, he sat stupidly in the saddle, the snow whirling about his face as he regained his bearings. He was in the hills east of the castle; its bulk and the near smudge of Needwood were only a short ride away. His mouth was dry and foul-tasting, and he was suddenly desperate for a long drink of water. The generous proportions of Needwood's big well rose temptingly in his mind. Still shaken and woozy, he nudged Malvo down the hill and onto the road toward town.

In Needwood's town square, everyone turned to look. He knew they were bowing, but all his attention was on the well in the middle of the plaza. A few women stood beside it with pails and pitchers at the ready, and the youngest of them, thick-set and plain, was cranking the windlass. When he reined up near them, the women drew back, dipping into clumsy curtsies, and one hissed a warning to the young woman, who had not noticed his approach. She looked up, saw him, and stepped back quickly, letting the bucket fall back into the well. The sound made him want to whimper; he was so terribly thirsty. He dismounted with difficulty, his legs buckling and shaking. He took hold of the windlass handle and tried to winch the bucket up, but its weight was too much for him, and he leaned on the handle and lowered his head.

"My lord . . ." the young woman said timidly. "My lord . . . may I help?"

"Yes, please," he almost whispered.

With a few economical turns of the windlass, she heaved the dripping bucket up and placed it on the edge of the well. She stepped back, then held out a plain earthen mug. "Would you like to use my cup, my lord?"

"Yes, please," he said again. He reached for the cup, and as he closed his hand about it, his fingers touched hers.

A fresh bolt of energy pierced him. The young woman's fear of him was a cold chill, but her pity for his weakness ran through the cold like a warm current. Beneath that, something else was stirring, something small and still that was part of her and yet separate, something that sent a buzzing up his arms and into his neck and head. Another life lay deep in the woman's belly, but it was motionless, dormant, as if waiting to die. At that moment, he knew the woman believed the baby was dead in her womb. *Like the others before it*, he thought, and realized the knowledge was not his, but hers. He suddenly knew her mind, her heart: how much she loved her husband, how she had kept the knowledge of the pregnancy from him, determined to suffer the certain miscarriage in silence to spare him the grief of another loss. His heart swelled with compassion for her sad courage, and for the stillness of the little life within her.

He put his other hand on the woman's belly.

She gasped; all the women gasped, and he knew he had frightened them, but then the child in the womb twitched, as if aware of his touch, and he felt the throb of its little heart. Tears welled in his eyes, and he smiled.

"This one lives," he said. "Tell your husband. This one lives."

The woman gaped at him, and at the same moment, the baby in her belly shifted again and every hair on his body prickled as he felt the woman sense the movement. Wonder and joy sparkled in her eyes. "I feel it," she whispered. She turned to one of the other women, one with the same square shape and plain face, only older. "Mother, it's moving. I feel it. I feel it."

The women surged forward, shouldering Kristan aside in their eagerness to place their hands on the young woman's belly. Some wept, and some laughed, and the mother-to-be raised her face to the slate-colored sky and closed her eyes as the tears ran down her cheeks and into the corners of her laughing mouth. Kristan turned to the bucket and dipped the homely little mug into the water, and he put back his head and drank gratefully, and no water had ever tasted so fresh, so cold, so bright with all the flavors of the earth from which it had sprung. He had only time to savor a mouthful before the young woman was kneeling before him. Knocking the cup to the ground, she caught his hand in hers and covered his scarred fingers with kisses and tears. "Thank you, StoneKing," she said in a choking voice. "Thank you."

The woman's mother was kneeling too, and she put her hand on his booted leg and a fresh tremor shook him, and her gratitude and her love for her daughter washed about him like a river, and then the other women were putting their hands on him.

Every touch sent a new jolt through him; each hand told him its owner's story, her wants and woes, her little joys and great griefs and everything in between. All their lives pulsed through his feeble frame and made his head spin and his heart pound, until he thought he might faint. He pulled free and was trying to mount Malvo when a stolid, stocky man elbowed through the growing crowd to the young woman's side. She pressed his work-thickened hand against her belly and pointed to Kristan, saying words that Kristan could not hear through the rising din. The man threw his arms around her and held her tight. Kristan gave up trying to get into the saddle and clung to Malvo for support as all around him people put their hands on him, patting his back, stroking his hair, clutching his wrists and elbows, sending wave after wave of life through him. Each touch was one more shock to his already exhausted mind and body; every hand told him of his people's longing; their need to believe he would be the kind and just ruler who would lead them out of poverty and barrenness and misery. The impact of each heart and mind, of each essence he absorbed, filled him with a shuddering exhilaration, but at the same time his body was failing, and his head swam. *So this is what Simeon meant,* he thought. *This is what avama is. If it goes on much longer, I may die of it.*

Then the stocky young man was elbowing the others aside. "StoneKing!" he cried, his face wreathed in a huge and foolish grin. "StoneKing, I . . ." Suddenly, the man burst into tears, even though he was still smiling. He grabbed both Kristan's hands and knelt before him, and Kristan, flooded with the man's joy, shivered and swayed on his feet. *Heather*, he thought. *I have to find Heather.* "Help me," he said, his voice no more than a gasp, but the man looked up and understood. With one hand he grabbed Malvo's bridle, then shoved a broad shoulder beneath Kristan's backside and heaved him onto Malvo with such force that Kristan nearly overshot the saddle. Other hands reached out to steady him as the stocky man took Malvo by the bridle and led him through the crowd. More hands reached toward Kristan, touching his legs and feet when they could, stroking Malvo's hide when they could not. Malvo pranced beneath their caresses, and his pleasure in being admired sent tingling waves through Kristan's body.

Someone began to cheer, and other voices joined in. "StoneKing! StoneKing! StoneKing!" rang through the streets, echoing in the morning air. The people made way for him, and many fell in behind, running after him as he rode up the street to the castle. Malvo crossed the drawbridge and the townspeople stood cheering at one end while the gatehouse guards gawped from the other. His knights were there too, on horseback as if about to ride out (*search party*, Kristan suddenly thought, and choked back a giggle of incongruous hilarity), and they stared at him as he rode past, Malvo nearly capering as the mob continued their refrain of "STONEKING! STONEKING! STONEKING!"

Serle, Desta, and Nolle came hurrying as he entered the courtyard. He reined up before the keep steps and was distantly amused to see how the three pushed and shoved to be the first at his side. Desta was quickest, grabbing Malvo's bridle with one hand and steadying Kristan's stirrup with the other. Even with her assistance, Kristan nearly fell as he dismounted. Instinctively, he grabbed Desta's shoulder to steady himself, and a new shock burst through him, this one a thunderclap of admiration and need and fierce devotion. *This child would go through fire for me*, Kristan thought, with mingled wonder and dismay.

Serle was at his other side then, murmuring encouragement as he took Kristan's elbow, but where Desta's essence was a thunderclap, Serle's was like a summer downpour; a warm, drenching surge of unreserved affection coupled with an earnest desire to both serve and comfort. *Such a kind boy*, Kristan thought. *Such an innocent.*

Nolle was in front of him then, hands on hips. "What happened?" she demanded. "What are all those people yelling about?"

He disengaged himself from Serle and Desta and, to Nolle's obvious discomfiture, placed his hands on either side of her face. He was rewarded with a snapping, sizzling awareness of her quick mind and impetuous nature, and beneath that, a fear of failure as deep as a well. *We have more in common than you know*, he thought as Nolle pulled free, frowning.

His head was spinning, and his legs wobbled. The stairs leading to the keep doors loomed before him like a mountain. *I'll never do it*, he thought, letting his gaze drift up each step. *I'm going to collapse right here in the courtyard.* He lifted his eyes to the doorway just as Colin came through it and stood, gaping at him.

Right behind him was Heather.

The roaring of the crowd outside the castle walls dwindled away, and Kristan became aware of the chiming hum of the Stone around his neck. Heather's eyes were bright with worry, but when she caught sight of Kristan, her expression shifted: from worry to relief, from relief to guardedness. His whole being yearned for her, and with the last of his strength, he mounted the stairs toward her.

As he gained the final step, she drew herself up with soldierly precision and raised her hand to salute, her lips forming words that he could not hear over the chiming of the Stone. He took a deep breath, braced himself, and caught her hand in his own.

Her essence exploded through him with such force that he nearly blacked out. He felt the heat of her, the crackle of her brain and the throb of her heart; he sensed her kindness and courage and loneliness and most of all her love, the love that had never cowered, never flinched, never faltered, in spite of his cruelty. As if in a dream, he saw her confusion; as if in a dream, he grasped her arm, her waist; he gathered her to him and bent his head to her upturned face. He kissed her and felt her gasp and *thought if I must die today, let it be like this. Let it end here, in Heather's arms.*

* * *

Kristan released her and took a reeling step back, and then the children were on him, grasping his hands, pulling and pushing at him, all talking at once. They bowled past Heather, past Colin, through the doors and into the keep.

Stunned, Heather stood, looking after them. It was only when her father turned to her, slack-jawed, that she realized her own mouth was standing open. She shut it so hard her teeth clicked.

"Now what in the world—" Colin said, but she was already shoving past. She rushed through the anteroom and into the great hall, but the children had gained the door to Kristan's chambers and were dragging his staggering figure down the corridor. She broke into a run, but Nolle spotted her and slammed the door shut.

"Wait!" Heather called, reaching for the handle, but the metallic scrape of a key in the lock told her Nolle had been too quick for her. In sudden rage, she hammered on the door with both fists. "Open up! Open this door, I tell you!"

"Clear off, or I'll turn you into a slug," Nolle shouted back.

"Why, you little brat—"

Sir Geoffrey hustled up, with the rest of Kristan's knights behind him. "Let me handle this, my lady," he said, and rapped sharply on the door. "Nolle, open up. Do as I say."

"Bugger off," Nolle answered smartly. Geoffrey swore under his breath. Walter and Matthew snickered.

"Let me try," Walter said. He tapped more gently, and said in a wheedling voice, "Come on, now, Nolle. Be a good girl and open the door for your friend Walter."

"Not for you, nor for any . . . what is it?"

Someone else on the opposite side of the door was murmuring urgently; Heather was sure it was Desta.

"Asleep?" Nolle said, and there was no mistaking the surprise in her voice. "That's all? Are you sure?"

There was more murmuring. Walter turned to the other knights, eyes wide. "Asleep. Did you hear that?"

Matthew shook his head. "Did you see him when he rode up? He looked like death. I've never seen anyone that pale." He knocked on the door, but quietly. "Nolle, are you sure? He's only sleeping?"

"Serle says he is."

"Serle doesn't know his ass from his elbow," Geoffrey muttered.

"Hush," Matthew said, and knocked again. "Nolle, let us in. Just to look. Just to make sure."

There was another murmured conference. "Mitchell can come in," Nolle announced. "Just him. Everyone else get away from the door."

"Now see here—" Geoffrey said.

"And be quiet or you'll wake him up."

"Come on," Walter said. "Do as she says. Everyone back away."

They crowded back, leaving Mitchell at the door. Heather found herself next to Kennet, who flicked a glance at her and just as quickly looked away. The hall was filling with people: her father, her own knights, Bayla, Lily, and Annys, servants and soldiers and courtiers all agape. Heather wondered how many of them had seen Kristan kiss her, witnessed how she had pursued him and hammered like a fool at his door. A hot flush of shame crawled up her cheeks, not helped when Alister squeezed up alongside her, smirking. "Sounds like I missed all the fun," he whispered. She turned a fierce glare on him, and his smile faded a bit. "It's madness outside," he went on. "The Needwood folk are saying he touched a woman and brought her unborn baby back to life, right in the womb."

"Nonsense." She turned her attention back to Kristan's door. Mitchell was still waiting, arms crossed, but he looked down as a mouse squirmed beneath the door. It peered at the crowd, then Mitchell, then wedged itself under the door again. A moment later, the door opened, just a bit, and Mitchell slipped inside. Everyone craned forward, as if by doing so, they could see down the corridor, but then the door closed and the key creaked in the lock. After a little while, the little mouse came out again. It sat up, tiny paws folded on its chest, beady eyes bold, as if daring anyone to come closer.

"Cheeky creature," Geoffrey growled. "Just look at her. Someone ought to go after her with a broom; that'd teach her."

Eventually, the mouse ducked beneath the door again, and shortly after Sir Mitchell came out and shut the door quietly. His fellow knights hurried to meet him, with Heather and Colin on their heels.

"Well, she wasn't lying," Mitchell said, keeping his voice low. "He's sound asleep. He seems all right to me—his breathing is even, and his color is better. I wanted to send the healer in, just to check on him, but the children said no."

Colin grunted. "Are those brats calling the tune now?"

"They may be right," Matthew said. "The StoneKing is exhausted."

"He needs sleep, not someone poking at him," Geoffrey agreed.

"But what are we supposed to do meantime?" Colin said.

"Tell everyone to go about their business, but be quiet about it," Walter said. "And assign some soldiers to send all those folk outside the castle home."

"I'll tell Sir Jerrold to take care of it," Kennet said, and before Heather could protest, he was gone. Kristan's other knights moved off together, talking quietly; Colin was already shooing the courtiers off, a finger to his lips. More than a few were whispering behind their hands and darting amused looks Heather's way. She felt herself blushing again, and averted her face. When at last the great hall was quiet, she moved toward Kristan's door again. She raised one hand to knock and realized she was trembling. *Fool,* she told herself. *What are you going to do, stand here and beg these children to let you in? Make yourself even more of a laughingstock?*

She dropped her hand and stepped back. Just then, the little mouse stuck its head from beneath the door again. Its whiskers seemed to quiver with amusement. With a muttered oath, Heather stamped her foot at it. It whisked out of sight, and with clenched fists, she stalked off, ready to find fault with the first slacking soldier she encountered.

CHAPTER FOURTEEN

The scrape and crackle of someone poking up the fire pierced Kristan's consciousness at last. He lay with his eyes shut, unwilling to waken fully, enjoying the warmth of the blankets, the softness of the pillow beneath his head, the smell of clean linen. He was dozing off again when a sudden realization struck him.

He was lying on his back.

He was so startled that his eyes popped open. For months, he had been unable to sleep any other way than on his right side, with his right arm curled protectively across his brow, the Stone clutched in his left hand and the covers drawn tight over his head. But now he was on his back, arms and legs sprawling, the covers half off, and the Stone shining somewhere in the vicinity of his left shoulder. By reflex, he held his breath, listening for the low, menacing laugh that had dogged him for so long. At last, he heard it, but it was no more than a faint, far-away mutter. *Not gone*, he thought, *but weaker. Much weaker.*

He sat up slowly, wincing in anticipation of pain, but there was none—at least not the cold, stiff ache he usually experienced on waking. Instead, he was pleasantly sore all over, as if muscles long tensed were now stretched and warmed and eased.

"Good morning, my lord," said a soft voice, and he turned his head to see Serle standing at the bedside. The boy was smiling, although he looked oddly weary.

Kristan threw back the covers and saw he was still dressed. "Sorry, my lord," Serle said. "I took your boots off, but that's all. You were so peaceful. I didn't want to wake you."

Kristan swung his legs out of bed and came carefully to his feet. His body felt light, his head almost weightless. "Gently now," Serle said, his hands outstretched as if he feared Kristan might fall. "Are you hungry? Desta just brought me some bread and cheese, but you can have it."

Bread and cheese sounded surprisingly good, but Kristan's dry mouth was the more pressing issue. "Just some water, please," he said.

As Serle busied himself with goblet and pitcher, Kristan lifted his hands and gazed at them. *Avama*, he thought. *Was all that real, or did I dream it?*

"Here you are, my lord."

Serle was extending the goblet to him. As Kristan took it, he deliberately let his fingers brush against Serle's.

Nothing happened.

With his free hand, Kristan gave Serle's shoulder a tentative pat. Still nothing happened, except for the delighted smile that spread across Serle's face. "Thank you," Kristan said. He took a sip from the goblet. The water was pleasant in his parched mouth, but there was no shock at the taste of it. It was just water, plain and simple. *It's over, then*, Kristan thought. *If it happened at all.* He squinted at the sun coming through the windows. "It's bright out. Is the storm past?"

"Yes, sir. It was a good one, though. The wind was so fierce last night that it rattled the windows, but you never stirred."

"Last night?" Kristan repeated. "How long have I been asleep?"

Serle's smile broadened. "Since yesterday morning, my lord."

"A whole day? A whole day I've been asleep?"

"Yes, my lord. Desta and Nolle and me, we wouldn't let anyone disturb you. Sir Geoffrey and the rest, they came wanting to know how you were, and Sir Colin too, and Lady Heather, of course; she came right away. She was mad when we wouldn't let her in."

The memory of kissing Heather rose up, as startling as a sudden slap.

What have I done?

"Serle, where is she now? Where's Lady Heather?"

"She was yelling at her men just before breakfast, my lord, and then they all went marching out. I like her, my lord, but she's got such a temper. I've never heard such language from a lady."

"Where? Where did she go?"

"I don't know, my lord—"

Kristan was already stumbling for the door. He threw it open so hard that it crashed against the wall. Desta and Nolle were sitting in the corridor, but they leaped to their feet, mouths full of bread and cheese. "Get Malvo," he snapped at Desta. "If he's not at the keep doors in three breaths, I'll have your hide. You," he said, turning to Nolle as Desta bolted off. "Lady Heather is out with her soldiers somewhere. Find her."

"Her?" Nolle's nose wrinkled with distaste. "What d'you want her for?"

"Now now *now!*" Kristan shouted. Startled, Nolle ran past him into the bedchamber. For once Serle was thinking as quickly as she was; he flung open the windows just as she shifted into bird-form. With a rattle of feathers, she launched herself from the room and was gone.

"BOOTS!" Kristan roared, rushing back into the room, but Serle had already produced them, and Kristan flung himself on the bed to drag them on. When he rose, Serle was waiting with his cloak, and even went so far to bat Kristan's fretful, fumbling hands away to fasten the clasp himself. Just then Nolle shot back into the room so wildly that she flew straight into Kristan. The shift collapsed, and she sprawled at his feet. "Off to the northwest," she panted. "Oh, she's in a temper. I could hear her yelling."

Kristan was already striding down the corridor. He burst through the door and found himself face-to-face with Geoffrey and Kennet.

"My lord, where are you going?" Geoffrey asked.

"Should we come with you?" Kennet said. "You shouldn't ride out alone, not after being mobbed yesterday."

"Get out of my way," Kristan said, plunging past. "By the Stone, I may already be too late."

"Let us escort you, at least."

"No! No! Leave me be!" He was practically running now; ahead, Matthew and Walter had shouldered the pages aside and were already holding the great doors wide open. Beyond them, at the bottom of the steps, Desta waited with Malvo, and Mitchell stood ready to help Kristan mount. Kristan brushed past him, swung himself into Malvo's saddle and snatched the reins from Desta. The other knights surrounded him, all talking at once. Kennet reached for Malvo's bridle, but as if sensing Kristan's agitation, Malvo reared and whinnied shrilly. The knights scattered, and Kristan turned Malvo toward the gatehouse and kicked him into a full gallop. "Here he comes again!" one of the guards shouted, and then Kristan was flying past them, over the bridge and out into the cold morning air.

* * *

"You there!" Heather reined Skapi up alongside a struggling soldier. "Straighten your belt, get into step, and wipe that smile off your face! Do you think this is funny?"

"No, ma'am," the soldier answered, but the quirk of his lips said just the opposite, and Heather ground her teeth in fury. No matter that they had been drilling in knee-deep snow all morning, deprived of their breakfast, and likely of their nooning as well, they kept on grinning. Even Skapi was cavorting and tossing her head as if the whole thing were a joke.

The whole castle seemed to be smirking at her. Like wildfire on the Plain, word had spread throughout the castle that their fierce little commander had been soundly kissed and left gasping like a landed fish. Since then everyone's eyes had been on her, from the giggling scullery maids to old Phelan, whom she'd encountered as she'd trudged downstairs after a sleepless night. "Knew it!" he'd cried, patting her head as if she was a little girl. "Knew it would come to this in time, my dear!"

Without answering, she'd stalked off in the other direction. Everywhere she went, knot after knot of chinwaggers and scandalmongers scattered at her approach. When she joined Colin and Alister in their private anteroom, Alister's greeting was accompanied by a knowing wink, and her father had dryly informed her that the StoneKing was still asleep, so no use banging on his door again. Escaping to her room, she had startled Bayla from a whispered conversation with Lily and Annys. Fleeing to the courtyard, she'd interrupted Sir Jerrold on the verge of a fistfight with a courtier who'd had the temerity to suggest that perhaps the StoneKing's long slumber was due to a visit to the town tavern and a drop too much of the local ale.

That had been the tipping point, and she had roared at Jerrold, Eaden, and Bran (newly returned from his trip to Norwinn and deeply confused by all the events that had occurred in his absence) to assemble every man not on duty, and now she was stuck out here in the snow, with her anxious knights, grinning soldiers, unruly horse, empty stomach, and ill temper. She wanted to throw something, hit something, scream her humiliation and rage at the bright blue sky. Instead, she ordered the troops to a halt and was in the midst of giving the whole company a tongue-lashing that would have made her father blanch when she realized the men were looking past her, faces tense with anticipation. She glanced over her shoulder. A single horse was approaching at a gallop, and her heart gave a wild leap as she recognized the rider. She took a deep breath and forced herself to speak calmly. "Sir Jerrold, call the men to attention."

The order was unnecessary; the men were already bolt upright with shoulders strained back. She turned Skapi to face the oncoming rider, and her knights brought their mounts in line with her. Motionless, the entire army waited as the rider reined up before them.

Kristan ran one hand through his untidy hair and tugged his wrinkled tunic straight. Heather studied his face, looking for any trace of the dazed look she had seen the day before, but there was none. His expression was troubled, but that was all.

"Good morning," he said softly.

"Good morning, my lord," Heather answered.

Her cold, formal tone seemed to startle him. "Good morning . . ." he said, and cleared his throat. "Yes."

Heather sensed her knights watching her sidelong. "How may I serve you, my lord?"

Kristan shifted uneasily in the saddle. "May I have a word with you? When you're finished, of course."

"We're finished now, my lord."

His brows knotted slightly. "In private, please . . . Commander."

Heather's pulse was jangling in her temples, but she turned to Sir Jerrold with as much composure as she could muster. He was grinning, but his smile vanished beneath her stare. "Sir Jerrold, march these men back to the castle, then dismiss them to their usual duties."

"Yes, ma'am." Jerrold saluted and wheeled his mount around to face the ranks. "All right, you lot. Quick march. Left, right, left!"

The soldiers set off toward the castle, stumbling in the snow but trying their best to step smartly as Jerrold called the cadence. Heather waited until they were no more than a shifting smudge in the distance, then straightened her shoulders and turned to Kristan.

He cleared his throat again. "About yesterday. I shouldn't have done . . . what I did. It was inappropriate."

Her throat knotted. "Inappropriate, my lord?" she managed to choke out. Skapi chose that moment to whinny and give her head an irritable toss. Heather reined her up sharply.

"Improper. Ill-timed." Malvo suddenly shifted sideways, as if he too, was growing impatient. "And I owe you an apology," Kristan went on, as he tried to bring the big horse under control.

"Oh, no, my lord," Heather said, through anger-tight lips. "It was my fault. I should have been on my guard. I should have known."

"I beg your pardon?"

"Every man with the power to do so has tried to undercut me." Heather's voice rose in pitch and volume, and in response, Skapi yanked at the bit again. "My father. Ravelin. Commander Callum and his captains in Stratheden. They've challenged me, belittled me, opposed me outright. They've tried to undermine my confidence and shame me before my men. And none of them have succeeded, not one—not until yesterday. Not until you."

"Heather—" Malvo took a sly nip at Kristan's foot, and Kristan jerked it out of reach. "Heather, listen—"

"My command is the one thing in my life that's given me any self-respect, any pride, any pleasure—and you took it away. I suppose it's your right; you gave it to me, you're the StoneKing and can do as you please, but I expected better of you, my lord. Whatever else you've taken from me, you always showed me respect as your commander, but now it's clear I've lost even that regard."

"By the Stone—" Kristan flung himself from the saddle, pushed Malvo away, and grabbed Skapi's bridle. "Get down. Get down from there."

"Why?"

"I'm not going to have this conversation while these horses are playing the fool. Get down." He reached for her, as if to pull her from the saddle. Heather planted her foot in the middle of his chest and shoved with all her might. Kristan reeled backward, lost his balance, and sat down hard in the snow.

The horses stopped cavorting. Heather clapped one hand to her mouth. For a long, long moment, Kristan sat, staring at her.

"Was I wrong?" he said at last. "I thought I felt it . . . I thought I knew. Was I wrong? About you? About all of it?"

His expression was so stricken that she wanted to leap from the saddle and run to him. Instead, she clenched her fists tight on Skapi's reins. "What do you mean?"

"I felt it." He got slowly to his feet, his shoulders hunched like an old man's. "All of it. I was floating in it, flooded with it, drowning in it. I thought I'd die of it. But I had to get back to you first." He stumbled to Malvo and took up the reins to mount, but then sagged against the horse's broad black side. "While it lasted, I had to get back to you."

"Why?"

"I had no right," he went on, as if he hadn't heard. "I know that. No right even to hope. But I had to touch you. I had to know."

"Know what?"

He looked at her then. "That you still love me."

She could not move. She could not even breathe.

"Heather," he said. "Heather, I love you. I always have. The words were always in my heart, even when I was too broken and spineless to say them out loud. Please, Heather." He took a faltering step toward her. "Please tell me I haven't destroyed your love the way I've destroyed everything decent and good in my life. Please tell me that what I felt was true. Tell me you still love me."

Something warm streaked down her face and landed on her gloved hand, leaving a round, wet mark on the leather, like a drop of summer rain.

"I love you," she said. "I didn't want to. I tried to stop but I couldn't. I love you. I always have. I always will."

He pressed one hand to the Stone over his heart. The other

he held out to her. "Come down. Come down to me. There's no one to see. No one here but us. Come down."

As if in a trance, she swung herself from Skapi's back. She let the reins drop. She put her fingers into Kristan's hand and stepped into his arms.

They stood holding each other for a long, long time, not speaking, not moving. His breath rattled in his chest, and he trembled like an injured bird. Through the padding of his tunic, Heather felt how thin he was, how wasted. He stank of dirty clothes and unwashed skin but all the same, she pressed close, burying her face in the crook of his jaw, inhaling his scent like perfume.

"I'm so sorry," he whispered in her ear. "So sorry for the way I've treated you. I've done terrible things, Heather, things I'm ashamed to tell you—"

"Hush."

"—but you have to know, you have to know so you'll understand—"

A gust of wind sent his hair tumbling into his face, and she raised a hand to brush it back. He flinched and threw up one arm. Bewildered, she stepped back, and his features twisted with wretchedness. "I'm sorry. You caught me off guard. I still can't bear being touched . . . where Daazna . . . where he put his hands on me."

"Oh, Kristan," was all she could say.

"This is what I am now, Heather." His breath hitched, his voice broke. "You have to understand what I am: a twisted, scarred, ugly little man, who's plagued by nightmares, and hears voices, and shies at shadows. You have to understand the danger—"

"Hush," she said, taking his hands. "I don't want to talk about any of that now."

"But Daazna—"

"Hush. We're not going to talk about Daazna now. We're not going to talk about anything. We're going back to the castle."

"I—"

"I haven't eaten today, and I'm hungry. I'm sure you are too."

He shook his head. "Heather—"

"We're going to have our nooning, and after that, you'll have a bath, and maybe a nap. I'll have Bayla sort out clean clothes for you; what you're wearing is so filthy it should be burnt."

"But you need to know—"

She planted her mouth on his, smothering his protests with a long kiss. "You love me," she said, when she finally released him. "That's all I need to know now. When you're better, you can tell me everything, but until then, I don't want to talk about it. Agreed?"

He nodded, bemused and a little breathless.

"Very good, my lord."

He winced. "Don't call me that."

"I will, and you're going to call me Commander, at least in front of others. We're going back to the castle, and we're going to behave as if nothing has happened, at least until I regain control of my men and you get Hogia back on course. Both our roads will be easier if we're not tripping over a lot of gossiping tongues."

He sighed. "Yes, Commander. Shall we shake hands to seal the bargain?"

"No, my lord. I want you to kiss me, but slower this time, and no running away after."

"Yes, Commander," he said again, but this time, he smiled.

* * *

They returned under a lowering sky, in comfortable, companionable silence. At first, they rode so close together that their knees brushed, but as they came within sight of the castle, they withdrew to a more decorous distance. On the approach to the castle gates, they were very nearly mobbed by a crowd of townsfolk, who surged forward, trying to touch Kristan, but a mounted guard led by Sir Kennet warded them off. At the keep doors, they were met by Sir Geoffrey, who inquired somewhat diffidently if the StoneKing was hungry, and whose face brightened with delight and surprise when Kristan acknowledged that he was indeed.

They found the rest of the court dining on slabs of pork and piles of roasted root vegetables, all swimming in a thick, oily sauce. Kristan's entrance made everyone jump; they got quickly to their feet, murmuring greetings and dabbing surreptitiously at their mouths as he took his seat at the head of the table. Heather found a vacant chair halfway down, nodded coolly to those who greeted her, ignored the sidelong glances and smirks, and tried her best not to look at Kristan.

It was difficult, if only because of the silent little drama playing out at the head of the table. Serle hurried to serve Kristan, but as usual, Desta was faster. With a flourish, she placed a tankard of ale and an enormous, steaming portion of meat before Kristan. He nodded his thanks but eyed the gargantuan serving without enthusiasm. On his right, Colin was digging into his own meal with gusto as he argued taxes with some of the other courtiers. Eventually, Kristan was drawn into the discussion, and, to Heather's dismay, pushed his plate aside. Desta's shoulders sagged, but Serle, with a decisive nod, slipped from the room.

The discussion continued, while Kristan's food cooled and congealed and Heather cursed her father silently, wondering what to do. Before she could decide on a course of action, Serle was back, bearing a small, covered plate. He replaced Kristan's untouched meal with the new plate and removed its cover, revealing a single hard-cooked egg, quartered and sprinkled with finely minced herbs. Accompanying it was a slice of toasted bread, cut in half and glistening with a faint sheen of butter. Completing the dish was a pretty piece of preserved quince. Serle placed a cup of what looked like mulled cider next to the plate, then stepped away, solemn as an owl.

A few moments passed before Kristan noticed the new plate. He picked up one of the egg quarters and popped it absently into his mouth. Another piece followed, then a bite of toast and a swallow of cider. The conversation grew more heated, distracting him, but eventually his hand wandered back to the plate. Four bites, and half the toast was gone, another bite took care of the bit of quince. Appetite renewed, Heather addressed herself to her own food.

As the meal concluded, Colin got to his feet, suppressing a satisfied belch behind his fist. "My lord, we can continue this discussion, if you like. I have all the figures written up for your perusal. And there are a number of other issues to be addressed."

Both Serle and Desta rushed to pull out Kristan's chair. "Perhaps later," Kristan said as he stood, seemingly unaware of the two elbowing each other. He stole a quick look at Heather. "Right now, I'm going to have a bath."

Heather ducked her head to hide her smile and went in search of Bayla. She discovered her maidservant in a quiet hallway, in Sir Walter's arms. The two jumped apart at the sight of Heather. Walter bolted, and Bayla turned to Heather, blushing. Her own embarrassment made Heather gruff as she gave instructions to assist in arranging a bath and fresh clothing for the StoneKing.

Her discomfiture continued when Eaden, Bran and Jerrold approached her, looking uncharacteristically timid. "My lady, we wanted to explain," Jerrold said. "About this morning. About the soldiers, and all."

"What do you mean?"

"My lady, they want you to know they didn't mean any disrespect," Bran said. "They were smiling because . . . well, because they were happy. For you." He quailed under her forbidding stare.

"Ma'am, no one wanted you to marry Ravelin," Eaden said, picking up the narrative. "We all thought you deserved better.

And yesterday, when the StoneKing . . . well." He grinned. "Ma'am, you can't do much better than the StoneKing, can you?"

His smile quivered and faded as she turned her glare on him. "You men always joke about gossipy women," she said, "but what a lot of clucking old hens you've turned out to be."

"Ma'am—"

"Not that it's any of your business, but what happened yesterday has been discussed and dealt with." She eyed her now-crestfallen knights. "It's clear my men have too much time on their hands. I'm tempted to run everyone out on maneuvers again, but to be honest, I'm sick of the sight of you all. So— those not on duty are restricted to barracks for the rest of the day. But there'll be no lounging around gossiping. I want that place cleaned from top to bottom, and other than what needs to be said to get the job done, I want it accomplished in silence. I'll hold an inspection first thing tomorrow morning, and there had better not be a speck of mud on the floor or a single cobweb in the rafters. And if I see one soldier with dirty boots or a scruffy beard or a buckle that doesn't shine until I can see myself in it, I'll personally kick his ass all around the courtyard. Understood?"

The knights slumped off. *That should keep things quiet so Kristan can rest,* Heather thought, and on the heels of that thought came an enormous yawn. She could not remember the last time she'd slept during the day. The idea of a nap was so delicious, so decadent that she could not resist it. With a light heart, she bounded up to her room, pulled off her boots, stretched out on her bed, and within moments, was fast asleep.

CHAPTER FIFTEEN

The next few days passed quietly. It did snow, but gently this time, big, feathery flakes that muffled everything in white, as if the earth drowsed beneath a thick blanket. In consequence, everyone lowered their voices and walked softly, and both castle and town took on an air of placid contentment.

Heather saw Kristan frequently: at meals he sat at the head of the table, still eating lightly but looking better now that he was washed, shaved, and combed. His color and energy improved daily. The terrible barking cough eased to an occasional throat-clear. Although he was not talkative, when he did speak, his words were considered and concise.

As agreed, they kept their distance, although often as not, when Heather allowed herself to sneak a glance at him, she found him looking back. Sometimes, when she passed him a dish or a document, their fingertips touched and then lingered a breath longer than necessary. One evening, they met unexpectedly in a deserted hallway and were instantly in each other's arms. They kissed and kissed until the sound of approaching footsteps sent them hurrying in opposite directions, breathless and wide-eyed, with never a word spoken between them.

When he called her "Commander," the formal title somehow sounded like the sweetest of endearments. When she called him "my lord," she was often unsure if she had said "my love" instead.

"Commander."

She hesitated, wondering how on earth Kristan had known she was passing his chamber. "My lord?" she called down the hall.

"Would you join us for a moment, please?"

She hurried down the corridor, both relieved and a bit disappointed he was not alone. Within the chamber, her father and Alister sat before Kristan's big worktable, looking somewhat disgruntled. "I won't keep you long," Kristan said, waving her to a vacant chair, "but I need your opinion about Stratheden. I think I handled my recent encounter with Aldo very poorly."

"Nigel didn't think so," Heather said. "'Masterful' was the word he used."

"Aldo didn't deserve better than you gave him," Alister said. "He treated you shabbily."

"And Stratheden is poor and its army ill-equipped," Colin said. "We have nothing to fear from them."

"This isn't about fear," Kristan said. "It's about common sense. Wouldn't it be better to foster more cordial relations with our neighbor?"

Colin only snorted, and Alister shrugged. "What did you have in mind, my lord?" Heather asked.

Kristan nodded toward a lumpy gray bundle at one end of the table. "What do you think of that?"

Unfolding it, Heather realized it was the cloak Kristan had worn on his arrival in Hogia. "It's an interesting fabric," Kristan went on. "I understand the wool comes from a kind of sheep peculiar to Stratheden's highlands."

"Fandrall produces better quality wool," Colin protested. "Why would we need to import this heavy, greasy stuff?"

Kristan smiled faintly. "As partial as I am to Fandrall's wool, it's not as durable as this. This cloak has kept me warm and dry since I left Stratheden. Commander, would this wool make good winter uniforms for your army?"

"It would, my lord," Heather said. "And I expect buying a large amount of it from Stratheden would go a long way toward improving relations with Aldo."

Colin grunted. "True. I hadn't thought of that."

Alister picked up the cloak and hefted it. "It's sturdy stuff. A shame it's so drab."

Colin reached across to rub the fabric between thumb and forefinger. "The greasiness of the wool probably makes it hard to dye."

"Mali Uzuri in Dyer might be able to solve that problem," Kristan said. "Alister, would you send her a sample and ask her to see what she can do with it? Colin, you can begin drafting a trade proposal for Aldo." The two men rose, and Heather got to her feet as well. "A moment, Commander," Kristan said. "There's another matter I'd like to discuss with you."

Heather sat down again, maintaining her formal manner as she waited for Colin and Alister to leave the room. Once they were gone, she turned to Kristan, smiling in anticipation of a few stolen moments together, but his expression was somber. "What is it, my lord?"

"So much damage to repair," he said, more to himself than to her. "So many broken fences to mend."

"My lord?"

"I need your opinion." He sighed and clasped his hands on the tabletop. "I assume you know about Olaf . . . about what happened to his brother Sigurd."

"He drowned."

"I let him drown. I could have saved him—Olaf begged me to save him—but I let him drown." He kept his gaze fastened on his hands. "I let Sigurd die and destroyed my friendship with Olaf. And there have been so many others I've wounded. I need to make amends. I have to right those wrongs." When she was silent, he finally looked at her. "Heather, what should I do?"

She breathed a little sigh of her own. "Olaf and Sigurd stole from your subjects. They kidnapped your sister and your companions to force you to follow them. Melissa deserted her post in Norwinn and defied you when you tried to send her back.

Marcus and Dell neglected their duty to both you and Dyer. Given the circumstances, your actions were entirely appropriate. To apologize for them now would be a sign of weakness. As your commander, my advice is to stand by your actions."

Kristan bowed his head. Heather reached out and placed her hand atop his. "But as your friend, I would say: do as your heart tells you. You're the StoneKing, and strong enough to show kindness. Do what you must to find peace of mind."

He caught her hand between his and raised it to his lips. "My wise commander," he whispered as he kissed it. "My best friend. Do you think Phelan could send one of his crows to find Olaf?"

* * *

Nolle accompanied Phelan when the old Wiche was summoned to Kristan's chamber, and stood by sullenly as Phelan slunk to a chair. He sat shivering and mumbling to himself, refusing to answer questions, avoiding Kristan's gaze. When Kristan extended a sympathetic hand, he actually shied back. "Don't!" he cried. "You're *avama*. You'll see. You'll know, and I couldn't bear it. I couldn't bear the shame."

He burst into tears and had to be escorted from the room. Nolle watched him go, amber eyes narrowed. "I'll go for you," she said. "I'll find old Olaf."

"You don't know where he went," Kristan said.

She shrugged. "He was heading east when he left us. I have two eyes in my head. I can find him."

Her manner was so offhand that it bordered on insolent. Heather bristled, but Kristan only looked concerned. "It might be a long way, across the sea. Are you sure you can travel that far?"

"Of course. Besides, it'll be a relief to get out of here. That old man hasn't taught me anything, and I'm tired of listening to his babble."

"Watch your mouth, miss," Heather snapped.

"Sorry," Nolle said, with another shrug that made Heather want to slap her.

"How soon can you be ready?" Kristan asked.

"I'm ready now."

"Let me write my message to Olaf first. While I do that, run down to the kitchen and tell them I said to give you whatever supplies you need. Dress warmly and make sure to pack a bedroll."

"I know, I know," Nolle said, and strode off. Kristan pulled a fresh piece of parchment from a nearby stack and unstoppered his ink bottle.

"I don't like the way she talks to you," Heather said.

"Quinn Logan once said the same thing about you," Kristan replied as he selected a quill. "But I'll put up with a certain amount of cheek if it means getting the job done." His slight smile faded as he contemplated the blank page before him.

"What will you say?" Heather asked.

"I scarcely know." He shook his head. "In one of my crueler moments, I refused to let Melissa go in search of Nigel. I told her to write a note for Olaf to carry to him instead and gave her almost no time to compose it. In spite of that, it was beautiful—the perfect combination of humility and brevity." He sat in silence for some moments, then finally dipped his quill, wrote a few careful lines and turned the page so Heather could see the words:

> *What I did was unforgivable.*
> *I will regret it until the day I die.*
> *Tell me how I can make amends.*

She nodded her approval. Kristan signed his name, folded the parchment into a neat packet, and sealed it. He sat regarding it with such melancholy that Heather hurried to change the subject. "Phelan called you that name."

"What name?"

"The one you said your teacher used to call you. *Avama.* You said you never knew what it meant. Maybe Phelan could tell you."

"I know what it means. Ariphele told me. But it wasn't until a few days ago that I truly understood."

She spread her hands in confusion. "You've lost me."

"I'm sure I have. You said you didn't want to hear explanations from me until I was better. I'm better, Heather, and we need to talk." Hurrying footsteps sounded in the corridor, and he added in a lower voice: "But not now. Tonight. We'll have dinner together, and I'll tell you everything."

Desta burst into the room. "My lord, let me go with Nolle," she pleaded. "You know she always fiddles about and does as she pleases. I can make sure she delivers your message promptly."

"I trust Nolle to do as she's promised," Kristan said.

"I could go as her guard."

"She'll be in shift form for a large part of her journey. You wouldn't be able to keep up."

"She can shift me too."

"You know how it tires her, Desta. It's kind of you to offer, but I think Nolle should travel alone."

Shoulders slumped, Desta stepped aside just as Nolle strutted back into the room, a cloak over her shoulders, a stuffed knapsack on her back. Serle was at her heels, looking both jealous and anxious. "I'm ready," she announced. "Where's the message?"

Kristan handed her the packet. "Be careful," he said. "If you don't find Olaf within a few days, turn back. And if you do find him, approach with caution. I doubt he'll be very welcoming."

Nolle grinned. "I'll get your message to him if I have to bounce it off his head. Serle, open the window. I'm off." Desta had the window open before she finished speaking.

"Safe journey," Serle said. He stepped toward Nolle, as if to hug her, but with a flash of feathers, a rattle of broad wings and a harsh screech, she was out the window and gone.

Heather snorted out a laugh. "What did she just turn into?"

"An eagle, I think," Kristan said.

"She just gets better and better," Serle said wistfully. "She didn't even say the spell that time."

"Close the window, Desta," Kristan said. "Serle, tell Cook that Commander Demitt and I will be meeting over dinner tonight. I'd like our meal served in the west anteroom."

Both children rushed for the door, collided at the doorway, and then continued down the hall, pushing and shoving. "Don't run—" Kristan called, too late.

"My money's on Desta," Heather said.

"No bet."

A crash and a roar of outrage at the far end of the corridor punctuated the children's departure and announced the arrival of Colin Demitt. Kristan breathed a little sigh. "There's your father with the trade proposal. Thank you for your advice, Commander. I'll see you at dinner."

* * *

Heather was late, which was so unlike her that Kristan was growing nervous. A crackling fire warmed the anteroom and a row of fat beeswax candles ranged down the dining table, casting a golden glow on snowy linen, shining bowls, pitchers, and platters. A cadre of silent servants stood ready to serve, but the sumptuous array only reminded Kristan uncomfortably of other recent dinners that had started well, only to end in disaster.

"Isn't it pretty, my lord?" Serle said. "And wait until you see all the delicious things Cook made for you."

"Will you sit, my lord?" Desta asked. Erect and proper, she stood at the ready beside his chair.

Kristan shook his head and clasped his hands behind his back to hide their trembling. He had tried to neaten himself as much as he could, but he was suddenly, acutely aware of his straggling hair, his borrowed clothing, his crooked figure and scarred face. *Jelena and Tansy were right*, he thought. *I'm an ugly little man.*

He was further rattled when at last Heather arrived, escorted by Sir Walter. Instead of her uniform, she wore a gown, beautifully made but high-necked and plain to the point of severity. Even so, the curves of her body, the regal set of her head, and the play of candlelight on her neat coronet of braids set his heart pounding. He was grateful for the distraction of Serle, who gasped. "Ooo, you look nice, my lady."

"Thank you, Serle," she replied coolly, but a faint blush colored her cheeks as she nodded to Kristan. "Good evening, my lord."

Wordless, he nodded back. Heather flicked a glance at Sir Walter, who stood in the doorway with an attitude of mingled diffidence and eagerness. "Thank you, Walter. Off to your own dinner."

"The rest of you go too," Kristan added, finding his voice. "Lady Heather and I will serve ourselves."

"Let me stay and serve, my lord," Desta protested as the puzzled servants filed out.

"Me too, my lord," Serle said, not to be outdone, but Kristan shook his head.

"Come on, you two," Walter said. He shooed them from the room but hesitated in the doorway, his hand on the door.

"Leave it open, please," Kristan said, "but pass the word that we're not to be disturbed."

They waited until the echo of his footsteps faded. "You're late," Kristan said, and immediately wished the words unsaid. Discomposure had given his voice a gruff edge.

"I apologize. Walter asked to speak to me and I lost track of time."

"He seemed troubled."

"'Troubled' is not exactly the word I'd use. He'd like to get married."

"Married? To whom?"

"My maidservant Bayla. The two of them have been writing since last summer. They've been inseparable since he arrived in Hogia." Heather smiled at his astonishment. "You've been preoccupied, my lord; otherwise you would have noticed. I'm sure he's been waiting to ask your permission."

"Ah."

The feeble response was all he could muster; he felt bumbling and foolish, especially when, after a brief silence, Heather gestured toward the table. "Shall we begin, my lord?"

They sat and spread their napkins in their laps. The silence hammered in Kristan's ears, but all the things he had planned to say were nothing but a tangle in his brain. He sensed Heather's gaze on him, but his throat was so tight that he thought he might choke. He lifted the domed lid from a nearby platter.

Before him lay a small game bird, its head turned to one side, its claws curled into knots of yellow, its poached breast a bulge of white between the plumage of its spread wings and tail.

"My lord?"

The lid slipped from his fingers and clattered to the table.

"Kristan?"

The room whirled, and he thought he might faint, but Heather's fingers on his wrist anchored him, brought him back. He raised his head and found her pitying gaze on him. "What's the matter?" she asked softly.

The sound of her voice unclenched his mind and voice. Words began to spill from him; not the careful, rational explanations he had rehearsed in his mind but a flood of confession: what he had done to Tansy, to Melissa, to Olaf and Sigurd and Nigel and even Jelena. Every malicious word, petty cruelty, and vindictive deed since his departure from Fandrall was blurted, in waves of shame and sorrow. At some point in his narrative, Heather thrust out an arm and dragged her chair close so that she could sit, but she never let go of him, even when he moved to what had happened the day of Ravelin's funeral. The fire died to coals and the candles guttered, but she sat perfectly still, holding his hand, listening until his voice cracked and failed and the river of words ran dry. She let go of him long enough to fetch her goblet and the pitcher of wine, and to pour for both of them, but then placed her fingers atop his free hand and watched as he drank. Her touch was comforting, and the wine pleasant on his tongue and warm in his throat and belly. He sighed and put the goblet down.

"Are you talked out now?" she asked quietly.

He nodded.

"Do you feel better?"

Oddly, he did. He nodded again.

She pulled the nearest platter closer and uncovered it. "Eat one of these little things. They're probably cold now, but you need to eat."

They were fritters, stuffed with minced meat and dried cherries, lukewarm but surprisingly tasty. He ate one as she watched.

"How are you sleeping these days?"

"Better. Longer."

"The nightmares?"

"Gone, mostly. I still have dreams, but nothing like before."

She nodded sternly toward the platter. Like an obedient child he ate another fritter as she poured more wine. She waited until he was finished, then hitched her chair a little closer. "So the power you told me about—this *Tabi'a* of destruction—it's gone?"

"Yes. I couldn't carry it any longer. You were right. It was destroying me. So I chose. I let it go."

"And when you let it go—that's when this *avama* overwhelmed you?"

"Not at first. When the *Tabi'a* was gone, my past—what was left of it—went too. All the bad memories turned to shadows, along with the good."

Her brow furrowed. "All of it? Gone?"

He nodded a third time. "Without the *Tabi'a*—without the rage that's driven me for so long—I was afraid. Empty and powerless. Too weak to even move. I curled up in the snow and wept like a child." He bit his lip for shame, but Heather only watched him with compassionate eyes. "But when I touched the Stone, it was warm. I felt like it belonged to me again . . . or I to it. And then the *avama* happened. It was as if the Stone heard, and released the *avama* to me, to fill the void. So I could finally feel all the world around me. Malvo, the trees, the snow, the people. All of it."

"And you used it to bring that woman's child back to life?"

"No."

Heather raised an eyebrow. "The townspeople think you did."

"I didn't use it. All I did was touch her. I felt the other life in her—the baby growing cold and weak, as if it had given up. But it was the *avama* that woke it, not me. And then everyone was touching me, and I could see into their hearts, and I thought my own heart would burst."

"And it hasn't happened since that day?"

"No. I think it's gone too."

"But Phelan still sensed it. He didn't want you to touch him." A look of sudden comprehension flooded her face. "And now I understand why. He was afraid you'd know what he did."

"What did he do?"

Heather smiled crookedly. "He cursed the Seachlans, long ago."

"What? How?"

"It's a long story. Phelan wanted to punish them. He cursed them with barrenness. It's why Ravelin couldn't sire an heir. Phelan kept the curse in place for years—all the time he was in the Exilwald."

"How do you know this?"

Heather lowered her gaze. "He told me . . . when he thought I was going to marry Ravelin. He offered to lift the curse, so I could bear Ravelin's child, if that's what I wanted. He said he was so weary of carrying the hatred. That it sapped his strength and dulled his wits and hurt others besides the Seachlans. I don't know what he meant by that."

Dumbfounded, Kristan stared at her. "I do," he said, when he could speak. "More than anything, Ravelin craved an heir. Through that craving, Daazna gained control of him. By cursing Ravelin, Phelan caused my father's death. And the fall of Hogia and Fandrall and Dyer."

Heather put one hand to her mouth. "No wonder he didn't want you to touch him. Think of it . . . all that suffering and sorrow from one little spell."

"It wasn't a little spell," Kristan said. "It was enormous—one that spanned miles and years. A spell of that magnitude takes a terrible toll on its maker. I'm amazed Phelan was able to control it for so long . . ." He tightened his grip on Heather's hand as a new thought struck him. "Or maybe he couldn't."

"What do you mean?"

"Maybe, as time passed and Phelan grew weaker, the spell got out of control. Leaked. Spread."

Heather's eyes went wide. "You think Phelan caused Hogia's barrenness too?"

"It's possible. Maybe it even affected the *Kentávron*. Wiche is a powerful force; it's foolish to think it can be controlled. I know—I made that mistake myself. *Avama*." The word was no more than a breath, a sigh, but it set his skin tingling. "Whatever it was, Heather, whatever happened to me that day—it felt *right*. Not like the other *Tabi'a*. The Stone accepted it. Maybe even wanted it. I think it was in alignment with the Stone's purpose."

"Whatever that is." She was smiling, but her eyes were anxious.

"I know it sounds like madness, all of it," Kristan said. "But I need you to know everything, so you can make a sound, sober decision."

"About what?"

He took a deep breath. "I want you to marry me."

"I will."

"Wait. First you have to understand the danger—"

"I said I will."

"—what it could mean when Daazna comes back—"

"I don't care about Daazna."

"But you have to care, you have to understand the danger of being with me, of loving me when Daazna still stalks me, waiting for a chance to strike—"

"Stop," Heather snapped.

Startled, he fell silent.

"I won't listen to this," she went on in a gentler voice. "I love you, Kristan, and I'll marry you, and I'll share your life, every part of it—but I won't live it cringing."

He stared at her. "You don't believe it, do you? That he's still alive?"

"I don't know. I don't know if what I saw below stairs was him, or you, or something else. This world is full of things that I don't understand, that frighten me, but if I let my fears consume me, then I'll have no life at all. I see what the fear of Daazna has done to you. It's weakened you, sickened you; it's kept you from being the just, strong king I know you can be."

He got to his feet. "You must think me a terrible coward."

"No." She caught his arm. "Kristan, I swear to you: if you're right—if Daazna isn't dead, if he returns—I'll be at your side, no matter what. I will always be there. But if being your wife means I have to live my life in dread, I won't do it. I won't marry you."

"Truly, Heather?" He began to tremble.

Tears welled in her eyes, but her jaw was firm. "I love you, Kristan. I always will. Living without you will break my heart. But I will not give Daazna that power over me." She let go of him. "Please, Kristan. I want to be your wife. I want to be with you always. I'll do it if you promise me you won't let the fear rule you. Maybe the Stone gave you the *avama* to help you fight it, to teach you to live again. I don't know. But promise me you'll put your whole heart and mind and all your strength into living as fully and happily as you can. Promise me you'll try."

Slowly, clumsily, he lowered himself to one knee and clasped her hands in his. "By the Stone—by the Stone you found and returned to me, Heather—I'll try. I can find the courage, if only you're with me. Say you'll marry me and be my queen."

"I will," she said again, and leaned in to kiss him as the last candle flickered out.

CHAPTER SIXTEEN

Fingers clumsy with anxiety, Bastian broke the seal on the parchment. As he read, his eyes widened. "What is it?" Quinn Logan demanded. "What fresh catastrophe is upon us?"

"It's not a catastrophe," Bastian said. "He says he's going to stay in Hogia a while longer. He says . . . he says he's getting married."

"What? To whom?"

"Lady Heather."

Quinn groaned, but Sir Randolf clapped his hands softly and chuckled. "Now that's a proper match," he said. "A far better choice than that Princess Jelena."

"He's appointing her father Reach in Ravelin's place. Sir Jerrold will assume command of Hogia's army."

"Thank goodness," Quinn said. "If she's to be queen, it's time she behaved in a more womanly manner."

Bastian grinned. "Oh, I don't think so. He's also making her High Commander of all his military. Alister is already sending out the proclamations," he continued, over Quinn's outraged sputters. "He says they'll be married within the fortnight, and come home by way of Norwinn. He says he needs to see his sister."

"They're going to reconcile," Randolf said happily. "I know they are. They were always so close as children; it broke my heart to hear of them quarreling."

"As long as she does her duty as Reach, I don't care if they kiss or curse each other," Quinn grumbled. "Well, we'd better start making preparations for their arrival. And I'd better write to Lockward in Malchea and give him the news. He'll be disappointed, but to be honest, I'm relieved. Lady Heather is headstrong, but she comes nowhere near Princess Jelena for sheer willfulness."

"She loves the StoneKing," Randolf said. "Headstrong or not, she'll make him happy—and that's the important thing."

* * *

"The important thing is that she'll be a steadying influence," Raul said, handing the parchment to Piri Neff.

"A queen who's also High Commander?" Fedro Vincenze said, his face twisted as if he'd tasted something sour. "A queen's job is to produce an heir. How's she going to do that if she's galloping around the countryside?"

"You don't know Lady Heather like I do. Anything she puts her mind to, she can do. Including riding into battle with a baby at her breast."

"Um . . . yes." Piri Neff cleared his throat. "This announcement finishes any hope of marriage to Lockward's daughter, though. A shame. A political match with Malchea would have strengthened the StoneKing's position and the realm's stability."

Mali Uzuri grinned. "A fresh stream of commerce will put this realm right faster than any political marriage could. The StoneKing's happiness aside, the best news in that letter is the trade agreement with Stratheden."

The other guild heads murmured their approval, although Fedro Vincenze remained sullen. "You only say that because you think the StoneKing is going to grant you the contract for dying that nasty, greasy Stratheden wool."

"I have to prove I can do it first." Mali looked at Fedro sidelong. "But I will, never fear."

"I underestimated how powerful your fawning and flattery

can be."

"It was more effective than you forcing your whore on him. That cost you the StoneKing's respect, and Tansy too."

"Best lay in the realm," one of the other guild heads muttered. "I'll miss her."

Fedro slapped the tabletop. "At least I didn't trick him, like you did. Foisting that peculiar cousin of yours on him."

"Guild masters, please," Piri said wearily.

The conversation shifted to more mundane matters, and Fedro joined in, although he was still sullen. Mali, however, clasped her wrinkled hands on the tabletop and studied them as the conversation swirled around her. "I tricked him for Desta's sake," she said, more to herself than the others. "For the child's good. Surely, he knows that. Surely, he'll understand, and forgive me."

* * *

"*Forgive me*," Melissa said. She stared at Nigel. "That's what it says. *Forgive me*." She pressed the message to her chest and burst into tears.

Vadden Yale gazed tactfully at the ceiling as Nigel took Melissa in his arms. "The prospect of marriage must have softened Kristan's heart at last," he said, grinning, but his own eyes were wet.

"He says they'll be coming here after the wedding."

"Excellent."

"But shouldn't we go to the wedding ourselves?"

"No. Steffen said you need to rest, and you know how snippy our royal healer gets when he's disobeyed."

"But it's my brother and your sister. We should be at their wedding."

"I'm sure Kristan will understand. I know Heather will."

"I have to agree with the First Advisor, Princess," Vadden said. "More winter travel would be a grave mistake."

Melissa sat up and wiped her face. "I can do it. It's not such a long trip."

"And there it is. The Gemeta stubborn streak," Nigel said. "Dependable as the morning sun."

"I'm not being stubborn—"

"Do you want me to bring Steffen into it? He's already beside himself at how frail you are."

"I can do it, I tell you."

"Princess, we're behind on everything," Vadden said a little desperately. "The country can't spare either of you right now. I know you want to be there, but duty comes first. Your brother would say the same thing."

Melissa clenched her jaw and glowered.

"My love," Nigel said softly, "do you still want to have a child one day?"

"You know I do."

"Then treat yourself more gently. For your sake and for mine." He kissed the top of her head. "The idea of losing you is more than I can bear."

Vadden busied himself shuffling papers as they embraced. When at last they parted, he passed a sheaf of documents across the table. "For your signature, Princess."

As Melissa applied herself to the papers, Nigel took up his own correspondence. "Here's a quick scribble from Heather. Mercy, her handwriting is still appalling. She says her maidservant and Sir Walter got married and have gone to visit his family. She says they'll be back before the wedding, but meantime she can't find a thing. Ah, and see here? She says neither she nor Kristan want us to risk the journey to Norwinn. She says they'll come visit us after the wedding. She sends her love." He shook his head, smiling, and opened another message. "And this one's from Alister. Castle and town are both in an uproar, he says. New people are arriving in Needwood every day. Marcus has opened an inn and a tavern to take advantage of the situation. No expense spared."

"Since it's Kristan's money he's spending, no wonder," Melissa muttered.

"Alister says every time Kristan leaves the castle, the people mob him."

"They're excited about the wedding."

"It's not that," Nigel said, his brow furrowing as he read. "He says they want Kristan to touch them. That's why so many strangers are in town. They think he has healing powers."

Vadden looked up from his own papers. "Why in the world would they think that?"

"He says Kristan touched a young woman and her unborn child came back to life."

The quill dropped from Melissa's hand, splattering ink across the topmost document. Vadden clucked and whisked the parchment away, but Melissa paid him no attention. "How . . . how . . ." she breathed. Her wan face was alive with sudden, stark hope.

Nigel put his hand over hers. "It's just a rumor, Missy," he said quietly.

"But Alister said—"

"People in Needwood can be very silly at times."

"But if Kristan—"

"I know what you're thinking, love. What you're hoping."

She clutched his hand in hers. "Stranger things have happened, Nigel. Maybe it's true."

"Maybe it is." He kissed the back of her hand with great tenderness. "I hope it is. We'll find out when he gets here, won't we? Meantime, we have to get everything ready for his arrival. He'll want to see an efficient, happy kingdom and a sister back in the bloom of health. So let's focus all our attention on achieving that, and let the rest sort itself out as it may."

* * *

"You know he's not right in the head," Colin said gruffly. "He's the StoneKing, and I know you're happy with him, but I wish you were marrying someone steadier."

Heather shrugged. "I knew you'd find something to complain about, Father."

"He's an improvement on Ravelin, at least," Alister said, grinning.

"I assume since Nigel isn't coming, you'll want me to give formal permission," Colin said.

"Actually, no," Heather said. Her father's jaw jutted in mingled surprise and hurt, and she hurried on: "My men will give permission, with Sir Jerrold leading them."

"Well, of all the—"

"I think that's rather fine," Alister said. "Who's going to speak for Kristan, since Melissa won't be here either?"

"The people of Needwood will give permission, on behalf of all his subjects."

"My goodness," Alister said, laughing.

"And where in the world will this enormous ceremony take place?" Colin demanded.

"On the castle drawbridge. My men on the battlements, the people ranged before it."

"And likely in a snowstorm," Colin snorted. "It's madness. You're both mad."

Heather turned her back on his objections and went in search of Kristan. When she finally found him on the battlements, her father's words echoed balefully in her brain.

He was right at the edge of the parapet, leaning into the brisk morning wind. His eyes were closed, his arms outflung, and his clothing whipped about his thin frame like rags on a scarecrow. Serle and Desta stood nearby, poised to drag him back from the edge. The guards on battlement patrol were watching him narrowly.

Heather approached carefully. "It's in the air," he said as she joined him. His eyes were still closed. "Can you feel it?"

It's happening again, she thought. *The avama.* She took gentle hold of his elbow. "What, my lord?"

"Waking," he said, and breathed deep. "Everything's waking." He turned his head toward her and opened his eyes, but it was as if he was seeing something else, something wonderful and yet faraway, and his features were soft with a strange, dreamy rapture.

Then he blinked, and was himself again. "Hello, Commander," he said, looking both pleased and a little surprised.

"Good morning, my lord. Step back from the edge, please; you're making everyone nervous."

"Oh," he said, finally noticing where he stood. "I had no idea . . ." His bemusement was so endearing that she wanted to throw her arms around him. "What was I saying?"

"Only that everything's waking, my lord." She inhaled deeply. "There's a whiff of spring in the air. Is that what you meant?"

"Maybe," he said, but sounded far from certain.

As she led him from the brink, she shot a pointed look at the guards, who quickly directed their attention elsewhere. Serle hurried up, proferring Kristan's cloak. "It's cold up here, sir; you should put this on."

"Allow me, my lord," Desta said, and with a single, fluid gesture, yanked the cloak from Serle and swung it around Kristan's shoulders. Its bedraggled fur lining reminded Heather of her mission.

"It's time you had some new clothing, my lord," she said. "The tailor in Needwood assures me he can outfit you handsomely, and the cobbler would be pleased to fit you with new boots. Both can come to the castle at your convenience."

Kristan gave himself a shake, the abstraction fading from his face at last. "Let's go to them now instead. I could do with an outing."

"You'll be mobbed again, my lord."

"The more often they see me, the less interesting I'll be."

"I'll get the horses, my lord," Desta said, and bolted for the stairs with Serle hard on her heels.

"Don't run," Kristan called, but they were gone.

"Their scuffling for the right to serve you isn't funny anymore," Heather said as they descended into the keep. "Serle's a nice boy, but Desta is far more skilled. Why isn't she your squire instead of him? Is it because she's a girl?"

Kristan heaved a sigh. "No. Serle was my squire well before I met Desta. I know he's a bit of a bumbler, but his kindness got me through some very dark times." He looked at her sidelong. "However, Desta is Gabriel's child, and I want to do right by her. I was thinking she'd make a good squire for you."

"I admit I could use the help, especially now that Bayla's married. But the StoneKing should have the squire who's most skilled."

"The StoneKing disagrees. The High Commander is a true soldier and should have the best squire. No arguing," he chided gently, as she opened her mouth to protest. "My mind is made up. Talk to Desta about it, won't you?"

Sir Jerrold met them at the keep doors. "Good morning, my lord. Good morning, Commander. I understand you're going into Needwood."

"Indeed, we are," Heather said. "Assign a unit to accompany us, please."

"It's done, and I've already sent troops into town to keep order. My lord, I took the liberty of informing your personal retinue as well. Sir Walter is still away with his new wife, but the other four will accompany you, along with Bran and Eaden."

The knights greeted them cheerfully as they stepped outside, except for Sir Kennet, who had been nearly silent since receiving word of the impending marriage. He nodded politely to Heather, pushed Desta and Serle aside, and assisted Kristan into Malvo's saddle himself.

As the company passed over the drawbridge, they met Dell Curry coming on foot from the east. "I was just coming to find you," he said to Kristan, without so much as a good morning. "You need to see something. Follow me."

"Can't it wait?" Heather asked. "We're on our way into town."

Dell ignored her. "Follow me," he said again, and headed back the way he had come. With a small shrug, Kristan nudged Malvo after him.

"But your errands, my lord," Sir Matthew protested.

"They can wait a bit," Kristan said. "I've learned that when Dell wants me to look at something, I'd better look."

Even though he was on foot, Dell stayed well ahead of them, with a long, effortless stride that never broke. The horses struggled in the knee-deep snow, but Dell never faltered, even when he ascended into the eastern hills. "What foolishness is this?" Sir Geoffrey muttered. Heather turned to Kristan to voice her own impatience, but he was gazing intently ahead, and she swallowed her protests.

"At least the snow is thinner up here, where the sunlight's been on it," Sir Mitchell said.

They urged their mounts carefully up the slushy hillside. Dell waited for them at the crest, and as they joined him, pointed at the ground at his feet. "Look," he said. "It's closing."

"What is?" Mitchell asked.

With a snort of exasperation, Dell jabbed his finger at the ground again. "The Crack. The *sprunga*. The Reaving. Last summer, this one spread from the castle right up through the trees behind me. But now this part has filled in."

He crouched and used the side of his hand to scrape away the melting snow as the others dismounted to look more closely. "See? Back at the castle, it's still wide open, but the further from the castle, the shallower it gets. It's collapsing in on itself. It's closing up."

"Like a healing wound," Bran muttered. "I've never seen one

do that before."

Eaden snorted. "We've had nothing but rain and snow the past few months. The ground has finally softened since last summer's drought."

Dell turned expectantly to Kristan, but he was studying the remains of the Crack in silence.

"Look!" Serle called, breaking the silence. The squire had wandered away from the others, but now he was hurrying back, waving something dark and dripping wet. "Look, my lord! I've found your gloves!"

"So you have," Kristan said. "I'd wondered where they'd gotten to."

"Well done, boy," Geoffrey said.

"They're sopping," Desta sniffed. "Ruined."

"I can save them," Serle said. "It'll take time and careful drying, but I can do it."

"What were you doing up here, Kristan?" Dell asked. "And how did you come to lose your gloves?"

Kristan glanced at him. The look was fleeting but managed to convey reprimand, warning and apology all at once. Dell's mouth tightened, but he did not pursue the subject.

"Maybe the rest of the Cracks will close in time too," Sir Matthew said.

"If you're finished here, my lord, I can send the horsemen ahead to Needwood to clear the way," Heather said.

As the horsemen thundered off and the rest of the party mounted up again, Kristan turned to Dell. "Thank you for showing me this," he said quietly. "I value your observations, Dell."

Dell only nodded. They left him standing on the hillside, still studying the Crack. The knights rode ahead with the children, maintaining a discreet distance so that Heather and Kristan could be alone. "Why did it close?" Heather asked in a low voice. "Do you think the *avama* caused it?"

"I don't know." Kristan looked over his shoulder at Dell's

solitary figure, then turned forward again, his face set in thoughtful lines.

"You don't need to worry about Dell. He may have his suspicions, but he'll keep them to himself."

"I'm not worried about Dell. I was remembering what he said once—about how the realm's messengers are always in a hurry, how useful it would be if they could slow down and really look at the country as they pass through. I appointed Reaches to extend and strengthen my hold on the realm. Maybe what I need now are people who can travel through it, observing and reporting back what they see." He nodded to himself. "Gazes, to broaden my vision. I'll give it some thought."

"Right now, my lord, you need to think about clothes and boots." They were entering Needwood, and troops were already lining the streets, holding back the crowds. The knights closed protectively around Kristan. "So many new faces," Heather muttered, keeping a wary eye on the people jostling for position. A one-legged man on a crutch forced his way past the soldiers and threw himself into Kristan's path. "StoneKing!" he cried. "StoneKing, heal me!"

"Get that fool under control," Sir Bran barked.

Soldiers surrounded the man, but he swung his crutch fiercely at them, hopping on his single foot while keeping up his cry: "StoneKing, heal me!" The crowd added their voices to the din.

"Get us out of this," Heather said to the knights.

"Wait," Kristan said. "Let me talk to him."

"My lord, no—" Mitchell cried, but Kristan was already out of the saddle.

"Everyone stand aside!" Geoffrey bellowed. "Let the StoneKing approach!"

To Heather's astonishment, soldiers and surging crowd alike obeyed, clearing a path for Kristan as he limped toward the one-legged man. "My lord," the man whimpered, and sagged onto his single knee, using his crutch for support. "My lord, heal my leg. Make me a man again."

The crowd fell silent. Kristan stood over the man for a long moment, then shook his head. "If I could heal you, don't you think I'd heal myself first?" he asked. "I can't magic you a new leg, any more than I can magic the scar off my face." He put his hand out. "Now get up from the mud."

Wide-eyed, the man took Kristan's hand and levered himself back onto his feet. Kristan put his head on one side and squinted at him. "Beating your wife makes you less of a man than the loss of your leg," he said. "Don't do it again, do you hear me?"

The crowd gasped. The man gaped. "Yes, my lord."

"Good. Now go home. Stop brooding over what you've lost and be thankful for what you have." He nodded to the soldiers, and as they escorted the man away, Kristan returned to Malvo. The crowd, subdued and murmuring, fell back, and the knights, too startled to lend a hand, gaped at Kristan as he struggled to remount. Even Desta sat dumbly in her saddle, but Serle quickly climbed down to assist. "Thank you," Kristan said when he was in the saddle again. "May we proceed?"

"So it's true, my lord?" Sir Mitchell breathed as they nudged the horses forward. "What the people say about you?"

"Nonsense," Geoffrey said, but his expression was uncertain. "He didn't heal the man, did he?"

"But how did you know, my lord?" Kennet asked with surprising eagerness. It was the first time in days he had shown interest in anything. "How did you know he beats his wife?"

Kristan nodded toward the one-legged man, who was sobbing in a woman's embrace. As they passed, she looked up. One eye was bright with tears, the other bruised and swollen shut. She pressed one hand to her lips and blew a kiss at Kristan.

"Well, I'll be," Sir Eaden said.

"You saw her before you touched him," Kennet said. "You reasoned it out." He shook his head in wonder, and Heather had to smile. *Poor Kennet. He needs someone to revere so badly. I'm glad it's Kristan instead of me.*

"Whatever the reason, it certainly took the wind from a few sails," Mitchell said. "See how the crowd is holding back now? All those people who wanted to touch him are afraid he'll see into their hearts and know their secrets."

Heather shot a quick look at Kristan, but his expression was unreadable.

Their retinue waited in the street as Heather and Kristan visited the tailor and the cobbler. Kristan suffered being measured with good grace, although Heather could tell it made him uncomfortable. "Don't you worry, my lord," the tailor assured him, mistaking Kristan's unease for vanity. "Some judicious padding here and there will give you a more striking figure, and with careful tailoring, I can offset the crookedness of your shoulders."

Heather wanted to slap the man, but Kristan only thanked him politely. The cobbler was no better, observing that Kristan's left leg was shorter than his right and offering to build up that boot's sole accordingly. "I can do it cleverly, my lord, so no one will be the wiser," he said in a conspiratorial whisper. Heather's own leg twitched with the desire to kick him, but again, Kristan's response was courteous.

It was only when they were headed back to the castle that Kristan's melancholy eyes gave his true feelings away. Breaking her own rule, Heather slipped her hand into his and squeezed it reassuringly. He gave her a rueful smile and raised her fingers to his lips. "I should heed my own advice," he said softly. "Because I am so grateful for what I have."

As the company dismounted in the castle courtyard, Kristan looked up. "She's back," he said, and raised one hand.

Overhead, a large bird drifted on an updraft of wind, but as if in answer to Kristan's gesture, it folded its wings and stooped straight at them. Instinctively, everyone ducked except Kristan, who never flinched as the bird landed an arm's length from him and suddenly materialized into Nolle—dirty, gaunt, and scowling.

"Did you find him?" Kristan asked.

"I found him. He was drunk."

"Did you give him the message?"

"I did." She pulled off her knapsack.

"What was his answer?"

She rummaged in the knapsack, withdrew a large, bejeweled medallion, and handed it to Kristan. "He threw that at me and told me to give it back to you. Then his men grabbed me and kicked me out of their camp. They chucked rocks at me until I flew out of range."

For a few moments, Kristan stood in silence, turning the medallion in his fingers. Finally, without a word, he mounted the steps and disappeared into the keep. Sir Kennet started after him, but Heather waved him back. "Let him be," she murmured.

Nolle snorted. "All that way, and that's the thanks I get?"

"Go and rest," Heather said. "Get something to eat; tell Cook I said you're to have whatever you like. Serle, see to Malvo. Desta, I'd like a word with you. You can help me with Skapi. The rest of you are dismissed."

* * *

"I suppose . . . I suppose I could."

Heather snorted a laugh as she brushed out Skapi's silky mane. "Well, I expected a little more enthusiasm."

"I'm sorry, my lady," Desta said quickly. "It would be an honor to serve you, of course. But . . ."

"But you've set your sights higher."

Desta rubbed at a nonexistent spot on Skapi's saddle and did not answer. Heather lowered her voice so that Serle, cleaning Malvo's tack at the other end of the stables, could not overhear. "Desta, the StoneKing has a squire. You know that."

"He deserves a better one, ma'am."

"No argument there. But he won't dismiss Serle so you can have the job. He told me so."

Desta's chin quivered, but she blinked back tears and continued to rub at the leather. "It's because I'm a girl. I know it is."

"Certainly, there are duties expected of a squire that might be considered inappropriate if the squire were female," Heather said. "Sleeping at the master's bedside, dressing him, helping him bathe—"

"Serle doesn't do any of that. He never has. The StoneKing doesn't like it."

"To be honest, I wouldn't like it either." Heather stroked Skapi's nose. "Is it the StoneKing or nothing, then?"

Desta heaved Skapi's saddle onto its rack. "Ma'am, it's just that . . . I want to be a knight. A real one. I don't want to be part of some women's unit, fighting in my spare time with brooms. I don't mean to offend," she added as Heather scowled. "Your Home Guard is fine, but it's not what I want. I hate it when people say 'you're good—for a girl.' I want to be treated the same as the boy squires, so I can be a knight, the same as them. I'm afraid if I squire for you, I'll still be set apart. I'll never be a real knight."

Heather gnawed on her lower lip and considered the girl. "I understand. What if I promised you I'd make sure you weren't set apart; that you were treated just the same as other squires?"

"Maybe . . ." Desta said slowly. "But ma'am . . . my father. Everyone told me my father was no good. Aunt Mali said he was a rascal and a disgrace." Desta swallowed hard. "She said the same thing about me. But the StoneKing said my father was a hero, and died a hero's death. No one ever said anything like that about my father before. That's why I want to serve him."

"I knew your father too," Heather said.

For the first time, the girl's face brightened. "You did?"

"Not for long, and not as well as the StoneKing, but I did." She smiled. "He was a handsome man. He had a wicked smile and he carried himself like a lord. You remind me of him."

"I do?"

"Not the smile—you don't smile nearly enough—but you've

got his looks and his long stride."

"Can you . . . can you tell me about him? I'd ask the StoneKing, but I think remembering my father makes him sad."

It's the not remembering that saddens him, Heather thought, and breathed a little sigh. "Your father rode and fought well. He liked to sing. His best friend was a hunchback named Martin. And he loved the StoneKing. He and Martin called him Kinglet. They found him in the Exilwald and looked after him all the time he was in hiding. They protected him from thieves and bounty hunters and even from me, when I came looking for him, to give him his Stone back. And when Daazna took their Kinglet, they went by themselves to rescue him. They died trying to save him. I wanted to go with them, but they wouldn't let me. Because I was a girl." She put her hand on Desta's shoulder. "So you see, I understand how you feel. Maybe being my squire wouldn't be so bad after all."

Desta pursed her lips. "May I think about it, my lady?"

"Take the time you want. Big decisions shouldn't be rushed."

On her way out of the stable, Heather passed Serle. He was hunched over Malvo's saddle, his thin shoulders jerking as he polished the leather. Suddenly, a tiny dark spot appeared on the gleaming leather, then another. Serle buffed them quickly away, but not before Heather recognized them as teardrops. With a guilty start, she realized her voice and Desta's had carried further than she thought. She paused, wondering what to say, but Serle ducked his head even lower, and with a shrug, she walked on.

CHAPTER SEVENTEEN

The next few days passed in a rush. In the tumult of wedding preparations, Walter and Bayla returned and immediately pitched in with a will. Their merry mood flooded the entire castle, so that everyone hurried about their duties laughing and joking, and even Colin was caught smiling at times.

Alister wrote out two copies of the wedding vows. One copy was posted near Needwood's great well, and the townsfolk who could read helped those who could not in memorizing the passages. Sir Jerrold posted the second copy in the barracks and drilled the men until they had the words by heart. Guards on duty recited them in a soft murmur as they paced the battlements; laundresses chanted them in rhythm with their scrubbing; merchants bringing supplies for the wedding crooned them to the teams drawing their wagons. The loving words were everywhere, floating on the breeze like snowflakes.

Real snow fell the morning of the wedding, but it was only a light coating, soft and fluffy as lambswool. It ended by noon, when servants and soldiers alike were decorating the drawbridge and the battlements with great swags of evergreen boughs, tied with bright ribbons. The ceremony was not scheduled until sunset, but long before then, the townspeople began gathering at the foot of the drawbridge.

Heather retired to her bedchamber with Bayla. She bathed—not her usual brisk splash with everyday soap, but a luxuriant, scented lathering. Afterward, she sat before the fire in her dressing gown while Bayla toweled her hair dry. Lily and Annys arrived soon after, bearing Heather's wedding clothes: stockings and a tight-fitting undergown of thin, soft white wool trimmed with embroidered lace, slippers of smooth, pale leather and over it all, a magnificent bronze gown embellished with beads of gold and whorls of blue and plum-colored thread. When Desta and Nolle peeped in shyly from the doorway, Heather motioned them toward a bench by the hearth, and the two girls perched there, side by side, watching the preparations with wide eyes.

The women dressed Heather before the mirror, and for once, she was happy with what was reflected back at her. The dress was beautifully fitted, and its rich color set off her hair, eyes, and skin in a way her other clothing never had. "You look splendid, my lady," Annys said as she turned back the gown's wide sleeves, the better to show off the embroidered arms of the undergown.

"What about your hair?" Lily asked. "Will you be wearing it up in braids, as always?" The slight emphasis on the last two words spoke volumes.

"Braid it as usual," Heather said, then caught sight of Bayla's disappointed face in the mirror. "But perhaps not as tight," she added, relenting a bit.

Smiling, Bayla caught up comb and brush. "You've got those pearl combs you never wear," she said in a wheedling tone. "They're just the color of your undergown."

"I don't need any fancy jewelry. I'll wear my best sword instead. I'm a soldier, remember?"

"You're the Lady of the Sword, and after today, the queen," Bayla said. "And the combs are just gold and pearls. Plain as plain."

"Oh, very well."

Heather had to admit the softer plaiting of her usual coronet, with the addition of the pearl combs, was very flattering, although hardly military. When she turned from the mirror,

Desta clasped her hands to her chest. "You look so pretty," she said, and then quickly added, "my lady."

Nolle eyed Heather with something like jealousy. "I'll tell the StoneKing you're ready," she said, and before anyone could say anything, she shifted into a dragonfly, all sparkling blue, and zipped from the room.

"Little show-off," Lily muttered.

When Heather descended to the great hall, Kristan was waiting before the throne, resplendent in a deep blue tunic embroidered in white and gold, dark leggings, and boots of fine, soft leather. On one hand, he wore a ring of silver centered with a bright blue gem, and the Gemeta Stone shone red from his chest. Serle was at his elbow, his knights ranged on either side of him, and Nolle stood nearby, looking a bit miffed. Colin, wearing the chain of office signifying his status as Reach of Norwinn, stood with Alister at the foot of the stairs. "There she is at last," he said. Kristan looked up at her, and a slow smile of delight spread over his face. The knights nodded and grinned, all except Kennet, who looked away, as if unable to bear the sight of her.

"You look lovely, cousin," Alister said.

"She'll do," Colin grunted, but his eyes were suspiciously moist. He offered his arm, and she took it, but her gaze was locked on Kristan. When she was within a few steps of him, she let go of Colin's arm and dipped into her deepest curtsey. He bowed low, leg extended with something like his old easy grace. "Commander," he murmured.

"My lord," she whispered back.

Bayla stepped forward with Heather's cloak—a new one, with plush fur lining. Serle helped Kristan into his own new cloak. Then Kristan took her hand, and together they walked out into the soft light of late afternoon. Malvo and Skapi waited at the foot of the steps, curried until they gleamed, with ribbons braided into their manes and tails. Kristan and Heather mounted up, and then nudged the horses across the courtyard, through the gatehouse, and onto the drawbridge.

A deafening roar made them both jump. Ranged before them were all the people of Needwood, and behind, the soldiers of Hogia lined the battlements. The cheering went on as Malvo and Skapi clopped across the drawbridge, tossing their heads at the noise. Colin and the other courtiers crowded behind, but Alister slipped past them, a rolled parchment in his hand, and took up a position at the far end of the drawbridge. Kristan and Heather reined up and waited.

"My lord Kristan Gemeta, king of Hogia, Fandrall, Dyer and Norwinn," Alister said, then turned toward the people of Needwood. He unrolled his parchment, nodded his head, and a multitude of voices rose to join his in reciting the vows:

"You have asked our permission to wed this woman you have chosen: Heather Demitt of Needwood, Hogia. Will you be both sword and shield to her, to protect and defend her?"

"I will," said Kristan. His eyes were shining.

"Both roof and door, to shelter and welcome her?" the townspeople chanted.

"I will."

"Both meat and drink, to sate and quench her?"

"I will."

"Both sun and moon, to light her comings and goings by day and by night?"

"I will."

"Then with great joy, we give consent to your marriage, and acknowledge Heather Demitt as your wife and our queen. May you warm together before one fire, dine at one table, embrace in one bed, cherish your children, and honor and love each other all the days of your life."

A few people cheered and were immediately shushed. As Heather and Kristan turned their mounts to face the soldiers on the battlements, a little breeze riffled the fur of his cloak and sent his dark hair tumbling across his face. Heather ached to smooth the errant curls but controlled herself. *Be patient,* she told herself. *In time, he won't flinch when I reach for his face; in time, I won't fear that a show of softness will make me less of a commander.*

On the battlements, Sir Jerrold raised his own copy of the vow. "High Commander Lady Heather Demitt," he barked out, paused meaningfully, then nodded.

"You have asked our permission to wed this man you have chosen: Kristan Gemeta of Kingsmere, Fandrall," the assembled soldiers thundered. "Will you be both sword and shield to him, to protect and defend him?"

"I will," said Heather.

"Both roof and door, to shelter and welcome him?"

"I will."

"Both meat and drink, to sate and quench him?"

"I will."

"Both sun and moon, to light his comings and goings by day and by night?"

"I will."

"Then with great joy we give our consent to your marriage, and acknowledge Kristan Gemeta as your husband. May you warm together before one fire, dine at one table, embrace in one bed, cherish your children, and honor and love each other all the days of your life."

Another attempt at cheering was stifled as Heather and Kristan turned the horses toward each other and nudged them forward, so they were face-to-face, knee-to-knee. Skapi whickered and nosed Malvo's rump, but he stood without moving, as if he understood the gravity of the moment. Kristan held out his hand, and Heather took it. For a long moment, they sat looking at each other, while the onlookers seemed to hold their collective breath.

"You are the core of my heart," Kristan said. His voice rang off the castle's stone wall.

"You are the song of my soul," Heather answered, her words equally strong.

"You are the brightness of my morning."

"You are the comfort of my night."

"My pride."

"My pleasure."

"My wonder."

"My treasure."

They took a deep breath and finished together: "And I will love you all the days of my life."

This time there was no stifling the onlookers' roar of approval. Kristan smiled and leaned forward to be heard over the tumult. "Shall we, Commander?"

"Indeed, we shall, my lord," Heather answered, with a smile of her own.

Their lips met in a brief, chaste kiss. In response, the soldiers pounded their pikes and stamped their feet. Phelan, standing with them on the battlements, sent balls of colored fire rocketing skyward, which burst into patterns of bright flowers and flashing stars. The people of Needwood applauded, threw their hats skyward, skipped and danced and embraced each other in their delight. In the castle courtyard and in the town square, musicians struck up lively tunes as the newlyweds nudged their mounts across the drawbridge and through the gatehouse.

In the great hall, the wedding celebration continued with feasting, toasts, more music, and dancing. Marcus made jokes and capered, the knights raised toast after toast to the couple, Lily and Sir Matthew sang a romantic duet, Alister recited poetry, and Annys coaxed Colin into dancing with her, leading him out onto the floor like a busy little hen herding a reluctant bear. Desta, Nolle, and Serle forgot themselves enough to act like real children, romping and giggling and chasing each other through the crowd. Phelan worked charming little spells for the company's amusement. Even Dell lost his usual faraway look as he laughed and talked with his tablemates. Only Kennet was somber. He sat with his wine goblet cupped in both hands, staring into its depths when he was not drinking from it.

Kristan and Heather sat at the center of the head table, nodding and smiling decorously, but beneath the table their hands sought each other again and again. When the carousing was at its peak, Walter came to Kristan's side and murmured in his ear. Kristan nodded and squeezed Heather's fingers. Together they rose and slipped unobserved from the table. Candle in hand, Bayla met them at the foot of the stairs. As they ascended, she led the way, and Walter followed.

In Heather's bedchamber, the mantel was decorated with more beribboned evergreens. A row of tall, creamy tapers in silver holders marched along its length. Their soft light danced off a silver pitcher of wine and a pair of goblets on a little table set invitingly near the bench before the hearth. At the other side of the room, moonlight shone from the window onto Heather's bed, its fur-lined blankets turned back to display snowy linens.

Heather stood just within the doorway, feeling suddenly at a loss. She and Kristan had decided to spend their wedding night in her bedchamber; his room downstairs, while larger, was too close to the festivities, and the great chamber formerly occupied by both Ravelin and Daazna held no attraction for either of them. But Bayla had tidied away all Heather's familiar little messes: the battered uniform and well-worn boots, the untidy stacks of rosters on her worktable, the little barrel stuffed with rolled maps, the scruffy quills and pots of ink. Kristan took a few steps into the room, then hesitated. "It's a pretty chamber," he said, and it was, but it was like a stranger's room now.

"Good night, my lady," Bayla said, and kissed Heather on the cheek.

"Good night, my lord," Sir Walter echoed. The two of them left, closing the door on the noise drifting up from the great hall.

Kristan held out his hand, and Heather came to his side. They sat before the fire, shared out the wine, and drank, watching each other over the rims of their goblets. Finally, Kristan put his aside. "I have something for you," he said, and pulled the blue ring from his finger. "This has had a somewhat checkered past," he went on, holding it up so the firelight played on it. "I bought it for myself in a moment of indulgence, because it reminded me of your eyes. Then I wished I hadn't, because thoughts of you were torture when I knew I could never have you. So I gave it to Astéria because she was sad. It was a simple gift between friends, but others misconstrued its meaning, and she gave it back to me. I've carried it in my pocket ever since. It's been dunked with me in the Mor and in the sea, and I very nearly threw it into the fire after I saw you with Ravelin. But I couldn't do it. Angry as I was, I couldn't let it go, any more than I've ever been able to let you go, try as I might." He took her free hand and slid the ring onto her first finger. "I thought about having Needwood's goldsmith put it in a more elaborate setting, something with diamonds, but then I realized it needed no diamonds, that it was beautiful without embellishment, just as you are. And I thought it would suit you."

Heather admired the ring in the firelight. "It does. It's beautiful, Kristan."

They kissed, long and lingeringly. Heather raised her hands to the fastenings of Kristan's tunic, but he put them gently aside and stood up. "Let me put out these candles first."

She caught his wrist. "Leave them. I want to see you."

"Heather." He swallowed hard. "I've told you . . . my body is ugly."

"I have scars of my own. I earned them in your service, and I'm not ashamed of them." She turned her back to him. "Unlace my dress. I want to show you."

Barely breathing, she waited as his fingers worked the broad embroidered lacings loose. As soon as the high neckline sagged away from her throat, she pulled it aside, then tugged the undergown off her shoulder, exposing her scars. Kristan sucked in his breath but said nothing.

"That's where Iele bit me," she said. "She held me under the water and tried to tear my throat out. If she'd been able to get a better grip, she would have too. Unlace the rest of it."

He was so close she could feel his breath on her bare skin. Her pulse hammered in her ears, drowning the noise of the celebration below. *Does he find me repulsive?* she wondered, and suddenly understood his fear of exposing his body to her. At that moment, he tugged the lacings completely out of the dress with a hissing sound that made her jump, and dropped them on the floor. The dress slid down to her waist, leaving her clad only in the white undergown. "Unlace the undergown," she said, her voice little more than a croak.

These lacings were of silky ribbon, and they whispered as he drew them from the fabric. When they were gone, she pulled the undergown down to her waist, exposing her back. "And that's where she stabbed me," she said, barely able to force the words from her throat. "There, on the left side. She had a little knife, and she stabbed me twice."

Still Kristan said nothing. His silence made her tremble. Then his fingers touched the wounds on her back, feather light. He stroked the scars, then slid his hand around her waist so it rested against her ribs just beneath her breasts. He drew her close. His soft curls brushed her skin as he bent his head to her neck. He kissed the scars left by Iele's teeth, again and again, then traced his tongue delicately along the rippled, pitted flesh. She gasped and arched her back, exposing her neck even further. His lips moved up her throat, and she turned her head to meet them with her own mouth. "You're so beautiful," he whispered between kisses. "Every part of you."

The hand at her ribs shifted, caressing her sides, then her belly, then the rounded flesh of her breast. He did not squeeze and grope and paw her, as Ravelin had; his touch was gentle, unhurried, tantalizing, and her body prickled with delicious gooseflesh. This was no lightning bolt of sheer bodily passion; this was a banked fire, long buried in ashes, slowly returning to heat and light.

Kristan's free hand was at her head now, plucking away the

combs and hairpins, pulling the braids down, shaking and stroking the hair loose so it tumbled over her shoulders and down her back. He buried his face in her hair and breathed deeply. "So beautiful," he murmured. She turned to him, and he caught her face in both hands and kissed her until she was breathless.

"Wait," she gasped as his hands cupped her breasts. "Wait. I want to see you first. I want to see all of you. Stand up."

He dropped his hands and rose, his features taut with reluctance. She stood before him and began to unfasten his tunic.

"Heather—"

"Hush." The heavy tunic was open now. She brushed the Stone aside, pulled the tunic off, and let it fall. Beneath it, Kristan wore a soft linen undershirt.

"Heather," he said again, but without answering, she slid her hands beneath the undershirt. He caught his breath and closed his eyes.

His flesh was traversed by long, thick welts. She ran her hands slowly up his belly, across his chest and down his sides, tracing the scars with tender, searching fingers. She slid her hands around to his back, holding him close as she continued her exploration. He went tense, as if keeping himself in place by sheer will.

The scarring on his back was worse, much worse. The welts criss-crossed so frequently that his flesh was knotted with them. Heather leaned into him, running both hands from the nape of his neck to the base of his spine, sliding her fingers into the waist of his leggings, letting her palms come to rest against the mutilated flesh of his buttocks. He shuddered, but at the same time she felt his growing hardness against the cleft of her legs.

"Do you want me to stop?" she whispered.

"No," he breathed. "No."

"Do you trust me?"

"With all my heart."

Gently, slowly, she pulled the linen undershirt up. His hand rose, long enough to catch hold of the Gemeta Stone as she pulled the undershirt over his head. He stood with it clenched in his fist as she dropped the clothing on the floor and studied him.

"I told you I was ugly," he said. His voice was hoarse with shame.

"I want you," she said. "All of you. Your body, and every scar on it. Your heart. Your mind. I want every part of you." She slid her dress down, so it pooled around her feet. She slipped out of her shoes, peeled off her stockings and stood before him naked, with the firelight dancing on her skin. "Do you want me, Kristan?"

"With all my heart," he whispered.

"Then put these where you want them," she said, and held out her hands.

He took them in his own. He touched his lips to every fingertip, turned her hands over, and placed a tender kiss in each palm. Then he took hold of her wrists, and with a quick intake of breath, pressed her hands against his forehead.

She bent over him as he sagged to his knees. She crooned wordlessly, stroked his hair, kissed the bruises Daazna's fingers had left on his brow. With trembling hands, he caressed her buttocks. He kissed her thighs and belly, caught her breasts gently in his mouth and rolled his tongue across each nipple. At last, he rose, and with sudden, surprising strength, lifted her off her feet. She locked her legs around his hips, her arms about his neck. "All of you, my lord," she whispered as he carried her to the bed. "I want all of you."

* * *

In the middle of the night, Heather woke to the sound of her own name. At first, she thought Kristan had spoken, but he was fast asleep beside her. Moonlight from the window washed his tranquil features in cold blue-white.

Deciding she had imagined the sound, she snuggled closer to Kristan and was just closing her eyes when she heard it again. Someone was calling her name from the courtyard below.

She slipped from the warmth of the bed and caught up her dressing gown. Clutching it to her chest, she crept to the window and peeped out. Someone was crouched at the bottom of the keep steps, groaning. On the battlements, two guards had paused and were watching curiously. The groaning man threw back his head and cried out her name again.

It was Kennet.

The keep doors opened and two people hurried down: Sir Walter and Bayla. They bent over Kennet, who had buried his face in his hands and was sobbing. Although Heather couldn't make out their words, their gentle tones and gestures told her they were trying to comfort him. After a few moments, Kennet staggered to his feet, and Heather realized with a start that Kennet—disciplined, dutiful Kennet—was reeling drunk. Avoiding Walter's extended hand, he stumbled to the edge of the staircase, bleated Heather's name one last time, and then vomited, suddenly and violently, into the courtyard. Walter caught him around the waist as he collapsed. With Bayla's help, he half dragged, half carried Kennet up the stairs and into the keep.

"Well," Heather murmured, pity mingling with exasperation. *I can't help his pain*, she thought. *I was always honest with him. I told him I could never love him.*

She turned back to the bed. In her absence, Kristan had changed position. Now he lay curled on his right side, one hand knotted around the Stone, the other wrapped around his head. His expression was no longer serene: his eyes were pinched shut, his lips pressed tightly together. Thinking he was chilled, Heather drew the covers over him, then hesitated, her gaze drawn to the hand that clutched the Stone.

He doesn't need that anymore.

The thought startled her. It was her own voice, in her own

head, but the idea seemed to come from somewhere else.

The danger is gone. Daazna is gone. He'll never be a great king until he can conquer his fear. Look at him, clutching his Stone like a child clutches its blanket for solace. He needs to stop hiding behind the Stone.

Kristan grimaced. She leaned over him, her hand raised to stroke his hair, to comfort him.

You can help him, just as you've always helped him.

Her hand twitched toward Kristan's, toward the Stone gripped in his fingers. At that instant, she was overwhelmed with a familiar sense that something was dreadfully, dangerously wrong. She pulled her hand back and stood upright, but her movements were labored, as if she was underwater, caught in a strong, icy current. *No,* she told herself. *It can't be. It can't be.*

Teeth chattering, she rolled her eyes longingly toward the hearth and wished for a blazing fire to warm herself, but the embers were nearly dead. Only two coals still gleamed through the ashes, but instead of glowing red, they were pale and still, like a pair of staring eyes.

Like eyes.

"No," Heather whispered. Her breath steamed in the icy air. She dropped her gown and forced herself toward the hearth, one slow step at a time, pressing through a wall of cold that prickled her skin and numbed her naked flesh and sank all the way into her bones. "No, you don't. Not this time."

Her fumbling fingers found the iron poker. Clutching it, she drew back, then thrust it with all her might into the fireplace, right between the two pale spots. They glared out brighter than ever, but she stabbed at them again and again, raising a cloud of ash and sparks. From deep in the embers, a red flame licked up, then another and another, and the pale glare flickered. Heather threw fresh kindling into the fire and thrust it deep with the poker. "Get out," she hissed. "Go back to your hole in the ground."

Roaring high, the flames smothered the lights in their fierce, hot glow. Heather stood over the fire, poker raised and ready, but at last, she returned it to its place and stepped back. Her knees were shaking.

"What are you doing?"

Kristan's voice was thick with sleep.

"Just poking up the fire," she answered. "I was cold."

"Come back to bed, then."

She stumbled across the room and slid in beside him. "You're shivering," he murmured, and pulled her close, tucking her into the warm spoon of his body. "Feet and backside like ice . . . poor darling."

He kissed her temple and the side of her neck just below her ear. His hand drifted across the curves of her body, from breast to belly to hip and back again. She felt him stir and rise against her buttocks, but she lay perfectly still, her eyes on the fire. His hand slowed, his breathing deepened, and finally his body relaxed into slumber, still holding her close, one hand cupping her breast.

She kept her gaze fixed on the fire. *I will fight you with the last breath in my body,* she told the vanished eyes. *If you want him, you'll have to go through me first. I swear it.*

She was growing warmer. The Stone, pressed between Kristan's chest and her back, seemed to give off a heat that seeped down her spine and into her chilled heart. She tucked her feet between Kristan's, folded her arms over his, and at long last, fell asleep.

CHAPTER EIGHTEEN

"Well?" Nolle said. "Are you going to do it?"

She and Desta stood on the keep steps, well out of the way of the subdued bustle of departure. The servants were doing their best to keep quiet as, out in the courtyard, the Lady of the Sword made her final inspection of Hogia's soldiers and its Home Guard. Men and women alike stood at precise attention as she moved through their ranks, stopping now and then to twitch a collar straight, adjust the angle of a pike, lay her hand on a shoulder and speak an encouraging word.

"She's a good commander," Desta said, in a small voice. "And she looks wonderful today."

"Fancy new uniform to go with all her fancy titles. Queen, High Commander, Lady of the Sword. You'd probably get a fancy uniform like hers."

"I don't care about fancy uniforms."

The Lady of the Sword was talking to Jerrold, Bran, and Eaden now, her weight on one hip, her gloved hand resting lightly on the hilt of her fine sword. At last, she drew herself upright and raked a stern gaze over the assembled ranks. "Ladies and gentlemen," she said, her voice clear in the crisp dawn air. "It's been an honor. I leave you in Sir Jerrold's capable hands."

A cheer rose as she saluted them. "You could be there," Nolle said. "You could be standing right there beside her."

"I know. But—" Desta broke off as the keep doors swung

open and the servants quickly drew back, nearly crowding them off the stairs. The cheering doubled as the StoneKing stepped out, drawing on his gloves. He nodded an absent acknowledgement to the ovation but continued his conversation with Sir Colin while his knights and the rest of Hogia's court crowded close. Serle squeezed through the throng and made a mad dash toward the stables. "Look at him," Desta muttered. "I'll bet he hasn't even saddled Malvo yet. And he'll probably make a hash of it. He always does."

"Jealous?"

"The StoneKing deserves better."

"He likes old Serle. You'd better take what you can get." Nolle's pulse quickened as Phelan tottered out of the keep and stood smiling and blinking at the tumult. "I'll be right back."

"Where are you going? We're about to leave!"

"I forgot something." She shifted quickly into a mouse, dodged nimbly past all the feet, and scuttled into the keep. Once inside, she changed into a dragonfly and zigzagged her way to Phelan's room. The door was shut, as she knew it would be, and a faint, acrid scent told her there was a locking spell on it as well. *Can't stop me, old man*, she thought smugly. With barely a pause, she shifted into a cockroach, found a crack in the wall, and squeezed through.

Once inside, she shook off the shift and ran to the bookshelves. She scanned the books, looking for the big hidebound volume Phelan had hidden so many days before, but it was not there. She rifled through the stacks of parchment on the worktable, but the book was not there either. She dropped to her knees to look under the bed and found only dust mice. On sudden impulse, she thrust one hand beneath the mattress and there, there was the book at last. She dragged it into her lap; it flopped open, and the battered little book with the rat-gnawed leather cover lay before her. With a little squeak of triumph, she thrust it beneath her skirts, jammed the big book back in its place, scrambled to her feet, and turned—

And found Phelan before her, leaning on his staff.

She leaped backward and nearly fell onto the bed. "You were outside . . . how did you . . ."

The old Wichearte came no closer. He seemed no more than a shadow, but his eyes were uncannily bright. "I'm still outside. Still standing on the steps, blinking like a fool." He cocked his head, like a hawk considering a cornered mouse. "I knew you'd try. I'm surprised it took you so long."

"I didn't do anything—"

"You have no use for it," he went on, his voice low with menace, not at all the sound of the daft old man she'd scorned. "You can barely read it. You have no idea of its import. But you knew I valued it, and for that reason alone, I knew you'd try to steal it."

"Steal? I never—"

"You have talent," Phelan said. "It could be a great talent, but you weaken it with your greed. You smear and sully every spell with your lies. You're a thief and a sneak, with a petty heart and a puny spirit. That's why you can't learn the great spells. That's why you'll never be anything more than a two-faced little Wiche shifter."

It was as if he had reached into her chest, pulled out her ragged, stained soul, and thrust it in her face. Her throat knotted, but she forced herself to sneer. "I don't have your book, you dotty old fool."

Phelan heaved a great sigh and pointed his thumb at her. "*Ya o.*"

An icy gust blasted up from the floor, knocked her into the air, and held her there, tumbling and shaking her, turning her upside down and right side up, yanking her clothes askew until every trinket, every trifle, everything she had snatched and secreted about her person juddered free and swirled around her, clouting her head, smacking her in the face, striking her arms and legs. Somewhere in the storm, Phelan spoke again, and the great wind lessened. It lowered her to the floor, gradually and gently, and with a final, cold puff, was gone.

Panting, Phelan hunched over and braced his hands on his thighs. With trembling hands, Nolle straightened her skirts and palmed her hair out of her face. All around her, the floor was littered with the things she had stolen, like a nimbus of her guilt. Just in front of her was the little book. Eyes welling with hot tears, she caught it up and held it out to Phelan. "Here," she said. "Take it back. I just . . . I just wanted to know."

Phelan raised his head. His wrinkled face was pale and sagging with exhaustion. Instead of taking the book, he considered the welter of items on the floor. "You stole all this?"

"Most of it." Phelan's gaze locked on the blue glass ball. "Not that. The StoneKing gave that to me."

"Did he?"

"I tried to steal it. He caught me, but then he said he'd give it to me if I helped him get Astéria to Dyer. So I did. But it's no good." A hiccupping sob escaped her, and she wanted to die of shame. "Aunt said it's a scrying ball, and you can see the future in it. But I can't. It won't work for me." Another sob blurted out, then another. "Nothing works for me. You're right. I'll never be a great Wichearte."

As she sat blubbering, Phelan straightened up, one hand pressed into the small of his back. "But you learned something today," he said. "Something new, I'll be bound."

She sniffed and eyed him suspiciously. "What?"

"Humility. It's a hard lesson to learn because it's impossible to teach." His figure suddenly wavered, like a distant mirage on a hot day. "Some never learn it. And some learn too late. Pick up your things, girl."

Nolle gathered up all the trinkets and baubles she had pilfered. There was no longer any pleasure in possessing them, only shame, but not knowing what else to do, she secreted them once more about her person. At last, the little book was all that remained. With downcast eyes, she held it out to him. He did not take it, nor did he speak. She glanced at him from beneath her brows and found his eyes on her, but he seemed to be looking right through her.

"I'd hoped to redeem myself, before my time ends," he murmured. "Translate the words so I could enlighten him, guide him, prepare him for what comes. But perhaps he doesn't need me after all. Perhaps he's already making his own way, just as the book has made its own way all these years. Perhaps it only fell into my hands so it could move on." Once again, his figure wavered, then faded until it was as if she was looking at a shadow. "Take it," he said, and his voice seemed to come from far off. "Take what you stole, girl, and go away."

The shadow flickered out, and Nolle was alone. The door creaked and swung open. Snuffling a bit, Nolle trudged downstairs, not even bothering to shift.

Outside the StoneKing's retinue was already mounted and waiting. Nolle shouldered her way through the crowd to Desta, already astride her own pony and holding onto Nolle's. "There you are at last!" Desta said, and passed Nolle the reins. "I was afraid we'd have to leave without you. What was so important?"

Nolle heaved herself into the saddle, feeling for the first time the clumsy weight of all her ill-gotten goods. "It wasn't so important after all," she said, but the words rang false.

At the head of the cavalcade, Sir Kennet called out the order to march. The onlookers cheered, and the column started forward. As she passed the keep, Nolle snuck a look at Phelan. He still stood at the top of the steps, but now his full weight was on his staff, as if it was all that kept him erect. He stared straight ahead, his face drawn with exhaustion but his eyes serene, like a footsore traveler who has, at long last, laid down his burden.

* * *

More than a whiff of spring today, Heather thought, breathing deep as the company left Needwood and headed across the Plain. The sun was bright and the breeze that fluttered the royal banner had a hint of softness beneath its chill. Most of the snow had melted, leaving a fair amount of mud to be slogged through, but she did not mind.

She turned in the saddle to check the cavalcade's progress. Had Kristan his way, the company would have been limited to the two of them, his five knights, Bayla, Dell, and the children, but Heather had insisted on increasing their complement with a dozen handpicked horsemen. "We should have more, but I don't want to leave the castle shorthanded," was her answer to his protest. "You're liable to be mobbed all along our journey, and we'll need the extra men to keep order."

He had acquiesced mildly enough, but as they passed through Needwood and the usual crowd came running, he had reined up. Heather had held her breath as he clasped some of the many hands that reached for him, but the contact, blessedly, seemed to have no effect.

She was not certain he shared her relief. Although he smiled readily enough whenever he met her gaze, his expression in repose was pensive, and his hand went again and again to the Gemeta Stone. *Still trying to make sense of it all*, she thought, and felt more protective of him than ever.

Most of the party was cheerful, although there were a few who seemed as preoccupied as Kristan. Dell studied the landscape without speaking, Kennet was more grave and proper than ever, and all three children seemed low-spirited. Serle rode just behind Kristan, his freckled face solemn, with Nolle slouched sullenly at his side. Desta rode a little apart, and while she sometimes brought her horse abreast of Heather, and smiled at her shyly, her eyes went again and again to Kristan. *She's trying too*, Heather thought and sighed. *Trying to come to terms with the fact that she'll never be the StoneKing's squire. Trying to make herself settle for second best.*

Sir Geoffrey, leading the column, adjusted their route to the southwest and Norwinn's border. Squinting against the bright morning light, Heather scanned the horizon. It was then that she spotted the donkey moving toward them from the west, laboring beneath the weight of its two riders. "There they are!" a child's voice cried. "There she is! Wait, wait!"

The donkey jumped as if it had been nudged, none too gently, and broke into an awkward trot. "What in the world..." Kristan muttered, reining up.

"Sir Geoffrey," Heather called. "A moment, please."

The company drew to a halt and waited. The donkey's short legs stuttered through the slushy mud, and as it drew closer, Heather could make out the riders: a thin, weary-looking woman and a small girl, who leaned forward, staring at Heather with a gaze of ferocious intensity. "Now who could that be?" she murmured to Kristan, but he was regarding the new arrivals with something like dismay.

Sir Walter burst out laughing. "I recognize them now. Let's hope the little girl hasn't found another stick, my lord!"

The donkey drew up just short of the company, and the little girl slid from its back and bent into a deep bow. The woman dismounted with far less alacrity and dipped into a clumsy curtsey. "My lord—" she said.

The girl interrupted. "It's me, my lady! Hilla Dunne! I'm ready now, my lady! I've done everything the StoneKing told me to do and I've been training and everything and I'm ready!"

Heather turned to Kristan with a sense of foreboding, which only increased at the sight of the faint rush of crimson coloring his pale cheeks. "What is she ready for, my lord?"

Kristan cleared his throat. "To be your squire, Commander."

Walter let out a snort of laughter and quickly turned it into a cough. Heather shot him a withering look, then turned back to Kristan. "I don't understand, my lord."

"He told me last summer I could be your squire, my lady!" The girl was beaming. "He took my stick and hit me on the head and said I was in training. He said—" She sucked in a deep breath and continued at a rattling pace: "He said I had to moderate my unruly behavior and honor my parents and help my elders and protect the weak and treat everyone with justice and kindness and comport myself in a manner befitting the Lady of the Sword's squire."

"Well done," Kristan said weakly.

"So can I be your squire now, my lady?" Hilla demanded.

The woman with Hilla—Heather assumed she was the child's mother—raised a timid hand. "My lord, Hilla's done everything you asked. Every single thing. Over and over and over again." She breathed a tiny sigh. "The village is so . . . grateful. So very, very grateful. They sent us to ask—no, they *beg*, my lord—that you reward Hilla by honoring your promise."

Kristan turned to Heather, mute apology in every feature. Heather blew out a sigh of her own and looked over her shoulder. Desta was upright in the saddle, head high, shoulders back, features composed in spite of the dull resignation in her eyes. She nodded—a short, sharp jerk of her proud head.

Heather turned back. "If the StoneKing made a promise, it must be honored," she said.

She was not prepared for the blaze of joy that lit Hilla's face, nor for both child and mother to sink to their knees in the mud. "Thank you, thank you, my lord," the woman murmured, but Hilla only stared adoringly at Heather.

"Get up, get up," Kristan said. "Hilla's very young, madam. Are you sure you're willing to let her leave home and go into the High Commander's service?"

"Absolutely sure, my lord." The relief in the woman's face was unmistakable. "I would never stand in the way of something Hilla wants so much."

Woe to anyone who does, Heather thought, but found herself admiring such determination in one so young.

"Do you want to take the donkey, Hilla?" the mother asked.

"You take it, mother. I'll walk behind the Lady of the Sword's horse." Hilla looked as if walking behind Skapi was the dream of a lifetime.

"No one needs to walk," Heather said. "I think we can make

room for you on one of the pack ponies."

"She's your squire and should have a horse, my lady," Desta said. "She can have mine. I'll take the pack pony."

Heather opened her mouth to protest, but Desta had already dismounted and was offering the reins to Hilla. Hilla hugged her mother fiercely, snatched the reins from Desta, and climbed into the saddle. Desta helped her adjust the stirrups, gave the horse a quick pat, then started toward the pack ponies at the rear of the column. Serle and Nolle watched her go. Serle's expression was stricken, but Nolle only glowered. "Share my horse, Desta," she said suddenly. "There's plenty of room. And I feel like flying right now, anyway." With a reproachful glance at Heather and Kristan, she transformed herself into a hawk and shot into the air. Hilla left off staring at Heather long enough to gape after it.

"Goodbye, Hilla," the woman said.

"Goodbye, Mama. I'll write you as soon as I learn how."

Kristan was murmuring to Sir Walter. The knight dug into his tunic, produced a few coins and passed them to the woman. "To ease your parting," he said.

The woman nodded her thanks and climbed aboard the donkey. Desta swung herself into Nolle's vacated saddle as Hilla nudged her new mount into position behind Heather. "Ready, my lady," she almost crowed.

Geoffrey shook his head. "A fourth brat—that's all we needed."

The cavalcade started south again; the figure of the woman on the donkey receded west. Kristan leaned close to Heather. "I'm so sorry. I should never have made such a promise on your behalf. And Desta—"

"Desta would never have been happy in my service," Heather answered, keeping her voice low. "This new girl wants nothing more. I think everything worked out for the best."

"Perhaps one of my knights could take Desta on."

"I think that would create more problems than it would

solve. A girl squire in service to a male knight is asking for a lot of gossip."

"You do realize I'm a man too?"

His muffled indignation made her smile. "All too well, my lord. But Desta's heart is set on serving you, and the StoneKing is in a position to rise above gossip. To defy custom. To set precedents."

"You think I should dismiss Serle and make Desta my squire."

"She's the better of the two."

"I made a promise to Serle." Kristan lowered his voice even more. "If I break my word, it'll break his heart."

"Someone's heart is bound to be broken over this business. Whether it's Serle's or Desta's comes down to you, my lord."

"My own heart may break in the process," Kristan said, and sighed. "All right, Commander. I'll give it some thought."

CHAPTER NINETEEN

By late afternoon of the second day, they were in sight of Norwinn's border. Ahead, in the spot where Norwinn's army had forded the Strath the summer before, stood a massive bridge. Shouts of welcome rang out across the water. A crowd was gathered on the opposite shore, and their cries swelled as the company clattered across. Resplendent in blue and silver, a contingent of Norwinn's knights and soldiers waited in ranks, with Nigel at their head. Although he was smiling, he shifted from foot to nervous foot as Kristan dismounted. "Welcome back to Norwinn, my lord," he said.

He bent into a bow, but Kristan stepped forward, his hand outstretched. "Brother," was all he said.

Nigel's entire face lit up, and he clasped Kristan's hand in both of his. But Heather's hand he ignored, and caught her up in a bear hug instead. "Queen and High Commander you may be," he whispered in her ear, "but you're still my little sister. Oh, welcome! Welcome!"

The warmth of their greeting spread through the rest of the company. Sir Geoffrey and Sir Mitchell were enveloped in a wave of blue and silver as their former comrades surrounded them, gripping their hands and pounding their backs. The common folk cheered even harder. "I confess I'd forgotten about the bridge," Kristan said, raising his voice to be heard. "It turned out well."

"When word went out last fall that you wanted a bridge over

the Strath, I think every builder in Norwinn submitted plans," Nigel said. "But it was Missy who thought to write Captain Ommald in Dyer to ask his opinion. He sent back a plan of his own—the only one that took into consideration what the Strath would be like at full force, not the little drought-strangled trickle we forded back in the summer."

Heather eyed the torrent tumbling past the bridge's massive piers. "Good thing you listened to him."

"Ommald is past due for knighting, I think," Kristan said. "Nigel, is my sister well?"

"Better every day. She wanted to come with me, but Steffen got all red in the face at the idea. She's waiting at the castle instead. Good heavens, what's gotten into these people?" he added as the crowd around them pushed closer, calling out for Kristan, and trying to touch him.

"The same thing that's gotten into everyone in every village we've passed," Heather said. "Sir Kennet, if you please."

Kennet barked out an order, and the royal escort herded the crowd back, none too gently.

Kristan's brows knotted. "Give me a moment or two, please. If I speak to them and touch a few, they usually calm down."

"Alister wrote us about the rumors circulating in Needwood," Nigel said to Heather. "They seem to have spread into Norwinn. Are they true, my queen?"

His joking words were belied by the wistfulness of his voice. "Are you asking if Kristan really does have a healing touch?" she asked a bit gruffly. "It seems to have happened once. Whether it can happen again, I don't know."

Nigel nodded toward Kristan, who had placed his hand on a palsied old woman's shoulder as he leaned close to hear her plaint. "What does he think?"

"He hasn't really said. Some strange things have happened, brother. I think he's trying his best to make sense of them."

"Whatever happened, he looks the better for it," Nigel said. "He's lost that half-crazed look. No more *ragis*."

"*Avama*," Heather said under her breath.

"What?"

"Nothing. Just more of what he's trying to sort out."

They watched in silence as Kristan spoke gently to the old woman. With an effort she raised her jerking, twitching head. It looked as if she was trying to smile. Her tremors slowed, and the crowd ooohed and pushed closer.

"Look," Nigel breathed, and stood almost on tiptoe to watch.

At that moment the woman's head twitched sharply, and her trembling resumed. Kristan shook his head and stepped back, and Nigel's eager posture sagged. Heather put her hand on his arm and gave it a light squeeze. "I know what you're thinking. If Kristan can help you, he will. But you and Missy shouldn't get your hopes up."

Their journey to Moordock was an erratic one. Every road was lined with cheering people, and many tried to shove past the soldiers in their eagerness to touch Kristan. Again and again, the procession was forced to stop until the escort cleared the way. A few times, Kristan dismounted in an attempt to calm the throng, slowing their progress even more. When his touch produced no miraculous results, the people quieted and allowed the company to pass, but Kristan grew more ashen with each encounter. "Is it happening?" Heather finally whispered as he climbed back into the saddle following another halt. "Is it the *avama*?"

He sucked in a deep breath and clasped the Stone in one hand. "A bit," he murmured. "Strong, but not like the first time. They want me to make things better, Heather; they're hoping so hard I can taste it, like a mouthful of sweet and bitter—"

"Everything all right?" Nigel asked, moving up beside them.

"Fine," Heather said. "But we're not stopping again. Sir Kennet!"

"Yes, my lady?" Kennet called from the front of the line.

"Let's get going. And keep everyone moving this time. Send a brace of riders ahead to clear the way. I want to be at the castle gates by twilight."

The sky was a deep, velvety blue by the time they arrived. Lights blazed from every window of the castle, and when they drew to a halt before the keep, Melissa was waiting for them. Vadden Yale stood smiling on her right, the healer Steffen on her left. Her face, framed in a fur-trimmed hood, was drawn and pale, and her soft mouth was trembling. Kristan dismounted, passed the reins to Serle and faced her. "My lord," she whispered, and dipped into a curtsey.

"No," Kristan said, and caught her by the elbow. "Don't bow to me; I can't bear it. Embrace me, Melissa, and let us be sister and brother again."

* * *

The company spent a few pleasant days in Moordock. There was work, of course; "There's always work," Kristan said, but meetings and inspections, council sessions and military drills were interspersed with celebrations, genial dinners and quiet conversations.

Steffen fussed and clucked over Kristan, finally bullying him into a complete examination. Afterward, he grudgingly admitted that the StoneKing, at long last, seemed to be on the mend. "If you and your sister would heed my advice, you'd both be the better for it," he said. "Proper meals, plenty of rest and delegation of duties so you don't work yourselves to death—that's what you need."

"Nigel and I will see to it," Heather said.

Steffen snorted. "Demitt determination against Gemeta stubbornness—I wonder which will prevail."

"The two will be working together, not against each other," Kristan said mildly. "Now I have a favor to ask of you, Steffen. Sir Dell has a new title, and new duties. He's the first of what I hope will be many Gazes, whose job it will be to travel to every corner of my realm and report what they see."

Steffen raised his eyebrows. "You mean spies, my lord?"

"No. Spies observe and report on human activity. A Gaze will observe the natural world of my realm: the rivers and lakes and streams, the mountains and valleys, the forests and meadows and swamps and all the wild things that live on and above and under it. You've been a keen observer of nature for years. Perhaps you'd share your insights with Dell."

"It would give me great pleasure, my lord. If I were a younger man, I'd be begging to be a Gaze myself."

"That takes care of Dell," Kristan said as he and Heather snatched a quick noonday meal in the privacy of their chambers. "How goes it with Hilla?"

"She's taken to both sword and saddle like a bird to the air," Heather said. "A bit of a bumpkin yet, and clumsy at jobs like serving at table, but I like her spunk." She looked at Kristan sidelong. "Desta has been helping her train."

"That's good of her," Kristan said, in what he hoped was a noncommittal tone.

"Kristan, what are you going to do with Desta? When we get to Fandrall?"

"My love, I don't know yet. Maybe she'd be of some help training other squires." He thought of the cocky, broad-shouldered boys he had interviewed before choosing Serle, and winced. "No, that won't work. Perhaps she'd be better off helping train the pages."

Heather raised one eyebrow but said nothing. Kristan reached for a second piece of bread. "I have to sort out Nolle as well."

"What's she up to this time?"

"Nothing. That's the problem. She's been very subdued. I sent her to the head scribe for instruction in reading and writing, and she didn't say a word. She didn't even roll her eyes."

"That's not like her."

"Oh, there's more. I've always suspected Nolle of petty pilfering. All through my journeys, little things have been disappearing: a silver toothpick of Walter's, a Stratheden coin Geoffrey carried for luck, a knife I gave to Serle. No one ever made any accusations, but I could tell they thought it was her."

"Did she ever steal from you?"

"She tried once, before we left Fandrall, but I caught her." He was surprised at the pang he still felt over giving up the scrying ball. "She never did it again, not to me, but it appears everyone else was fair game. Yet, now all those missing items are reappearing. Serle found his knife tucked inside a spare shirt yesterday. Walter's toothpick turned up last night in the bottom of his pack, and Geoffrey's coin was back in its usual pocket. And this was on the throne this morning." He showed her the large, glossy pearl he had found nestled like an egg on the throne's cushion.

"Whose was that?"

"I'm not certain, but I think it came from a pearl circlet Princess Jelena wore when she visited Fandrall."

"I'll take it, then," Heather said, grinning as she plucked the pearl from his hand. "So Nolle's had a change of heart, it seems."

"Now if I can only decide what to do with her when we get back to Fandrall. She worked in the kitchen before, but after all she's done, I can't put her back there."

"You'll figure something out." Heather drained her goblet and stood. "I'm going to gather up Hilla and a few knights and go down to the docks to make sure everything's ready for our journey tomorrow."

"Shall I come?"

"With all due respect, my lord, I'd rather you didn't. You'll attract a crowd and it'll take us 'til nightfall to fight our way back."

She leaned down, kissed him thoroughly, and strode from the room. As he sat blinking and catching his breath, there was a cursory knock at the door and Serle poked his head into the room. "Sorry to disturb you, my lord, but your sister was hoping you could spare her a few moments."

Kristan resisted the urge to moan. He had avoided being alone with Melissa, all too aware of the naked hope in her gaze. *She believes the rumors,* he thought miserably. *She's going to ask me to make her well, so she can bear children.* He considered making yet another excuse to evade the encounter, then sighed and thrust the idea aside. "Clear away these dishes please, then send her in."

Melissa arrived, with a speed that told Kristan she must have been waiting nearby. He motioned her to the seat Heather had vacated.

Serle still lingered by the door. "May I bring you anything, Princess? My lord?"

"Thank you, no," Kristan said. "Aren't you supposed to be training with Sir Geoffrey this afternoon?"

Serle's shoulders sagged. "Yes, my lord."

"Then don't keep him waiting. I won't need you until dinnertime."

"He's a sweet boy," Melissa said, as Serle's dragging footfalls faded. "He reminds me a little of William."

"William?" A sliver of memory flickered through Kristan's brain and was gone.

"Father's manservant, don't you remember? He had freckles like Serle's . . . he was so fond of you . . ." Melissa's voice faltered. "No. No, of course you don't. I'm so sorry, Kristan, I wasn't thinking. I didn't come here to cause you grief—"

Kristan put his hand over hers. "You didn't. What grieves me is not being able to give you what you want so badly."

Her chin trembled. "Then the rumors aren't true?"

"No, Missy."

"You can't heal people?"

"No, Missy."

"And you didn't bring a woman's baby back to life?"

"No, Missy."

"Then why do they act the way they do? Why do they gather in mobs and push and shove and try to touch you?"

He squeezed her hand. "Because they're hoping."

"Then why don't you tell them they're wrong? That you can't help them?"

"I've tried. But people keep on hoping, no matter what I say."

"But you touch them. You stop, and dismount, and you touch them. You're giving them hope. Why?"

Why, indeed? Kristan sat back, put his hand to the Stone and tried to shape his thoughts into words. "I was with Steffen earlier today," he said at last. "He felt my forehead to see if I was feverish. He listened to my chest, thumped my back, and peered down my throat. And he poked and prodded all the wounded, broken parts of me, so he could tell if I'm healing properly."

"He does the same thing to me," Melissa said impatiently. "What of it?"

"When I stop to touch someone, that's what I'm doing. I'm putting my finger on the pulse of my realm: to see what my people need, what they fear, what they hope. Sometimes I can help them; more often I can't. But I can, at least, let them know that I see them. That I hear them. That I care. Because it would be wrong to destroy their hope. If people didn't hope for something, they'd just . . . give up." Another memory glimmered in his brain, but this time he was able to catch it before it faded. "*Hope holds the key.*"

"What?"

"It was in that book . . . the book that set everyone looking for me last summer. I wonder what happened to it." He gave himself a little shake. "Never mind. It isn't important. What's important is that you don't lose hope. And while you wait to become a mother in fact, be a mother in spirit to the people of Norwinn. This part of the realm is yours, to guide and shape and mold as you see fit. Will you do that for me?"

She nodded. He rose and held out his hand. She gazed at it, then raised beseeching eyes to his. "Will you try, Kristan?" she whispered. "Will you at least try?"

A refusal was on his lips, but then he remembered how he had rebuffed Olaf's plea for help. *If only I'd said yes*, he thought, overwhelmed with regret. "Yes, Missy," he said. "Of course I will."

She stood up, took his hand in both of hers and pressed it against her belly. Clasping the Stone in his other hand, Kristan closed his eyes and waited.

Nothing happened, not even the tiniest tingle. The room was silent but for Melissa's quiet breathing and the thrum of his pulse in his ears. *Please*, he thought, gripping the Stone tighter. *If there's even a chance. Please.*

Finally, Melissa heaved a little sigh and released him. "Thank you for humoring me, brother."

"I'm sorry, Missy. Truly, I am."

She tried to smile. "You told me it wouldn't work. I should have believed you." She put one hand to his face. "Don't look so sad, Kristan. You have a realm to rule; I have a country to mother, and we've had enough grieving for two lifetimes. It's time to leave all that behind. It's time to begin again."

* * *

"No, no, not like that," the head scribe squawked, and snatched the quill from Nolle's fingers. "See, you've bent the nib. How many times do I have to tell you not to bear down so hard—"

"Pardon me, master." One of the apprentice scribes stood in the doorway. "You're wanted in the throne room, sir."

"Oh, for—" The head scribe threw the ruined quill aside. "Take up a fresh one, girl, and start the exercise again. How in the world I'm supposed to teach someone to read and write in the space of a few days is beyond comprehension . . ." His carping voice receded down the hall, and after giving Nolle a wry look, the apprentice left as well.

Nolle sat for some moments, studying the scribe's work chamber. Every corner held barrels stuffed with maps, every flat surface was piled high with stacks of parchment, every wall from floor to ceiling was lined with shelves crammed full of books, the topmost accessible only by means of a tall, wheeled ladder. Nolle fastened her gaze on the highest, dustiest shelf. "Right, then," she muttered, shifted into a moth, and fluttered upward, dodging cobwebs. When she reached her destination, she landed and shifted back, scrabbling for hand- and toe-holds. Panting a bit, she fumbled the little rat-gnawed book from its hiding place in her clothing. She scowled at Phelan's bits of scribbled parchment still wagging from the book's pages, like taunting tongues. "I'm not carrying your stupid book any further, old man," she said, and wedged it between two fat, tattered tomes. Dust rose in waves, making her sneeze, but as she poked the little book out of sight, she grinned. "Free now," she whispered, and indeed, she felt light as air. She shifted again, this time taking the form of a wasp, and made three quick, triumphant circuits of the room before buzzing through the open door and out of sight.

CHAPTER TWENTY

In spite of an early morning drizzle, a boisterous crowd thronged the docks as the royal party prepared to depart Norwinn. "Safe journey to you both," Melissa said, raising her voice to be heard over the cheering. "I wish you were taking a bigger ship."

"This cog will be fine. Anything bigger and we wouldn't be able to land on Fandrall's shore," Kristan said.

"Is everyone here?" Heather asked. "Where are the children?"

"I've got Hilla," Bayla said, grabbing the girl's shoulder as she wandered too close to the dock's edge. "Careful, child, or you'll end up in the water."

"I don't know how to swim," Hilla said.

"Well, maybe Nolle can turn you into a fish and you can learn," Nigel said.

Sir Matthew laughed. "How about it, Nolle? Why don't we all swim to Fandrall instead?"

"I'm not going," Nolle said.

Everyone wheeled to look at her. "What do you mean, you're not going?" Sir Geoffrey demanded.

"Why not, Nolle?" Kristan asked more gently.

She shrugged. "I'd be bored, hanging around Kingsmere learning lessons. I thought I'd go with Dell when he sets off to start his Gazing. Maybe I could be a Gaze too. I like traveling."

"It's scarcely proper, a girl your age traveling alone with an older man," Melissa protested.

Heather raised her eyebrows and turned to the new Gaze. "Dell?"

"I have no objection," Dell said. He cleared his throat, rather pointedly. "And Nolle has nothing to fear from me. I swear it."

"Very well," Kristan said, although the thought of losing Nolle, even with all her quirks, was strangely painful. "If that's what you want to do, Nolle, I won't stand in your way."

"Thanks. Oh, I nearly forgot. Here." She dug in her clothing, pulled out the scrying ball and handed it to Kristan. "You can have the old thing back."

"Don't you want it anymore?"

"It's no use to me. Besides, it weighs me down."

"We wouldn't want that," Heather said with a wry grin.

"You've been a great help to me, Nolle," Kristan said. "I'll miss you."

"Oh, I'll come visit you at Kingsmere once in a while." She gave Serle a friendly swat. "So long, friend. Goodbye, Hilla. Goodbye, Desta. Have fun in Fandrall."

"I'm not going to Fandrall either," Desta said.

"Oh, now what?" Sir Geoffrey said under his breath.

"Of course you are," Heather said. "We talked about this, Desta. You were going to help me train the Kingsmere pages."

"I know, my lady. But I . . . it's not what I want to do. I wouldn't be happy." Her jaw was set hard and her eyes were bleak. "I'll just go home to Seagirt."

"You don't fit in there," Nolle said gruffly.

"I don't fit in anywhere."

Kristan raised a hand, intending to put it on Desta's shoulder, but to his astonishment, Serle pushed between them. "My lord, please don't let her go," he said, tears in his eyes. "Desta is better than me—at everything. She's better with Malvo, better at archery and swordplay, better at everything a squire is supposed to do. She should be your squire, not me."

Desta's head came up. Her eyes were wide with hope.

"Everything you say is true, Serle," Kristan said. "But your training has been spotty, and that's my fault. When we get back to Fandrall—"

"When we get back to Fandrall, I'll still be useless and fumbling!" Serle cried. "I'll never make a squire, nor a knight. I won't shame you anymore by rewarding your patience with mistakes. Make Desta your squire."

"Are you sure, Serle? Are you absolutely sure?"

Serle took a deep, hitching breath. "I'm absolutely sure, my lord."

"Very well." The pang at losing Nolle was nothing compared to the misery of losing Serle. "If you're sure, I'll release you from my service and take Desta as my squire."

Desta caught her breath so hard that it sounded like a squeak. Serle tried to smile. "Thank you, my lord. It's only right and fair."

"But Serle—what will you do?" Nolle said. "Where will you go?"

"I'm a shepherd. I should go back to my family and look after our flock."

An idea was taking shape in Kristan's brain. "Perhaps you could have a flock in Kingsmere."

"Sir?"

"Just a small one. Only one sheep, but he takes a lot of looking after, as you already know. I still need a manservant, Serle—someone who can tell when I'm cold and build a good fire, knows when I'm tired and can keep everything quiet, and sees when I'm hungry and makes me eat even when I say I'm too busy."

Serle gaped at him. "But you . . . you have a wife for that, my lord."

Heather let out a snort, even though her eyes were suspiciously bright. "Boy, if you think I'm the type to wait hand and foot on my husband, you're much mistaken."

"There, you see?" Kristan said. "I'd be most grateful if you'd take the job, Serle."

Serle wiped his eyes and straightened his shoulders. "I would be proud to be your manservant, my lord."

"Even if there's no knighthood in it?"

"Yes, my lord. 'Sir Serle' sounds silly, anyway."

"Then that's settled. Here, take this ball and put it in my pack." Scrying ball in hand, Serle ran up the gangway as Kristan eyed the rest of the group. "Now, if there are no further objections, may we start our journey?"

After a final round of farewell embraces, Kristan and Heather boarded the ship. They stood at the rail, waving to the crowd, with the members of their party clustered around them. "We're moving!" Hilla cried as the crew cast off. "But why are we going so slow?"

"Look ahead, you little lubber," Sir Mitchell told her. "See those rowboats, and the towlines that lead to our ship? They'll row us out of the harbor until we're clear of all these other boats, and then our crew will put up the sails and away we'll go."

Hilla stayed obediently at Heather's side, but she still stood on tiptoe to watch. "Off with you," Heather said. "Go and see how they do it."

Kristan waved his hand at Desta and Serle. "You too. Be children for a while. But stay out of the way of the crew," he called as the three dashed off. A white-feathered, wavering blur flashed past: Nolle, in seagull-form. She joined the other children in the bow and shifted back, and all four children crowded in the bow, pointing and chattering.

"They're so young," Bayla said with a little sigh.

Walter put his arm around her. "We're all young, my love. Except Geoffrey, of course."

"Whippersnapper," Geoffrey grunted, but he was grinning.

Everyone laughed, even Kennet. Kristan drew in a deep breath, grateful for their high spirits, for the start of the journey home, for the soft spring rain pattering on his cloak and hat of Stratheden wool. Heather caught his eye and winked. He yearned to take her in his arms but controlled himself.

"The forecastle has been prepared for you, my lord," Kennet said. "No need for you to stand out here in the rain."

"Thank you, Kennet, but for the moment, it's rather refreshing."

Matthew leaned on the rail. "The air's softer. Spring's coming."

"It usually does, Matthew," Kennet said dryly.

"Kennet! Did you just make a joke?"

Kristan inhaled again. A sudden tingle ran up his spine. The air was filling a new scent, a heady mingling of musk and spice. At that moment, Mitchell pointed to port. "Look!" he cried. "Look!"

A flotilla of ships was approaching from the south. At the fore was one of Norwinn's warships; ranged behind it were five smaller, very familiar vessels.

"It's the *Kentávron*," Kristan whispered. The tingling was spreading across his chest, into his arms and legs, warming him from within.

"Do you think they were successful?" Heather said. "Do you think they found the rest of Astéria's people?"

"I'll wager they did," Sir Walter said. "Listen!"

The *Kentávron* were singing. Full-throated, joyous, and sure, their voices rang across the water. The sound resonated, bell-like, through Kristan's body. *Avama*, he thought. *It's happening again.* He sucked in another deep breath. *Don't resist it. Open to it.*

Everyone on board was waving and calling to those on the warship. The men in the rowboats stopped to gape, oars arrested in mid-stroke. The warship's sail fluttered and sagged as it swung into the wind, and the song gave way to shouts of recognition. Centaurs lined the rails, grinning and waving back. Many stood in couples, arms slung about each other's waists, and their happiness and pride and passion swept over Kristan like a wave. *So strong*, he thought. *The life in them is so strong, I can feel it without touching them.*

"Kreestan!" someone cried. Astéria was pushing her way to the rail, with Torrin right behind her. "Kreestan, you are married!"

"Congratulations, my friend," Torrin called. "Heather, I wish you all the joy in the world."

"How did you know?" Heather shouted back.

"Raul told us. We stopped in Dyer to revictual."

"You stopped in Dyer?" Sir Walter laughed and slapped one leg. "You must have shaken the place up!"

"No more hiding for the *Kentávron*," Torrin said. "There's enough of us now to take our place in the world. Kristan, haven't you anything to say?"

"Congratulations," Kristan croaked, so overwhelmed with sensation that he could barely form words. Torrin grinned and put his arm around Astéria's shoulders; she hugged him back and raised her face to be kissed. As their lips met, Kristan tasted their desire like a mouthful of new honey, thick and sweet. His body responded with such sudden, surprising vigor that he was grateful for his heavy cloak.

"But what are you doing here?" Heather asked.

"Returning Melissa's ship. It was a good thing she loaned us her largest; we're chock full. Eighty-seven new centaurs! We'll have to offload in Moordock and sort everyone into our own vessels for the trip back to *O Tópos*; thank goodness the wine ship we loaned you last summer is still docked there—we'll need it."

"Melissa and Nigel will be so happy to see you."

"We can't linger, not this time. Father is waiting for us back in *O Tópos*, to begin our own wedding ceremonies and celebrations. You should come, Kristan. You and Heather."

"Not this time," Kristan echoed. "Mitchell, send word to the captain to have our rowers cast us loose and guide our friends into port. Torrin, my friend, safe journey home. I wish every happiness to you and Astéria. Every happiness to your people."

As the *Kentávron* flotilla made its way into Moordock, Nolle shifted back into a gull and flew after them, dodging and weaving among their sails. The rest of the company moved into the stern to watch them go and leave the deck clear as the crew hoisted the sails. Kristan, however, slipped into the forecastle. He was hot, too hot, and he tore off his hat, threw it aside, and braced his hands on his knees. His breath came in deep heaving gasps. Every part of him felt heavy, swollen with desire, as if the smell of the centaurs' passion had filled him to bursting.

"Kristan?" Heather was in the doorway, looking concerned. "Are you all right?"

Without answering, he caught her arm, pulled her into the room, and shut the door. She let out a muffled squeak of surprise as he kissed her, parting her lips with his tongue. He pressed her backward, toward the forecastle's narrow bed, and they tumbled onto it in a tangle of cloaks, boots, buckles, and belts. He mashed her into the mattress, fumbling their clothing open, aside, away; her hands joined his and from her throat came a deep, animal grunt. The smell of damp wool, leather, and sweat filled the small, close room, mingling with another scent: the pungence of sheer, single-minded lust. This time there were no whispered endearments, no featherlight kisses and caresses; this time their lovemaking was urgent, ravenous, all hungry mouths and greedy hands. When he finally plunged into her, she grabbed his buttocks and sank her fingernails into his flesh. With each thrust, he pushed deeper and deeper; with each thrust she opened wider, pressing her face into his neck to stifle her moans. At last, a strangled cry burst from her. She shuddered and shook beneath him, but still he pounded on, his pulse thundering in his ears like hoofbeats until, brain whirling and lungs bursting, he arched his spine, threw back his head, and with a guttural groan, spent himself deep inside her.

For some time afterward they lay entangled, panting, their bodies sticky with drying sweat. Finally, Kristan rolled onto his back. Heather heaved herself onto one elbow and with one fingertip, traced a lingering path from the middle of his chest to his navel. "Now what was that all about?" she murmured.

He snorted out a laugh. "I have no idea."

"Ah." She grinned wickedly. "In that case, can we do it again and find out?"

* * *

"There it is," Sir Matthew said, topping the last rise. "There's Kingsmere."

Sir Geoffrey stood up in the stirrups. "Look at the castle. Now that's an improvement."

Kristan's vision blurred, but he quickly blinked the tears away. The castle stood on its hill, surrounded by win-ter-browned grass washed with a faint tinge of green where the spring growth had already begun. The keep rose from behind the curtain wall, its stone surface clean and bright in the late afternoon sun.

Serle caught his breath. "Look how pretty, my lord."

"All the soot stains are gone," Sir Mitchell said. "It's like new."

Sir Kennet turned to Kristan and nodded gravely. "Welcome home, my lord."

"Welcome home," the other knights echoed.

"Welcome indeed," Kristan said, and breathed a grateful sigh.

"It's beautiful, my lord." Heather said, smiling. "No wonder you missed it so."

"I know it hasn't the size of Hogia's castle, or the elegance of Norwinn's, or the grandeur of Dyer's—"

"It's better than those," Serle protested. "It's *home*."

Kristan nodded. "It's home. And I hope with all my heart you'll be happy here, Commander. Bayla, Desta, and Hilla too."

"What are we waiting for?" Sir Walter demanded. "Let's go!"

"I do believe Kingsmere has gotten bigger," Matthew said as the company trotted westward, squinting against the lowering sun. "Look at all the new buildings."

"And more going up yet," Walter said. "Hear all the sawing and hammering?"

A sudden shout went up from the town, and Geoffrey shook his head. "We've been spotted. Commander, shall I send the escort forward as usual?"

"If you please." Heather leaned toward Kristan and lowered her voice. "I suppose there's no point in asking you not to stop to greet the crowd."

"None at all. I know these people, Heather; they're not going to mob me."

"Sure about that, are you?" A flood of people surged onto the road ahead, cheering and waving. Heather tightened her grip on Skapi's reins. "Here we go. Hilla, stay close."

The mounted escort held the people back, so the royal party could pass, but here and there people burst through and flung themselves at Kristan, touching his legs, his arms, any part of him they could reach. Malvo rumbled low, almost as if he were growling, and Desta brought her mount to his left and slightly ahead, ready to deflect the eager throng.

There was nothing for it but to rein up and dismount, and with Walter and Kennet flanking him, make contact with the crowd. Some people cried out as he touched them, and others knelt at his approach, clasping their hands in supplication, while still others, familiar faces, called out greetings.

"Welcome home, Gemeta!"

"Happiness to you and your new queen!"

"Three cheers for the StoneKing!"

A cluster of young women, dressed in an extravagant manner unusual for Kingsmere, bent into deep curtsies. "High-class doxies," Walter muttered in Kristan's ear. "I suppose it was inevitable, but I hate to see it here."

The last woman in the group caught Kristan's hand and pressed it to her lips. As he tried to disengage himself, the woman raised her eyes and fixed him with a mocking gaze.

"Welcome back, StoneKing," she said.

It was Tansy.

Before Kristan could react, Desta squeezed past him and thrust her face right into Tansy's. "Don't you touch him," she hissed, flashing just the tip of her knife beneath Tansy's nose. Tansy stood up quickly, snapped her fingers at the other women, and led them out of the throng.

Stunned, Kristan made his way back to Malvo. Still glaring after Tansy, Desta held the stirrup so he could mount. "Desta, you mustn't—" Kristan said.

Desta shook her head. "She's a bad woman, my lord. You shouldn't let her anywhere near you."

"Who was that?" Heather asked when they were on their way again.

"Tansy Yeomans." The encounter had shaken him; it was an effort to smile and wave.

"The woman you told me about?" Heather looked over her shoulder, her expression a sudden echo of Desta's glare. "What's she doing here?"

"I don't know," Kristan said, but he was weighed down with foreboding.

The cavalcade continued toward the castle. Kristan did not stop again, although when he spotted Feva and Lyko Yeomans standing well back in the crowd, he hesitated. The couple nodded when he raised a hand in greeting, but their smiles were forced and melancholy.

Up the castle road, over the drawbridge, past guards grinning at attention and soldiers cheering on the battlements, across a courtyard freshly laid with a thick layer of white gravel, everything fresh and clean and welcoming. Servants stood in neat rows beside the keep steps, and at the very top, in front of the doors flung wide in welcome, were Quinn Logan, Bastian, and Sir Randolf. The old knight was the first down the steps, holding out his arms. "Welcome, welcome, a thousand welcomes!" he called, and the genuine happiness on his face warmed Kristan's chilled heart.

"Sir Randolf," Heather said, smiling as he handed her down from Skapi, with a bow as elegant as any Dyerian courtier.

"The place is much improved," Kristan said, handing Malvo off to a waiting stablehand.

"That's all Randolf's doing, my lord." Bastian was lumbering down the keep steps, with Quinn following more sedately. "As soon as weather permitted, he had an army of workers up on scaffolds, scrubbing down the exterior walls."

"We were going to whitewash, but your friend, Mali Uzuri in Dyer, sent us three barrels full of some stuff she'd concocted," Randolf said. "Took the skin off your hands if you weren't careful, but it did the trick."

"She also sent two bolts of the most beautiful cloth, my lord," Bastian said. "One pale blue, and one the darkest red I've ever seen. A wedding gift, her letter said."

"How kind. I'll have to write and thank her."

"You've many thank-yous to write, my lord. We've been inundated with wedding gifts. The great hall is full of them. I've logged them in as they arrived and drafted responses for your signature."

He moved off to greet Heather, whom Randolf had drawn away to meet Fandrall's captains. Quinn Logan looked Kristan up and down. "Marriage seems to agree with you, my lord," he said. "Like your castle, you're much improved."

"I am indeed, Quinn. Very much improved."

"Where is Nolle? And who are these new children?"

"Nolle decided she'd rather accompany Sir Dell, who'll be exploring the realm on my behalf. I'll tell you more about that later. The loud little girl is Hilla; she's the High Commander's squire. The tall girl is Desta, a relation of Mali Uzuri's. She's my squire." He met Quinn's gaze squarely, daring him to protest.

Quinn only nodded, inscrutable as an owl. "Very well, my lord. And what of Serle?"

"Serle is now my manservant. I think the job will be a

happier fit all around."

"Indeed, my lord." Quinn bowed low as Heather rejoined them. "How good to see you again. Welcome to Fandrall, Queen Heather." His polite façade faltered a bit as Heather frowned. "I beg your pardon; have I offended you somehow?"

"No offense, Councilor Logan, I'm just not used to being called that. To be honest, when I'm in uniform, I prefer 'Commander.'"

"As you wish, Commander," Quinn said smoothly. "May I escort you inside?"

With Hilla trailing them, Heather and Quinn ascended into the keep. Kristan followed, with Serle and Desta close behind, then Walter and Bayla arm-in-arm, with Bastian and the other knights bringing up the rear, all talking at once. Just inside the door there was a brief scuffle as both Serle and Desta tried to take Kristan's cloak, but before Kristan could quell it with a glance, Desta stepped back, raising her hands as if in surrender. "You have him inside, then, but outside he's mine," she murmured.

"Fair enough," Serle answered, and Kristan was hard-pressed not to laugh.

"... quite torn up about it," Randolf was saying to Sir Kennet. "The two of them were beside themselves with happiness when she reappeared, but when word got out that she was opening a doxy-house in Kingsmere, well . . ." He became aware of Kristan's gaze. "Lyko and Feva Yeomans, my lord. Their daughter, Tansy, came back, about a month ago. She's been in Dyer all this time. Little Tansy a doxy; can you imagine—"

"I saw her," Kristan said, more brusquely than he intended, and Randolf fell silent.

"Kristan, come look at this," Heather called from the great hall.

He hurried to join her. She and Quinn Logan were standing before a row of tables ranged along the western wall, each piled high with wedding plunder. Gold, silver and jewels glittered in the light filtering through the windows, dazzling Kristan so that he had to blink. "Much of it's from the guild heads in Dyer," Quinn said. "Here's the cloth from Mali Uzuri, and a rather gaudy set of jeweled goblets from Fedro Vincenze. Reach Ferrador sent those magnificent arrases. The necklace with the opals is for the High Commander, from King Aldo in Stratheden, and that gold coffer with the emeralds is from King Lockward in Malchea. Oh, and this," he added, laying his hand on an enormous square object stitched into a canvas covering. "This is from Princess Jelena."

"What is it?" Kristan said, eyeing the massive thing with trepidation.

"I don't know, my lord. It arrived covered up, on a cart pulled by a half-dozen oxen. It took twenty men to get it up the keep steps, and then it barely fit through the doors. Sir Velios was in charge of the shipment; he said the princess gave instructions that it was only to be uncovered by you."

"Open it, Kristan," Heather urged.

"Very well," Kristan said. "May I borrow your knife, Serle?"

He sliced the canvas cover from corner to corner, and with everyone lending a hand, managed to pull it off. Beneath was a single gigantic block of green-blue granite. "This came with it," Quinn said, and handed Kristan a piece of parchment, folded and sealed with red wax. Kristan broke the seal.

"What does it say, my lord?" Sir Randolf asked.

"*To replace what was destroyed*," Kristan read. "*May your warrior woman bring you happiness, and your plate be ever full.*" He let the parchment drop.

"But what is it?" Heather asked, looking as if she could not decide to be flattered or miffed.

"It's a throne." Kristan ran one hand down the rough stone surface. "Or it will be, when it's carved. This must be from the same quarry that produced Fandrall's original throne."

"What a splendid gift, my lord," Sir Kennet said.

"It is indeed."

"You'll have to reciprocate appropriately, my lord," Quinn said. "She's getting married herself."

"Really? To whom?"

"Sir Velios."

"Poor fellow," Sir Walter muttered.

"I've never seen a man so transported," Quinn said a bit primly. "He was almost giddy when he was here."

"Well, I'm glad for them both," Kristan said. "The rest of these gifts can wait until later, I think."

"May I show you both to your chamber?" Sir Randolf asked. "I think you'll be pleased at the change since you last occupied the room, my lord."

The chamber, once so cold and drafty, was already warm from a new fire crackling in the hearth. A magnificent canopied bed stood near it, draped with curtains embroidered in gold and green. A fat bolster ran along the headboard, with plump down pillows propped against it. The brocaded bedcover was turned back invitingly to expose a soft, white woolen blanket and bright new linens beneath. Randolf cleared his throat diffidently. "The bed is from Princess Melissa and Sir Nigel. The curtains and bolster and bedcover are from Quinn, Bastian, and me. The linens, featherbed and pillows are from Fandrall's household servants."

Too moved for words, Kristan managed a nod. Heather took over, thanking Randolf so earnestly and effusively that the old knight blushed and shuffled his feet like a boy. "Well, I'll let you get settled in, then," he said, edging toward the door. "Dinner will be ready whenever you want it."

"I'd like to inspect the troops first," Heather said.

"I'll arrange it now, High Commander. Ah, here are your things." Randolf stepped out of the way as Serle, Hilla and Desta came in, staggering under the weight of packs, bundles and bags.

"Put everything over there," Heather directed. "Hilla, I'm going to hold an inspection, and I'd like you and Bayla to accompany me. I'll be down directly, so have my cloak and gloves ready. Desta, perhaps you'd like to come as well?"

Desta looked to Kristan. He nodded his assent, and the two girls dashed from the room. Serle diplomatically busied himself unpacking the bags as Heather put her arms around Kristan. "Will you come too, my lord?" she asked softly.

"No, you go ahead. Everything is so different. I think I'd like a few moments just to take it all in."

"As you say." She kissed him and hurried from the room.

Kristan stood at the window, his hands clasped behind his back, watching as dusk crept across the rolling meadows of Fandrall. Serle moved quietly around the room as he unpacked, but then he paused and let out a little chuckle. "What is it, Serle?" Kristan asked, without turning around.

"I was just putting your scrying ball away, my lord, and remembered my first night here, when I met Nolle. It seems like a long time ago."

"It was a long time ago," Kristan said. "Ages, in fact. Let me have the ball a moment, Serle."

Serle brought it to him, buffing it lightly against his tunic. "It looks the same as ever," he said. "You'd never know the adventures it's had. I'll be right back, my lord; there's a few more bundles downstairs yet."

Would that we all could come away from our adventures so unmarked, Kristan thought as Serle's footsteps faded. He held the ball up to the window, so the last few rays of sunlight set it gleaming. On a whim, he brought the ball close to his eye and peered through it. The world outside turned a deep, murky blue: meadows, roads, town, battlements. He smiled, but the smile faded as a shadow moved along the top of the castle wall. It was a lone figure, bent with sorrow and yet hurrying, as if trying to outpace whatever grieved it. Kristan lowered the ball and squinted toward the same spot on the battlements, but there was nothing there.

Once more, he raised the ball to his eye; once more, the

mysterious figure moved across the battlements. He found himself holding his breath, overwhelmed with sudden, terrible dread as the shadow paused at the very brink of the parapet. It pulled itself upright, then took one step forward and disappeared over the edge.

"*He jumped, my lord.*"

The sobbing, grief-stricken voice echoed through his brain. The scrying ball slipped from his hand. It struck the edge of the windowsill and with a loud crack, broke into two pieces. They fell to the floor and lay like two blind eyes gazing sightlessly at the ceiling. Paralyzed with nameless, reasonless horror, Kristan stared at them.

And at that instant, from some dark corner of the room, came a long, low chuckle.

THE END

RAGIS
BOOK FOUR OF THE GEMETA STONE

DONNA MIGLIACCIO is a professional stage actress with credits that include Broadway, National Tours and prominent regional theatres. She is based in the Washington, DC Metro area, where she co-founded Tony Award-winning Signature Theatre and is in demand as an entertainer, teacher and public speaker.

ALSO BY
DONNA MIGLIACCIO